LINDA LAEL MILLER

MONTANA CREEDS

Logan

HQN™

HQN™

ISBN-13: 978-0-373-78845-3

Montana Creeds: Logan

This edition published by arrangement with Harlequin Books S.A.

For questions and comments about the quality of this book,
please contact us at CustomerService@Harlequin.com.

www.HQNBooks.com

Printed in U.S.A.

Dear Friend,

Welcome (or welcome back) to Stillwater Springs, Montana, home of the Creed men.

This is Logan's story. The oldest of three estranged brothers, he returns to the small town and to the run-down ranch that's been in his family for well over a century. He's determined to rebuild both the ranch and the Creed name. He soon meets his fiercely independent neighbor, Briana Grant, and her two spirited sons, and the word *family* takes on a whole new meaning.

The Creed stories illustrate—and I hope affirm—the important things in life. Family, in all its guises. Love and marriage (of course!). Community. Friendship. Respect for the land we're so fortunate to live in. Forgiveness and the ability to compromise, to see the other person's point of view (and that's especially true of these stubborn brothers as they find their way back to each other). Also critical for me and I'm sure for you is our responsibility toward animals. Oh, and a sense of humor—nothing helps us through the hard times more than a few friends and a few laughs.

You probably know that Western settings, Western stories, are among my favorites. In these books the setting is Montana, with its beauty, its grandeur and wide-open spaces.

I think it's fair to say that the Western as a genre in both books and movies expresses one of the founding myths of America. Perhaps Westerns in their classic form aren't as popular as they once were. (And admittedly, these books, movies and TV programs were sometimes careless with the facts about Native Americans—something that more recent versions have tended to address.) But in newer versions of the Western (like mine, for instance), we still have many of the classic themes: the relationship between the land and the people who work it, the conflict between good and evil (with good winning out, needless to say!), the opposing desires for journey and adventure on the one hand, and for home on the other. The need to stand up for self and others… See how many of those themes echo the things that remain so important to us?

The era of TV shows like *Bonanza*, *The Lone Ranger* and *Rawhide*, movies like *The Searchers*, *Hondo* and many others, and novels like those of Owen Wister, Louis L'Amour and Zane Grey, may be part of our past—but they're still read and watched. They're truly classics! The world portrayed in these Westerns (or a contemporary version of it) still has relevance for us in North America. Relevance and fascination. And I predict that Western settings will *always* be a favorite with romance readers.

That world is where my characters, the Creeds, belong.

As always in these letters, I want to make my appeal on behalf of the animals we love and especially the ones who *need* our love. Support your local animal charities. Please make sure you spay and neuter, vaccinate and keep your pets safe—and encourage other people to do the same. Have cats and dogs microchipped if you can; it's not expensive and can really make a difference if—God forbid—they happen to get lost.

I hope you enjoy this story. Drop by my website, lindalaelmiller.com, and feel free to leave a comment. Tell me if you have a favorite Western location and why. I'd love to hear!

All my best,

Linda Lael Miller

For Steve Miller—

gifted Western artist,
cherished friend and
incredibly generous spirit.
10,000 thanks for
showing a country girl and her
loved ones the
Big Rodeo, in style!

CHAPTER ONE

Stillwater Springs Ranch

THE WEATHERED WOODEN sign above the gate dangled from its posts by three links of rusty chain. The words, hand-carved by Josiah Creed himself more than 150 years earlier, and then burned in deeper still with the edge of an old branding iron, were faded now, hardly legible.

Logan Creed, half inside his secondhand Dodge pickup—"previously owned," the dealer had called it—and half outside, with one booted foot on the running board, swore under his breath.

Startled, the bedraggled dog he'd picked up at a rest stop outside of Kalispell that morning gave a soft, fretful whine, low in his throat. Little wonder the poor critter was skittish; he'd clearly been from one end of lost-animal hell to the other.

"Sorry, ol' fella," Logan muttered, his throat constricted with a tangle of emotions, sharp as barbed wire. He'd known the family ranch—a legacy shared equally with his two younger brothers, Dylan and Tyler—would be in sad shape. The whole spread had been neglected for years, after all…ever since they'd had that falling out after their dad's funeral.

He and Dylan and Tyler had gone their stubborn, separate ways.

The dog forgave him readily, that being the way of dogs, and seemed sympathetic, sitting there on the other side of the gearshift, his brown eyes almost liquid as he regarded his rescuer.

Logan grinned, settled himself back into the driver's seat. "If I were half the man you think I am," he told the mutt, "I'd be a candidate for sainthood."

The idea of any Creed being canonized made him chuckle.

The dog responded with a cheerful yip, as if offering to put in a good word with whoever made decisions like that.

"You'll need a name," Logan said. "Damned if I can think of one right off the top of my head, though." He turned in the seat, facing forward, cataloging the fallen fences and disintegrating junk, and sighed again. "We've got our work cut out for us. Best get started, I guess."

The sign bumped the truck's roof as Logan drove beneath it, and the rungs of the nineteenth-century cattle guard under the tires all but rattled his teeth.

Weeds choked the long, winding driveway, but the ruts were still there, anyway, made by the first vehicles to travel that road—wagons. Mentally, Logan added several tons of gravel to the list of necessities.

There were three houses on various parts of the property and, because he was the eldest of the current Creed generation, the biggest one belonged to him. Some inheritance, he thought. He'd be lucky if the place was fit to inhabit.

"Good thing I've got a sleeping bag and camping gear," he told the dog, leaning forward a little in the seat as they jostled up the grassy rise, peering grimly through the windshield. "You okay with sleeping under the stars if the roof's gone, boy?"

The dog's eyes said he was game for anything, as long as the two of them stuck together. He'd had enough of being alone, scrounging for food and shelter when the weather turned bad.

Logan told himself to buck up and reached across to pat the animal's matted head. No telling what color the mutt was, under all that dirt and sorry luck. As for the mix of breed, he was probably part Lab, part setter and part a whole slew of other things. His ribs showed and a piece of his left ear was missing. Yep, he'd been nobody's dog for too long.

When he'd pulled into the rest stop to stretch his legs after the long drive from Las Vegas, he hadn't counted on picking up a four-legged hitchhiker, but when the dog slunk out of the bushes as he stepped down from the truck, Logan couldn't ignore him. There was nobody else around, and if there had ever been a tag and collar, they were long gone.

Logan had known he was that dog's last hope, and since he'd been in a similar position himself a time or two, he hadn't been able to turn his back. He'd hoisted the critter into the pickup, and they'd shared a fast-food breakfast in the next town. The dog had horked his chow up, in short order, and looked so remorseful afterward that Logan hadn't minded stopping at a car wash to scour out the rig.

Now, several hours later, as he steeled himself to lay eyes on the ranch house for the first time in a lot of eventful years, Logan was glad of the company, though the conversations were distinctly one-sided.

They finally crested the last hill, and Logan saw the barn first—still standing, but leaning distinctly to one side. He forced himself to swing his gaze to the house, and his spirits rose a little. Part of the roof was sagging, but the rambling one-story log structure, originally a one-room cabin smaller than most garden sheds, had managed to endure. None of the three stone chimneys had crumbled, and the front windows still had glass in them, the old-fashioned kind with a greenish cast to it and little bubbles here and there.

Home, Logan thought, with a mixture of determination and pure sorrow. Such as it was, Stillwater Springs Ranch was home.

It was probably too much to hope that the plumbing still worked, he decided, but he'd called ahead and had the lights and the telephone service turned on, anyhow. His sidekick was in sore need of a bath, and hiking back and forth to the springs for water would be taking the whole back-to-basics thing too far. His luxurious Vegas lifestyle hadn't prepared him for roughing it.

"Sidekick," Logan mused, as he climbed out of the truck. "Suppose you go by that for a while?"

Apparently overjoyed, Sidekick leaped across the gearshift and the console into the seat Logan had just vacated. Logan chuckled and lifted him gently to the ground. Soon as he got the chance, he'd take the animal to a vet for a checkup and some shots. There might be a microchip implanted somewhere under his hide, identifying him as someone's lost pet, but Logan doubted it.

Most likely, Sidekick had been dumped, if he'd ever belonged to anybody in the first place.

The dog did some sniffing around, then lifted his leg against an old wagon wheel half-submerged in the ground. As Logan approached the house, with its drooping front porch, Sidekick trotted eagerly after him.

Any sensible person, Logan reflected ruefully, would bulldoze the once imposing shack to the ground and start over. But then, he wasn't a sensible person— he had two failed marriages, a career in rodeo and a lot of heartache to prove it.

He shouldered open the front door, causing the hinges to squeal, and, after another deep breath, stepped over the threshold. The place was filthy, of course, littered with newspapers, beer cans and God knew what else, but the plank floors had held, and the big natural-rock fireplace looked as sturdy as if it had just been mortared together.

Standing in the middle of the ancestral pile—and *pile* was definitely the word—Logan wondered, not for the first time, if there weren't as many rocks in his head as there were in that fireplace. Ever since he'd tracked down his distant cousins, the McKettricks, six months back, and visited the Triple M, down in northern Arizona, questions about the state of this ranch, and what was left of his family, had throbbed in the back of his mind like a giant bruise.

And that bruise had a name. Guilt.

He crossed the large room, sat down on the high ledge fronting the fireplace and sighed, his shoulders slackening a little under his plain white T-shirt. He shoved a hand through his dark hair and smiled sadly when Sidekick came and laid his muzzle on his knee.

"Some people," Logan told Sidekick, "just can't get enough of trouble and aggravation. And I, old buddy, am one of those people."

Ranches in Montana, in whatever degree of disrepair, were golden on the real estate market. Especially if they had a rip-roaring history, like this one did. Movie stars liked to buy them for astronomical prices, put in tennis courts and soundstages and square-acre swimming pools. He and Dylan and Tyler could split a fortune if they sold the place. Cut the emotional losses and run.

Just about the last thing Logan needed, though, besides a dog and that old truck he'd bought because it would fit in in a place like Stillwater Springs, Montana, was more money. He had a shitload of that, thanks to the do-it-yourself legal services Web site he'd set up fresh out of law school and recently sold for a mega-chunk of change, and so far, all that dough had caused him nothing but grief.

But there was a deeper reason he couldn't sell.

As run-down as the ranch was, seven or eight generations of Creeds had lived and died, loved and hated, cussed and prayed within its boundaries. Folks had gotten themselves born in the houses, run hellbent for the closing bell through whatever years they'd been allotted and been laid to rest in the cemetery out beyond the apple orchard.

Logan just couldn't leave them behind, any more than he'd been able to get into his truck back there at the rest stop and pull out without Sidekick.

They were his, that horde of cussed, unruly ghosts.

So was their reputation for chronic hell-raising.

Seeing the Triple M, something had shifted in Logan. He'd decided to stop running, plant his feet and put down roots so deep the tips might just pop up someplace in China. The Creed legacy wasn't like the McKettrick one, though, there was no denying that.

The McKettricks had stayed together, the line unbroken all the way back to old Angus, the patriarch.

The Creeds had splintered.

The McKettrick name was synonymous with honor, integrity and grit.

The *Creed* name, on the other hand, meant tragedy, bad luck and misery.

Logan had come back to take a stand, turn things around. Build something new and durable and good, from the ground up. His own children, if he was ever fortunate enough to have any, would bear the Creed name proudly, and so would his nieces and nephews. Not that he had any of those, either—Dylan and Tyler, as far as he knew, were still following the rodeo, at least part of the time, chasing the kind of women a man didn't want to impregnate, and brawling in redneck bars.

He had no illusions that it would be easy, changing the course the Creeds had taken, but at the brass-tacks level, wasn't it a matter of making a choice, a decision, and sticking by it, no matter what?

Dylan wasn't going to do any such thing, and neither was Tyler, and there wasn't anybody else who gave a damn.

Which meant Logan was elected, by a one-vote landslide.

He stood and headed for the kitchen, which was in

worse shape by half than the living room, but when he turned the faucet in the sink, good Montana well water flowed out of it, murky at first, then clear as light.

Cheered, Logan scouted up an old mixing bowl in a cupboard, washed it out and filled it with water for Sidekick, then set it on the grimy linoleum floor. The dog lapped loudly, and then belched like a cowboy after chugging a pint of beer.

They prowled through the rooms, dog and man, Logan making mental notes as they went. Once he'd bought out the local Home Depot and hired about a hundred carpenters and a plumber or two, they'd be good to go.

BRIANA DIDN'T GET to the cemetery until late afternoon, and once she arrived, she wondered why she'd come at all, just like she always did. While her sons, Alec, eight, and Josh, ten, ran between the teetering headstones and rotting wooden markers, she spread the picnic blanket on a soft piece of ground and got out the juice and sandwiches. Her old dog, Wanda, a portly black Lab, watched placidly as the boys raced through the last blazing sunlight of that warm June day.

"I don't even know any of the people buried here," Briana told Wanda. "So why do I break my back pulling weeds and planting flowers for a bunch of dead strangers?"

Wanda regarded her patiently.

For the past two years, since the night her now ex-husband, Vance, after a lengthy argument, had abandoned her, along with the boys and Wanda, in front of the Stillwater Springs Wal-Mart store, Briana had been busy surviving.

At the time, she'd thought Vance would circle the block a few times in their asthmatic old van, letting off steam, then come back for them. Instead, he'd left town. By the time he'd shown up again, three months later, magnanimously ready to let bygones be bygones, Briana had filed for a DIY divorce, found a place to live and landed a job at the tribal casino, serving free sodas and coffee for tips. At first, the few dollars she'd earned in an eight-hour shift had barely put food on the table, but she'd worked her way up to clerking in the players' club, then dealing black-jack. Finally, she'd become a floor supervisor, making change and paying out the occasional jackpot.

Floor supervisors made a decent wage. They also had health benefits, sick leave and paid vacations.

She'd made it on her own, something Vance had had her convinced she couldn't do.

Soon after they'd all moved into the house across the creek, Alec and Josh had come across the cemetery in their wanderings, and she'd come to check the place out, make sure it was safe for them to play there. Briana was big on safe places, though they'd proved pretty elusive so far. At thirty, she was still looking for one.

Nothing could have prepared her, she supposed, for the effect the first sight of that forgotten country graveyard had had on her. Lonely, overgrown with weeds, strung from end to end with the detritus of a thousand teenage beer-and-reefer parties, the place had somehow welcomed her, too.

Ever since, tending to the abandoned cemetery had

been her mission. She and the boys had cleaned up the grounds, scythed the grass and then mowed it, planted flowers and straightened markers. The work parties always ended with the boys playing tag to run off their excess energy, then a picnic supper.

She hadn't expected today to be different from any of the ones that had gone before it, which only went to show that she still had the capacity to be surprised.

A lean, shaggy-haired man in jeans, boots and a T-shirt came strolling out of the woods, a reddish-brown dog at his side, and stopped in his tracks when he saw Briana.

She felt an odd little frisson of alarm—and something else less easily defined—at the first glimpse of him.

His hair was dark, and though he was slender, he was powerfully built.

Wanda gave a low, uncertain growl, but didn't move from her customary spot on the picnic blanket.

"Hush," Briana said, aware that the boys had stopped their game and were gravitating toward her, curious and maybe a little worried.

The stranger smiled, spoke quietly to his dog and kept his distance.

Alec went straight to him. "Hi," he said. "I'm Alec Grant. That's my mom, Briana, and my brother, Josh, aka Ditz-butt. Who are you?"

"Logan Creed," the man replied, with a slight smile. "Nice to meet you, Alec." He was looking at Briana, though, his gaze speculative, but languid, too. He took in all five feet, seven inches of her, clad in worn blue jeans and a pink ruffly sun-top, with green eyes and freckles and her long, strawberry-

blond hair pulled back, as always, in a French braid.
Inspected her as if he might have to identify her in a
lineup later on.

Briana hesitated, uncomfortable as she registered
the familiar last name, then advanced, working up a
neighborly smile. She put out a hand as she introduced
herself. "Briana Grant."

"We know somebody named *Dylan* Creed," Alec
said. Her younger son had never met a stranger, a
fact that both pleased and troubled Briana. The don't-
talk-to-people-you-don't-know lecture was wasted on
Alec. "Mom and Josh and me take care of his house.
He's got a bull, too. Cimarron."

Up close, Logan Creed was even better-looking
than he had been from a distance. His hair, a little too
long, was ebony, and his eyes were a deep, searching brown, full of intelligence and a few secrets. His
cheekbones were high, hinting that there might be native blood somewhere in his background. He looked
nothing like his blue-eyed, fair-haired brother, Dylan,
and yet there *was* a resemblance—something in his
temperament, perhaps, though she knew little enough
of that yet, admittedly, or the way he stood.

"So Dylan hired a caretaker, did he?" he asked
lazily. "And he owns a bull?" His gaze moved past
Briana to the graveyard. "Is my kid brother paying
you to look after the cemetery, too? If so, he ought to
give you a raise. The place looks a lot better than it
did the last time I was here."

Briana blushed a little, unsure how to answer, and
still feeling oddly exposed under this man's steady re-
gard. Dylan hadn't mentioned the cemetery when he'd
hired her, outside of Wal-Mart on that fateful night.

He'd been in town briefly, on some kind of personal business, and happened to see Vance toss a couple of twenty-dollar bills out of the truck window and speed off with his tires screeching.

Sizing up the situation, Dylan had probably felt sorry for Briana, the kids and the dog. He'd handed her a set of keys, given her directions to the place and strolled off without a backward glance. Warned her about Cimarron, a white bull recently retired from rodeo life; said a neighbor fed the animal and Briana ought to stay clear. She'd taken a cab to the ranch, furious with Vance and really hoping he'd come back after he'd cooled off and find them gone. Serve him right.

Instead, he'd kept right on going.

The next day, a load of groceries had arrived, via a delivery service, along with a note from Dylan saying there was an old Chevy truck parked in the barn and she could use it if she could get it running. Since then, they'd had no communication beyond the occasional e-mail or phone call. When something needed fixing and the job was beyond Briana's limited home-repair skills, Dylan was quick to send a check, and Briana was careful to provide a receipt, though he'd never asked for one.

Now, Josh stepped up, stood close to her side. The polar opposite of Alec, Josh considered *everyone* a stranger and thus potential trouble, and proceeded accordingly until they'd proved themselves. "Nobody pays us to take care of the cemetery," he said. "We do it because it needs doing."

Logan's smile came suddenly, and it set Briana back on her heels a little. She added very white teeth to the inventory she'd taken of him earlier, while he was taking *her* measure. "Well," he said, "I appreciate it. And that's as good a reason to do a thing as any."

Cautiously mollified, Josh softened a little, but he didn't quite smile. He was letting Briana know, by his stiff stance and knotted fists, that he'd protect her, and Alec and Wanda, too, if necessary. Thanks to Vance, Josh was half again too manly for a ten-year-old, too serious and too sad.

"Where do you live?" he asked Logan solemnly.

Logan cocked a thumb over one shoulder. "At the main ranch house," he said.

"Nobody lives there," Josh argued.

"Josh." Briana sighed.

"Someone lives there now," Logan replied affably. "Sidekick and I moved in today."

Josh looked at the copper-colored dog. "He's skinny. Don't you feed him?"

"He and I just recently met up," Logan answered. His voice was easy. "He'll fill out as time goes by."

Wanda bestirred her considerable bulk and ambled over to sniff at Sidekick's nose. Sidekick sniffed back. Then both of them lost interest in each other.

"I still think he could use one of our bologna sandwiches," Josh insisted sagely. Then, as a concession, he added, "He looks pretty clean."

"Half drained the well getting *that* done," Logan said. "About exhausted the soap supply, too."

Josh broke down and grinned.

It finally occurred to Briana that Logan must have come to the cemetery to visit someone's grave. And a pilgrimage like that, especially after a long absence, might require privacy.

"Maybe we should go," she said.

But Logan shook his head. "Stay right here and carry on with your picnic," he told her. Then, addressing Josh, he added, "Sidekick can have that sandwich if the offer's still good, but it's only right to warn you that he might hurl. Seems to have a delicate stomach."

Hurling being serious business to a ten-year-old, Josh nodded. "Dog food would be better," he said. "We could lend you some of Wanda's kibble if you need it."

Logan chuckled, looked as though he'd like to ruffle Josh's hair, but didn't. "Thanks," he said. "But we made a run to town for grub earlier, and we're all set."

Briana smiled, herded Wanda and the boys back toward the picnic blanket. Sidekick stayed with Logan, who went to crouch beside one of the graves.

"Can I take Sidekick some bologna?" Alec whispered.

"No," Briana said, watching Logan. "Not now."

"It's a *private* moment, doofus," Josh told his brother.

"Dogs don't *have* private moments, stink-breath!" Alec countered.

"Be quiet," Briana said, wondering why her hands shook a little as she poured drinks and unwrapped sandwiches.

LOGAN'S EYES BURNED as he ran the tips of his fingers over the simple lettering chiseled into his mother's headstone. *Teresa Courtland Creed. Wife and Mother.*

He'd been three years old when his mom lost her battle with breast cancer, and there'd been a gaping hole in his life ever since. His dad, Jake Creed, never a solid citizen in the first place, had gone on a ten-year bender starting the day of the funeral. His grief hadn't kept him from marrying Dylan's mother six months later, though. Poor, sweet Maggie had died in a car accident four days after her son's seventh birthday. True to his pattern, Jake had married again before the year was out—this time to Angela, an idealistic young schoolteacher with no more sense than to marry a raging drunk with two wild kids. Doubtless, she'd thought all Jake needed was the love of a good woman. She'd been a fine stepmother to Logan and Dylan, and had soon given birth to Tyler.

She'd lasted a whole five years, Angela had.

But Jake's carousing had just plain worn her out. One fine summer day, she'd made a batch of fried chicken, told Logan and Dylan and Tyler to be sure to do their chores and say their prayers, and left.

Jake had turned the whole countryside upside down looking for her. Enraged, he was convinced she'd left him for another man, and he meant to drag her home by the hair if it came to that.

Instead, Angela had had herself a first-class nervous breakdown. She'd checked into a motel on the outskirts of Missoula, swallowed a bottle of tranquilizers and died.

Such, Logan thought, was the proud history of the Creeds.

After that, Jake had given up on marriage. When Logan was a junior in college, the old man had gotten himself killed in a freak logging accident.

Remembering the funeral made Logan's stomach roll. As ludicrous as it seemed in retrospect, considering the havoc Jake's drinking had wreaked on all their lives, the three of them had swilled whiskey, then gotten into the mother of all fistfights and ended the night in separate jail cells, guests of Sheriff Floyd Book.

They hadn't spoken since, though Logan kept track of his brothers, mostly via the Internet. Dylan, four-time world champion bull-rider, was apparently a professional celebrity, now that he'd hung up his rodeo gear for good. He'd even been in a couple of movies, though as far as Logan could tell, Dylan was famous for doing not much of anything in particular.

Only in America.

Tyler, whose event was bareback bronc busting, was still following the rodeo. He'd been involved in a few well-publicized romantic scrapes, invested his considerable winnings in real estate and signed on as a national spokesman for a designer boot company. Though he was the youngest, Tyler was also the wildest of Jake Creed's three sons. He had issues aplenty, between the way Jake had raised them and his mother's death.

But his brothers' stories were just that—their stories. Logan knew he'd have his hands full straightening out his own life, and while he regretted it, the fact was, the Creed brothers were estranged. And the estrangement might well be permanent. Given the family pride, not to mention inborn stubbornness, "Sorry" just wasn't enough.

Logan was about ready to leave—he had several other places to go. Briana and the kids were folding up their picnic blanket. The younger boy, Alec, approached with a slice of bologna for Sidekick.

"You a cowboy?" the kid asked, taking notice of

Logan's worn boots while the dog feasted on lunch meat, downing rind and all.

Logan thrust a hand through his hair. "I was, once," he said, aware of Briana—now, where the devil had she gotten a name like that?—looking on.

"My dad's a cowboy," Alec said. "We don't see him much."

"I'm sorry to hear that," Logan replied.

"He rodeos," Alec explained. "Mom divorced him online after he left us off in front of Wal-Mart and didn't come back to get us."

Something bit into the pit of Logan's stomach. He felt fury, certainly—what kind of man abandoned a woman and two little boys *and* a dog?—but a disturbing amount of relief, too. Once again, his gaze strayed to Briana, who was just opening her mouth to call Alec off. Damn, but she was delectable, all curves and bright hair and smooth, lightly freckled skin.

"Mom takes real good care of us, though," Alec went on, when Logan didn't—*couldn't*—speak. Old Jake hadn't been the father of the year, either, but for all his womanizing, all his drinking, all his brawling, he'd worked steadily and hard up there in the woods, felling trees. On his worst day, he wouldn't have left his woman or his kids to fend for themselves.

"Bet she does," Logan managed to respond, as Briana drew closer.

"She's a supervisor over at the casino," Alex stated, speeding up his words as his mother got nearer.

Briana arrived, placed a slender hand on Alec's T-shirted shoulder. Both boys had dark hair and eyes, in contrast to their mother's fair coloring. A picture of her ex-husband formed in Logan's mind. He was probably a charmer, one of those gypsy types, with a good line and a sad story.

"That's enough, Alec," Briana said calmly. She kept her eyes averted from Logan's face, as though she'd suddenly turned shy. "We have to go home now. You have chores to do, and lessons."

Alec wrinkled his nose. "Mom home-schools us," he told Logan. "We don't even get a *summer vacation.*"

Logan arched an eyebrow, perched his hands on his hips. Resisted an urge to rub his beard-stubbled chin self-consciously.

"That," Briana said, squeezing the boy's shoulder gently, "is because you goof off so much, you have to put in extra time."

"I wish we could go to school in Stillwater Springs, like the other kids," Alec lamented. "*They* get to play *baseball*. They ride a bus and go on field trips and *everything.*"

Briana's face tightened almost imperceptibly, and that flush rose again, along the undersides of her cheekbones. "Alec," she said firmly, "Mr. Creed is not interested in our personal business. Let's run along home before the mosquitoes come out, okay?"

"Mr. Creed" was, in fact, interested, and out of all proportion to good sense, too. "Logan," he said.

Briana checked her watch, nodded. "Logan," she repeated distractedly.

"Can Josh and me call you 'Logan,' too?" Alec asked, his voice hopeful.

A woman who home-schooled her children might have some pretty strict ideas about etiquette. Logan didn't want to step on Briana's toes, so he said, "If it's all right with your mother."

"We'll see," Briana said, still flustered. Then, like a hen, but without the clucking, she gathered her brood and herded them off toward the creek. Dylan's place was just on the other side of a rickety little wooden bridge, hidden from sight by a copse of birch trees in full summer leaf. The black dog waddled after them.

Logan felt strangely bereft, watching them go. Sidekick must have, too, because he gave a little whimper of protest.

Logan bent, reassured the dog with a pat on the head. "Let's go home, boy," he said. "By now, word will have gotten around that I'm back, and we're bound to get company."

But neither of them moved until Briana, the boys and the dog disappeared from sight.

Logan paused, thinking he ought to stop by Jake's grave before he left, but he was afraid he'd spit on it if he did. So he headed toward the orchard instead, Sidekick hurrying to keep up.

Sure enough, Cassie Greencreek's eyesore of a car sat beside the house. It sort of classed up the place, which was a sad commentary by anybody's standards.

Cassie was waiting for him. She'd settled herself on the top porch step, looking resplendent in a purple polyester dress big enough to hide a Volkswagen. Her waist-length black hair was streaked with silver now, and her brown eyes glinted with a combination of welcome and bad temper.

"Logan Creed," she declared, receiving the dog graciously when he went to greet her. "I never thought you'd have the nerve to come back here, after all the goings-on at Jake's funeral."

Logan grinned sheepishly, pausing on the weed-choked walk. Spreading his hands in the time-honored here-I-am gesture.

"When was the last time you shaved?" Cassie demanded, making room for Sidekick on the step. "You look like some saddle-bum."

Logan laughed at that, drew near and bent to kiss the old woman's upturned face.

"I love you, too, Grandma," he said.

CHAPTER TWO

THE HOUSE THAT had sheltered Briana Grant, her sons and her dog for just over two years looked the same as ever, in the gathering dusk, and yet it was different, too.

A strange little thrill, not in the least unpleasant, danced in the depths of her abdomen as she looked around.

Same noisy, dented refrigerator, its front all but hidden by Alec and Josh's artwork.

Same worn-out linoleum floors.

Same old-fashioned harvest-gold wall phone with the twisty plastic cord. Beneath it, on the warped wooden counter, the red light on the answering machine winked steadily.

What had changed?

It wasn't the house, of course. *She* was different, altered somehow, and on a quantum level, too, as if the very structure of her cells had been zapped with some dangerous new energy.

What the *hell?* she wondered, biting down hard on her lower lip as the boys engaged in their usual coming-home chaos—Josh logging on to the computer at the desk under the kitchen window, Wanda barking and turning in circles around her water dish,

Alec diving for the answering machine when he saw that the tiny red light was blinking.

"Maybe Dad called!" Alec shouted, punching buttons.

"Maybe the president called," Josh mocked bitterly.

"Shut up, poop face!"

"Shut up, *both* of you," Briana said, drawing back a chair at the table and dropping onto its cracked red vinyl seat, feeling oddly displaced, as though she'd accidentally stumbled into some neighboring dimension.

Vance's voice, rising out of the answering machine like a smoky genie promising three wishes—none of which would come true, of course—sounded throaty and cajoling.

Wanda stopped barking.

"Hello, family," Vance said, and Briana glanced in Josh's direction, saw his sturdy little back stiffen under his striped T-shirt. "Sorry about that child-support check, Bree. I figured I'd have the money in the bank before it cleared, but I didn't make it."

Briana closed her eyes. Vance loved to toss the word *family* around, as if just by using it, he could rewrite history and undo the truth—that he'd virtually thrown his wife and children away, like the candy-bar wrappers and burger cartons that collected on the floorboards of his van.

"I might be passing through Stillwater Springs in a week or so," the disembodied voice drawled on. "I'll bunk in on the couch, if it's all right with you, and see what I can do about making that check good." A slight pause. "The couch folds out, right?"

The graveyard supper of bologna and juice roiled in Briana's stomach.

Alec erupted with joy, jumping all over the kitchen like one of those Mexican worms trapped inside a dry husk.

"If *he's* coming here," Josh huffed, fingers flying over the computer keyboard, "*I'm* running away from home!"

"See you soon," Vance crooned. "Love you all."

Click.

See you soon. Love you all.

Right.

Briana swore under her breath. The earlier, almost mystical sense of profound change receded into the background of her mind, instantly replaced by a tension headache, bouncing hard between her temples.

"Go *ahead* and run away," Alec taunted his brother. "I'd like to have the bottom bunk, anyway!"

Briana sighed. "Enough," she said, rising weakly from her chair, going through the motions. She filled Wanda's water and kibble bowls, but her gaze kept straying to the answering machine. Vance hadn't left a number, and she didn't have caller ID, since the phone was vintage. "Do either of you have your dad's cell number?"

Vance used cheap convenience-store phones, mostly. To him, everything was disposable—including people and a dog he'd raised from a pup.

"Like I'd call the jerk," Josh muttered. He put up a good front, but there were tears under all that scorn. Briana could relate—she'd cried a literal river over Vance herself, though the waterworks had long since dried up, along with everything else she'd ever felt for him. She was so over him—in fact, she'd been

looking for a way out long before the drop-off outside of Wal-Mart.

"Why do you want Dad's number?" Alec asked,
red behind his freckles, practically glaring at Briana. "You're not going to call him and tell him not to
come, are you?"

That was exactly what Briana had intended to do,
but looking down into Alec's earnest little face, she
knew she couldn't. Not while he and Josh were within
earshot, anyhow.

"He probably won't show up, anyhow," Josh observed, still busily surfing the Web. What exactly
was he *doing* on that computer? "With his word and
one square of toilet paper, you could wipe your butt."

"Joshua," Briana said.

"I hate you!" Alec shrieked. "I hate both of you!"

Wanda whimpered and flopped down by her water
dish in dog despondence. When Alec pounded into the
bedroom just off the kitchen that he and Josh shared,
Wanda didn't pad after him, which was unusual.

Briana sighed again, pulled the carafe from the
coffeemaker and went to the sink to fill it, glowering
at the nearby answering machine. *Damn you, Vance,*
she thought grimly. *Why don't you just leave us alone?
That's your specialty, isn't it?*

"He's a cowboy, all right," Josh said, sounding almost triumphant. The keyboard clicking had ceased,
definitely a temporary phenomenon. Josh was online
way too much, and he was way too skillful at covering his tracks for Briana's comfort.

She frowned, still feeling disconnected, out of step.
Went on making coffee, even though she didn't need
the caffeine. After the bomb Vance had just dropped,

she wasn't going to get any sleep that night anyway. "Your dad?" she asked.

Josh echoed the sigh she'd given earlier. *"Logan Creed,"* he said, with the exaggerated patience of a Rhodes scholar addressing a blathering idiot. "I ran a search on him. He's been All-Around Cowboy *twice*. He's been married twice, too, no kids, no visible means of support."

"He's a...cowboy?" Briana echoed stupidly. In a way, she found that news even more disconcerting than the threat of Vance's imminent arrival.

"He does have a law degree," Josh said, hunching his shoulders to peer at the monitor screen. "Maybe he's rich or something."

The Creeds were legendary in and around Stillwater Springs. Even as a comparative newcomer, Briana had heard plenty about their exploits, but if the state of the ranch was anything to go by, they not only weren't rich, but they'd also been lucky to escape foreclosure.

"Now why would you run a search on Mr. Creed?" Briana asked, with an idleness she didn't feel, as she took a mug down from the cupboard and dumped in artificial sweetener and fat-free cream.

Creed is a cowboy, said a voice in her head. *Consider yourself warned.*

"He said we could call him Logan," Josh reminded her.

"Logan, then," Briana said, filling her mug even though the pot wasn't finished brewing. The stuff had that strong, bottom-of-the-pot taste, fit to curl her hair, but it steadied her a little. "Why check him out online?"

"It was the boots," Josh reminisced, either hedging

or ignoring Briana's question entirely. "They weren't fancy, like the ones that guy at the Ford dealership wears, with stars and cactuses and bears stitched on them—"

"Cacti," Briana corrected automatically, ever the teacher.

"Whatever," Josh said, turning to face her now. "Logan's boots are beat-up. Anybody with boots like that probably rides horses and works hard for a living."

Briana thought of Vance's boots. He'd had them resoled several times, and they were always scuffed. "Maybe he's just poor," she suggested. "Logan, I mean."

Josh shook his head. "He's got a law degree," he repeated.

"And 'no visible means of support,' as you put it. Stop evading my question, Josh. Why did you research our neighbor?"

"To make sure he isn't a serial killer or something," Josh answered.

Briana hid a smile. In a few minutes, she'd check on Alec. Right now, she suspected, he needed some alone time. "And what's your assessment, detective? Is the neighborhood safe for decent people?"

Josh grinned. His smiles were so rare these days that even the most fleeting ones were cause for celebration. Some inner light had dimmed in Josh, after Vance's desertion, and sometimes Briana feared that it would go out entirely.

"At least until Dad gets here, it is," Josh said.

Ignoring that remark, Briana flipped on the overhead lights, sent the twilight shadows skittering. "You wouldn't really run away, would you?" she asked carefully, making the artwork flutter like ruffled feathers on some big bird when she opened the refrigerator door again. Bologna sandwiches aside, the boys would need a real supper. "If your dad comes to visit, I mean?"

The silence stretched thin between her question and Josh's answer.

Still in the chair in front of the computer, he looked down at the floor. "I'm *ten,* Mom," he said. "Where would I go?"

Briana set aside the package of chicken drumsticks she'd just taken from the fridge and went to her son. Moved to lay a hand on his shoulder, then withdrew it. "Josh—"

"Why can't he just leave us alone?" Josh broke in plaintively. "You're divorced from him. I want to be divorced from him, too."

Briana bent her knees, sat on her haunches, looking up into Josh's face. He was one very worried little boy, trying so hard to be a man. "I know you're angry," she said, "but your dad will always be your dad. He's not perfect, Josh, but neither are the rest of us."

A tear slipped down Josh's cheek, a little silvery trail coursing through an afternoon's worth of happy dirt. "I still wish we could trade him in for somebody different," he said.

Briana's chuckle was part sob. Her vision blurred, and her smile must have looked brittle to Josh, even forced. "Cardinal cosmic rule number one," she said. "You can't change the past—or other people. And the truth is, while things were pretty hard a lot of the time, I don't regret marrying your dad."

Josh sniffled, perplexed. "You don't?"

Briana shook her head.

"Why not? He's chronically unemployed. When he does send a child-support check, it always bounces. Don't you ever wish you'd married another kind of man? Or just stayed single?"

Briana reached up, ran a hand over Josh's ultra-short summer haircut. "I never wish that," she said. "Because if I hadn't married your dad, I wouldn't have you and Alec, and I can't even imagine what that would be like."

Josh ruminated. They'd had the conversation before, but he needed to be reminded, even more often than Alec did, that she was there for the duration, that she'd fight monsters for him, or walk through fire. For a year after Vance had left them, Josh had had nightmares, woke screaming for her. Alec had suffered, too, wetting the bed several times a week.

"We're a lot of trouble," Josh said finally. "Alec and me, I mean. Fighting all the time, and not doing our chores."

"You're the best things that ever happened to me," Briana said truthfully, standing up straight. "It *would* be kind of nice if you and your brother got along better and did your chores, though."

The door to the boys' bedroom creaked partway open, and Alec stuck his head out.

"I'm done being mad now," he said. His glance slid to Josh. "Mostly."

Briana laughed. "Good," she replied, getting out the electric skillet to fry up chicken legs. "Both of you need to clean up. Josh, you go first. Shut down that computer and hightail it for the bathroom. Alec, you can wash here at the kitchen sink, and then we'll go over your multiplication tables."

For once, Josh didn't argue.

Alec dragged the step stool over to the sink, climbed up and scrubbed his face and hands. "It's *summer,* Mom," he protested. "I bet the kids who go to *real* school aren't worrying about any dumb old multiplication tables."

"Alec," Briana said.

"One times one is—"

"Alec."

Alec rattled through his sixes, sevens and eights, the sequences that usually gave him trouble, before he got down off the step stool. Then he stood facing Briana, hands and face dripping.

"I know Dad's cell-phone number," he said.

Briana's heart pinched. Alec lived for any kind of contact with Vance, no matter how brief or limited. He probably expected her to shoot down the visit like a clay bird on a skeet-shooting range, but he was willing to give her the information anyway.

"That's okay," she said, a little choked up. Alec was only eight. Even after all the disappointments, and all Briana's cautious attempts to explain, he simply didn't understand why the four of them plus Wanda didn't add up to a family anymore. "You know, of course, that your dad…changes his mind a lot? About visits and things like—"

Alec cut her off with a glum look and a nod. "I just want to see him, Mom. I know he might not come."

Briana's throat cinched tight. Vance was always chasing some big prize, some elusive victory, emotionally blindfolded, stumbling over rough ground, trying to catch fireflies in his bare hands. Their marriage was over for good, but he still had their sons. They were smart, wonderful boys. Why were they always at the bottom of his priority list?

"I know," she said, at last. "I know."

CASSIE STROKED THE dog as she regarded Logan in her thoughtful way, seeing way inside. She looked completely at home in her skin, sitting there on the porch step. Unlike most of the women Logan knew, Cassie never seemed to fret about her weight—it was simply part of who she was. To him, she'd always been beautiful, a great and deep-rooted tree, sheltering him and his brothers under her leafy branches when they were young, along with half the other kids in the county. Giving them space to grow up in, within her constant, unruffled affection.

"You look so much like Teresa," she said quietly. "Especially around the eyes."

Logan didn't answer. Cassie was thinking out loud, not making conversation. She *never* made conversation, not the small-talk variety, anyway.

Teresa, his mother, had been Cassie's foster daughter, so they weren't really related, he and this "grandmother" of his. Still, he loved her, and knew she loved him in return.

Cassie looked around, sighed. "The place is a shipwreck," she said, still petting Sidekick, who was sucking up the attention, snuggling close against Cassie's side. "You should come and stay in my guest room until the contractors are through."

"Your guest room," Logan said, "is a teepee."

Cassie laughed. "You didn't mind sleeping out

there when you were a boy," she reminded him. "You used to pretend you were Geronimo, and Dylan and Tyler always fussed at me because you wouldn't let them be chief."

The memory—and the mention of his brothers—ached in Logan's rawest places. "You ever hear from them, Cassie?" he asked, very quietly and at a considerable amount of time.

"Do you?" Cassie immediately countered.

Logan shoved a hand through his hair. He still needed a trim, but there were only so many things a man could do on his first day home. "No," he said. "And you knew that, so why did you ask?"

"Wanted to hear you say it aloud," Cassie said. "Maybe it'll sink in, that way. Dylan and Ty are your *brothers,* Logan. All the blood family you've got in the world. You play fast and loose with that, like you've got all the time there is to make things right between the three of you, and you'll be sorry."

Logan approached at last, found a perch on the bottom step. His first inclination was to get his back up, ask why it was his job to "make things right," but the question would have been rhetorical bullshit.

He *knew* why it was up to him. Because he was the eldest. Because nobody else was going to open a dialogue. And because he'd been the one to start the fight, the day of their dad's funeral, by speaking ill of the dead.

Okay, he'd been drunk.

But he'd meant the things he'd said about Jake— that he wouldn't miss him, that the world would be a more peaceful place without him, if not a better one.

He'd meant them *then,* anyway.

Cassie reached out and mussed his hair. "Why did you come back here, Logan?" she asked. "I think I know, but, like before, I'd like to hear you say it."

"To start over," he said, after another hesitation.

"Sounds like a big job," Cassie observed. "Getting on some kind of terms with your brothers—even slugging terms would be better than what you have now—that'll be part of it."

Logan nodded, but he didn't speak. He didn't trust his voice beyond the three-word sentence he'd offered up last.

"I'll give you their numbers," Cassie said, shifting enough to extract her purse from between her right thigh and the porch rail, taking out a notepad and a pen. "You call them."

"What am I going to say?"

For all the figuring he'd done, all the planning and deciding, he'd never come up with a way to close the yawning gap between him and Dylan and Tyler.

Cassie chuckled. "Start with hello," she said, "and see where it goes from there."

"I shouldn't need to tell you where it *might* 'go from there,'" he replied.

"You'll never know if you don't try," Cassie told him. She scrawled two numbers onto the notepad, quickly and from memory, Logan noted, and tore off the page to hand to him. Having done that, she stood with the elegant grace that always surprised him a little, given her size. She patted Sidekick once more and descended the steps with the slow and purposeful motion of a glacier, leaving Logan to step out of her way or get run over.

Sidekick remained behind on the porch step, but he gave a little snort-sigh, sorry to see Cassie go.

Logan opened the door of her car, like a gentleman. Why Cassie didn't buy herself something decent to drive was beyond him—she received a chunk of the take from the local casino twice a year, as did the other forty-odd members of her tribe.

"Next time I see you," she said, shaking a finger at him, "you'd better be able to tell me you've spoken to Dylan and Tyler. And it wouldn't be a bad idea to shave and put on something with a collar and buttons." She paused to tug at his T-shirt. "In my day, these things were *underwear*."

Logan laughed. "I've missed you, Cassie," he said, leaning in to kiss her cheek. "Sidekick and I will stop by tomorrow—I'm taking him to the vet and I have a meeting with my contractor. I can promise the shave and the button-down shirt, maybe even a haircut, but whether I'll have called my brothers or not…well, that's a crapshoot."

"Longer you put it off, the harder it will be," Cassie said, making no move to get into the car. "Are you going to stay, Logan, or are you just blowing through to spit on your father's grave and sell your share of this land to some actor?"

"I hope you're not going to stand there and pretend you were the president of Jake Creed's fan club," Logan said.

"We had our tussles, Jake and me," Cassie admitted. "But he was your father, Logan. In his own crazy way, he loved you boys."

"Yeah, it was right out of *Leave it to Beaver,* the way we lived," Logan scoffed. There was a note of respect in his tone, but it was for Cassie, not Jake. "I guess you've forgotten the year he cut the Christmas tree in half with a chainsaw. And how about that wonderful Thanksgiving when he decided the turkey was overcooked and threw it through the kitchen window?"

Cassie sighed, laid a hand on Logan's shoulder. "What about the time you and Dylan decided to run away from home and got lost up in the woods? It was November, and the weatherman was predicting record low temperatures. The sheriff gave up the search when the sun went down, but Jake...? He kept looking. Found you and brought you both home."

"And hauled us both off to the woodshed."

"If he'd given up, you'd have been hauled off to the morgue. I know he took a switch to you, and I'd have stopped him if I'd been here, but it wasn't anger that made him paddle your hind end, Logan Creed. It was plain old ordinary *fear*."

"Today, they call it child abuse," Logan pointed out.

"Today," Cassie argued, "they've got school shootings and kids who can't be graded on a test because their self-esteem might be damaged. They call in the social workers if the screen on the TV in their bedroom is too small, or their personal computer isn't fast enough. I'm not so sure a good switching wouldn't be a favor to some of those young thugs who hang out behind the pool hall when they're supposed to be in class."

"That is so not politically correct," Logan said, though secretly, he agreed.

"I don't have to be politically correct," Cassie retorted, with a sniff.

She was right about that. She didn't. And she wasn't.

She ducked behind the wheel of her car. "Welcome back, Logan," she said, watching him through the open window. "See that you stay."

He thought of Briana Grant, her lively sons and her fat black dog. The idea of sticking around didn't seem quite so daunting as before.

"I guess Dylan's been back," he ventured. "Long enough to hire a caretaker, anyway."

Cassie merely nodded, waiting.

"Is he… Are Dylan and Briana…?"

Cassie's brown eyes warmed with humor and understanding. "Involved?" she said. "Is that what you mean?"

"Yes," Logan grumbled, because he knew she was going to leave him hanging there if he didn't respond. "That's what I mean."

She lifted one shoulder in a half shrug. "You know Dylan. When he goes after a woman…"

Logan's knuckles ached where he gripped the lower edge of Cassie's car window.

Cassie smiled and patted one of his hands. "If you want to know about Dylan and Briana," she said sweetly, "you'd better ask one of *them*. I'm just an old lady, minding my own business. How would I know what is—or isn't—going on between those two?"

"You know everything," Logan said. If he hadn't been wearing a T-shirt, he'd have been hot under the collar. "About everybody in Stillwater Springs and for fifty miles in all directions."

Cassie sighed. Shifted the car into Reverse. "You'd better step back," she said, "if you don't want me to run over your toes."

Logan, being no fool, stepped back.

He watched Cassie whip the little car around and chug back down the driveway at a good clip, exhaust pipe belching blue smoke, loose parts rattling. When she topped the rise, then dipped out of sight, he looked down at the paper she'd handed him earlier.

Dylan's number.

Tyler's.

Sidekick came down the porch steps to nudge Logan in one thigh, as if urging him to get it over with.

Cassie had been right, of course. It wasn't going to get any easier.

He got out his cell phone, thumbed in Dylan's number, half hoping he'd get voice mail.

"Yo," Dylan said, live and in person. "Dylan Creed."

Logan plunked down on the porch step, right where Cassie had been sitting earlier. Cleared his throat. "Did you check caller ID before you answered?" he asked.

Silence.

Then, "Logan?"

"It's me," Logan said, bracing himself. Prepared for either a backlash of profanity or an instant hang-up.

Neither one came. Dylan seemed stunned, as much at a loss for words as Logan was.

"I'll be damned," Dylan said finally. "Where are you?"

"On the ranch," Logan replied, relieved.

"What are you doing there?" Now there was an edge to Dylan's tone; he sounded vaguely suspicious.

"Not much of anything, right at the moment," Logan said, scratching Sidekick's ears. "The place is going to hell in a wheelbarrow. Thought I'd fix it up a little—my part of it, anyway."

Another silence followed, pulsing with all the things neither one of them dared say.

"What've you been up to, Logan?"

Was it brotherly interest, that question, or an accusation? Logan decided to give Dylan the benefit of the doubt. "Quit the rodeo, got married and divorced a couple of times, started a business. What about you?"

"There are similarities," Dylan said quietly. "I'm not rodeoing anymore, either. No wives, current or ex, but I do have a two-year-old daughter. Her name's Bonnie—or it was the last time I heard. Her mother's changed it half a dozen times since the kid was born."

Logan closed his eyes. His own brother had a child, his *niece,* and he hadn't known the little girl existed. "The last time you heard? Don't you see Bonnie, Dylan?"

For a moment, the connection seemed to crackle, then Dylan took a breath. "Not much," he admitted. "Sharlene's supposed to share custody, but she doesn't."

"Maybe I could help you with that," Logan heard himself say.

"Yeah," Dylan retorted, and the edge was back in his voice. "You're a lawyer. I keep forgetting."

I'm also your brother.

"Look, if you decide you need legal advice, give

me a call. If not, that's okay, too. I just called be-cause—"

"Why *did* you call, Logan?" A challenge. That was like Dylan—to assume Logan must be up to some-thing, if he'd made contact after all this time.

"I guess being back home made me a little nostal-gic, that's all," Logan said.

"Home?" Dylan echoed, downright testy now. "Where's that?"

Logan said nothing.

"What do you want?"

The words hurt Logan a lot more than he would have admitted. "Nothing," he said. "I just thought we could talk."

"You're planning to sell your share of the ranch, aren't you? That's why you're hiring contractors and buying lumber. So you can nick some Hollywood type for a few million?"

Ah, the grapevine, Logan thought. Dylan knew he was fixing up the ranch house, because he still had sources in town. Asking where he was had been a formality.

"I'm not selling," he said evenly. "I'm here to stay. And if you're thinking of liquidating your share of the place, I'll match anybody else's offer." That train of thought led to Briana Grant, since she was living in Dylan's house, and following it got Logan into trouble. He was a beat late realizing he'd said the wrong thing.

"If I was going to sell my ten thousand acres—and I'm not—I sure as hell wouldn't let you buy me out."

Here we go, Logan thought. "Why's that?"

"You *know* why. Because of the things you said about Dad."

"I was wrong, okay? I should have been more respectful—kept my opinions to myself. I'm sorry, Dylan."

More silence. Dylan would have been prepared for a counterattack, but the left-field apology probably threw him a little.

"Dylan? Are you still there?"

Dylan sighed audibly. "I'm here."

"And 'here' is where?"

"L.A.," Dylan said. "I had a meeting with my agent and a few studio people—I'm doing some stunt work for a movie. They're filming up in Alberta, starting next week."

"You like that kind of work?" Logan asked. He couldn't imagine why anybody would, but then it couldn't be any more dangerous than rodeo, and they'd both taken a turn at that.

"It's a living," Dylan answered. "Pays my child support."

Logan took the plunge, though he knew the water would be cold. "I'm thinking of running some cattle on the ranch. Buying some horses, too. Maybe you'd like to be a partner?"

"We wouldn't get along for ten minutes," Dylan said, but there was something wistful in the way he said the words.

Logan laughed. "We never did," he replied. "But we had a lot of fun in between brawls."

More silence.

Then Dylan laughed, too. "Yeah," he said.

It was the first thing they'd agreed on in a decade.

"You going to call Ty?" Dylan asked.

"At some point."

"Well, tread lightly when you do. And don't give my name as a reference—he's seriously pissed at me right now."

"Why?" Logan asked, though he could imagine a thousand reasons—not the least of which was Tyler's tendency to be a hothead.

But Dylan shut him down. "Too personal," he said coolly. *This is between Ty and me. You're on the outside, looking in.* "Look, Logan, it was good to hear from you, but I've gotta go. Big date."

"Right," Logan replied. He and Dylan had been civil to each other. When he saw Cassie the next morning, he could honestly say he'd tried. "Good luck with the movie."

Dylan said thanks and hung up.

Logan looked down at Sidekick, who was gazing soulfully into his eyes.

"One down, one to go," he told the dog.

Sidekick whimpered.

Logan consulted Cassie's note again, then dialed the number scrawled next to Tyler's name.

One ring.

Two.

Three.

Then, the recording. "This is Tyler Creed. I'm busy right now, but I'll call you back unless you're selling something. In that case, you're SOL. Wait for the beep, and spill it."

Logan chuckled, waited for the beep.

"This is Logan," he said. He recited both his cell number and the new one for the ranch phone. "Call me. I'm not selling anything."

Like hell he wasn't.

CHAPTER THREE

SOLEMNLY, ALEC PRESENTED Briana with a tattered piece of notebook paper. The pencil marks forming Vance's number were pressed in hard, as though Alec had been afraid they would fade if he didn't copy them down with all his might.

The sorrow Briana felt in that moment weighed down her heart. Even Alec, Vance's most loyal supporter, knew that the precious digits in that phone number were elusive. Like his father.

Tears scalded the backs of her eyes, and she touched the pendant she always wore—she'd made it herself, scanning an old photo of her dad, resizing it, setting it in resin. He'd been a rambler, too, Bill McIntyre had, a well-known rodeo clown following the circuit during the season, parking his camper in his sister's backyard in Boise when there were no rodeos to perform in. The difference was, he'd taken Briana on the road with him, after her mother died. She'd been Alec's age then.

Her aunt Barbara had objected, of course, to all the travel and Briana doing her schoolwork by correspondence instead of attending a real school. A young girl needed friends, Barbara had argued. Needed dance lessons and Sunday school and security.

Every time they'd returned to Boise, Briana's bossy

but beloved aunt had hustled her off to the school for tests; every time, Briana had proved to be far above her grade level. In fact, she'd completed high school by the time she was fifteen. Bill had immediately signed her up for college-level courses, and she'd aced those, too, with his help.

She treasured the recollection of the two of them sitting at the little fold-down table in the camper, lamplight casting a golden benediction from over their heads, bent over one textbook or another.

Now, with her son standing hopefully before her, she missed her dad more poignantly than ever. Sure, he'd dragged her all over the United States in that old camper, but he'd been rock-solid, too. There for her, no matter what.

Her greatest regret, where her children were concerned, was that she hadn't given them the kind of father Bill had been to her. Instead, she'd been swept away by Vance's good looks, charm and easy drawl.

"Are you going to call Dad?" Alec asked, his voice small.

Briana smiled. "Yes," she said. "But only to ask how long he'll be staying."

Alec looked desperately relieved. His gaze slipped to the pendant, on its simple leather cord, and the image of Bill "Wild Man" McIntyre, clad in full clown regalia. "You miss Grampa, huh?"

"Lots," Briana admitted. Her dad had retired from rodeo soon after she married Vance, giving up his beloved camper for a modest house a few blocks from Barbara and her family, saying he was all set to fish every day and wait for his grandchildren to come along.

A month later, he'd passed away very suddenly, after a particularly nasty case of the flu had turned to pneumonia.

The irony of that still bothered Briana. Her dad had been gored by bulls and trampled by broncs in his long career as a rodeo clown, and in the end, he'd died of an ailment a simple injection might have prevented.

Alec leaned in, planted a kiss on Briana's cheek. "'Night, Mom," he said. "And thanks."

Briana waited until Alec and Josh had both settled in for the night, keeping herself busy by puttering around the kitchen, washing up dishes she'd left in the sink that morning, making up a grocery list, checking and rechecking her work schedule for the coming week. Finally, sweaty-palmed, she took the phone receiver off the hook on the wall and called Vance.

"That number," an automated operator responded, after three rings, "is no longer in service."

Of course it wasn't, Briana thought, hanging up with a slight bang, feeling both relieved and annoyed. Vance would have had to buy more minutes to keep that particular line of communication open; instead, he'd simply gotten another phone, in another convenience store, with a new number he hadn't troubled himself to share with her.

She rarely had anything to say to Vance, but suppose one of the boys were sick or hurt? How would she reach him?

Resigned, Briana sighed and checked the clock on the stove. Too early to turn in, especially with all that caffeine coursing through her system, and she didn't feel like watching television or cruising the Internet.

Wandering into the living room, she peered through

the lace curtains toward the main ranch house. Saw its lights shining through the trees in the orchard for the first time since she'd moved into Dylan's place as caretaker-in-residence. The sight was comforting, made her feel less isolated and alone. Not that she meant to get too friendly with Logan Creed—he was easy on the eyes, and she'd liked him right away, even if he did make her nervous, but he was a cowboy.

Like Vance.

He'd blown in on a stray wind, like some tumbleweed, Logan had, and he was likely to blow right out again, when the right breeze came along.

Biting her lower lip, Briana turned away from the window.

In the distance, the phone jangled.

She ran to answer, smacking her shin on one of the kitchen chairs as she passed. Wincing, she grabbed up the receiver and said, "Hello? Vance?"

Silence.

"Hello?" Briana repeated.

"It's Logan," her neighbor said quietly.

"Oh," Briana said.

"I'll make this quick, since you're expecting another call," Logan replied affably. "I checked out Dylan's pasture fence, and I don't think it would hold that bull if he decided to charge. Since I'm planning to do a lot of work around the place anyway, I'm having new posts and rails put in. Just thought I'd let you know before the work crews showed up."

I'm not expecting another call. That was what Briana wanted to say, but she couldn't bring herself to let on that she was glad he'd phoned, glad to hear another adult human voice on a dark summer night. He'd think she was needy if she did. In the market for a man.

"Did you clear that with Dylan?" she said instead, rubbing her bruised shin, and then wished she'd gone the needy route anyway. That would have been better than the unintentionally snippy way she'd put the question.

Logan waited a beat before answering, to let her know he'd registered the tone. "I don't imagine he'd object, since I'm footing the bill. If that bull got out and did some damage, it would be Dylan's hide the lawyers nailed to the barn wall, not mine."

The thought of Cimarron running amok, with Josh or Alec in his path, pushed all concerns about how she might have sounded to Logan right out of Briana's mind. Having watched hundreds of rodeos in her time, she'd seen bulls send cowboys and clowns into midair somersaults and, once or twice, cave in their rib cages when they landed.

"You really think he could get loose? Cimarron, I mean?"

"Yeah," Logan replied. She heard *Isn't that what I just said?* in his intonation, though that part went unspoken.

"Oh my God," Briana murmured, closing her eyes. Child care was hard to find in Stillwater Springs, so when she couldn't take the boys to work with her, leaving them to study or play handheld video games in the casino's coffee shop, she left them home to play, study or do chores. They had strict orders to call at any sign of a problem, and stay close to the house while she was away, but they were boys, after all. Lively and adventurous. She knew they probably ranged over most of the ranch when she wasn't around.

"Is something wrong?" Logan asked moderately.

"I was just worrying," Briana said, trying to smile, though she couldn't think why, since she was alone in the kitchen and Logan couldn't see her. "It's a mother thing."

"I'll take care of the fence," Logan assured her. "In the meantime, see that the boys stay clear of Cimarron." A pause. "Dylan did warn you about the bears, didn't he?"

Briana gulped. "Bears?"

"They like to raid the orchard every now and then," Logan said.

"In two years," Briana said, her stomach doing a slow backward roll, "I haven't seen a single bear."

"They're around," Logan replied. "Mostly browns and blacks, but there is the occasional grizzly, too, and they're bad news."

"G-grizzlies?" Briana echoed stupidly.

Logan sighed. "Dylan should have told you," he said.

Briana barely knew Dylan Creed, but she had every reason to be grateful to him since he'd given her a place to stay when she needed it most, along with a generous supply of groceries and an old pickup to drive, and the faintly critical note in Logan's voice put her on the defensive. "I guess the subject never came up," she said stiffly.

"With Dylan," Logan countered dryly, "the most important subjects often *don't* come up."

"I'll watch out for Cimarron *and* the bears," Briana said.

There was more Logan wanted to say—she could sense that—but he must have quelled the urge. "Good," he said, after several seconds had ticked by. Nothing more, just *Good*.

A man of few words, then.

Call-waiting clicked in. Since Briana didn't have caller ID, and since her better angels whispered that Logan *had* warned her and she had no cause to be hostile, she ignored the beeps. "Maybe you'd like to join us for supper tomorrow night," she said, to make up for her bad manners.

A flush climbed her neck while she waited for Logan's reply.

"Can I bring anything?" he asked presently.

"No need," she said, strangely jubilant at his tacit acceptance. It was only supper, a simple neighbor-to-neighbor courtesy. Mustn't make a big fat deal of it. "Sidekick's welcome, too, of course. Six-thirty? I get home from work at about five-fifteen, and I'll need time to shower and cook and everything."

More information than he needed, Briana reflected, blushing even harder. What was the *matter* with her?

"Six-thirty," he agreed, with a smile in his voice. It was almost as if he *knew* she was red from her throat to the roots of her hair.

They said goodbye and hung up, and the instant the connection was broken, the phone rang again.

"Hello?" Briana said. Had Logan changed his mind about supper already? Remembered a previous commitment?

"Hey," Vance said. "I just tried to call and—"

Briana let out a long breath. "I was on the other line."

"Did you get my message?"

"Yes. You're thinking of dropping in for a visit." She lowered her voice, since the boys' room was nearby and she wouldn't put it past either or both of her sons to be glued to the other side of the door with their ears on broadband. "Alec is going to be *seriously* disappointed if you don't show up."

"How about you, hon?" Vance drawled, playing up the cowboy routine that had sucked her into his orbit the first time. "Would *you* be disappointed if I didn't show up?"

Briana's blood pressure surged. She waited for it to peak and go into a decline before she answered. "Not in the least," she said. "We're divorced, Vance. D-I-V-O-R-C-E-D."

Atypically, he backed off. He was playing it cool, which meant he wanted something.

"What's up, Vance?" she asked, as calmly as she could. If she came on too strong, he'd simply hang up on her, but she wasn't going to roll over, either. "You didn't make it to Stillwater Springs when Josh had his tonsils out last fall. You were a no-show at Christmas, Thanksgiving and both the boys' birthdays. What's so important that you're willing to swing this far off the circuit to sleep on my couch?"

Vance's answer was underlaid with one big, silent sigh of long-suffering patience. He was *so* misunderstood. "I just want to talk to you face-to-face, that's all. And see the boys."

And see the boys.

Always the afterthought.

"About what?" Briana demanded, still struggling to keep her voice down. "So help me, Vance, if it's about wriggling out of paying your child support again—"

"It isn't," he interrupted, sounding put-upon. "Why does everything always come down to money with you, Bree?"

"If everything 'came down to money' with me, Vance Grant, you'd be in jail right now. Josh and Alec are your *sons*. Don't you feel any responsibility toward them at all?"

"I love them," Vance said, going from put-upon to downright wounded.

"Talk is cheap," Briana said.

"Do you want me to come or not? I can be there Saturday."

"I work on Saturday."

"That's okay," Vance responded, magnanimous now. "I can hang out with the boys until you get home."

Briana thought of Alec, his face so full of hope, and then of Josh, who'd threatened to run away if Vance made good on the visit. "Alec will be thrilled," she said, in all truth. "Good luck with Josh, though."

"What's up with my buddy Josh?"

"I'd say he sees right through you, Vance," Briana said. Josh didn't need a buddy, he needed a dad—a concept well beyond Vance's capacity to grasp.

"And that's supposed to mean *what?*" Vance asked furiously.

True colors, Briana thought. No more Mr. Nice Guy.

Stop baiting him, said the better angel.

Sometimes she'd like to throttle that better angel.

"You figure it out," she said.

"Look, I don't need this. Maybe it would be better if I just stayed clear."

Briana closed her eyes, but Alec's image was still there, yearning for a visit from the father he adored. She had to stop thinking about what she wanted— never to lay eyes on Vance Grant again—and consider her children's needs. Right or wrong, Vance was their dad, and as much as Josh protested, he wanted a relationship with him as badly as Alec did.

"I'm sorry," she said, nearly choking on the words.

"You know what's wrong with you?" Vance countered. He'd changed tactics again, turned the dial to "charm." "You need sex."

Instantly, Logan Creed came to mind. Would his chest be hairy or smooth, when he took off his shirt?

Briana gave herself an inward shake. "Maybe I do," she admitted. "But not with you, so don't get any ideas. You *are* sleeping on the couch."

"I'd planned on that anyhow," Vance said. "Which reminds me—does it fold out?"

He'd asked that same question in the message he'd left on the answering machine. Briana was puzzled, and a little alarmed.

"Yes," she said slowly. "Why do you ask?"

Vance's chuckle sounded false. "I've been thrown from a lot of broncs in my time," he replied. "Have to think about my back, now that I'm getting older."

"Right," Briana said, still curious, but unwilling to pursue the subject any further. She'd been talking to Vance too long as it was. Twenty minutes out of her life, and she'd never get them back.

"See you Saturday," Vance said cheerfully, like she was looking forward to his arrival instead of dreading it with every fiber of her being.

"See you Saturday," she confirmed glumly.

And then she hung up.

"I OUGHT TO PUNCH you in the mouth," Jim Huntinghorse said, the next morning, when Logan tracked him down at the Council Fire Casino.

Logan grinned. "I'm real glad to see you again, too, old buddy," he said, drawing back a chair at one of the tables in the coffee shop and signaling the waitress for a cup of coffee. Since Sidekick was out in the truck, he didn't plan to stay long. He'd get the java to go. He ran his gaze over Jim's fine black suit. "You've come up in the world," he said. "General manager. Who would have thought?"

"Who would have thought," Jim retorted, softening a little, but not much, "that you'd leave town without saying goodbye to your best friend? No calls. No e-mails. No nothing."

"When the judge let me out of jail after that brawl with Tyler and Dylan, he told me not to show my face in Stillwater Springs until I'd cooled down."

"It took you *twelve years* to cool down?"

"Chip off the old block," Logan said as he nodded his approval when the coffee arrived in a take-out cup and reached for his wallet.

Jim waved both the waitress and the money away.

"You can say that again." Jim scowled, still glowering. He stood beside the table, showing no signs of sitting down, his big fists bunched at his sides as though he might carry out the original threat. "You're as crazy as your dad was."

"I'm back," Logan announced, after taking a cautious sip of the steaming brew. "And except for buying grub at the supermarket and taking my dog to the vet for a checkup, this is my first stop."

"Is there a compliment lurking in there somewhere?" Jim frowned.

"Sit down. You cast a shadow like a mountain with the sun behind it."

"I'm working," Jim pointed out. But he pulled back a chair and sat.

"You're a priority. There's your compliment."

"Gee, thanks. I get married. No best buddy since kindergarten to stand up with me. I get divorced. Nobody to drown my sorrows with. But I'm a 'priority'?"

"Take it or leave it," Logan said. "Best I can do."

At last, Jim relented. A grudging grin flashed across his chiseled Native-American face. "You just passing through—looking for a fight with one or both of your brothers maybe? Or did you finally come to your senses and decide that *somebody* ought to come back here and look after that ranch?"

Logan put a tip on the table for the waitress, who was ogling them from the other side of the service counter. During the millisecond it took to lay the money down, Jim's face changed. Went dark again.

"You're not going to sell out to some movie yahoo, are you?"

Logan shook his head. "I'm staying for good." That refrain was becoming familiar, like a commercial heard once too often on the radio or the TV.

Again, the dazzling smile. All those white teeth

and all that handsome-savage bullshit had sure gone over with the women when they were young and on the prowl. It probably still worked, Logan reflected.

"You mean it?" Jim asked.

"I mean it."

"You meant it when you promised to be best man in my wedding, too," Jim pointed out.

"I was in Iraq," Logan said.

"*You* were in Iraq?"

"Didn't I just say that?"

"Just because you say something, Creed, that doesn't mean it's true."

"When my stuff gets here, I'll show you the documentation. Honorable discharge. Even a couple of medals."

Jim gave a low whistle. "So *that's* why you dropped out of the rodeo scene. You always got a lot of play on ESPN. Then, all of the sudden, you're just not there. You got drafted?"

"I enlisted," Logan said. "Can we not talk about Iraq right now?"

Jim frowned, obviously confused. He was a veteran himself, and in buddy world, guys swapped war stories. "Why not?"

"Because I need booze to even *think* about combat, let alone talk about it, and given my illustrious history, not to mention the high incidence of alcoholism in the Creed clan, I try to limit myself to the occasional beer."

"Oh," Jim said. "Bad, huh?"

"Bad," Logan admitted.

"You were special forces, right?"

"Right. And this constitutes talking about Iraq. I'm stone-cold sober and I'd like to stay that way."

"Okay," Jim agreed hastily, putting up both hands, palms out. "Okay."

Logan stood. "I just came by to say hello and let you know I'm back. My dog's in the truck and I have contractors to meet with, plus I promised to stop by Cassie's before I head for home."

Jim grinned, rising, too. "You have a dog *and* a truck? You really *are* going redneck."

"Nah," Logan said, giving the waitress a wave as he turned to go. "I still have both my front teeth."

"Not for long," Jim quipped, "if either of your brothers gets a wild hair to come back home the way you did."

Jim was only joking, but the words jabbed at a sore spot in Logan. It was too much to hope that Dylan's and Tyler's personal roads might turn and wind homeward, and the three of them could come to some kind of terms, but Logan hoped it would happen, just the same.

His friend walked him to the front doors of the casino, slot machines flashing and chinging all around them. Logan wondered how anybody could work in the place, with all the noise.

"I'm off at six," Jim said, as they parted. "Want to play some pool, swig some beer and catch up?"

"Not tonight," Logan answered, remembering the unexpected invitation to have supper at Briana's. She'd clearly been pissed off when he mentioned Dylan, and then she'd turned right around and offered him a meal. There was no figuring women. "Already made plans."

"Soon, then," Jim said. "I promise—no combat stuff. Unless you count a detailed description of my divorce as a war story, that is."

Logan laughed, slapped Jim on the shoulder. "Any time after tonight," he said. "You know where I live. Stop by when you get a chance."

Jim nodded, and then Logan headed for his truck, and Jim went back inside the casino to do whatever the general manager of a casino did.

So, BRETT TURLOW THOUGHT, just getting into his car after a brutal all-night poker game in which he'd lost his ass, he wasn't the only one who'd returned to the old hometown after a long absence. Difference was, he'd come back with his tail between his legs. Logan Creed looked a mite too cheerful for that to be the case with him.

Brett slid behind the wheel of the dented Corolla he'd borrowed from his sister. Watched as Creed climbed into a respectably battered pickup truck, ruffled his dog's ears and started the engine.

Most likely, Logan meant to sell the ranch, since nobody appeared to give a good goddamn about the place, and get on with his life.

That would be a good thing, if he left.

If Creed stayed, on the other hand, it meant trouble, pure and simple.

Bleary-eyed, half-sick because he hadn't eaten in twelve hours and he'd gambled away most of his unemployment check, Brett made a mental note to ask around a little. Find out what Creed's intentions were.

In the meantime, he needed to crash.

BRIANA STAYED CLEAR of the coffee shop until Logan was gone. Then she wandered nonchalantly in to say hello to Millie, the sole waitress on duty, and snag a nonfat latte to keep her going through the morning.

She'd been up late the night before, on a jangling java-high, worrying that Vance would show up on Saturday, worrying that he wouldn't. She needed caffeine, fast. Hair of the dog that bit her, so to speak.

The boys were still at home, warned on pain of death to stay away from Cimarron and the orchard, where there might be bears.

"Did you see that guy talking to Jim?" Millie enthused, automatically starting the latte. "Mucho *cute*."

Briana felt a sting of proprietary annoyance and a boost to her spirits, both at once. "The cute ones are deadly," she said lightly.

"Yeah," Millie answered, looking back at Briana over one shoulder while the milk foamed under the sputtery nozzle on the fancy coffee machine, "but what a way to go. I'm going to ask Jim what his name is."

"No need," Briana said. "It's Logan Creed."

Millie's eyes widened. "As in Stillwater Springs Ranch?"

"As in," Briana confirmed. Like her, Millie was relatively new in town. She'd heard about the Creed brothers, though; they were almost folk heroes, like certain outlaws in the old west.

Famous for raising hell, mostly, from what Briana had been told.

"So you know him, then?" Millie fished, handing over the latte.

"I live on the ranch," Briana reminded her friend.

"That makes us neighbors." She hugged the rest of the story—that Logan was having supper with her and the boys that night—close, like some delicious adolescent secret.

Silly.

Just then, Briana's radio, buckled to her belt, crackled to life. A disembodied voice informed her that someone had just hit a jackpot on the newest bank of slot machines—time to attend to business.

She thanked Millie for the latte and hurried off.

The jackpot was a big one, it turned out. A little blue-haired lady off the senior citizens' bus had struck gold on the Blazing Sevens, and Briana spent the next forty-five minutes handling the paperwork.

Jim, being the manager, paid out the booty in crisp hundred-dollar bills, beaming for the camera right along with the lucky winner.

After all the hoopla died down, Briana pulled her boss aside for a word. "I need Saturday off, if that's possible," she said.

Jim frowned. He was a good man, serious about his work and goal-oriented. There was even some talk that he might run for sheriff, if old Floyd Book retired early, on account of his heart condition.

"Saturdays are pretty busy," he reminded her.

"I know," Briana said.

He flashed her the grin that made a lot of women's knees buckle. She and Jim had gone out a couple of times, after their separate divorces, but there was no spark, and when he got promoted to his present lofty position, they'd decided to stop dating and be friends.

"Hey," he said. "I know you. If you're asking for time off, it's important."

Was it important? Vance was supposed to arrive on Saturday, and she was nervous about his spending the day with the boys without her there. There was no physical danger—Vance had never raised a hand to her or their sons—but Alec and Josh could so easily be hurt in other ways.

"My ex-husband is coming back then," she confided.

Jim's grin faded. "Oh."

Realizing what he was thinking—that there was a reconciliation in the offing—Briana blushed. "It's nothing like that," she said quickly. "I'm just worried about the boys being alone with him all day. Alec is suffering from a bad case of hero worship, and God knows what ideas Vance might put in his head, and Josh told me he'd rather run away—"

Jim put up a hand. "You can have Saturday off," he interrupted. "I'll fill in for you myself. But you owe me an extra shift."

Briana nodded, deeply relieved. "Thanks, Jim."

He smiled, but his dark eyes were worried. "Josh threatened to run away?"

Jim knew Briana's sons, since they were in the casino coffee shop so often, and he'd been remarkably tolerant of their presence. Lots of bosses wouldn't have been so understanding, but Jim had a boy of his own. Four-year-old Sam lived with his mother now, in Missoula, and didn't visit often.

Briana patted his arm. "I don't think Josh would really hit the road on his own, but I'd rather not take the chance."

Jim heaved a heavy sigh, shoved a hand through

his longish, blue-black hair. "Kids do stupid things sometimes," he said.

Briana thought of the bull in Dylan's pasture, and the bears that apparently fed in the orchard on occasion. She glanced at her watch. It was almost lunchtime; she'd call home from the employees' lounge behind one of the casino's three restaurants and make sure Alec and Josh were following orders.

"Yeah," she agreed belatedly. "Sometimes they do."

She and Jim parted, and she headed for the lounge, went straight to the pay phone. She needed a cell, but it wasn't in the budget.

Josh answered on the third ring. "Alec is a buttface," he said, without preamble.

"Be that as it may," Briana answered, used to the running battle between her sons, "he's your brother. What are you two up to?"

"Alec is doing his math, and I was on the Internet until you called. Wanda ate a woodchuck or something, and her farts are, like, *gross*."

"I feel your pain," Briana said cheerfully. "And how could Wanda have eaten a woodchuck?"

"I said 'or something,'" Josh pointed out.

Briana smiled. "Joshua?"

"Okay, it was the bratwurst left over from night before last," Josh said. "It wasn't *my* idea to give it to her. Alec did that."

Situation normal.

"Will you come and get us?" he asked. "It's boring around here, when we can't even go outside."

"No time," Briana said. "You'll have to tough it out

until I get home. I'm stopping off at the supermarket after work, so I might be a few minutes late."

"Alec really thinks Dad's coming on Saturday."

Briana closed her eyes. "Maybe," she said evenly. "*Maybe* he's coming on Saturday."

"With Dad, it's always 'maybe,'" Josh replied.

"True enough. Do me a favor, though, and hold the remarks. It really upsets Alec."

"He's living in a fantasy world."

"You're Alec's big brother," Briana said. "Be nice to him."

Josh sighed dramatically. "Okay, but only until you get home," he said. "Then all bets are off."

"Fair enough," Briana said, with a smile.

Josh responded with a disgusted wail.

"What?" Briana asked anxiously, thinking the house had caught fire or a serial killer was trying to break down the back door.

"Wanda just cut one," Josh lamented. *"Again!"* In the background, Alec whooped with manic delight.

"Butt-face!" Josh yelled.

"No name-calling, Josh," Briana said. "You promised."

"All right," Josh countered, "but if you're not here by five-thirty, I'm going to have to kill him."

"I've only got one word for you, Joshua Grant."

"What?"

"Babysitter," Briana replied. Then she said good-bye and hung up.

CHAPTER FOUR

THERE WERE TWO cars parked in front of Cassie's ramshackle place at the edge of town, and she'd scrawled *With a client* on the whiteboard nailed up beside the front door. Logan took the marker, dangling from a piece of tattered baling twine, and added *I was here. Logan.*

That done, he turned and swung his gaze across the property.

Sidekick was sniffing around the edge of the teepee, the closest thing to a tourist attraction that Stillwater Springs, Montana, had to offer. It was authentic, built in the old way, by Cassie's father, of tree branches and buckskin, and she charged fifty cents per visit.

Logan approached, dropped two quarters into the rusty coffee can that served as a till—Cassie believed in the honor system and so did he—and ducked into the cool, semidarkness where he and Dylan and Tyler had played as boys.

Except for the long-cold fire circle in the center, rimmed by sooty stones, the teepee was empty. Gone were the ratty blankets he remembered, the gourd ladle and wooden bucket, the clay cooking pots. No sign of the mangy bearskins, either.

He sat down, cross-legged, facing the fire pit, and

imagined the flames leaping before him. Sidekick took an uncertain seat beside him, leaned into his shoulder a little.

Maybe the animal knew that in the old times, he might have been on the supper menu.

Logan wrapped an arm around the dog, gave him a reassuring squeeze. "It's okay, boy," he said. "Nobody's going to boil you up with beans."

Sidekick stuck close, just the same.

As Logan sat, he drifted into a sort of meditation, recalling other visits, sometimes alone, sometimes with his brothers. They'd always built a fire, filling the place with hide-scented smoke, and taken off their shirts. Sometimes, they'd even painted their chests and faces with cosmetics left behind by one or the other of their mothers.

Jake never threw anything away.

Except, of course, for three wives and three sons.

Something tightened inside Logan, and Sidekick seemed to feel it, as though the two of them were tethered together by some intangible cord. The dog gave a low, throaty whine.

The warp and woof of time itself seemed to shift as Logan sat there, waiting. It stretched and then contracted, until, finally, he could no longer measure the passing of seconds or minutes or even hours.

Outside, car doors slammed.

Engines started.

Sidekick eased away from his side, restless, and headed for the opening to look out.

And still Logan didn't move.

He knew the bulky shadow at the entrance was Cassie, but he didn't look up or speak.

"You'll have to make peace with him, you know," she said quietly.

Logan didn't respond, even to nod, nor did he meet her eyes. He knew she was referring to Jake, the man he both loved and hated, with such intensity that most times, he couldn't separate one emotion from the other.

"He won't rest until you do," Cassie went on. She stepped into the teepee then, sat down on the ground across from him, graceful despite her size.

Logan blinked, came out of the meditation, or whatever it was. He smiled. "Still telling fortunes, I see," he said, referring to the client she'd been with when he arrived.

"It's a living," she said, with a little shrug and a partly sheepish smile.

"You don't need to read cards to make a buck, Cassie," he pointed out, as he had at least a hundred times before. "You get a regular check from the tribal council."

"Maybe it isn't about the money," Cassie suggested mildly, laughing a little when Sidekick gave her a nuzzle with his nose and tried to sit in her ample lap.

"What do you tell them?" Logan asked. "Your clients, I mean?"

"Depends," Cassie answered, "on what I think they need to hear." She regarded him with a focus so sharp that it was unsettling. "Did you call Dylan and Tyler?"

"Yes," he replied. "Dylan basically blew me off. I left a message for Ty, but he hasn't called back." He grinned. "Off the hook," he finished.

"In your dreams," Cassie said.

"Is this the part where you tell me what you think I need to hear?"

"Yes," she replied succinctly.

He huffed out a sigh.

Sidekick arranged himself on Cassie's broad thighs, and she didn't push him away. Instead, she stroked his back idly, though her attention was still on Logan, one hundred percent. It felt a little like a ray of sunlight coming through the lens of a magnifying glass, searing its way through the brittle inner shell meant to hide his secrets.

"Jake won't rest until you've come to terms with being his son," Cassie said.

Logan bristled. "What do you mean, he won't rest? He's dead, gone, crossed over, whatever. Maybe they let him into heaven, but I'm betting he gets his mail in hell."

"So bitter," Cassie said, in a tsk-tsk tone. "No one is all bad, Logan. Including Jake Creed."

"He was a son of a bitch."

Cassie frowned. "Wrong. Your grandmother was a fine woman."

Logan said nothing. He'd never known his grandmother, or his grandfather, either. They'd both died long before he was born, and Jake neither told stories about them nor kept their pictures around.

"People come into this life with agendas to fulfill, Logan," Cassie told him quietly. "Sometimes they're simple. Sometimes they're complicated. Jake did what he was supposed to do."

"What? Raise hell?"

"He made you strong. You and Dylan and Tyler.

You're as tough as the walls of this teepee, all three of you."

"It would have been easier," Logan said, "if he'd just named me Sue."

Cassie laughed. "Easier isn't necessarily better," she pointed out.

Logan wanted to refute that statement, but even with all his legal training, he couldn't come up with a solid argument. "I called my brothers," he said. "The ball is in their court. What else is there to do?"

"You haven't been to Jake's grave, have you?"

Logan stiffened, shook his head. Cassie, it seemed, had eyes everywhere, in the bushes, in the trees, in the walls. She'd always known, somehow, what he'd done and what he hadn't done. Worse, she believed she had the right to comment.

"His things are still packed away, too. That's convenient, isn't it? Because then you don't have to remember quite so readily."

"I came back here, didn't I?"

Again, Cassie executed a half shrug. "You won't stay if you don't settle things with Jake," she said. "I know what your dream is—to make the name Creed mean something good—and I can tell you that it's more than just a dream. It's a quest—the most important thing you'll ever do." At this, she paused and looked up and around at the interior of that teepee, as though her ancestors were hovering in the air or something. When her brown gaze collided with Logan's, he felt like a butterfly with its wings pinned to a mat. "You'll fail if you don't own who you are— all of it. Not just the law degree, and the fancy silver belt buckles you won at the rodeo, and all that money you're pretending you don't have. You've got to accept that you're flesh of Jake Creed's flesh, bone of his bone, blood of his blood, and nothing is going to change that."

Logan shifted, got to his feet. "He was a bastard," he said. "If I could be anybody else's son—*anybody's*—I would."

"Well," Cassie said implacably, moving Sidekick gently off her lap and then accepting Logan's hesitantly offered hand so she could stand, "you're not. That's one thing I know for sure."

"Maybe you should have told *him,*" Logan said, seething. "He used to say otherwise. He said Teresa was a whore—did you know that? Practically every time he got drunk, which was often, he told me she'd been catting around, and I probably wasn't his." He leaned in a little, despite the flinch he saw in Cassie's broad, kindly face. "And you know what? I wished to God it was true back then, and I wish it now!"

Cassie stood her ground, like she always had. It was a trait he blessed her for, even when he hated what she said. "How's that working out for you, Logan?" she asked quietly. "All that wishing?"

He glared at her.

She waited.

"You're so sure he wasn't telling the truth, for once in his miserable, worthless life?"

"Teresa was faithful to her husband. She loved him. She loved *you*." Cassie drew in a long, somewhat quivery breath. "Besides, you have Jake's bone structure. His temper, too, and that mile-wide stubborn streak that ought to be in every dictionary under 'Creed.'"

"Great," Logan said, sagging a little on the inside, now that he'd let off steam. "And what am I supposed to *do* with all this information, oh, great medicine woman?"

"Break the curse," Cassie answered. "Make different choices than Jake did. Find a woman, love her with your whole heart and mind and body and spirit. Make babies with her. Stick with her—and the children—for the duration." She paused, regarded him with a kind of warm sorrow that got under his skin in a way her challenges hadn't. "You've been running ever since the day they put Jake in the ground," she went on, touching his arm. "Coming back here was a big thing. I know that. But until you can forgive Jake—really forgive him—you'll be stuck, no matter where you go or what you do."

Logan thrust a hand through his hair. "I can't," he said.

"Then you and your dog might as well get back in that old truck and move on, because you're wasting your time here." Tears glittered in Cassie's wise brown eyes. "In all the ways that really count, Teresa was my daughter. I know what Jake put her through— Maggie and poor Angela, too. I had to let it all go, Logan—the hatred, the need for revenge—because it was devouring me from the inside.

"*Look* at your life. Your brothers are strangers to you. Twice, you married the wrong woman. The ranch—*your legacy*—is practically in ruins. You can't just ignore all of that. You have to make it right."

"How?" Logan demanded, furious because it was all true. Both his wives, Susan and Laurie, had been good women. He'd never raised a hand to either one of them, barely raised his *voice,* in fact. But in his own way, he'd been no more available to them than Jake was to Teresa or Maggie or Angela. "Short of committing bigamy—"

Cassie smiled. "Those marriages are behind you," she said. "Did you part friends?"

Friends? Logan ached. He'd loved Susan, or thought he did. And when they weren't having monkey sex, they'd been giving each other the cold shoulder. Now, she was happily married to a balding dentist with a slight paunch, and expecting her second child. He'd given her a settlement when his company took off, several years after their divorce, and she'd put it in trust for her children. Still, the last time he'd seen Susan, he'd known by the look in her eyes that she could barely restrain herself from spitting in his face.

"Not so much," he admitted. He still talked to Laurie sometimes—usually when she needed something. She'd used *her* divorce settlement to open a hair salon in Santa Monica, and the last time they'd spoken, she'd told him all about her recent wedding ceremony on a beach at sunset.

She'd married herself. White dress, veil, cake and all.

Still, it had to be an improvement over being married to *him,* Logan reflected ruefully. Except, if he did say so himself, for the sex.

That had been beyond good, with both Susan and Laurie.

It was also pretty much all he missed about being married.

"Are they happy?" Cassie asked, ostensibly asking about his exes.

He nodded. "Nothing like divorcing one of the Creed men to improve a woman's outlook on life," he said.

Cassie laughed. Dusty light poured into the tee-pee as she pulled the flap aside to step out. Sidekick preceded her—Logan followed.

The sun dazzled him, made him fumble for his sunglasses, which he'd left on the dashboard of the Dodge.

Another car pulled into the driveway, parked beside his truck.

"That's Elsie Blake," Cassie said, with a philosophical sigh. "She's going to ask if I see a man in her future, the way she does every time she comes for a reading. I ought to tell her she'd be better off marrying herself, like Laurie did."

Logan blinked. "You knew about that?"

"Of course I did," Cassie answered brightly, and the dismissal was as clear as if she'd flat-out told him to get his butt into his truck and go home already. "She mailed out announcements, with a picture of herself on the front, wearing a white dress. I sent her a toaster."

Logan was rolling his eyes as Cassie walked away.

RUSHING INTO THE kitchen with a grocery bag in each arm, Briana surveyed her surroundings. The counters were clear, except for the vestiges of lunch—grilled cheese sandwiches, she guessed, by the burned crusts of bread—sneakers were neatly lined up just inside the back door and both boys looked angelic enough to light candles for a Vatican Mass. Only Wanda was her regular self.

"Okay," Briana said suspiciously, juggling the bags and heading for the table to set them down. "What have you guys been up to?"

"I've been doing my history homework on the computer," Josh said loftily, and whatever Web page he'd been looking at faded into cyber-oblivion at the click of the mouse.

"And I swept the floor," Alec volunteered. "After I did *my* homework, of course. Not that stink-face would let me use the computer."

"What did I say about name-calling?"

The boys exchanged poisonous glares.

"Don't do it," they chorused dolefully.

Briana had been concerned that Alec and Josh might head for the orchard—it was infested with bears, to hear Logan tell it—or dash off to Cimarron's pasture to play matador the moment she'd driven out of sight that morning. Instead, they'd probably watched something they weren't supposed to on TV, or gotten into her secret stash of snack-size candy bars.

Or both.

"What are we having for supper?" Alec asked, as Briana began taking things out of the bags—milk, oversize cans of soup, packages of hamburger and chicken breasts, bread and fresh fruit, frozen potatoes compressed into little cylinders.

"A casserole," she said.

Alec frowned in obvious disapproval while Wanda scratched hopefully at the back door, asking to be let out. "You *do* remember that we're having company tonight?"

Briana smiled hurriedly, went to open the door

for Wanda, and then put away everything except the soup, two pounds of lean hamburger and the potato chunks. "Yes, Alec," she said. "I remember."

"I think cowboys eat steaks," Josh observed, drawing nearer. This particular casserole was Briana's specialty—her dad had taught her how to make it—and both boys loved it.

Usually.

"Not tonight, they don't," she replied, going to the sink to wash her hands before assembling the meal. She would shower while the dish was in the oven, and put on fresh mascara and lip gloss, too. There was no time for a shampoo, so she'd wind her braid into a chignon at her nape, pin it into place and hope for the best. "Tonight, it's Wild Man's Spud Extravaganza or nothing."

Alec made a face. "Josh is right," he said, in an I-hate-to-admit-it kind of tone. "Cowboys like steak and stuff like that."

"Sorry," Briana said, sounding a bit manic. Wanda was scratching at the door again. "No steak. Somebody let the dog in, please."

Josh did the honors, after a brief stare-down with Alec.

"And then feed her," Briana added.

"We've been cooped up in the house all day," Josh said, looking like a slave hauling construction materials to a pyramid as he dipped Wanda's bowl into the kibble bag, brought it out overflowing and set it down on the floor for her. "I was hoping we could have another picnic at the cemetery."

"I told you what Mr. Cre— Logan said about bears."

"When was the last time you saw a bear, Mom?" Josh persisted.

Briana sighed. She'd *never* seen a bear, at least not around Stillwater Springs, which was probably why Dylan hadn't warned her when she and the boys moved in. He *had* told her, during one of their rare phone conversations, that the cellar floor was rotting in places and the furnace needed three good kicks to get going when the temperature fell below freezing in the winter and that she should let the neighbor feed Cimarron and keep away from him herself.

If bears were a threat, wouldn't he have said something?

Wouldn't Jim Huntinghorse or one of the dozens of other people she knew in town have said something?

Her mood, already slightly frenzied, darkened a little. Logan was either paranoid about bears, or he simply didn't want her and her sons having the run of the property.

For a moment, she wished she hadn't invited him over, that or any night. What *other* ridiculous fears was he going to plant in her head?

"When, Mom?" Josh prodded, because he never let any subject drop before he was satisfied that all the angles had been covered.

"Okay," she said. "We can still go to the cemetery for picnics—but not tonight. I am not lugging a hot casserole across the creek."

Josh and Alec gave each other high fives, in an unusual show of accord.

Hastily, she browned the hamburger in a cast-iron skillet, drained it, mixed it in with the cream of mushroom soup and a few dehydrated onions, poured the potato thingies over the top and put the whole concoction into the oven at three-fifty.

The phone rang as she was stepping out of the shower.

Vance, calling to say he'd be arriving early or not coming at all?

Logan, begging off on supper?

The bathroom door creaked open and Alec stuck his head through the crack, his eyes squeezed tightly shut. "Mom!"

Briana, wrapped in a towel, chuckled at the sight. "What?"

"We won a week's vacation at Lake Tahoe," Alec said. "All we have to do is look at a time share and watch a video. They'll even fly us down there!"

"It's a sales pitch," Briana said, reaching for her robe with her free hand. "Hang up."

"But I told the guy you were in the shower and I'd come and get you. Mom, we *won*."

Briana was in her robe by then, belt pulled tight. "You can open your eyes now, Alec," she said. "I'm decent. Go back, tell 'the guy' we're not interested and hang up."

Alec dragged off to the kitchen to do as he was told—Briana hoped—and she slipped into her bedroom to put on clean underwear, cut-off jeans and a white tank top. She slipped her feet into sandals, pinned up her hair, applied a spritz of the drugstore perfume the boys had given her for Christmas and examined her reflection in the blurry mirror above the bureau.

She definitely needed mascara and lip gloss, she decided.

The savory scent of the casserole filled the kitchen when she made her entrance. She drew up, a little thrown, when she saw Logan sitting at the kitchen table, with Josh seated at his right side and Alec at his left.

"I'm early," he said, looking apologetic as he rose from his chair. He'd brought wildflowers in a canning jar and a bottle of light wine, both of which were sitting on the table.

She gave him credit for good manners. But he looked too fine in his new jeans and pressed white shirt, open at the throat. His dark hair was still damp from a shower, and there were little ridges where he'd run a comb through it.

The back door was open, and through the screen, Briana saw Sidekick sleeping contentedly on the porch. She'd had to look away from Logan for a moment, in order to steady her nerves, but now she made herself look back.

"That's okay," she said, too brightly and a beat too late. "Supper's ready."

"Smells good," Logan said. He sounded shy.

She knew he wasn't.

Was he putting on an act?

"It's Wild Man's Spud Extravaganza," Alec announced proudly, evidently over his earlier fixation about serving steak.

Logan, sitting down again at a nod from Briana, raised an eyebrow, and a slight grin quirked one corner of his mouth. "Who's Wild Man?" he asked.

"Our Grampa," Josh answered. "He was a famous rodeo clown."

"Oh," Logan said, his eyes never leaving Briana's face. "*That* Wild Man."

"You *knew* him?" Alec asked, hyperintrigued. This, his expression seemed to say, was even better than "winning" a free trip to Lake Tahoe. Even his freckles were jazzed.

"I saw him perform a few times, when I was about your age," Logan answered, shifting his gaze to Alec, somehow managing to pull Josh into his orbit, too. "I wanted to be Wild Man McIntyre when I grew up. Turned out to be myself instead."

Briana busied herself setting the table. Logan had probably eaten off the same dishes they'd be using that night, she thought fitfully, back when he and Dylan were like regular brothers. If indeed they'd ever *been* regular brothers.

"We've got a whole album *full* of pictures of him!" Alec said.

"After supper," Briana interjected, her smile a little tight-lipped.

The boys missed it.

Logan didn't. His eyes lingered on her face, making every single cell in her body throb before going back to Alec. "I'd like that fine," he said. "When the time is right."

Briana gave herself strict orders to calm down, stop being such a ninny, but herself didn't listen. This was just supper with a neighbor, that was all, but it felt like more.

It felt like some kind of beginning.

Briana didn't like beginnings, because they inevitably turned into endings. Given her druthers, she'd have spent the rest of her life somewhere in the middle, between major events. The present, for all its problems, was a terrain she knew.

She had her boys, and a place to live, and a job that paid the bills.

And that was enough—wasn't it?

The casserole went over big. Logan had two helpings, though he didn't touch the wine. Since he'd opened the bottle at some point, Briana accepted a glass, took a couple of jittery sips and decided she'd be better off without a buzz. Even a very mild one.

The truth was she had enough of a buzz going in her nerve endings already, without adding alcohol to the mix. Maybe Vance had been right, when he'd accused her of being sex-starved.

She went weeks without thinking about sex.

Now, with Logan Creed sitting at her table, looking ruggedly handsome in his cowboy dress-up clothes, something primitive was streaking through certain parts of her anatomy.

It simply wouldn't do.

As soon as everybody was finished eating, Briana jumped up and started bustling around, cleaning up. Usually, she made Alec and Josh do the dishes, but tonight she needed to be busy.

So she bounced around that kitchen like a bumblebee trapped in a sealed jelly jar. Even Wanda regarded her with curiosity.

Logan tried to help with the dishes, but she sort of elbowed him aside. All she needed was that man standing hip-to-hip with her in front of the sink, or anywhere else. The scent of his cologne—if that was what it was—made her feel light-headed. He smelled like sun-dried sheets, fresh-cut grass and summer.

Josh fetched the photo album from its honored place in the living room, and opened it on the freshly cleared table. "This is him," he told Logan, tapping at a faded black-and-white image with one index finger. "This is my Grampa, Bill 'Wild Man' McIntyre."

Briana had long since come to grips with the fact that her boys would never actually know their grandfather. Just the same, her eyes were suddenly scalding, and her throat was tight.

The angle of Logan's head, bent over the album, touched something tender inside her. She wished he'd just get up and leave. Wished even more that he would stay.

She *was* losing her mind.

As if he'd felt her watching him, Logan lifted his eyes.

"Mom says the clowns are the bravest men in rodeo," Alec said, preening a little.

"She's right about that," Logan said, still watching her. "They've saved my…life a time or two."

Briana tried her damnedest to look away, found she couldn't.

"See?" Josh chirped, delighted to be right. "I *told* you Logan was a cowboy!"

Briana's cheeks stung. *Look away,* she pleaded silently, *because I can't.*

As if he'd heard her, Logan averted his eyes. Fixed his attention on Alec and Josh. "I *was* a cowboy, once upon a time," he told the boys quietly. "Gave it up to join the service."

"Were you in the war?" Alec asked, impressed again. Or still.

"Yeah," Logan said. His voice came out sounding hoarse, and he cleared his throat. "Didn't care much for that."

Didn't care much for that.

The very way he'd said the words marked them as the understatement of the ages.

"We usually take Wanda for a walk after supper," Josh said.

Logan was clearly grateful for the change of subject. He pushed back his chair, smiling. "Sounds like a good idea," he replied. "Maybe Sidekick and I could tag along?"

"What if we should stumble across a *bear*?" Briana asked, raising both eyebrows. She'd finished with the washing up by then, draped the dish towel over the plates and glasses and silverware stacked on the drain-board.

Logan chuckled. "Well," he said, "I wouldn't recommend running. A bear can beat a fast horse. Climbing a tree is out, since they're pretty handy at that, too. Guess I'd just have to grin him down, like ol' Dan'l Boone."

"We're related to Daniel Boone," Josh said.

"Isn't everybody?" Logan teased.

Josh laughed.

Logan opened the screen door, and they all went out, Briana bringing up the rear.

She would have sworn Logan was looking at her—well, *rear*—as she passed.

Sidekick and Wanda trotted ahead, happy at the prospect of a walk, with the boys close behind them.

"They like you," Briana told Logan.

"That's a good thing, isn't it?"

She turned her head, looked up at his face. "Depends," she said. "They miss their dad. It would be easy for them to—"

"To what?" Logan asked quietly.

"To like you too much," Briana answered, embarrassed.

"I'm harmless," Logan said.

"I don't think so," Briana replied.

And they walked in silence for a while, watching the two boys and the two dogs cavorting up ahead.

Although the sun would be up for at least another hour, the first stars were popping out, and the moon was clearly visible. The country air smelled of hay and grass and fertile earth.

Or was that Logan?

She'd barely touched her wine, but Briana Grant felt moderately drunk. "Why did you tell me to watch out for bears?" she asked. "I was almost afraid to let the boys leave the house."

He didn't take her hand, but he moved closer, their knuckles touched and a hard, burning thrill ripped through Briana's system.

"I wasn't trying to scare you," Logan said. "Bears feed at the landfill, mostly, on the other side of town. But once in a while, they pay a visit to the orchard. I'd say it was because of people encroaching on their habitat, but the fact is, they've been raiding those pear and apple trees since the first season they bore fruit. And that was back in old Josiah Creed's time."

Briana shivered, hugged herself, though the night was warm.

"Bears are like most wild animals," Logan went on. "They're only dangerous if they feel threatened, and that happens when you take them by surprise."

"I guess I could beat a spoon against the bottom of a pan or something," Briana said seriously. "When we go to the cemetery, I mean. We don't have much reason to pass through the orchard."

Logan grinned. "You could do that," he said.

Was he laughing at her?

Briana got her back up a little. "I don't want my boys to be afraid," she said. "Not even of bears."

"A little fear is a healthy thing sometimes," Logan retorted. "Especially where bears are concerned. And that old bull of Dylan's."

She stole a sidelong glance at Logan, but whatever she'd heard in his voice as he mentioned his brother didn't show in his face or bearing. "We've never had any trouble with Cimarron," she said.

"God only knows why he keeps that bull anyhow," Logan mused, with a distracted shake of his head. "He doesn't run cattle. It would make sense if he had heifers to breed."

"You don't like him much, do you?"

"Cimarron?" Logan asked, hedging.

"Dylan," Briana said.

"I wouldn't say that."

"What *would* you say, then?"

"That we had a falling-out a long time ago," Logan told her. His tone was stiff; she'd crossed a line. "It happens with brothers."

Briana looked up ahead, at her boys, and felt the usual surge of wild, helpless love for them. "Alec and Josh argue all the time," she confessed. "But if they grew up and hated each other, I don't think I could stand it."

Logan didn't answer for a few moments. "I don't hate Dylan," he said.

Briana glanced at him, saw that his jawline had tightened. Since she'd already said too much, she decided to hold her tongue. No sense in digging herself in deeper.

Logan whistled, the sound low and distinctly masculine, and both boys and both dogs turned at the sound, sprinted back toward him.

"Thanks for supper," Logan said. "Sidekick and I had better be getting back home now. Big day tomorrow."

Briana merely nodded.

Logan said goodbye to the boys, and then he and Sidekick headed off toward the orchard. If either one of them were worried about encountering a bear, it didn't show in the easy way they strolled that country road.

CHAPTER FIVE

LOGAN'S CELL PHONE rang as he walked through the twilight-shadowed orchard, the dog prancing briskly alongside. He squinted at the caller ID panel, swallowed hard and thumbed the appropriate button.

"Hello, Ty," he said.

The responding chill was transmitted in milliseconds, bouncing from Tyler to some satellite and straight into Logan's right ear to pulse through his whole head.

"You left a message?" Tyler asked. His voice was deep—the last time they'd spoken, it had still been changing.

Logan suppressed a sigh. "We need to talk," he said.

"Maybe *you* need to talk, big brother," Tyler countered, "but *I've* got nothing to say to you."

Logan stopped in the middle of the orchard, looked up into the branches arching over his head, in case a bear was about to land on him. The weight of what lay between him and Tyler was heavier than anything that could have dropped out of a tree, though.

"Don't hang up, okay?" he asked. He'd had to swallow a measure of pride before he could get the words out.

"Give me one good reason why I shouldn't," Tyler

snapped, but at least he was still there. Still listening—if that stony stillness could be considered listening.

"Because we're brothers?"

Ty laughed, but there was no humor in the sound, only the numbing coldness that had greeted Logan's initial hello and expanded like a low-crawling fog drifting over a rain-soaked landscape. "That was a reach," he said. "And we're *half* brothers. Guess which half is my favorite?"

"Too easy," Logan said, moving again, but slowly. Sidekick was looking up at him, every few steps, in that worried way of his. "The half that isn't related to me."

"Right. What do you want, Logan? It can't be money—you've got plenty of that. If it's my signature on a sales contract for the ranch, you can forget it."

Logan had to unclamp his back molars to go on. "Nobody said anything about selling the ranch," he snarled. "Dylan reacted the same—"

"You talked to Dylan?"

"Yeah, yesterday."

"If you talk to him again, tell him he's a chickenshit son of a bitch."

In spite of everything, Logan grinned. He and Sidekick cleared the orchard, and the dog dashed ahead to sniff at the mega-load of steel fence rails, lumber and other building materials that must have been delivered while he was having supper with Briana and her kids.

"Tell him yourself," he said.

A second silence ensued. Then Tyler repeated the pertinent question. "What. Do. You. Want?"

Logan had given that a lot of thought, since he and Dylan had had a similar conversation. He didn't exactly know, specifically, so he made something up. "I'm planning to renovate the main house. Build a new barn. Replace some fences. Since you and Dylan own equal shares of the ranch, I thought you might want to look things over. Approve the changes."

Another silence.

"Are you still there?" Logan finally asked. He'd reached the front porch by then, but he wasn't ready to go inside, so he sat down on the step. Sidekick chased a low-flying bug through the high grass, snapping his jaws and missing every time.

"I don't have any say in what you do with the main house," Tyler said, at long last. His voice was even, but charged with resentment. "Build a barn if you want to. And you've never needed my approval before, so why start now?"

"I plan to run cattle," Logan answered. "If I want to keep them from straying, I'll have to put up new fences around the grazing section, and part of that land is yours."

"Suppose I don't want you to graze cattle on my share of that section?"

You little rooster, Logan thought, sourly amused. "Then I guess you'd better get your ass back here and try to stop me," he said. "And while you're telling Dylan he's a 'chickenshit son of a bitch,' pass that on to him."

Tyler swore. But he still didn't hang up.

Logan wondered if that was a good sign, or if his youngest brother was simply spoiling for a fight, even by long distance. Maybe the people he associated with now were too nice to provide an opportunity.

Not likely.

"No fences, Logan," Tyler said. "Not on my land, at least."

"Too late," Logan retorted. "The supplies are here and I've already hired the crew. They start tomorrow morning, bright and early."

"*No fences.* Do you hear me, Logan? If you put them up, I'll make you take them down again."

"Big talk for a little brother," Logan said, knowing full well that he might just as well have dropped a lighted match into a gasoline tank. "I'm a lawyer, remember? By the time you untangle yourself from all the red tape, I'll have the biggest cattle operation in the state of Montana."

"God*damn* it, Logan—"

Logan stretched luxuriously, and made the sigh-like sound to go with it. "Nice talking to you, Ty. Say hello to Dylan for me."

"*Logan—*"

Logan yawned. "I'm a rancher now," he said. "We get up early, if you'll recall. So I guess I'll turn in."

"Do *not* hang up on me—"

Logan thumbed the end button.

The cell immediately rang again.

Logan checked caller ID. Tyler.

He ignored the ringing, whistled for Sidekick.

And the two of them went inside.

The old house seemed to echo around them, empty of furniture and pictures and all the knickknacks several generations could accumulate. The soles of Logan's boots made a lonely clunking sound on the plank floors.

The phone stopped ringing, started up again.

Again, Logan looked at the tiny panel.

Sidekick turned his head to one side, perked up his ears. He might have been on his own for a long time—as Logan had expected, the vet hadn't found a microchip—but he knew a ringing phone was supposed to be answered. Feeling guilty for confusing a dog, Logan shut the cell off and set it on the mantelpiece above the empty fireplace.

"It's okay," he told Sidekick, flipping the light switch next to the door that led into the dining room. The pale glow only made the house look worse.

He thought of the album Alec and Josh had shown him over at Briana's, earlier that evening. And a lonely feeling welled up inside him.

His mother and both his stepmothers had been big on taking pictures—there were scores of photographs, if not hundreds, chronicling his childhood, Dylan's and Tyler's.

Where *was* all that stuff?

He had most of the furniture carted off to storage a year after Jake died. Had the albums and the trunk full of family papers gone with it?

He couldn't remember—if he'd ever known in the first place.

He had a key to the storage unit in town, but he didn't feel like driving in there and going through a bunch of old junk with a flashlight. He wanted the pictures, though—because all of the sudden he felt strangely insubstantial, almost as though he didn't have a past, didn't exist at all.

He and Sidekick might have been ghosts, the pair of them, haunting that run-down ranch house. All they lacked was chains to rattle and somebody to scare.

Knowing he wouldn't sleep anytime soon, Logan decided the attic was the logical place to start the search for the pictures. He headed for the back of the house, and Sidekick tagged along, still afraid, apparently, to let Logan out of his sight.

The attic steps were concealed behind a trap door in the kitchen ceiling.

Tall as he was, Logan had to jump, lay-up style, to catch hold of the rope handle and pull them down.

Dust billowed out of the space overhead as the heavy stairs struck the floor, causing Sidekick to leap backward in alarm and Logan to cough until his eyes watered.

"Stay here," Logan told the dog, before he started the climb, lowering his head to keep from banging it against the heavy timbers edging the opening.

Sidekick ignored the order and scrambled nimbly up behind him.

Logan ran a forearm across his face. He should have brought a flashlight, he thought, but since that would involve descending the stairs again and going all the way out to the truck, he decided to make do with his eyeballs.

There was stuff in that attic, all right.

Trunks. Boxes. A long plastic toboggan with a crack down the middle. An old aluminum Christmas tree, catching stray, winking glimmers of light from outside.

At least the old man hadn't been able to saw *that* tree in half, Logan reflected. He'd bought it himself when he was twelve, with money he'd saved mowing lawns and shoveling snow in town and doing odd jobs on neighboring ranches. Gone right into the hardware store and plunked down the cash. He'd even gotten one of those funky lights that rotated, casting a red glow over the tree, then green, then gold. Damn, but Dylan and Tyler had loved that tree.

They'd been too big to believe in Santa Claus—with Jake Creed for a father, they probably never had—but Logan could see the gleam of that garishly lighted silver tree reflected in their eyes as clearly as if he'd gone back in time.

He felt a grinding ache in his throat, remembering.

Back then, he and his brothers had been close. They'd had to be—it was the three of them against the old man and a hard world.

Sure, they'd fought with each other, the way boys do, more for sport than out of any particular hostility, but when there was trouble—and that was often—they'd stood shoulder-to-shoulder to face it down.

When had that changed?

It must have happened before Jake's funeral, or they wouldn't have been ready to go for each other's throats the way they had, but for the life of him, Logan couldn't remember a turning point.

"Shake it off," he told himself aloud. The words, like so many things, were an unwanted legacy from Jake.

Shake it off, boy. That had been Jake's answer for everything.

Dylan's broken arm, in fifth grade, so bad that the bone came right through his skin.

Tyler's screaming nightmares, after Sheriff Book

came to tell them his mother had been found dead in a distant motel room.

Logan's emergency appendectomy, the night of his senior prom. He'd damned near died in the ambulance.

Shake if off, boy.

"Fuck you, old man," Logan said. *"Fuck you."*

Far in the back of his brain, he thought he heard Jake laugh.

He started opening boxes and trunks.

Papers. Journals so old the pages were crumbling. Deeds and maps and what appeared to be a family tree, rolled up scroll-style and tied with a disintegrating ribbon.

He set those things aside and moved on. He'd come in search of the albums kept by Teresa, Maggie and Angela, and he was nothing if not single-minded.

He found the fat books inside a large plastic container with a snap-on lid, the word *pictures* scrawled on the side with a black marker. The handwriting was Jake's bold, slanted scribble.

Logan didn't allow himself to wonder—not consciously, at least—if that meant anything, Jake's apparent effort to preserve the albums he'd always scorned. Even without refreshing his memory by looking, Logan knew he probably wouldn't find a single picture of Jake simply smiling for the camera, like anybody else. He always had to mug, scowl or duck out of the frame at the last second before the flash went off.

Always had to screw it up somehow.

Logan attributed the burning in his eyes to the free-range dust he and Sidekick stirred up with every movement. After blinking a couple of times, he hoisted the surprisingly heavy container, into which much of his, Dylan's and Tyler's lives were compressed, and started for the stairs.

In the kitchen, he set the plastic box on the only original furniture left in the place—the round oak table and mismatched chairs that had belonged to every generation of Creeds since Josiah.

Sidekick's toenails made a clicking sound on the linoleum as he leaped over the last couple of steps, did a Bambi-on-ice thing and finally righted himself in a way that said "I *meant* to do that" as clearly as if he'd spoken in a human voice.

Logan chuckled hoarsely and bent to muss up the dog's ears.

"I'm not sure I'm ready for this," Logan said.

At the same moment, the wall phone rang. It was old, so he couldn't screen the call. In case Briana had bears on her back porch, or Cimarron had escaped the pasture to go on a rampage, Logan answered.

Dylan launched right in. "What the hell are you doing out there?" he demanded.

Logan smiled. Dylan and Tyler might have been on the outs about something, but Tyler had obviously passed on the news about the pasture fences. "Right now? I'm standing in my kitchen."

"Tyler said you're fencing off the whole ranch so you can run cattle," Dylan accused.

"That's right," Logan said. "I might even breed some of my heifers to your bull, since he doesn't seem to be serving any other purpose besides burning through a lot of grass and grain."

"You own a *third* of that ranch, not the whole thing!"

"What is the big deal about fences?" Logan asked, popping up a corner of the container lid and peeking in at the dusty cover of an old album. *Our Family* was stamped on the front in flaking gold letters. "It'll be an improvement, and I didn't ask either you or Tyler to contribute a dime."

"Just leave my third of the ranch alone, okay?"

"I might do that, if it weren't for your bull." He paused, letting that sink in, subtext and all. "I shouldn't have to tell you, Dylan, even considering how many times you've had your brains rattled by rodeo stock, that if Cimarron gets out and hurts somebody, there *will* be a lawsuit. And the plaintiff isn't going to give a rat's ass which of us owns the animal. If it happens anywhere on the property, it'll be our responsibility, since we own it jointly. Maybe you don't mind taking that chance, but I do."

Dylan was still seething, but the mention of a lawsuit must have reined him in a little, the way it did most people. "I've been paying Chet Fortner two hundred bucks a month to make sure Cimarron's looked after," he said. His voice had shrunk a little.

"Well," Logan answered, "Chet hasn't been mending fences—for two hundred a month, I don't blame him. Just the same, the rails are old and some of them are rotting. A couple of good kicks or a head-butt, and that bull will be out and about, looking for trouble and bound to find it. That's why I ordered enough steel posts and pipes to enclose the whole pasture."

Dylan must have used up all his hot air. "How much do I owe you? For the fencing, I mean?"

"I won't know until the job's done," Logan lied. He had an estimate, to the penny, and he'd made sure the contractor understood he was getting the figure inked in on the bottom line. Any cost overruns were going to be *his* problem, not Logan's. But he didn't want Dylan to write a check; he wanted him to come home, if only long enough to see what was going on.

"Oh," Dylan said.

"I've seen your house," Logan told him. This, too, was a calculated remark, meant to smoke his brother out on the subject of a certain very pretty neighbor. "Briana's taking good care of it."

Nothing from Dylan. Logan knew he was chewing on the information, deciding whether he ought to be pissed off or not. With Dylan, it could go either way.

"Hello?" Logan said.

"You're already visiting Briana?" Dylan asked. "Pretty fast footwork."

"'He who hesitates is lost,'" Logan quoted blithely, but inside he was as uneasy as he had been in the bad old days, when Jake was late getting home on payday and the current stepmother was trying to put a good face on things. If Dylan had something going on with Briana, it would change things, and not for the better.

"She's a nice woman, Logan," Dylan said, testy again. "Do her a favor and leave her alone."

"You sound like a man with a claim to protect."

"I barely know her. But she's decent and she works hard, and from what I've heard, she's had all the man-trouble she needs. If you have any ideas, back off."

"Not a chance," Logan said.

Dylan swore and broke the connection.

Logan smiled down at Sidekick, who'd been watching with interest the whole time. "So far, so good," he said.

Sidekick whimpered. It was a good bet he didn't agree.

Logan put a bowl of kibble on the floor for the dog, then went to the kitchen sink to wash the attic dust from his face, hands and arms. That done, he dried off with a wad of paper towels and returned to the business at hand.

He took the lid off the container, imagining the scene in one of the Indiana Jones movies, when somebody had opened the Ark of the Covenant. He couldn't shake the feeling that he'd just turned loose a lot of howling spooks and specters.

Logan lifted the *Our Family* album off the top, shaking his head at the naive optimism that title expressed.

He turned back the cover, and felt a pinch in his heart at the inscription he found on the first page. *For Jake and Teresa, on your wedding day. With love, Cassie.*

So, Cassie had been the optimist who'd bought the *Our Family* album. She'd lived in Stillwater Springs all her life, so she had to have known what Jake was like. Maybe back then, unlike now, she'd believed that wishing could make it so.

Thick-throated, Logan pulled back a chair and sank into it, knowing he wouldn't be able to look at the pictures stuffed into that album while he was standing up.

Sidekick rested his chin on Logan's thigh and made a sympathetic sound.

Logan braced himself, turned the first page.

Right off, he was proved wrong—there *was* at least one smiling photo of his dad. Jake, very young and bearing a strong resemblance to Dylan, clad in what he would have described as a monkey suit later in his life, gazed joyfully out of a cheap wedding portrait. Beside him, Teresa beamed, a dark beauty, proud of her new husband and her mail-order wedding dress.

Logan's eyes smarted again.

He curved the fingers of his right hand, touched her face, almost expecting to feel the soft warmth of living flesh. Teresa couldn't have been older than seventeen, if that. She'd been pregnant with her first and only child, but if either she or Jake regretted that, their smiles gave no sign of it.

On that day, at least, they'd both expected to lead long, happy lives.

Teresa had probably believed her love would change Jake, inspire him to give up his wild ways.

Maybe Jake had believed that, too.

Swallowing hard, Logan turned the page.

There were more pictures of the wedding—old-fashioned snapshots with yellowing, zigzag edges, some in color, some in black and white, all of them fading, slowly disintegrating.

As painful as it was to look at those images— Logan could barely manage it without flinching— he knew he couldn't let them be lost. As soon as his desktop and scanner arrived, he'd preserve every one, store them on a disk.

For now, all he could do was look.

Had he ever seen these pictures before? If so, he didn't remember.

Slowly, he turned another page, and then another.

Teresa in a polka-dot sundress, posing beside a tree, magnificently pregnant.

Jake, grinning as he sudsed an old jalopy, the spray from the hose frozen forever on the paper.

And then the first baby picture.

Logan looked down at his bald and patently unremarkable infant self. Teresa was in the picture, too, still in her hospital bed, holding her baby and glowing as if she'd just given birth to a second savior.

Jake's arm was visible—it must have been his, the hand resting on Teresa's shoulder.

Dear old Dad, Logan thought. Already easing out of the picture.

After that, he couldn't turn any more pages.

He closed the album, noticing that it was jammed at the front, and empty at the back. Put it back in the box and snapped on the lid, as if to corral the ghosts again, trap them in plastic.

But there was no containing the retro-spooks now, he knew. They were out for good, and sure to haunt him.

Wishing he'd never come back to Stillwater Springs Ranch, never opened this particular can of worms, Logan pushed back his chair and stood. Ran one forearm across his face, and almost stumbled over Sidekick, who'd been lying patiently at his feet, waiting for whatever came next.

The jolt put things into perspective.

If he hadn't headed for home, he wouldn't have found the dog. And as short as their acquaintance was, Logan couldn't imagine how he'd gotten along without Sidekick for company.

He frowned. Briana called her dog Wanda. Maybe

he should have given the critter a "people" name, like Gus or Bob. Something, well, *chummy*.

Logan still wasn't ready to sleep—he was keyed up from supper with Briana and the telephone conversations with his brothers and looking at all those old pictures. Like his computer gear, his TV hadn't arrived yet, not that he would have watched it, anyhow. He just missed having the option.

He found his duffel bag, ferreted through it for the spy-thriller he'd bought somewhere along the way home and stretched out on the sleeping bag on the floor of his old room.

The ranch house might have been about to fall down around his ears, but it was big. He and Dylan and Tyler had each had a room to call their own, though when he was little, Ty had often sneaked in in the middle of the night and curled up on the rug next to Logan's bed, much as Sidekick might have done if there'd *been* a bed. Let alone a rug.

The recollection choked Logan up all over again and, as lonesome as he felt, he was glad it was just him and Sidekick. If somebody had been around to ask him what was wrong, he might have broken down and told them.

Or just plain broken down.

Sidekick curled up close against his legs.

Logan opened the book, found his place and read.

At some point, he fell asleep, but all night long, the ghosts kept poking him awake. Once, knowing he was dreaming, he'd seen Jake—the prime-of-his-life Jake, from the album—peek in at him from the hallway, smile and shut the door again.

In the morning, letting the dog out and then back

in, starting the coffee brewing, he recalled the dream as clearly as a mystic would recall a visitation.

"Why couldn't you love us, old man?" he asked the sunrise, standing on the back porch and watching fingers of peach-colored light reach over the eastern hills.

He didn't know the answer, but he had a theory.

Jake Creed hadn't loved his wives, or his children, because he hadn't loved himself.

THE FENCING CONTRACTOR and his crew arrived at seven, just as Logan was finishing breakfast, and started work. The freight truck came at nine-thirty, to Sidekick's great excitement, and two men got out to unload Logan's computer, camera gear, books, bed and dressers, clothes and assorted household stuff.

He was on the bedroom floor with a screwdriver, setting up the metal frame that would hold the mattress and box springs, when he heard voices out in the living room.

Sidekick, a little slow on the uptake when it came to guard-dogging, rose to his haunches and gave a tentative bark.

"Logan?"

He recognized the voice. It was Josh, Briana's older boy.

"In here!" he called. "End of the hall, on the right!"

Footsteps pounded along the wide corridor, and Josh and Alec appeared in the open doorway, flanked by Wanda.

"Everything okay?" Logan asked. Given the time, their mother was probably working. Did these kids run loose all day, on their own, with only a fat old dog for protection?

You did, said a voice in his mind.

The reminder made him smile.

"Sure," Alec said. "We just came to visit, that's all. It's okay, isn't it?"

"Yeah," Logan replied. "It's okay provided your mom doesn't object."

The boys exchanged guilty glances.

Logan decided to pretend he hadn't noticed. "Did you come through the orchard?" he asked casually, concentrating on turning the last screw. Tonight, he'd be sleeping in his own comfortable bed. Things were looking up.

"Nope," Alec said helpfully. "Mom said there might be bears, or Cimarron might get loose and charge us, so we took the main road."

"Maybe you ought to call your mother at work. Let her know where you are."

"We're not supposed to bother Mom unless one of us is bleeding or we smell smoke," Josh said.

"That's reasonable," Logan answered, getting to his feet. "Let's go see how the new fence is coming along, then we'll rustle up some lunch."

The boys looked delighted.

Spotting his cell phone on the mantel as they entered the living room, which was piled with boxes from the freight truck, Logan snagged it and turned it on.

Five messages—three from Dylan, two from Tyler. He smiled and slid the phone into his jeans pocket. Let them stew.

"Mom says we're going to have a cell phone when she either gets a raise or wins the lottery," Alec said.

"Hmm," Logan said. Things must be pretty tight if Briana couldn't afford a cell phone. Hell, even kindergarteners had them these days.

"She's not going to win the lottery, stupid," Josh said, giving his brother a shoulder shove. "She doesn't *buy tickets*."

"You called me a name," Alec protested. "I'm *telling*."

Logan whistled through his teeth, a surefire attention-getter.

The boys stared at him in admiring surprise.

"Chill, my brothers," Logan said. Then he gestured toward the open front door. "Let's go."

BRIANA FROWNED AT the phone receiver before she hung up.

Millie, on her break, sat on one of the couches thumbing through an old copy of *People,* but otherwise, they had the employees' lounge to themselves.

"Is something wrong?" she asked.

Briana tried to ignore the incipient panic forming into a little whirlwind in the pit of her stomach. "I've called home three times since I got to work this morning," she murmured. "Nobody answers the phone."

"Maybe Josh is on the Web," Millie said. Most people had high-speed Internet connections, but Briana still used dial-up, and there was only one phone line in the house.

"You're probably right," Briana admitted, wondering why she hadn't thought of that perfectly obvious possibility.

Because she'd thought of Logan Creed and practically nothing else since the night before, *that* was why. She'd tossed and turned and gone to the living room window twice, when she should have been sleeping, hoping to see the lights of his house gleaming through the trees.

Still, she felt uneasy, and if she hadn't already pushed the envelope by asking Jim for Saturday off, she'd have made a quick trip home, just to make sure nothing was wrong.

And so many things *could* be wrong.

The boys might have left the house, bored with chores and daytime TV and the computer, and gone to the orchard, figuring they could "grin down" any bear they might encounter.

They might have gone to the pasture, to look at the bull.

Or Vance might have come, knowing she'd be working, and stolen them. Granted, that one was a stretch, since stealing Alec and Josh would also involve feeding and clothing them, but stranger things had happened.

Vance loved getting a rise out of her, and abducting her children would certainly do the trick.

She folded her arms and bit down hard on her lower lip. Bills or no bills, she was getting a cell phone as soon as her shift ended.

The yogurt Briana had gobbled down in her car on the way to work curdled and tried to climb into the back of her throat.

"Bree?" Millie fretted. "You don't look so good. Want me to ask Jim if you can go home sick?"

Briana was sorely tempted, but in the final analysis, she couldn't bring herself to lie to Jim, even indirectly. He'd promoted her twice and given her Saturday off, even though they were always short-handed on the weekends. He didn't deserve to be jerked around.

She shook her head, drew a deep breath and headed back out onto the casino floor to pay out jackpots, make change and keep an eye out for trouble.

She was near the front entrance, half listening to an old man insisting that the slot machines were rigged and half worrying that her sons were on their way to God knew where in Vance's old van, when she spotted Logan coming into the nearby restaurant, through the "family entrance."

Alec and Josh were with him, both of them grinning cheerfully.

The first thing Briana felt was relief. Her boys were safe, close enough to see and touch.

The second thing was a slamming fury that shook her bones and then rushed through her bloodstream like venom.

Who the *hell* did Logan Creed think he was, taking *her children* anywhere without her knowledge or permission?

CHAPTER SIX

"INCOMING," JOSH INTONED, peering over the top of his menu.

Logan had already spotted Briana out of the corner of his eye, steaming toward them like a freight train on a downhill grade. He grinned a little, anticipating the inevitable collision, complete with sparks. "Think I'll have the beef enchilada-tamale combo," he said.

Alec shifted uncomfortably in his seat. "Mom looks *pissed,*" he whispered.

"You're not supposed to say 'pissed,'" Josh told him.

"Pissed," Alec repeated, jutting out his chin. "Pissed, pissed, pissed."

Briana strode through the wide doorway in the long glass wall separating the Mexican restaurant from the rest of the casino.

Logan calmly closed his menu.

Stood.

Briana glared at him, then, hands on her hips, turned to the boys, both of whom were cowering behind the giant menus, their eyes wide with both alarm and defiance.

"What," she began, "did I tell you about riding in cars with strangers?"

"Logan isn't a stranger," Josh said. "He's our neighbor."

A waitress approached, cautiously, hovering at a safe distance.

"Join us for lunch?" Logan asked Briana.

Color surged into her cheeks. She always looked good, but being mad gave her a fiery quality that made Logan want to take her to bed, ASAP.

That would probably happen later, rather than sooner.

If at all.

"I'm *working*," she said.

"And that means you can't eat?"

Clearly flustered, she turned to her sons again. "You're supposed to be at home," she said. "You know the rules."

"We got lonesome," Josh said.

"It's hard being a latchkey kid," Alec added. He'd have a big future in any business involving manipulation-by-bullshit, that one. Probably make a good lawyer—or a politician.

"So we went over to Logan's place to see what he was doing," Josh went on, as though Alec hadn't spoken.

"We stayed *completely* away from Cimarron and the orchard," Alec added, his tone and expression earnest. "We took the county road."

Briana consulted her watch, the motion of her arm slight but jerky. She started to say something, then stopped herself. Sighed.

"Guilt won't work with me," she told Alec, a little late.

On the contrary, Logan thought, Alec's latchkey remark had struck the bull's-eye.

She looked up into Logan's face, and he saw pain in her eyes. Pain and fear and a kind of weariness that even a long vacation couldn't cure. "I have to work," she said.

And Logan wanted to draw her into his arms, hold her. Tell her everything would be all right.

He had no business doing any of those things, so he just stood there. "No harm done," he said quietly. "When the boys showed up at my place, I figured the best thing I could do was bring them here. To you."

She let out her breath, and her stiff shoulders slackened a little. "Thanks," she said, without much conviction. And then she looked at her watch again. "I'd better get back on the floor," she said. Pride had replaced the pain in her eyes. "I don't get off work until five. Alec and Josh can wait in the coffee shop until my shift is over."

Logan nodded, registering that she didn't trust him to hang out with her children for the rest of the day, and reconciling himself to that. He was a stranger to her; caution was more than reasonable.

"Can't we go back to the ranch with Logan?" Josh asked. "It's no fun sitting in a casino all day."

"I guess you should have thought of that," Briana told her son, "before you broke rule number one—when I'm not home, you don't go any farther than the yard." A pause. "And where, pray tell, is Wanda?"

Alec grinned broadly. "She's home. We dropped her off before we came to town, but Sidekick is out in the truck. He's even got a water dish."

"Can't you just have lunch with us?" Josh's voice held a pleading note.

"I owe you a meal," Logan said, referring to last night's supper.

But Briana just shook her head. Then, after fixing each of them with a warning glance—first Josh, then Alec, then Logan—she turned and went back to work.

The boys were a little subdued after that, but they ordered the beef enchilada-tamale combo, as Logan did, and ate as if they'd been locked away someplace and starved for a week.

They'd almost finished their lunch, and Logan was gearing up to leave the boys behind at the casino— a thing he would find hard to do—when he spotted Brett Turlow watching him from a table on the far side of the restaurant.

Turlow immediately looked away.

He was sitting alone, a smaller man than Logan remembered. In his midforties, old Brett wasn't aging well. He'd evidently done some hard living since taking over the family logging business, running it into the ground and declaring bankruptcy.

Logan knew all that because he'd kept up a subscription to the *Stillwater Springs Courier* after he left home the first time, and because he had several good reasons to dislike Brett Turlow.

They went way back, he and Brett, though there was a decade's difference in their ages.

Way, way back.

Logan paid the lunch check, left a tip for the waitress and walked Alec and Josh to the coffee shop to wait out the rest of Briana's shift. Mindful of Sidekick out in the truck with a partially rolled-down window and a limited supply of water, Logan took the time to backtrack for a word with Brett.

Somewhat to Logan's surprise, Turlow was still sitting at his table, the remains of an order of nachos in front of him, along with a glass of beer.

Turlow looked up at him, and the old mean streak coiled in his eyes. Back in the day, he'd been a hardass and a bully, the boss's son. Now, his skin didn't fit his face, but hung loose on his bones.

He'd beaten the hell out of Logan once. And then Jake had beaten the hell—and then some—out of *him*.

Turlow had wanted his dad to fire Jake, on the spot.

But whatever else he might have been, Jake Creed was the best logger in the woods. He felled three trees to everybody else's one, and he wasn't afraid of anything. Not the giant pines they called widow-makers, because they had a way of splitting from tip to trunk and crushing any man setting chain somewhere along their length, and certainly not Deke Turlow's son. Ever mindful of his profits, Deke had ordered Brett out of the woods instead of Jake.

He hadn't come back until after Deke turned a bulldozer over on himself and died, and even then, the old man's will prevented him from getting rid of Jake. That must have been hard to swallow, working day after day with a man who'd kicked his ass in front of half of Stillwater Springs.

"You come over here to gloat?" Brett asked wearily.

"Now why would I want to do that?" Logan countered.

"You know I lost the logging outfit. All that competition from overseas, and the environmentalists always making a fuss over some owl—"

"Bad things happen," Logan said. Like that chain snapping at the wrong time, he thought, and spilling a few tons of logs off the truck bed to crush Jake to a pulp.

"You and your brothers got the insurance money," Brett said, as though that made it all right, the way Jake had died. He'd been alive under all that timber when the other loggers got to him, according to the sheriff. The pain must have consumed him like a fire, but he'd laughed. He'd looked up at old Floyd Book, bloody as a chunk of raw hamburger, and *laughed.*

"This is how it ends, old buddy," he'd told Floyd. "This is how it ends."

They'd settled Jake's personal debts with the insurance check, he and Dylan and Tyler, and divided what was left. Logan had used his to pay off the loans he'd taken out to go to college.

"You were there that day, weren't you, Brett?" Logan asked. "The day that logging chain broke?"

Turlow squirmed a little, then pushed back his chair and stood.

Logan stood a head taller, and he didn't move to let the other man pass.

"I was there," Turlow said. "So what? So were the other eight men on the crew."

"They were still in the woods."

Turlow flushed a dull, sickly red. His breath smelled rancid, and he seemed to exude the sour stink of yesterday's beer from every pore. "There was an investigation," he spat. "I was cleared."

"He was sleeping with your girlfriend," Logan said. "Jake, I mean."

Turlow's flush deepened to dark crimson. "She was a tramp."

Logan shrugged one shoulder and stood solid as a totem pole. "Maybe so," he allowed. "But it must have made you mad, just the same. Your girl, pounding a mattress with a man twice your age—"

"Logan?"

Distracted, he turned. Saw Sheriff Floyd Book standing behind him. Speak of the devil.

Turlow skittered past him and beat feet for the outside door.

"If I thought it would do a damn bit of good," Book said, hooking his thumbs in his service belt, "I'd tell you to stay away from Brett Turlow for the sake of the peace." Floyd had always had a belly—now it hung lower and strained the buttons on his brown uniform shirt. His badge was as shiny as ever, though, and when he took off his round-brimmed hat, Logan saw that he still had a thick head of iron-gray hair.

"No worries, Sheriff," Logan said. "I've said what I wanted to say."

"I don't want any trouble around here," Book went on, sounding tired to the marrow. "Things have been relatively calm in Stillwater Springs since your daddy was killed—God rest his obnoxious soul—and you and your brothers lit out for parts unknown. At the risk of sounding like a character in a corny black-and-white western, I'd like to keep it that way."

Logan smiled. He'd always liked Floyd Book, thought he was a fair man. Now, though, he was mindful of Sidekick, alone in the truck. Brett Turlow probably wouldn't bother his dog, but Logan didn't want to take the chance. "I'll mind my manners," he said, starting to walk away.

Book sat down at a nearby table, nodded a good-bye. "Stop by my office when you get the chance," he said. "We'll jaw awhile."

Logan nodded back and left.

Out in the parking lot, Sidekick greeted him eagerly, sticking his nose through the opening in the window and barking in ecstatic welcome.

Logan felt a rush of relief as he unlocked the truck, shouldered the dog back off the driver's seat and climbed behind the wheel. He supposed running into Brett Turlow had been inevitable, given the size of Stillwater Springs, but the experience had nettled him, just the same. Brought back a lot of gut-grinding memories.

He'd rushed back to Montana when word of his dad's accident had reached him, and found Jake in the intensive care unit of a hospital in Missoula, veritably holding on to life by the tips of his fingers.

There had been no part of Jake that wasn't bruised a pinkish-purple. His legs and ribs had been smashed by the weight of those rolling logs, and the distortion was visible even under the blankets. Tubes and wires snaked from him in every direction—he'd seemed tangled in them, like a fly caught in a spider's web.

Only Jake's eyes, fiercely blue and snapping with obstinate pride, had been the same.

Jake hadn't been able to talk—his voice box and virtually every bone and organ in his body had been broken or ruptured—but those eyes had said plenty.

You're too late.

I'm disappointed in you. Always was.
Yes, I'm going to die.
Shake it off.

"Shake it off," Logan repeated aloud.

Jake had kept his unspoken promise. He'd died before Dylan and Tyler could get there, and that was when the blaming had started. They'd both been furious with Logan for being in that hospital room when Jake breathed his last—maybe because it wouldn't have seemed right to turn that fury on a dead man.

Especially when that dead man was their father.

Sidekick whimpered.

Logan reached out to tousle his ears.

And then they headed back to Stillwater Springs Ranch, where they belonged.

Or did they?

Just then, Logan wasn't sure *where* he belonged.

THE REST OF Briana's day crawled by.

She made brief but regular visits to the coffee shop, to make sure the boys were still there, and Jim even offered to let her leave early. Since she was about to make a purchase she hadn't budgeted for, getting docked on her pay didn't seem like the best idea in the world. Besides, with every other child-support check bouncing to the ceiling, she was barely making it as it was.

At ten minutes after five, Briana collected her boys, now sheepish and cranky from cooling their jets in the coffee shop for several hours, got into the dented, primer-splotched extended-cab pickup truck Dylan had left behind at the ranch, and started the engine while she waited for Alec and Josh to buckle themselves in. She could drive the old rig if she could get it running, Dylan had said, and she had, with most of her first paycheck from the casino and a lot of help from a mechanic in town, but after two years, *keeping* it running was the challenge.

Briana had been saving up to buy a decent used car, but it was three steps forward, two steps back. Every time she got a little ahead, some unexpected expense came up—medicine and veterinary bills when Wanda tore a ligament in one hind leg; the window Josh had broken out, playing baseball with Alec in the side yard; a donation at work when one of the other employees lost everything in a house fire.

It never stopped.

And now she *had* to get a cell phone. Josh and Alec would be able to call her directly, instead of going through the casino switchboard. They were good boys, and they probably would have contacted her before striking out for Logan's place via the county road, where they could have been run over, kidnapped or attacked by a wild animal.

They *probably* would have contacted her.

"What you did today was not cool," she said, speaking for the first time since they'd left the casino as she pulled into the parking lot at Wal-Mart. She shopped there a lot, but every visit brought back stinging memories of the night Vance had bailed on her and the kids and Wanda.

"We're sorry, Mom," Alec said.

"It was no big deal," Josh argued.

She turned in the seat, looked back at them. "It *was* a big deal, Josh," she said. "And, Alec, 'sorry' comes cheap. You guys are both grounded until further notice."

"Like *that's* going to change our lives," Josh said. "We're *grounded* all the time, because you make us stay in the house if you're not with us. It's like we're *babies* or something."

He had a point, but short of putting them in child care, which would not only finish off the car fund but also make them both severely unhappy, she didn't know what else to do.

Alec eyed her, then agreed with his brother, a rare occurrence in itself. "Yeah," he said. "We're *already* grounded. When Dad gets here, I bet he *takes* us places."

Vance. He would be in town Saturday, he'd said, and that was tomorrow. Briana's mood, already low, plummeted.

"Wait in the car," she said. "I won't be long."

"Mom, we're *always* waiting," Josh protested. "We just got *through* waiting all afternoon in the coffee shop!"

Briana sighed, and relented. "All right, but no wandering off. If I have to hunt all over the store for you guys, I'm not going to be a happy camper."

"What else is new?" Josh asked, pushing open his door and jumping to the ground before she could change her mind. "You're *never* a happy camper."

"Yeah," Alec agreed, though cautiously.

Briana rolled her eyes. "Let's just do this, so we can go home and feed Wanda, all right?"

"All right," Josh agreed, as though he had any say in the matter. "What is it we're going to do, exactly?"

"I'm getting a cell phone," Briana said. They were

in the crosswalk now, the very spot where Vance had told her to get out of the car and take the kids and the damn dog with her because he had better things to do than listen to a nagging woman.

She'd wanted to stop and buy fried chicken in the deli, because it would be cheaper than going to a restaurant, and she and the boys were sick of drive-through hamburgers. Did that qualify as nagging?

Alec wrenched her back to the present moment with a yelp of delight. "We're getting a cell phone?"

"*I'm* getting a cell phone," Briana corrected. "And you two are going to call me on it and ask for permission before you go hiking off down the road."

When they were younger, she would have held their hands until they were safely inside, but they both kept a manly distance now.

"All the kids at swimming lessons have their *own* cell phones," Josh told her.

Briana swallowed her stock response—*we can't afford it*—because she was tired to the bone of that answer, and so were the boys.

Inside the store, she headed straight back to the electronics department. Josh and Alec didn't agitate to head off on their own, probably because they were fascinated by the array of flat-screen TVs, laptops, DVD players and the like.

All that stuff was out of Briana's financial reach—she'd bought their computer from one of those low-monthly-payment mail-order outfits, because it was necessary for the boys' schooling, and it was a tur-key—and today, being perennially poor got her down more than usual.

Alec and Josh lobbied for the newest phenomenon,

with a camera, MP3 capability, video games and a touch screen.

Briana chose the supereconomical model—all it did was make and receive phone calls. No walking the dog. No wallpapering the living room. Just phone calls.

It did have one redeeming feature, though. It came with a free companion phone, and that mollified the boys a little. They promised to share, but she knew they'd probably come to blows over the thing before they pulled into the driveway at home.

With her umpteenth sigh of the day, Briana wheeled a cart to the grocery section to buy a bag of kibble for Wanda and a gallon of milk—she'd forgotten both the day before, when she stopped after work to pick up the ingredients of Wild Man's Spud Extravaganza—and after waiting in line to pay, they were on their way out.

Miraculously, they made it all the way home with no hostilities breaking out in the backseat. After carrying in the kibble and the milk, and letting Wanda out for a few minutes, Briana put the leftover casserole into the oven to warm up, Alec checked the answering machine and Josh settled down at the table with the new cell phones and accompanying instructions.

"We have to charge them first," he said. "That will take *hours*."

"We'll survive," Briana said, washing her hands at the sink.

"You said we could picnic in the cemetery tonight," Alec reminded her. "Last night, when you were making the casserole, you said that."

"I did not," she retorted. "I said sometime."

"That isn't fair."

"Sorry. That's the way it is."

"Why?"

"Because I said so."

"That *so* isn't fair. How come kids always have to do stuff because grown-ups say so?"

Briana laughed, starting to feel better now that they were home, doing normal things, like feeding Wanda and heating up leftovers. "Because most of us are bigger than you are," she said.

"Someday," Alec vowed, "I'll be bigger than *you* are."

"No doubt about it," Briana agreed. "But by then you'll be too much of a gentleman to argue with me."

"Fat chance," Josh contributed.

"Get ready for supper, both of you," Briana said.

"I'm not hungry," Alec retorted.

"You're just mad because there weren't any messages from Dad," Josh told his brother.

"Hold it right there!" Briana interrupted, gliding between the boys like a referee in a hockey game. "If this argument goes any further, neither of you get to use the extra cell phone. *Ever.*"

"It would be more effective," Josh remarked, looking up at her in solemn certainty, "if you could whistle like Logan does. That really shuts us up."

"What are you talking about?" Briana asked, baffled.

"Today in the Mexican place at the casino," Josh answered importantly, "me and Alec got into it, and Logan whistled. Through his front teeth. It was *really loud.*"

"And that's good?"

"It worked," Alec said, with a verbal shrug. "If I didn't already have a dad, it would be cool to be Logan's kid."

Briana slumped into a chair, forestalled Josh's inevitably sarcastic comment before he could get it out of his mouth with a pointed look.

"Do you think Logan has kids, Mom?"

She needed a few moments to recover. Why had Alec's words thrown her like that? *If I didn't already have a dad, it would be cool to be Logan's kid.*

"Huh?"

"Do you think Logan has kids?" Alec repeated patiently. He'd probably use that same tone when she was an old woman, forgetting things. She hoped she'd live long enough to be a problem.

"I have no idea," Briana said.

"Next time he comes to supper, I'll ask him," Josh said.

"There might not be a next time," Briana replied. "I only invited Logan over last night because it was the neighborly thing to do."

Alec's face clouded. "You're mad at him because he brought us to town today. You should be mad at *us,* not him."

That earned Alec an elbow jab from Josh.

"You're right. I should be mad at you." She kept a straight face. "But I'm not."

"Really?" Alec looked astounded.

It wasn't as if she lost her temper on a regular basis, Briana thought indignantly. If anything, she was overindulgent, letting them get away with too much. So what was with all the surprise?

"Really," Briana said.

"Don't push it, geek-face," Josh counseled.

Briana skewered her elder son with another look.

"Sorry," Josh said meekly.

The phone rang while they were having supper, and Alec knocked over his chair getting to the receiver.

His whole face shone when he said, "Dad! Hi!"

Briana waited uneasily, as did Josh. If past history was anything to go by, Vance was about to burst the bubble, make some excuse for not coming to visit. She'd be relieved, Alec would be devastated. The jury was still out on how Josh would react.

"You're almost to Stillwater Springs right now?" Alec nearly shouted.

"Sure, sure, I'll put her on— Mom! He wants directions!"

Briana rose slowly from her chair, crossed the room, took the telephone receiver and put it to her ear. She had to clear her throat once before she could say anything.

"So—you're almost here."

"We are," Vance answered.

We?

"Tell me how to get to your place, Bree. I'm real anxious to see my boys."

Alec was jumping around the kitchen.

Josh had probably ducked into his room. He'd have had to pass her to use the back door.

Calmly, Briana told her ex-husband which turns to take on which roads.

She was numb when she hung up.

She went straight to the boys' bedroom.

Sure enough, Josh was on his bed, a lump under

the bump-chenille spread he hated because it had a teddy bear on it and that was babyish.

"Josh?" Briana sat down gingerly on the edge of the mattress, laid a tentative hand on her son's back. "Wanna come out and talk to me for a minute?"

"No." The word was muffled. "Can I go live with Logan until Dad leaves?"

"Honey, he *is* your father."

Josh yanked the spread down and scowled at Briana, nose and forehead crinkled in disgust. "He's a *jerk!* He left us at Wal-Mart, Mom!"

"We've done okay since then, haven't we?" Briana asked, very softly.

"What if he stays?"

"I won't let him stay, Josh. Your dad and I are divorced."

"He should have just kept going. He *wants* something, Mom. That's why he's coming here." Josh's lower lip trembled. "What if he decides to take Alec and me away with him?"

"He's not going to do that, Josh," Briana said, as a piece of her heart quivered and then fell off. How long had Josh been worrying about this? "I have legal custody. That means you and Alec stay right here with me until you're old enough to be on your own."

Just then, Josh did something he hadn't done since the night Vance deserted them. He threw both arms around her neck and clung for dear life.

Briana held him tight. Kissed the top of his head. His buzz cut felt prickly against her lips, and that made her smile, even though her eyes were full of tears.

"It was scary, getting left like that," she said, after a

long time. "I'm really sorry that happened. But we're all right now, you and me and Alec and Wanda. We have a nice place to live, and I have a job and—"

Josh reared back. "Don't let him take us away, Mom," he begged. "He might get mad and leave us someplace, like he did before, only you wouldn't be there to take care of us—"

Briana was near tears herself, but she didn't dare let it show. She had to be strong for Josh, and Alec, too. She couldn't afford to cry any more than she could afford a big-screen TV or fancy computer or a cell phone with all the latest bells and whistles. "I promise that won't happen, Josh."

He sniffled, wanting to believe her. Struggling to believe her.

"Swear?"

"Swear."

"What do we do now?"

Briana smiled, risked a forehead kiss, was glad when Josh didn't pull away to avoid it. "I go back to the kitchen and make coffee, and you go to the bathroom and wash your face."

Josh nodded glumly.

Briana started a pot of coffee and found clean sheets, a blanket and pillows for the fold-out couch. Vance had said *we,* which probably meant he was bringing one of his rodeo-bum buddies along to run interference, keep the little ex-wife from getting on his case. Well, he could just share the thin couch mattress with his pal, because there was nowhere else to put him.

Vance rolled in in the same old van; Briana recognized the belching sound the muffler made.

"He's *here!*" Alec whooped, flinging open the back door and darting out of the house with Wanda right behind him, barking her brains out.

Fickle dog.

"Yippee," Josh murmured miserably, slumped in front of the computer.

Briana tossed him a sympathetic glance and made herself go to the door.

It was almost dark, but not so dark that she couldn't see Vance climbing out of the van, stepping down with that patented grin on his face to scoop Alec up and swing him around once.

When the other door opened, though, Briana's breath caught.

A woman—more of a girl, really—rounded the front of the van, smiling nervously. She was super-skinny, wearing one of those clingy tops that don't quite cover the territory, tight jeans and boots. A little silver hoop glinted from her naval, and her hair was bleached, yanked up into something resembling a ponytail, seeming to sprout from the top of her head.

Vance set Alec on his feet, looked up to meet Briana's gaze. At the same time, he stretched out an arm in the girl's direction, and she hurried to him, snuggled close against his side. Stared at Briana with enormous, frightened eyes.

"You look good, Bree," Vance said.

She couldn't speak. It didn't bother her to know that Vance had a girlfriend—that was old news. It *did* make her want to bite through a nail that he'd brought the squeeze-du-jour to the house, that he obviously intended to sleep with her under the same roof with their sons.

"This is Heather," Vance said. "Heather, my ex-wife, Briana. That's my boy Alec." He frowned, idly stooping to pet Wanda's head. "Where's Josh?"

"Inside," Briana managed to say.

"Hi, Briana," Heather chimed. She sounded so desperate to please that Briana felt sorry for her. The poor kid probably had no clue what she was in for with Vance.

"Come in," Briana said.

They all went into the kitchen, and the next few moments were awkward in the extreme. Josh didn't make a move to greet Vance, and both he and Alec gaped at Heather as though she were a curiosity on display at one of those roadside places where they sell dusty, dog-eared postcards and plastic paperweights with dead snakes coiled inside.

"This is Heather," Vance said, for the second time.

Heather blushed, looking as though she wished the floor would open under her feet.

Briana's sympathy deepened to pity. "Would you like some coffee, Heather?" Then, belatedly, added, "Sit down. Please. Sit down."

In the light of the kitchen, she could see that Heather was older than she'd seemed outside. Over twenty-one, anyway, which was good, because Briana would have called the sheriff if she wasn't.

"Thanks," Heather said, sort of collapsing into a chair.

She patted her hair, and that was when Briana noticed the slim gold wedding band on her left hand.

Vance puffed up like a rooster. "Heather," he announced to Alec and Josh, "is your new stepmother."

CHAPTER SEVEN

"AREN'T YOU EVEN going to say howdy to your old daddy, boy?" Vance asked, turning to Josh, who remained at the computer on the far side of the kitchen, looking stricken and furious.

"Howdy," Josh said dully.

Alec, meanwhile, was sitting on Vance's lap, but even he, the perpetual optimist, seemed a little thrown by the announcement that he now had a stepmother.

Vance sighed. Tossed Heather a knowing glance. "Guess I've got some fences to mend," he said.

"Guess so," Heather agreed readily. She probably agreed with everything Vance said, at this point. That, Briana knew, would change in time.

Her hand shook a little as she poured fresh coffee for Heather and Vance. She'd offered to rustle up some supper for them, but they'd demurred, said they'd already eaten on the way.

"Just so happens," Vance drawled, rubbing the top of Alec's stubbly head with his knuckles, "that we brought presents."

Irritation swamped Briana, made her nerve endings twitch. Presents? Vance didn't even pay his child support most of the time. He didn't buy the shoes and jeans and T-shirts the boys were constantly outgrowing. He didn't even send birthday cards.

How could he manage *presents?*

But, then, presents made him look good. He evidently regarded thankless necessities as *her* responsibility.

Alec brightened at the mention of gifts, of course, and even Josh seemed intrigued.

"They're in the van," Vance said. "What do you say we go unload them?" He turned, smiled easily at Josh. "We could use your help."

Alec was already on his feet and racing for the door. Josh followed, but only after a silent signal from Briana.

Vance got up, too, and the three of them went outside.

Heather shifted nervously in her chair. "We got them bicycles," she said shyly. "Found them at a garage sale in a little town outside of Vegas, but Vance fixed them up and they look like new."

Briana's heart did a slippery little sidestep. Bicycles. The boys had been asking for bikes every Christmas and every birthday for years. She'd never managed to come up with the money. How ironic was it that Vance would be the one to make that old and persistent dream come true?

"You don't mind, do you?" Heather asked.

Briana blinked, confused. "Mind?"

"That Vance brought me here. We won't be staying long—just 'til tomorrow afternoon."

Briana *did* mind, actually, but she wasn't mean enough to say so to Heather. The woman was scared to death.

Outside, Alec shouted with joy.

The bikes had been unveiled, then.

"Where will you be going next?" Briana asked, just to make conversation.

The bombshell, when it dropped, took Briana completely by surprise. "Oh, we're planning to stay right here in Stillwater Springs," Heather said brightly. "Vance hit a royal flush on a poker machine in Vegas the other day, and he said it was a sign from God that we ought to settle down someplace." Probably privy to the child-support situation, Vance's bride blushed and bit down hard on her plump lower lip. "It isn't a lot," she hastened to add, "but there's enough to pay rent and a cleaning deposit, and keep going until we both get jobs."

"There aren't a lot of those around Stillwater Springs," Briana said, feeling dizzy. Life. It could go along the same for years, then make a sudden one-eighty. "Jobs, I mean."

Heather contradicted her immediately. "We stopped at the auto repair place in town to get some new spark plugs," she said, "and there was a Help Wanted sign taped to the door. They need a mechanic, and Vance is a good one. The man asked him to come by tomorrow for an interview."

Briana resisted an urge to close her eyes and shake her head. Vance, living in Stillwater Springs? Actually working nine to five instead of following the rodeo?

Alec would be thrilled. Josh would probably adjust.

But everything would change.

Everything.

Briana was still processing the news when Vance appeared in the open doorway, standing on the back porch. In the glow of the outside light, he looked the same as always—and different.

Had he found religion, or something?

If she circled his van, would she find a Honk if You Love Jesus sticker on the bumper?

"Come see the bikes," he said.

Briana had no idea whether he was addressing her or Heather or both of them. But she waited until he and Heather were outside before following to stand on the porch.

Alec and Josh were riding around in wide, wobbly circles on their "new" bikes.

"Picked it up pretty fast," Vance said proudly, looking on.

The boys had ridden other kids' bikes whenever they got the chance, but it had been a while. Evidently, riding a bike really *was* something you never totally forgot how to do.

"I've got something for you, too, Bree," Vance told her.

Heather headed for the van to fetch her overnight case.

"What?" Briana asked warily.

Vance steered her back inside, and they stood in the kitchen, momentarily alone. He took out his wallet and counted several crisp one-hundred-dollar bills into her hand.

She stared.

"Child support," Vance said.

"Oh," Briana said, stunned. Knowing Vance, he'd probably want to borrow it back before the weekend was out. The bank was open Saturdays until noon, though, and she intended to be there when they un-locked the doors the next morning. "Th-thanks."

"That makes us square, doesn't it?" Vance asked, watching her closely.

What did he expect? Tears of gratitude? Maybe that she'd drop to the floor and wrap her arms around his knees, weeping with joy and relief? He'd *owed* her this money, and taken his sweet time paying up.

"Thanks," she repeated, hastily folding the bills, tucking them into the pocket of her work slacks. "Yes. It makes us square." *For now.* "Heather says you're planning to stay on in Stillwater Springs."

Vance nodded, cast a sidelong glance out the door. Something moved in his face as he watched the boys trying out their bikes, an emotion Briana had never seen there before.

"I blew it with Alec and Josh, and with you," he said, without meeting her eyes. "I still have a chance with my kids."

Briana's throat felt as if she'd swallowed a boul-der. When she could speak, she said, "Don't get their hopes up, Vance. Don't make them think you're going to stay and be part of their lives, okay?"

Before Vance could do more than look at her, with the expression of a man who'd just been slapped across the face, Heather was back, lugging in her overnight bag and her bulky purse.

"Would it be all right if I took a bath?" she asked Briana.

"Sure," Briana said, but she was still looking at Vance.

He moved past her to the porch, told the boys to put their bikes next to the house and come on in.

Instead, they wheeled them up the steps and parked them in the kitchen.

Briana shut the door slowly, her gaze going from boy to boy, and bike to bike. Even Josh looked cautiously delighted, and Alec was glowing.

"They might get stolen if we leave them outside," Alec said. He had the red bike; the handlebars gleamed, and the paint job looked fresh. Josh's blue bike had metallic flakes in the paint, and racing stripes.

"Put them in the utility room for now," Briana said. "And be careful not to scratch the washer and dryer."

Her sons nodded and wheeled the bikes out of the kitchen.

After that, things got awkward again.

Heather said she was tired, after her bath, and made out the couch bed to crawl in.

The boys sat at the table, all ears while Vance brought them up to speed on his latest adventures. He'd met Heather in Butte, he said, at a rodeo, and he'd known it was love. Married her before he left town.

Inwardly, Briana sighed.

Josh still looked careful; he was holding back. Two years older than his brother, he'd had more experience with Vance and his high-flown promises, but the bike had gotten to him a little, too. Briana could see that he *wanted* to believe in Vance, and didn't quite dare.

Alec's heart was wide open. All was clearly forgiven—not that he'd ever really held a grudge against his dad. He'd always seen something in Vance that eluded Briana.

"We'll get you some groceries tomorrow," Vance

told her quietly, well after midnight, when he'd herded Alec and Josh to their room and maybe even tucked them in.

Had he heard a word she'd said, about getting their hopes up?

Did he have the first clue how crushed they'd be when he broke his word, the way he always did?

"Sure," Briana said. "Good."

Vance crossed the room, took her shoulders in his hands, turned her from the sink, where she'd been filling the coffeepot for morning, and looked down into her eyes.

Briana shrugged free, moved just out of his reach.

In the living room, Heather either slept blissfully away on the Hide-A-Bed or lay wide-awake, listening.

"Briana, I was just—" Vance's voice sounded gruff, weary. "I wasn't going to do anything."

"You could have mentioned Heather on the phone, Vance. Given me a chance to prepare the boys."

"The boys," Vance said, as a muscle bunched in his square jaw, "seem to be handling it fine. And this is the kind of thing a man has to do in person, not over the telephone."

Briana looked away. Didn't speak. If Vance thought *she* was upset because he'd remarried, she'd die of mortification.

"I'd better turn in," Vance told her. "Good night, Bree."

Briana still didn't speak, still didn't meet his gaze. She just nodded.

Vance headed for the living room, murmured something husbandly to Heather, who sighed sleepily and murmured something back.

Good God, Briana thought, diving for the doorway to her room, Wanda close on her heels, *they aren't going to have sex, are they?*

If they did, she sure as hell didn't want to know.

After changing into a cotton nightgown and sneaking down the hall to use the bathroom, barely able to keep from covering her ears with both hands lest she hear something embarrassing, she dashed back to her room and turned the radio on low.

Wanda, curled up in her usual spot on the mattress, buttressed against the headboard, gave her a curious look, yawned and settled down to sleep.

Briana snuggled in, too, but sleep escaped her, tired as she was.

Besides the fact that the boys might hear any hanky-panky that went on, did she really give a damn if Vance and the missus made love?

No.

Then what was the problem?

She tossed onto one side, then the other. A smoky voice flowed out of the radio, singing the kind of song that made a woman want a man, a glass of wine and candlelight.

Briana stretched to crank the dial to another station.

Hog futures. That was it.

Nothing romantic about hog futures.

Whatever the heck *they* were.

A soft knock sounded at Briana's door.

She sat up, yanked the covers to her chin. "Yes?"

The door creaked open, and Josh stood in the opening. She could almost see him growing out of his pajamas.

"Can I sleep in here?"

She usually discouraged that, but the look on Josh's face gave her pause. "What's the matter, honey? Did you have a bad dream?"

Josh nodded, gulped. "I dreamed Dad took us away. I couldn't remember your cell-phone number, because it's new and—"

"Shh," Briana said, patting Wanda's side of the bed.

Accommodatingly, the dog moved to the foot of the mattress, so Josh could crawl in beside Briana.

"I'm too big to be sleeping with my mom," Josh lamented.

"Once won't hurt," Briana said.

"Is it okay to be happy about the bike?"

Briana's eyes stung. "Yeah. It's okay."

"Do you think he'll make us call Heather 'Mom'?"

"It's up to you what you call Heather, as long as you're respectful," Briana said carefully. The thought of Alec or Josh addressing another woman as Mom settled into her heart like an anvil, but she was determined to be fair.

On top of that, she sort of—well—*liked* Heather.

Josh lay there for a while, silent in the spill of light from the bedside lamp and the soft drone of the radio. Then he said, "How come you're listening to the farm report?"

The announcer was saying there would be a big stock sale in Choteau the next day as Briana smiled and shut it off.

"I just wanted sound," she said.

"Oh," Josh said, sitting up and throwing back the covers. "I think I'm okay now," he told her.

"Good," Briana said, watching as he left the room, headed for his own bed. Wanda nonchalantly reclaimed her place on the other pillow.

Briana turned the light switch, and the room went dark.

"WHAT I NEED," Logan told Sidekick, watching through the windshield of his pickup as a second construction crew swarmed over the barn first thing the next morning, "is a horse."

Sidekick didn't venture an opinion, one way or the other. He was probably hoping for a fast-food breakfast in town, or another visit from Alec and Josh and Wanda.

"Yes, sir," Logan repeated, mostly because he wanted to hear somebody's voice, even if it was his own, "I surely do need a horse."

He'd already been to check out the work on the new pasture fence. The workmen were a little scared of Cimarron, but so far, the old bull had kept his distance, eyeing the proceedings from a copse of birch trees and only pawing the ground once or twice. Short of drugging the critter and shipping him someplace for the duration, working around him seemed the most viable option.

So far, so good.

The barn wouldn't be fit to house any horses for a week or two, at the least, but there was a stock auction going on over in Choteau, twenty miles away, and Logan couldn't resist going.

As a kid, and later, in the rodeo, he'd ridden a lot. Jake had kept two old nags, Shadow and Dynamite, and he and Dylan and Tyler had virtually grown up on their backs. Logan smiled, remembering how it always pissed off Tyler that he had to ride double with either Logan or Dylan. He'd hated being the youngest, hated always having to follow when he wanted to lead.

Shadow and Dynamite had both died of old age long ago, but the loss seemed fresh that morning, as if they ought to have been waiting at the corral gate, ready to be saddled for the day.

Logan swallowed the lump in his throat and shifted the truck into gear. He could sit around here all day, crying in his beer, or he could make something happen.

He damn near hit Alec and Josh at the base of the driveway, where the top of the old gate still hung by the same three links of chain. They whizzed past on bicycles while he slammed on the brakes, simultaneously stretching out an arm to keep Sidekick from crashing into the windshield.

Alec and Josh slowed, made a wide loop in the road.

His heart pounding, Logan breathed deep as he rolled the window down. "You might want to be a little more careful in the future," he said.

"Sorry," Josh told him.

Alec's grin went from ear to ear. "We got new bikes!" he crowed.

Logan chuckled. "I see that," he said. "Way cool."

"Our dad bought them at a garage sale," Josh explained.

Their dad. It was a perfectly normal thing for a man to visit his kids, buy them bicycles. So why did he feel like dropping in on Briana so he could size up the situation?

The *situation,* whatever it might be, was none of his damn business.

"Does your mom know you guys are out here?" he asked, recalling the dustup the day before over their coming to town with him.

"She was going to take the day off from work," Alec said, "but Dad's watching us, so she went in after all. After Dad's job interview, he's taking us to look at a rental he saw in the newspaper."

It was a lot of information to take in and sort out, but Logan had had three cups of strong coffee that morning, so the mental cogs were working fine. "Where's your dad now?" he asked, just as a tall man rounded the bend on foot. He wore old boots, jeans and a blue chambray shirt, Western cut.

Alec cocked a thumb. "That's him," he said proudly.

Logan worked up a smile, got out of the truck.

"This is our neighbor, Logan Creed," Josh told his father. "He came to supper at our place night before last."

"Did he now?" The other man's blue gaze took Logan in as they shook hands. "Vance Grant," he said. "Good to meet you."

Logan merely nodded. Grant didn't like it that he'd paid a social visit to his ex-wife, Logan could see that. There was a chill of suspicion in those icy eyes.

"I'll be around from now on," Vance said. "If that makes a difference to you."

Logan raised an eyebrow, conscious of the boys standing nearby, with their new bikes, listening. "Should it?" he asked evenly.

Vance's grin didn't make it to his eyes. Before he could respond, somebody's cell phone rang.

Josh quickly extracted a model one step up from a toss-away out of his jeans pocket and answered.

"It's Mom," he told the assembled crowd, with a roll of his eyes, though Logan could tell he felt important. "Yes, Dad's here—he's *with us,* Mom. So is Logan." A pause. "Heather was still asleep when we left the house."

Who the hell, Logan wondered, was Heather?

"We ought to head home now," Vance said, as Josh hung up the cell phone, held it out of Alec's reach for a few seconds, then put it back in his pocket. "We're due in town in half an hour."

Alec and Josh both said goodbye and pedaled back toward Dylan's place. Logan got into his truck, the window still down, and Vance lingered a moment.

"My boys," he said, "have a dad."

Logan felt his ears burn. He'd had supper at Briana's once, and taken Alec and Josh to town the day before to have lunch and, as it turned out, wait for their mother. Did this yahoo think he was moving in on his turf or something?

The kids were definitely Vance's; they looked just like him.

But Briana wasn't his wife. Where she was concerned, turf wasn't an issue.

"Look," Logan said, resting his arm on the window ledge and gripping the steering wheel a little too tightly with the other hand, "we just met, so I'm going to give you the benefit of the doubt and not assume you're a prickly son of a bitch with a chip on your shoulder. Alec and Josh are nice kids. You're lucky to have them."

Vance huffed out a breath, relaxed a little. Took off his hat to shove a hand through his hair, half turned to follow the boys and then turned back again. "I guess I *am* a little prickly," he admitted. "I've made a lot of mistakes, and I'm trying to set things right. That's going to take some doing and the plain truth is, I don't need any competition just now."

Logan didn't say anything. He meant to listen, nothing more.

But Vance didn't add anything to the speech he'd just made. He turned again, saw that the boys had disappeared around the bend and followed them.

I don't need any competition just now.

What the hell did *that* mean? Was Vance trying to win his family back, Briana included? Or was he just talking about establishing some kind of relationship with his kids?

Key word *his,* Logan thought grimly.

The gears ground a little as he shifted into First, and the tires screeched as they grabbed the pavement on the county road.

He hardly knew Briana Grant. If she wanted to reconcile with her ex-husband, that was her prerogative.

Just the same, as he drove through Stillwater Springs, and then past the city limits, headed toward Choteau, it was all he could do not to turn in at the casino, find Briana and ask her what was going on. All that stopped him, in fact, was the recollection that Josh had mentioned a woman.

Heather.

He drove on to Choteau, found the stock auction,

signed up for a number. He and Sidekick walked past all the pens, examining the cattle and horses that would be up for sale that day.

Once the auction actually started, the bidding was fast and furious. By the time he loaded Sidekick into the truck, after writing a whopping check to the auction company, he was in the ranching business for real, to the tune of twenty heifers and four horses.

The cattle would be delivered in ten days, the horses in one.

Leaning forward in the seat, Logan peered up at the sky through the windshield. The weather was good. The cayuses would be fine in the corral until the barn was habitable.

He'd had to pay extra to delay the arrival of the cattle, though, since the pasture fence wasn't finished.

He grinned at Sidekick, panting in the passenger seat while the night scenery flew by. "How are you at herding cattle, boy?" he asked the dog.

Sidekick merely watched him, eyes luminous with devotion.

"One thing's for sure," Logan went on. "Cimarron is going to be one happy bull."

His cell phone rang.

Because he was driving, Logan answered without IDing the caller first.

"Logan Creed," he said, out of long habit. Until recently, when he'd sold his company, just about every call had been business.

Laurie laughed, and the rich, warm sound made him miss having a woman in his life, if not her specifically. "Most people just say hello," she told him.

"All right, hello," he said.

"Cranky."

"How's the marriage going?" he asked, to lighten things up. And maybe to get under her skin just a little, even though they were on friendly terms. Pretty much.

"I'm thinking of divorcing myself," she said. "We don't get along very well, me, myself and I."

"Sorry to hear it," Logan replied, but he had to chuckle. There were all the normal, ordinary people in the world. And then there was Laurie.

When she didn't make an immediate comeback, he thought he'd better jump-start the conversation. He didn't feel like chatting, and getting it going was the only way to get it over with.

"What do you want?" he asked.

Dylan's voice echoed in his mind, and then Tyler's.

What do you want?

Laurie started to cry.

Shit, Logan thought. "Laurie?"

"I can't keep my dog," she said.

"What?" Logan asked, confounded.

"I just moved into this condo, and they won't let me keep Snookums."

Logan glanced toward Sidekick. "That's rough," he said sincerely. Was she just venting? Or did she expect him to do something?

"I was wondering if you'd take him," Laurie said. "He's a good dog."

"Laurie, you live in California, and I live in Montana—"

"I could put him on a plane. Logan, you've got to do this for me. I can't move right now, and I'm going to be evicted if I don't find Snookums another home and I can't just hand him over to strangers—"

"Snookums?" Logan echoed stupidly. He could feel himself being sucked into a vortex reserved for people who love dogs. All dogs—big, small and in between.

"You'll do it!" Laurie cried, with such joy that Logan couldn't think of anything to say. "Are you still there?" his second wife, now married to herself, asked.

"I'm here."

"I'll put him on a plane as soon as possible."

"Snookums?" Logan repeated.

"You can change his name if you want to," Laurie said, sounding hurt.

"Laurie, can't you—"

She started to cry again. "Please, Logan. Please?"

He sighed audibly. "Okay," he said. "What kind of dog is—"

"I'll call you as soon as I've booked the flight," Laurie broke in, sniffling, her voice radiant with gratitude. "Thanks, Logan."

And with that, she hung up.

Logan closed his phone, looked into the rearview mirror, meeting his own gaze.

"Sucker," he said.

Sidekick made a soft sound in his throat.

"You're getting a brother," Logan told him. "Snookums."

The dog tilted his head to one side.

"Yeah," Logan confirmed. "You heard me right. I said *Snookums*."

"DAD GOT THE JOB!" Alec announced the moment Briana stepped into the house that night, after work. "And we found them a great trailer to live in, too!"

The van was in the backyard, but there was no sign of the happy couple. "Where are your dad and Heather?" she asked, bending to pat Wanda in greeting.

"They're taking a shower," Alec said.

Behind him, Josh made a face. *"Together,"* he said.

I'll kill him, Briana thought, setting her purse aside with a thunk.

"Heather found a job, too," Alec blathered on, the whole shared-shower thing going right over his head. Thank heaven. "She's going to be doing hair at the shop in the strip mall."

Heather was a hairdresser? Briana sincerely hoped the woman's own strawlike tresses weren't typical of her work. "That's great," she said, because Alec was so happy.

"They can't move into the trailer until tomorrow," Josh said, raising his eyebrows to give the statement adequate portent.

"But we got some groceries!" Alec chimed, swinging open the fridge door as proof. Briana saw a six-pack of beer, a package of lunch meat, salad makings and one of those bake-it-yourself pizzas.

She hadn't slipped into a parallel universe after all. Vance had bought beer.

In the distance, the shower stopped, and a few moments later, Heather padded into the kitchen, bundled in a skimpy pink bathrobe, her geyser ponytail hanging limp from the steam and moisture.

"Hi, Briana," she said cheerfully. "You go put your

feet up or something, because *I'm* cooking supper tonight."

Briana opened her mouth, closed it again. It wouldn't be right to tell the woman to cover up, for God's sake, because there were children in the room. Would it?

Vance appeared, shirtless, buttoning up the fly of his jeans. "I hope you don't mind if we stay one more night," he said easily. "Can't get the keys to the trailer until they turn on the water and the lights, and that'll be tomorrow."

Briana did the fish thing with her mouth again.

Open.

Closed.

Open again.

"Good," Vance said, heading for the laundry room. He came out a moment later, buttoning up a clean shirt. Evidently, he and Heather had done a little washing in between getting jobs and renting themselves a trailer. "Heather!" he called. "Get a move on with this pizza! I'm a working man now, and I have to eat!"

Briana booked it for her bedroom, shut the door and swapped out her casino getup for shorts and a T-shirt.

When she got back to the kitchen—and she had to force herself to come out of hiding—Heather was semi-decently dressed in a pair of skin-tight white jeans and another huggy top that left her belly bare. She popped the pizza in the oven and gave Briana a thoughtful once-over.

"You should cut your hair," she said.

Briana grabbed protectively at her braid. Why did

hairstylists always want to cut long hair short? It was like a challenge or something—Mount Everest to a climber.

"I'd be glad to do it for you," Heather went on. "No charge."

"Thanks," Briana said. "But I like it this way."

Heather frowned prettily. "When we get older," she said sweetly, "we really shouldn't wear our hair long."

The remark was so outrageous—and so guilelessly sincere—that Briana didn't even get mad. "I'll keep that in mind," she said.

Heather smiled, pleased, and started the salad.

Vance and the boys were in the living room now, watching a game of some kind of TV.

"Isn't there something I can do to help?" Briana asked. "With supper, I mean?"

"You could set the table," Heather said sunnily.

Briana went to the cupboard for dishes.

"This is nice, isn't it?" Heather asked, whacking away at the green onions.

Briana didn't answer.

Heather turned, looked back at her over one shoulder. "I'm so proud of Vance," she said. "He got the first job he applied for."

"Imagine," Briana agreed, biting the inside of her lower lip to keep from saying more.

Heather squinted at her. Maybe her sarcasm detectors were going off. But then she smiled again, shooting down Briana's theory. "We have an extra bedroom at the trailer," she said. "Vance and I hope the boys can stay with us sometimes, on weekends and after school."

That was a bridge Briana didn't intend to cross

until she got to it. "The boys don't go to school," she said. "I teach them at home."

Heather turned back to the salad greens, chopping harder. "Vance says he'll have to put his foot down about that," she replied, in a rush of words. "Anyhow, Alec and Josh want to be like other kids. Play baseball and stuff. I mean, you've done a good job as a mother and everything but—"

"Heather." It was Vance's voice.

Briana, frozen, turned only her eyes in his direction. Nothing else would move.

"Well," Heather burst out, "you said you were afraid to say anything about putting the boys in a real school, so I—"

Vance stood in the doorway to the living room, with Alec and Josh squeezed in on either side of him. "Heather," he repeated.

She broke into tears and fled to the bathroom, since there wasn't really anyplace else to go.

"That went well," Briana said, meeting her ex-husband's eyes at last. "And Alec and Josh are doing just fine with their schoolwork."

"They need to be around other kids, Bree," Vance said. "Get involved in sports. Go on field trips. Stuff like that."

"So now you're suddenly the caring father?"

Stop, said the good angel. *Stop now. The kids are listening.*

"I know your dad home-schooled you," Vance said quietly, letting her question pass without comment, "and it worked out fine. But Alec and Josh are my kids, too, and they're going to school this fall, like everybody else."

Alec peered around Vance's elbow. Josh took a step forward.

"Dad's right, Mom," Josh said. "We want to be regular kids."

"Alec?" Briana asked softly.

"I wanna be on a baseball team," Alec told her. "I wanna ride a yellow bus and eat lunch at the cafeteria."

Briana sat down, closed her eyes.

Everything was changing, and it was happening too fast.

Way, way too fast.

CHAPTER EIGHT

BRIANA HAD SUNDAY OFF, and when it dawned, she stretched luxuriously in bed, thrilling to the mistaken idea that she could sleep in.

Then she remembered. Vance and Heather were moving into their rental that day, and Alec and Josh had insisted on helping. Which meant they'd be going into town to spend the day at the new place.

He's their father, Briana reminded herself. *And this is what you wanted—isn't it?*

From the kitchen, she heard cooking noises. Wanda stirred, got up and jumped heavily off the bed. Went to the door and stuck her nose against it.

With a sigh, Briana got up, pulled on her ugly yellow bathrobe with the pink chenille roses on the back, cinched the belt and came out of hiding.

Vance was fully dressed and busy making breakfast—pancakes and sausage patties, his specialty.

Heather was in the shower.

"Where are Alec and Josh?" Briana asked, as she opened the back door to let Wanda out.

"Riding their bikes up and down the driveway," Vance answered, letting his gaze drift slowly over Briana before shaking his head and looking away. "Met your neighbor yesterday. Logan Creed."

Briana merely nodded, made her way to the coffeepot. Even though there was nothing going on between her and Logan, she wasn't comfortable discussing him with Vance.

"I probably didn't make the best impression on him," Vance said, flipping a pancake.

Briana went still, her coffee mug halfway to her mouth. "Meaning what?" she asked.

"I might have seemed a little...territorial."

Briana waited, but Vance didn't go on. So she prodded him. "Territorial? How so?"

"The boys talk about him a lot," Vance said, concentrating on the pancakes. "So I just reminded him that they're *my* boys."

Briana couldn't think of a response that wouldn't start a yelling match, so she kept her mouth shut.

Vance turned, just as Heather entered the kitchen from one side of the room and Alec and Josh and Wanda came in from the other.

"We can talk about it another time," Vance said.

Subject dropped. It was probably for the best, Briana thought.

The pancakes were good, like always, and so was the sausage. Briana wasn't hungry, but she ate because she knew she was going to need her strength. Every new day, it seemed, brought fresh challenges, flaming hoops to jump through, higher hurdles to clear.

"Want to come into town with us and see the new place?" Heather asked Briana, when the meal was over and the clearing-up had begun.

Alec looked at Briana in happy expectancy. Josh mouthed, "Please."

"Okay," Briana said. Whether she liked it or not, the boys would be spending a lot of time at Vance and

Heather's, for the time being at least, and she needed to know exactly what sort of place it was.

Briana washed dishes while Heather dried. Vance, having cooked breakfast, went outside with Alec and Josh to get the van ready. The old beater always seemed to need tinkering with before it would run— that, at least, hadn't changed.

"I'm—I'm sorry about the things I said about the boys going to regular school," Heather ventured, as soon as they were alone. "I was out of line."

"No harm done," Briana said. She'd had most of the night to think about the home-versus-regular-school question, and she'd decided to give in. She'd home-schooled the boys from first grade on, because she and Vance had followed the rodeo for most of the year. Then, when they'd wound up in Stillwater Springs, she'd continued, partly because Alec and Josh were doing really well in their studies, and partly because it was a new place and she'd felt overprotective.

"It'll give you more free time," Heather suggested. "Come fall, anyway."

Free time? What would she do with that?

Outside, the van's engine roared to life.

Alec rushed in; Josh followed slowly, with Wanda.

"Can I ride with Dad and Heather?" Alec asked eagerly.

Briana felt a pang. "I guess so."

"We could all go together," Heather put in.

"I have some errands to do," Briana said quickly. It wasn't a *complete* lie; the Stillwater Springs Library was open on Sundays during the summer, because of the influx of RVers and casino patrons. She had a stack of books to return, and wanted to check out more.

"I'll ride with Mom," Josh said quickly.

Thus, Briana and Josh followed Vance, Heather and Alec into town.

"You're all right with this?" Briana asked her son, as they passed the entrance to Stillwater Springs Ranch.

When was somebody going to fix that dangling sign over the gate?

"All right with what?" Josh asked, somewhat snappishly. The night before, he'd wanted to sleep in her bed. Now, in the bright light of day, he was probably embarrassed.

"Spending the day at your dad and Heather's new place," she said patiently. "You don't have to, you know."

Josh heaved a great, shoulder-moving sigh. "Maybe it won't be so bad," he said. "And all you're going to do is go to the library."

"What's wrong with going to the library? We've been there at least once a week ever since we moved to Stillwater Springs."

"We didn't move here, Mom. Dad *dumped* us here."

"What does that have to do with the library?"

In truth, Briana's emotional survival had had *everything* to do with the library, before *and* after Vance had done his vanishing act. Libraries were warm, spacious, bright places, full of books—and money, the one thing Briana didn't have, wasn't required. Josh and Alec had loved the local librarian, Kristy Madison, and sat in on story hour sometimes, even though they considered themselves too big for "that stuff."

Was this going to change, too?

Briana's heart sank a little.

"I guess it doesn't have anything to do with the library," Josh finally conceded. "Alec is going to ask if he can spend the night with Dad and Heather."

Briana wasn't surprised to hear that last part, but it still made her heart skitter a little. What would she do if Alec decided he'd rather live with his father and stepmother full-time?

"Mom?" Josh prompted, when she didn't answer.

They cruised past a series of signs, strung Burma-Shave style alongside the road.

Special
Election
July 1st
Have
You
Registered
To Vote???

"What?" Briana asked. She'd heard Sheriff Book was planning to retire, and she wondered who would run for his office when he stepped down.

"Will you be okay?"

She looked at Josh, saw the concern in his face.

"With Dad living in Stillwater Springs and everything," Josh clarified, studying her anxiously.

The question wasn't whether she'd be okay or not. It was whether *Josh and Alec* would. Vance had a new wife, a job and the best of intentions, but he liked the free life too much to stay in one place for long—especially a little town like Stillwater Springs. One day, sure as sunrise and taxes, he'd kick the dust of that rural burg off his feet, jettison both Heather *and* the job, and hit the road.

Heather would be on her own, but *Briana* would be the one who had to put Alec and Josh back together.

Her hands tightened on the steering wheel.

"*Will* you be okay, Mom?" Josh persisted.

"I'll be fine," she managed to say.

They'd passed the road leading into the casino, and she could still see Vance's van up ahead, belching smoke from the exhaust pipe. He *was* a good mechanic, if he'd kept that rig running all this time.

The trailer still had a For Rent sign in the overgrown front yard, and junk spilled out the front door—old toys, clothes and various kinds of garbage—as though the place had thrown up.

"Wonderful," Briana muttered. Okay, her place wasn't a palace. But she kept the lawn mowed and the yard cleaned.

"Needs a little work," Vance enthused, walking toward her when she got out of the truck.

"Yuck," Josh said.

Heather stepped from the van, after Alec had bounded down from the side door, holding a big box of supersize garbage bags in one hand and smiling happily.

"Let's get some sprucing up done around here," Vance said.

Josh groaned as he got out of the truck, but he didn't change his mind about going to the library with Briana, and she knew that was significant.

"It looks pretty bad right now," Vance told her.

"But it's okay on the inside. Come on in and have a look."

Her boys would be spending time in this trailer, Briana reminded herself. Swallowing a sigh, she got out of the truck and followed Vance around the spill of trash, up the porch steps and through the front door.

"Shouldn't the landlord have cleaned up a little?" she asked.

"He gave us the first month free for doing it ourselves," Heather said, as the three of them stood in the tiny living room. There was a galley kitchen, an area just big enough for a couch and a TV, and presumably bedrooms and a bath down the hallway to the left.

The floor was so littered with beer bottles, empty cereal boxes and other evidence of wild living that Briana didn't attempt to go any farther than just inside the door.

She glanced at her watch. "Well," she said, with a smile, "I guess I'd better get those errands done."

She wouldn't be far away, she told herself.

The library was two blocks down and one block over.

One SOS call from Josh, who still had possession of the extra cell phone, and she'd be back in a trice. Mommy to the rescue.

"See you later," Vance said.

At least he hadn't expected her to stay and help.

That would have been over-the-top, even for Vance, but Briana felt a little guilty for not offering, just the same.

As she backed the truck out, she saw Heather present Vance, Alec and Josh with a garbage bag each, and they all began to pick up garbage.

Five minutes later, she pulled into the parking lot at the library—a small, one-story brick building dating from the Roosevelt administration, according to the brass plaque beside the double doors. Just the sight of the place made her feel better, and she was gathering her return stack from the backseat when Sheriff Book pulled in beside her, behind the wheel of his squad car.

Briana smiled and nodded.

Sheriff Book nodded back and rolled down his window.

"I've got a couple of CDs here," he told Briana. "Wife borrowed them. Wonder if you'd mind taking them inside with your stuff."

"No problem," Briana said, juggling half a dozen books to take the CDs. "I hear there's going to be a special election," she added, recalling the progression of signs along the road outside of town.

"Yes, ma'am," Sheriff Book said. "I announced my retirement this morning, and the election committee wasted no time getting out the word. It's enough to make a man think folks will be glad to get rid of him."

Briana would miss the sheriff. He reminded her a little of her dad, despite the differences in their looks, and she liked his wife, Dorothy. "Any idea who your replacement will be?"

He looked surprised, and when he spoke, she found out why. "Jim Huntinghorse is the only candidate to file so far."

Briana's mouth dropped open. She worked with Jim five days a week, and they were friends. He hadn't said a single word about running for the sheriff's job. "Oh," she said, taking a moment to recover. "I didn't know."

"That much," Sheriff Book said kindly, "was obvious by the look on your face. I think Jim would do a good job, but there are bound to be some who'll vote against him on prejudicial grounds. Even if his is the only name on the ticket—and I doubt it will be—he'll need a certain percentage of votes to win."

"He's got mine, anyway," Briana said.

The sheriff chuckled, popped the squad car into Reverse. "Tell him that, and you'll probably wind up managing his campaign," he teased. "Thanks again for taking Dorothy's CDs inside."

Briana nodded and watched as Sheriff Book backed out of his parking space, made a wide turn and hit the main road.

More change.

She was happy for Floyd and Dorothy. Happy for Jim, too, if being sheriff was what he wanted, though she knew he'd be leaving the casino once he took office. They'd all have a new boss then, and that was always a scary prospect for people who lived from paycheck to paycheck, the way she did.

She held the stack of books and CDs a little more tightly as she headed for the library entrance.

Kristy Madison smiled at her from behind the main desk.

A lifelong resident of Stillwater Springs, Kristy wasn't the stereotypical librarian. Tall and slender, she kept her blond hair in a perky chin-length style, and her eyes were china blue. She wore jeans, a blouse or sweater and boots to work most days, and this one was no exception.

"Hey," she said, with a warm smile.

Briana set the books and CDs on the counter, next

to the hand-lettered sign that read Returns. "Hey, yourself," she responded. Now that her hands were free, she shifted her bag to the other shoulder and pulled her new cell from the pocket of her jeans, switching it to Vibrate, since ringing phones were verboten in the library.

Kristy took the top book off Briana's stack and held it up. "What did you think of this?" she asked. "I haven't read it yet."

"Well," Briana said slowly, "I finished it."

"Now there's a ringing endorsement," Kristy remarked, smiling. She'd invited Briana out to lunch a couple of times, but Briana had always made some excuse. Restaurant lunches weren't in the budget, along with a lot of other things. Anyway, she liked to spend her free time with the boys.

Now, as then, she wondered if Kristy thought she didn't want to be friends.

"Some books are better than others," Briana conceded.

"We're starting a once-a-month reading club," Kristy said. "Our first meeting is Tuesday night. I was going to suggest this book, since we have several copies of it, but now I'm not so sure."

Briana, who had been about to excuse herself and head for the new releases shelf—a person had to be quick to get the latest books—stopped. "A reading club?"

"For adults," Kristy replied, with a nod. In high school, according to Dorothy Book, who played penny slot machines at the casino on a fairly regular basis, Kristy had been a cheerleader, queen of the winter carnival and the drama group's favorite leading lady.

Briana didn't hold any of that against her.

"Really?"

Kristy nodded again. "Would you be interested?"

Briana was so used to turning down things like that that she almost said no. But Heather was right—she was going to have more free time. "I'd like that a lot," she said.

"Tuesday at seven," Kristy reiterated. "We'll meet in the community room in back, after the library closes. I guess we can all decide that night what we want to read first."

"Sounds good," Briana said, feeling reckless. Reading was nothing new—she'd been doing that voraciously since she was five years old, thanks largely to her dad—but doing something just because she wanted to was.

An older woman approached the desk to ask Kristy where to find a certain reference book, and Kristy zipped off to help her.

Briana zeroed in on the new releases. There was a one-book limit, and the return time was shorter, but she snatched up the latest Nora Roberts novel and felt rich.

She checked out several other books—a western, a thriller and a memoir—and left the library, resisting the temptation to drive by Vance and Heather's trailer to make sure the boys were okay.

Wanda was home alone.

She'd head for the ranch, let the dog out, make herself a grilled cheese sandwich for lunch and *read* until Vance either brought the boys home or called and asked her to come and get them.

She was getting the hang of this not-being-a-mother-hen thing.

Sort of.

LOGAN SAW THE dust roiling up from behind the truck and horse trailer when they were still a mile away, and he and Sidekick were waiting by the corral gate when it arrived.

When Briana pulled in right behind though, in the old pickup Dylan used to drive, he was a little surprised.

The truck driver climbed out of his rig, tugged at the brim of his billed cap to greet Briana and went around to the back of the trailer to open it up.

"You've got horses?" Briana asked, shading her eyes from the sun. Her tone was breathless, almost reverent.

"Do now," Logan said. "Excuse me for a second. I've gotta help unload."

Briana stayed on his heels. "I was just passing by, on my way home, and I saw the trailer—"

Logan grinned, glad she was there. She stayed close while he and the driver—Bob, according to the name stitched on his shirt—put halters on the new horses and brought them down the ramp, one by one. Sidekick kept a wise distance, retreating to the porch to watch the proceedings.

The big, heavy-shouldered buckskin gelding came first, and Briana was right there to greet him. She was comfortable around horses, Logan thought, impressed. But then she was Wild Man McIntyre's daughter. Of *course* she knew horses.

He felt a wrench just looking at her, standing there

in all that road dust, her attention completely focused on the buckskin, tendrils of her strawberry-blond hair escaping the braid to glitter in the sunlight.

His first wife had been terrified of horses.

His second was allergic.

But here was Briana, nose-to-nose with one, and obviously communicating. Maybe even bonding.

Logan shook off the vision, turned back to the task at hand. Bob brought the brown-and-white pinto mare out next, then the gray gelding, and by the time Logan had unloaded the fourth animal, a black filly still too young to ride, Briana had already led the buckskin into the corral.

She greeted each horse as they were turned loose, carrying on some kind of silent conversation, and Logan wanted in the worst way to know what she'd said to them.

He paid Bob for the delivery and waited until the truck and trailer were headed back down the driveway before approaching the corral. By then, Briana was outside the fence, perched on the lowest rail, admiring the new arrivals.

"They're *beautiful*," she whispered.

They were good-looking horses, sturdy and, as far as Logan could tell, even-tempered…but beautiful? He didn't see it.

Maybe he was too stuck on the realization that *Briana* was beautiful. He'd thought she was attractive before, but seeing her with the horses—well, there had been something mystical about that. Something that touched him, way deep, and left an imprint.

"Do you ride?" he asked, climbing up beside her, standing close enough that their upper arms touched.

He knew the answer—he'd only asked the question to get the conversation rolling.

She nodded, swiped a coppery-blond tendril of hair back from her forehead and never took her eyes off the horses. They were running around the corral, kicking up dust and generally celebrating being out of the trailer. Later, they'd establish a pecking order, which would involve some squealing and nipping, but the pinto mare would win out.

The oldest mare always called the shots.

"About the only thing I miss about the rodeo, besides my dad," Briana said, without looking at him, "is the horses."

"I've got to take the rough edges off them first," Logan said, "but if they're gentle enough, you can ride anytime you want."

She turned her head, and he saw a variety of emotions, none of which he could readily identify, flicker in her spring-green eyes. "Oh, these horses are gentle," she told him confidently. "They're just excited, that's all."

Logan felt like a fool, though he wasn't sure why. On top of that, he wanted to kiss Briana Grant, right then and there.

He didn't, because even though there was nobody else around, the barn crew having refused to work on Sunday, time and a half or not, he wanted privacy when he kissed Briana.

She looked toward the house, then met his gaze again.

All he'd have to do was lean in, just a little—

He realized he was staring at her mouth.

Not good.

He stepped down off the fence rail. He'd already filled the water trough, and put some hay in the rusty feeder. Now, there was nothing to do but wait for the horses to settle down.

"Where are the boys?" he asked, because he couldn't think of anything else to say. He'd sound like an ass if he invited her inside for a cold drink, wouldn't he? Might as well suggest that they skip the preliminaries and head straight for his bed.

Nix on *that* thought.

It was only too easy to imagine stripping off their dusty clothes, making love with the windows open to a summer afternoon's breeze. Skin slapping skin.

"They're with their dad," Briana said. "And their stepmother."

"Heather," Logan said, hoping she couldn't tell by the sound of his voice how relieved he was.

Briana raised a questioning eyebrow.

"Alec mentioned her yesterday," he explained. Hot damn. There was no reconciliation in the offing. Vance Grant had a wife.

"I'd better go," Briana said. "Wanda's home alone."

Logan found himself hurrying to catch up with her as she zoomed toward Dylan's truck. "Briana—"

She stopped, the truck door open, and looked up at him. She was coated with dust, like he was, and he wished he could lick her clean.

"You and Vance—"

"Over," she said. "He's married, remember?"

Did he remember? He felt like hiring a sky-writer to let the whole county know. "I was thinking of firing up the barbecue tonight," he said. Barbecue? Was there a grill anywhere on the place? "It would be great if you and the boys could come to supper."

She took so long to respond that Logan started to wonder if he'd said the words out loud or only thought them.

"Okay," she said. "What time?"

He had to hit town, get a barbecue grill and something to put on it. That would take an hour, tops.

"Six o'clock?" he asked, picking a time out of the air.

"I'll be here," she said. "Shall I bring anything? I make a mean potato salad."

"Potato salad," Logan agreed, almost tripping over his tongue.

"See you later," Briana answered. Then, after closing the door, she started up the old truck and drove away.

Logan waited until she was out of sight before jumping up and punching the air with one fist.

"The place is pretty clean," Josh said, whispering into his cell phone. "We picked up all the stuff and hauled it to the dump in Dad's van, and Heather is making spaghetti and meatballs for supper and—"

Listening to all this while she mixed up the mustard sauce for potato salad, Briana knew what was coming.

"And they want to know if Alec and me can spend the night."

"Alec and *I*," Briana corrected automatically.

"Can we?"

"May we?"

Josh huffed out a sigh. "*May* Alec and *I* spend the night?"

Briana frowned, recalling Josh's earlier misgivings. "You're sure you'd be okay with that?"

"We've got cell phones now, Mom," Josh said. "If it gets weird, I can call you."

She smiled, albeit a little sadly. "What's your definition of *weird?*"

Josh lowered his voice another notch. "Well, if Dad packed everything in the van and said we were going for a ride, or something."

"You can spend the night," Briana said. Her eyes burned with tears and her throat was thick, but she was smiling.

"She said yes," Josh told his brother.

Alec let out one of his famous whoops.

"What about toothbrushes and pajamas and stuff?" Briana asked, suddenly practical again.

"Dad said we could each use one of his T-shirts, and Heather got extra toothbrushes when we went to the grocery store."

"Okay," Briana said, feeling suddenly superfluous.

"Bye, Mom," Josh said.

"Wait," Briana interjected. "What time should I pick you guys up tomorrow?"

Josh relayed the question, and then Vance came on the line.

"You have to work tomorrow, right?" he asked.

Briana nodded, then remembered that Vance couldn't see her. "Yes," she answered. "But you and Heather do, too, don't you?"

"I have to be at the shop by eight," he replied.

"Heather doesn't start her shift until around two in the afternoon. What if she brought the boys by the casino before she goes to work?"

Briana closed her eyes. This was how things were going to be for a while and she'd better accept it. Still, Heather was a stranger to her, and to the boys. What if she had a dark side, or slept until noon, letting Alec and Josh run wild? What if she drank, or took drugs?

What if she was simply a bad driver?

"I don't know," Briana said uncertainly.

"You don't trust Heather?" Vance asked. He'd whispered the words, but everyone in the trailer had probably heard them. After all, it wasn't a big place.

"I didn't say that, Vance," Briana responded. "I don't *know* Heather, that's all."

"Well, I do, and if I trust her with my kids—"

Like he'd been a devoted father, showing concern for Alec and Josh's well-being. Like he hadn't—

Vance sighed. "If the kids are uncomfortable for any reason, Briana," he said carefully, "they can call you and you can come and get them."

Briana blinked, ran a forearm across her eyes. "I guess that's fair," she said.

Vance was still angry, she could tell. But he kept his temper, and that alone showed progress.

Maybe he really *had* changed.

And maybe if she put on ruby-red slippers and tapped the heels together, she'd wind up in Kansas.

"Goodbye, Briana," Vance said, and then he hung up with a clunk that made the inside of her eardrum vibrate.

She replaced the receiver and looked down at

Wanda, who was standing close and wagging her tail tentatively.

"I guess it's you and me tonight, girl," she said.

Then she went back to work on the potato salad.

It wouldn't be just her and Wanda that night, she recalled, with mingled excitement and dread.

She'd accepted an invitation to a barbecue at Logan's.

Of course, at the time, she'd thought Alec and Josh would be going with her, as well as Wanda.

Would she even know what to say to Logan, when it was just the two of them? What should she wear?

She looked good in her blue polka-dot sundress, but she didn't want her clothes to say *come hither*.

Did she?

What if he kissed her?

What if it led to sex?

She was *definitely* not wearing the sundress.

Jeans, that was it. Hadn't he promised her a horse-back ride? Surely the buckskin and the others had mellowed out by now, gotten used to the new place.

Jeans would say good sport, not hubba-hubba.

Did *anybody* even say hubba-hubba anymore?

She took a shower at five-thirty, keeping the cell phone nearby, on the back of the toilet, in case things *got weird* at the trailer in town. She put on black jeans and a blue pullover shirt, as planned, then wavered and changed into the sundress after all. Even slipped her feet into a pair of high-heeled sandals.

At six-fifteen, she and Wanda and the potato salad got in the truck and headed next door.

It was too soon for sex, she told herself, sundress or

no sundress. She hadn't known Logan long enough to go to bed with him. This was just a friendly barbecue.

No, sir, they were *not* going to have sex tonight. Probably not, anyway.

CHAPTER NINE

OKAY, LOGAN TOLD HIMSELF, as he marinated steaks for the barbecue in his unrenovated kitchen, it was too soon for a seduction, anyway. He'd only known Briana Grant for a few days, though it felt like much longer—a sort of cosmic, multiple-lifetimes thing—and he fully expected her to bring the kids along to supper.

If that hadn't been enough to dampen the action, Jim Huntinghorse would be. He'd called half an hour before to say he wanted to take Logan up on his offer to drop in at any time.

"Any time" turned out to be tonight.

On top of that, the folks at the airport in Missoula had contacted him, as well. Laurie's dog had arrived—Laurie-like, she'd forgotten the promised heads-up on the airline, flight number and ETA—and he'd arranged, at considerable cost, for the mutt to be delivered to the ranch by private courier.

"The best laid plans," he told Sidekick, who was keeping a close eye on the steaks as Logan slopped them from one bowl of previously bottled goop to another. Good thing he'd snagged a few extra T-bones at the supermarket—the way things were going, he wouldn't be surprised if half of his high school class showed up, too, for an impromptu reunion.

While the steaks were soaking up sauce, Logan

went out to feed his horses. It felt good to have that to do—all the other work on the ranch was, for the moment, being handled by contractors.

That, of course, would change when the cattle arrived.

He'd found his dad's old saddle under a pile of junk in the barn earlier in the day, along with some other tack, and brought it inside, meaning to clean it up a little. In the morning, he intended to ride. Get a *real* look at the state of Stillwater Springs Ranch in the time-honored way—from the back of a horse.

He was tossing hay over the corral fence when Briana drove in, alone except for Wanda riding shotgun in the passenger seat.

No kids, Logan thought, both intrigued and disappointed.

Briana about stopped his heart when she got out of Dylan's ancient truck, wearing a sundress that left her shoulders bare and showed a lot of leg. She even had on high-heeled sandals, and she looked embarrassed as she tottered toward him. She was a boots-and-jeans kind of girl, uncomfortable in big-city shoes, he thought, and the realization jarred something deep inside him.

He wished he could call Jim, ask him to come another time, but it wouldn't be right to put him off. Huntinghorse had been his best buddy ever since kindergarten, after all, though they'd been out of touch for a long while. He'd made a lot of other friends, rodeoing and building his company, but he'd never made a better one than Jim.

Logan met Briana in the middle of the yard, inclined his head toward Wanda, forgotten in the old beater, pawing at the side window and barking eagerly. "I'll get her," he said.

Briana blushed—even her shoulders glowed a fetching shade of pink. It would have been too obvious to check if her legs were affected, too, but he surely wanted to.

"Thanks," she replied, watching him as he went to the truck, opened the door and hoisted Wanda down to the ground.

"You need to cut back on the chow," he told the dog. He was painfully aware, the whole time, of his own work clothes, covered with hay dust, in contrast to Briana's fragrant skin and hair.

There was some guilt, too—always some guilt. Inadvertently, he'd put her on the spot. Jim, after all, was Briana's boss, and she didn't know he'd be joining them.

"Thought you'd bring Alec and Josh," he said, approaching her. He offered his arm because those heels of hers had sunk into the dirt and she looked stuck.

"They're with their dad," she replied. Then, with a wince, leaning against him a little, so wildfire raced through every part of him, she added, "Damn these stupid shoes."

"You could take them off," Logan said. Oddly, the moment felt as intimate as if he'd asked her to strip to the skin, not just kick away her shoes. They *were* pretty silly, but sexy as hell. There was another side to Briana Grant, and he was ready to explore it.

She looked at the rough ground, still littered with broken glass here and there, despite the admittedly half-assed clean-up effort he'd been making since he arrived. Shook her head. "I shouldn't have worn them," she said. "I don't know what I was thinking."

"You look really...*really* nice," Logan told her.

"Maybe I should go home and change," she fretted, biting at her lower lip in a way that made it swell slightly and look highly kissable. And in need of serious nibbling by him.

Logan wanted to shoot down the leaving idea, and pronto. If Briana went home, she might not come back, especially if he told her that Jim was probably on his way to the ranch at that moment. "Stay," he said, and his voice came out sounding hoarse, not at all like his usual Montana-boy drawl.

She looked up at him, and he wondered what was going on behind those spring-green eyes. Was she wishing she hadn't come?

Just then, before he could warn her, Jim's sleek black Porsche came over the rise.

"You've got to fix that sign," Huntinghorse said as he got out of the car, carrying a six-pack of beer in one hand. "It almost scratched the roof of my ride."

Briana didn't actually stiffen—odds were, she liked Jim, since most people did—but Logan felt her reaction to his arrival, just the same. A sort of tightening up, so subtle that if he'd been standing even an inch farther away, he wouldn't have caught it.

"I didn't get a chance to explain," Logan said quietly, close to her ear. That wasn't the whole truth, of course—he hadn't *taken* the chance to explain. He'd been too busy gaping at her, and wondering if the f-me shoes were meant to convey the message they did.

Jim's smoky, savage gaze took in Briana's sundress, and probably the shoulders and legs, too.

Logan felt an elemental stab of purely territorial irritation, the emotional equivalent of pissing a circle around Briana Grant to warn off any male who might catch her scent on the breeze.

"Jim," Briana said, with friendly surprise.

Jim's eyes shifted to Logan's face. "I didn't mean to intrude," he said, putting a point on the words.

"It's just a neighborly barbecue," Briana said brightly, still standing there looking delicious, with her shoes sunk deep into the Montana dirt. With the next rain, it would turn to the gluey mud natives called gumbo. She turned her head, looked up into Logan's face; he saw confusion in hers. "Isn't that right, Logan?"

"It's right," Logan said, taking care not to sigh the words. Then, on a reckless impulse, he scooped Briana up into his arms and carried her toward the house, leaving Jim to follow. If he'd been asked, he'd have said it was because she could break an ankle hiking across a barnyard in those lame shoes, but that wasn't the whole reason, and he knew it.

Jim followed, probably amused, as did Wanda and Sidekick.

Logan set Briana back on her feet when they reached the front porch.

She looked ruffled and pink all over, and immediately tugged at the sides of her dress, as if afraid it had ridden up. But she hadn't protested, Logan noted, and that felt better than winning the lottery.

After he'd led Jim and Briana through the house to the kitchen, he dodged into the main bathroom for a quick shower and a change of clothes. When he came out again, both his guests were seated at the picnic table out on the adjoining patio, sipping beer. The dogs lay companionably at their feet, and the whole picture was just a little too cozy for Logan's liking.

He put down the surge of jealousy he felt, knowing it was stupid. Jim was his closest friend and, besides, he had no claim on Briana Grant.

The smile she turned on Logan as he stepped out the side door soothed him in a way that troubled him even more than the rush of possessiveness had.

"It's official," she said. "Jim's going to run for sheriff."

She'd taken off her shoes. They lay at a helter-skelter angle under the table.

Heat surged through Logan again. Again, he waited it out.

"That's…good," he said, after a protracted silence, during which Jim raised one eyebrow and crooked up a corner of his mouth in a too-knowing grin.

"It'll be a tough race," Jim said. "Want a beer?"

Logan shook his head. "Maybe later." He approached the grill he'd bought that day at the hardware store, lifted the shiny new lid and was assaulted by roiling smoke.

"Guess the fire's ready," Jim observed dryly. Then he winked at Briana. "I know these things. It's the Indian blood."

Briana laughed.

Logan was not amused, but he grinned at his friend. "I'll get the steaks," he said. *You're a conversational genius, Creed,* he told himself.

Jim got up and followed him into the kitchen.

"Want me to get out of here?" he asked, as Logan

took the marinating steaks out of the fridge. By then, he figured they'd soaked up enough goop.

"No," Logan replied, but the word came out sounding peevish. He hadn't intended that, and sighed, setting the baking dish with the steaks in it on the counter with a thump. Shoved a hand through his shower-dampened hair.

Jim chuckled, then let out a low whistle. "Lighten up, man," he said. "Your primitive masculine instincts are showing."

"Shit," Logan said.

Jim laughed, shook his head. "Why didn't you just tell me not to come, Logan? I would have understood."

Logan thrust out another sigh. He'd been doing a lot of sighing, since he got back to Stillwater Springs. More accurately, since he'd met Briana Grant, picnicking with her kids and her dog in a graveyard, of all places. "Maybe, on some level," he admitted, "I didn't trust myself to be alone with her."

"She scares you?" Jim asked, grinning, his expressive dark eyes glinting with amusement. "Oh, brother, you *are so* gone on this woman."

"I just met her."

Jim folded his brawny arms. He was wearing, Logan finally noticed, a short-sleeved white polo shirt, neatly pressed black slacks and polished loafers. He looked like…a politician.

"Doesn't matter," he said. "I know that look when I see it. Reminds me of a bull stuck to the cow-catcher on the front of a speeding locomotive."

"You're really going to run for sheriff," Logan said, but he smiled at the image Jim had raised in his mind's eye. He *felt* like that imaginary bull, off his feet, whizzing along an unknown track toward God knew what end.

"Think I can win?" Jim asked, and he sounded serious now. Set his hands on his hips, elbows jutting out.

"Why not?"

"Well, for one thing, I'm a redskin."

"Very un-PC," Logan told him, picking up the dish full of steaks. "You're supposed to say 'Native American.'"

"Thanks, white eyes," Jim retorted, grinning. "I'll remember that."

Logan started for the back door. Briana was out there, looking all soft and fluffy and good, pulling at him like a magnet, all the more powerful because she didn't seem to have a clue she was having that effect on him.

He felt another catch, this time in the middle of his chest, when he saw her bending to stroke Sidekick's ear, the one with a chunk missing. He must have stopped, too, because Jim slammed into him from behind.

Practically sent him sprawling down the steps.

Picturing himself landing face-first in the dish of raw steak and goop, he jarred loose of the stupor he was in, as best he could.

"You'd better let Big Chief cook the meat, paleface," Jim said under his breath, easing past Logan and then taking the dish out of his hands. "You seem to be a little off your game tonight."

He *was* distracted—he'd probably burn dinner. He took one of the beers Jim had brought and sat down next to Briana at the picnic table, though not too close.

They ate salad, the three of them, and talked about ordinary things, and the steaks turned out okay.

Jim took his time leaving, though. Even when the meal was long over, and the mosquitoes were out, and the dogs had gnawed the steak bones down to nothing, he hung around.

Only when they went inside, to get away from the bugs, did "Big Chief" bid them adieu, head for his Porsche and drive away.

But he'd no more than pulled out when the courier arrived from the airport, bringing Snookums.

The crate looked small, Logan thought, as he went out to meet the guy and accept the delivery. He was conscious of Briana, standing on the porch watching, the whole time.

He sighed, took the crate by the handle and looked inside.

Snookums, it turned out, was one of those prissy little dust-mop terriers with hair that scraped the ground and a blue ribbon tied into his topknot. The kind of dog that yaps at every sound.

"Great," he muttered.

"What a cutie," Briana said, when he reached the porch.

For one moment of unadulterated stupidity, Logan thought she was talking about *him.* He'd been called a lot of things in his life, but a cutie wasn't one of them. *She means the dog, dick-brain,* he told himself.

"Meet Snookums," he said.

She giggled. Looked up at him. "'Snookums'?"

"Hereafter," Logan decided aloud, "Snooks. He'll get laughed out of Montana otherwise."

He set the crate down on the porch, and Sidekick

and Wanda sniffed curiously, causing Snooks to retreat to the back of the plastic box.

"Oh, he's scared," Briana said, gently shooing Sidekick and Wanda back and plunking herself on the top step to open the door on the crate and reach inside.

The little dog quivered, licked her face anxiously.

Logan wished he could do that. Lick, not quiver.

Briana laughed softly. "It's all right," she told Snooks. "Nobody's going to hurt you."

Sidekick and Wanda eased forward to sniff some more, then lost interest and went to chase bugs in the yard.

Belatedly, Logan sat down opposite Briana, on the top step, and interlaced his fingers, letting his hands dangle between his knees. Briana seemed oblivious to the mosquitoes now—all her attention was focused on that hairball of a dog.

"A Yorkie," she said, still admiring Snooks. Holding him up, the way she might have held a baby, just lifted from a crib. "Not the kind of dog I'd expect you to choose."

"I didn't choose him," Logan grumbled, though he was softening toward the poor little critter, despite the fact that he'd be in for some ribbing when Jim and the construction crews got a look at cutie-pooch. "He was my ex-wife's dog. She couldn't keep him because of her lease or something."

Briana didn't answer right away, didn't look at him, either. The flush blossomed again, along her jawline, under her ear. A need to kiss her there ground through Logan like some kind of heavy equipment in low gear.

"Josh and Alec were wondering if you had any children," she ventured, and blushed harder.

"I haven't been that lucky," Logan said. "Shouldn't we go inside, Briana? Before the mosquitoes eat you alive?"

She met his gaze then. Set Snooks in his lap and stood up, but not to go inside, like he'd suggested. She had the look of a woman headed home, ready to wind things down.

"It was nice," she said. "Tonight, I mean. Thanks."

"I should have warned you that Jim was coming. It was a last-minute deal, and—"

"No problem," she replied. "I like Jim."

How much? Logan wanted to ask, but he didn't. He rose slowly off the porch step, careful not to jostle the nervous Yorkie, nearly lost in his hands. The thing was hardly bigger than a rat. What kind of ranch dog would he be?

"Want me to carry you to the truck?" Logan said, without thinking, and then could have kicked himself for sounding like such an idiot.

"I think I can make it on my own," Briana told him, and though her mouth didn't change, her eyes sparkled with laughter. "Thanks for the offer, though."

He watched as she teetered toward the rig Dylan had driven in high school, Wanda tagging after her. She paused once, probably to regain her balance, and looked toward the horses standing quietly in the corral, the sun setting behind them, rimming their manes and the lines of their bodies with gold.

Was it that peculiarly Montanan sight that made Logan's breath catch, or was it the woman gazing at them with one hand shading her eyes?

The moment seemed eminently precious, the kind of thing a man remembered for a lifetime. Logan knew he would sit on this porch, as an old, old man, remembering the way it all was, the horses and the sunset and Briana standing there like that, stilled by grace.

Too quickly, it was over.

Snooks squirmed in his hands, and he put the dog down on the floor of the porch. The Yorkie lifted a hind leg and let fly against a flowerpot with some long-dead plant inside.

And Briana waved, got into the truck—a delightful maneuver in itself, considering how short that sundress was—and drove away.

Logan watched her out of sight.

Maybe Jim was right, he thought. He'd always been confident around women, known what to do and say. With Briana it was different—she made him feel awkward and, at the same time, more of a man.

Was he "gone on her," as Jim had put it?

He pondered the possibility, then shook his head.

"Nah," he said to Sidekick, and they both went back inside, Snooks bouncing along behind them.

THE HOUSE WAS too quiet, with just her and Wanda there.

First thing, Briana got rid of the shoes. Not only took them off, but dropped them into the trash bin for good measure. She'd probably looked ridiculous, mincing around in those things like some *Sex and the City* wannabe.

Briana wandered into the living room and switched on the TV. Flipped through a few channels. As usual, there was nothing on but news and no-brainer sitcoms.

Without cable or a satellite dish, the Discovery and History channels, her favorites, didn't come in.

With a sigh, she shut the set off and meandered over to the window. The lights of Logan's house twinkled like yellow lanterns through the branches of the venerable apple trees in the orchard.

Briana smiled, recalling how incongruous Logan and the Yorkie looked together. Wondered what kind of relationship he had with his ex-wife, too. Obviously, they were friendly enough that he'd been willing to take in the woman's dog on short notice.

A muffled ringing sound reached her from the kitchen.

She frowned, then realized it was her cell phone, jangling in the depths of her purse. Since only Vance, Heather, Josh and Alec had the number, she ran to answer, scrabbling through her purse to find the thing.

The ringing stopped, then immediately started up again.

"Hello?" Briana blurted, suddenly anxious.

"B-Briana?" It was Heather's voice, and she sounded choked up.

The room whirled around Briana. "Yes! Heather, what is it—?"

Heather began to sob.

Oh my God, Briana thought, her heart cramming itself into the back of her throat. *I knew it, I knew it— something is wrong—*

Vance came on. "Alec's all right," he said quickly, but his voice was deeper than usual, and grave.

"Alec's— Vance, *what's happened?*"

"He's got a broken arm, that's all," Vance answered wearily. "Fool kid ran behind the van when Heather was backing out to go to the store for milk—must have been in her blind spot. Anyhow, she hit him, and we're in the emergency room at the clinic."

Briana gripped the edge of the table, waiting for the kitchen to stop doing its tilt-a-whirl thing. "A broken— She *hit* him—?"

"Take a breath," Vance broke in. "It was an accident, and it isn't serious. He'll be in a cast for the rest of the summer, that's all."

Briana began to hyperventilate. She had to get to the emergency room, but she was shaking so hard, she thought she might faint and run off the road if she tried, and besides that, she'd had a couple of beers next door, at Logan's.

"They're not keeping him overnight or anything?" she heard herself ask. It was the strangest sensation, as though she'd separated into two people, one calm and matter-of-fact, the other bouncing off the walls like a human ping-pong ball.

"No," Vance said. "He's pretty shaken up, but he's all right."

"Josh—how is Josh?"

"He's fine," Vance answered. "If they admit anybody, it will probably be Heather. She's a real mess. I'd better get off the phone and try to calm her down a little."

The woman had backed a van into Briana's son. Who cared if she was a mess?

"I'll be right there," Briana said.

"It might be a few hours before Alec is released," Vance told her.

Briana asked to talk to Alec.

He was in an exam room.

She asked to talk to Josh.

"M-Mom?" her elder son said shakily. "Alec got hurt."

"I know, babe," she said, pacing. "I'll be there as soon as I can, so hang on, okay?"

"O-okay," Josh said. "But come quick, will you?"

Logan. She would call Logan. Ask him to drive her to the clinic in town.

"I'm on my way, honey. Tell your dad that, and Alec, if they let you see him. All right?"

"All right, but hurry. Heather's freaking out, and Dad's face is this funny gray color and I'm scared he's going to have a heart attack or the doctor will come out and say Alec is worse—"

Me, too, Briana thought wildly. *Me, too.*

She ended the conversation as quickly as she could, realized she didn't know Logan's number and called information to ask for it. Thank God he was listed, and he answered on the second ring.

"Dylan?" he said.

Of course, Briana thought distractedly. He had caller ID, and the call would ring in under Dylan's name, not hers.

"It's Briana," she said quickly, but then got so tangled in the phone cord that she felt as though she'd been lassoed. "Alec's at the clinic in town. His arm is broken and I—"

"I'll be right over," Logan said. The calm strength in his voice brought tears to Briana's eyes—tears of relief. She still had to be strong, but for once, somebody would be there to help her.

Logan hung up without saying goodbye, and Briana hurried into her room, stripped off the sundress and wiggled into the jeans and lightweight sweater she'd meant to wear earlier. She put on socks and her tennis shoes, grabbed her purse on the way through the kitchen.

Logan was just rolling in when she reached the back porch.

She ran across the yard, leaped in on the passenger side. "I could have gone on my own, but I'm sort of shaken up and I didn't think…"

"You made the right decision," Logan said, when her voice fell away. He shifted gears, turned the truck around and started for the main road. "Just how badly is Alec hurt?"

Briana was shivering now; her teeth chattered so hard that Logan reached out and turned on the heater, even though it was a warm summer night.

"Vance says it's 'just' a broken arm," she answered, breathing deeply and slowly, really trying not to lose it and get hysterical. "Heather was backing the van out and Alec ran behind her. She didn't see him and she…she—" Briana stopped, put both hands over her face, pressing hard.

Logan leaned sideways to give her nape a squeeze with one hand.

"She hit him," Briana finished, sputtering out the sentence as though it were a fish bone she'd nearly choked on.

Logan's profile was grim. *"Damn,"* he whispered, with a shake of his head.

They barreled over those country roads, the headlights piercing the thickening twilight, slicing into the night, carving out a path for them to follow.

When they pulled into the clinic's parking lot, Briana was out of the seat and ready to leap off the running board before Logan brought the truck to a full stop.

"Remind me to tell you that that was a *really* stupid thing to do," he said, catching up to her and taking hold of her arm as they both sprinted toward the nearest entrance.

Josh spotted them first, charged into Briana's arms, nearly knocking her over. She hugged the boy hard, searching over his head for Vance or a doctor or a nurse—*anyone* who could lead her to Alec.

"I yelled at him, Mom," Josh half cried, his face buried against Briana. "I yelled at Alec to look out, but he didn't *stop*—"

"It's okay," Briana said. Vance was coming toward her by then, and she saw his gaze trip from her face to Logan and back again.

"This way," he said, turning on one heel.

"You stay with Logan," Briana told Josh, gripping his shoulders.

Her son hesitated, then nodded.

Briana hurried away with Vance.

Everything was a blur around her—people in scrubs, equipment, tile walls. The lights were too bright, the noise too loud.

And then a curtain was pulled aside, and there was Alec, looking small and as fragile as a baby bird, with his right arm in a cast. His face was as pale as the plaster, and at the sight of Briana, he gave a heart-rending little wail and tried to get to her.

She gathered him close.

"It was an accident," Vance said, from somewhere

in the pulsing void surrounding Briana and her little boy.

She ignored him.

"Heather didn't mean—"

Briana looked up. Without speaking, she made it perfectly clear that she wanted him to shut up about Heather. This wasn't *about* Heather, it was about Alec.

"Can I go home, Mom?" Alec asked, his voice so small that Briana had to strain to hear it. "Will you take me home?"

She stroked his cheek, kissed his forehead. "I have to talk to your doctor first," she said. "If he says it's okay, we're out of here."

Alec's smile was wobbly, but real. "Okay," he said. "I came here in a real *ambulance,* with lights and sirens and everything."

"Dandy," Briana said, and while her tone was geared to Alec, the look she gave Vance over the boy's head was different.

The doctor appeared shortly, told Vance he'd given Heather a sedative and finally turned to Briana and Alec.

"You're a very lucky young man," Dr. Elliott said, smiling at Alec. He was the boys' pediatrician, and thus familiar with their medical histories. "I trust you'll be more careful in the future?"

Alec nodded solemnly. "Can I go home with my mom now?"

Dr. Elliott nodded. Handed Briana a brown plastic prescription bottle. "These are for pain," he said. "He may not need more than one or two doses. I'll need to see Alec again in a week, in my office. Sooner if he hurts too much or develops any signs of infection, such as a fever."

Briana nodded numbly. Stuffed the bottle into her jeans pocket.

A nurse brought a wheelchair, and she and Vance eased Alec into it. He'd been frightened when Briana arrived, but now he seemed to be enjoying the attention. As for Briana's state of mind, well, she was already thinking in practicalities. Her insurance was good, thanks to the casino's generous benefit package, so there wouldn't be any significant doctor or hospital bills to pay, but she wouldn't be ready to leave Alec and Josh with Heather anytime soon, nor could the boys stay home alone.

Which meant she'd be missing who knew how much work, and she couldn't qualify for sick leave because she wasn't the one who'd been hurt.

So much for the car fund.

She gave herself a mental shake. Nothing mattered except that Alec was okay. Tonight's scenario could have been tragically worse, if Heather had run over Alec, instead of bumping him with the rear fender.

Logan and Josh were in the waiting room, and they both jumped out of their chairs at Alec's approach. Vance had stayed in the back, probably seeing to Heather.

Heather.

Briana bit down on her lower lip. "I'll be right back," she said.

The patient was lying on a gurney in an exam room, Vance leaning over her.

"I'm so sorry," Heather said. Her eyes were like two burned holes in a blanket, as Briana's father used to say. She was as white as the bedding except for her lips, which were a scary shade of lavender. "Oh, Briana, I'm so sorry—I didn't see him. There was this awful thud and I slammed on the brakes, but—"

Briana took the other woman's hand. Squeezed it. "Alec will be fine, Heather," she said. Actually, it was the better angel talking, not her. Inside, she didn't feel gracious at all, didn't want to forgive or even try to understand. "I know you didn't mean to hurt him."

A big tear rolled through the smudged makeup on Heather's cheek. Her grip was strong, crushing Briana's fingers together. "You'll still let the boys come to our place, won't you?"

Briana swallowed, looked up to meet Vance's eyes, looked down at Heather again. After a long time, she nodded. That was the better angel in action, too. Another part of her seethed.

Without another word, she left the examining room. Stopped at the desk to show her insurance card and sign the necessary papers.

Logan, Josh and Alec had already left the reception area when she got there, so she hurried to the parking lot.

Josh and Alec were settled in the backseat of Logan's truck. Logan himself was leaning against the left front fender with his arms folded. When he saw Briana, he gave her a wan grin and straightened.

"Ready?" he asked.

She nodded.

He opened the passenger-side door for her and helped her in. Even buckled her seat belt.

She couldn't remember the last time she'd felt so, well, taken care of. She straightened her spine, told herself not to be a sap. Logan Creed was a nice man; like any good neighbor, he'd been ready to pitch in and help out in a crisis.

It didn't mean a thing, beyond that.

It really didn't mean a thing.

Send For
2 FREE BOOKS
Today!

I accept your offer!

Please send me two free novels and two mystery gifts (gifts worth about $10). I understand that these books are completely free—even the shipping and handling will be paid—and I am under no obligation to purchase anything, ever, as explained on the back of this card.

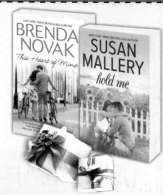

194/394 MDL GHQR

Please Print

FIRST NAME

LAST NAME

ADDRESS

APT.#   CITY

STATE/PROV.   ZIP/POSTAL CODE

Visit us online at
www.ReaderService.com

Detach card and mail today! No stamp needed.

Send For
2 FREE BOOKS
Today!

I accept your offer!

Please send me two
free novels and two mystery
gifts (gifts worth about $10).
I understand that these books
are completely free—even
the shipping and handling will
be paid—and I am under no
obligation to purchase anything,
ever, as explained on the back
of this card.

194/394 MDL GHQR

Please Print

FIRST NAME

LAST NAME

ADDRESS

APT.#   CITY

STATE/PROV.   ZIP/POSTAL CODE

**Visit us online at
www.ReaderService.com**

CHAPTER TEN

ALEC NODDED OFF on the way home, probably swamped by excitement, exhaustion and the medications he'd been given at the clinic. Logan parked the truck as close to Briana's back porch as he could, got out and lifted the sleeping child gently off the seat.

The little boy smelled of fresh plaster, kid sweat and the greasy burgers Logan had bought for him and Josh at the drive-through place on the way out of town.

Standing there in the moonlight, Briana looked poised to take Alec, carry him herself.

Logan put a finger to his lips and shook his head. Even Josh was quiet, scrambling out of the rig to head for the house. Briana and Logan were still standing there in the yard, looking at each other, when he flipped on the lights.

"I can take it from here," Briana whispered.

"I know," Logan answered, and went past her with the boy. Carried him all the way inside, Josh leading the way, to the smaller of two bedrooms.

Clearly shaken, Josh looked as though he'd been hit by a car, too. "He can have the bottom bunk," he said, gesturing. It was a major concession, Logan knew, and it touched him. "He might fall out of the top one."

With a nod, Logan laid Alec down, passed Briana in the doorway as he left the room.

"Don't go yet," she told him. "Please."

He nodded, waited in the kitchen.

The place was familiar, yet strange, too. Dylan owned the house, but as far as Logan knew, he'd never lived in it. Back when they were still speaking, Dylan had been hell-bent on renovating the place one day. He'd planned to add on bedrooms and a couple of baths, build a barn and keep horses.

Now, in the postemergency quiet, Wanda gave Logan an imploring look, and he assured her that Alec would be okay. You never knew what animals understood; more than they were given credit for, that was for sure.

Presently, Briana came out of the boys' room. Stood looking at Logan from the doorway into the narrow hall.

"Thanks," she said. Her eyes were enormous, and full of things she wanted to say, but couldn't—or wouldn't. Maybe it was pride, maybe it was just good judgment.

"You're welcome," he answered. Such ordinary words, not even skimming the surface of what seemed to be happening between them. He finally crossed to her, kissed the top of her head. Lord, he wanted to do so much more, though. "Get some sleep."

She leaned into him a little, not quite touching, and then withdrew. Looked up at him. Her mouth moved, but no words came out.

The need to kiss her for real was almost palpable, but it wasn't the time.

Briana gave a belated nod, as though just then registering the sleep remark. "I could make some coffee," she said, sounding bemused. Alec's near miss had taken a lot out of her—she seemed literally beside herself. Another reason to leave her alone—or to stay the night.

Logan grinned. "The *last* thing you need right now is caffeine," he told her. "Lock up behind me, and then go get some shut-eye. Things will look better in the morning."

"Will they?" she asked.

Logan had turned to go, but he stopped and looked back at her, his heart snagged on the soft, sad way she'd spoken. "Bring the boys over, if you have to work," he said, determined not to take advantage, but tempted, too. "I'll keep an eye on them."

He saw the struggle in her face—need against pride, fear against courage. What a brave little thing she was—the kind of woman who had helped build the west. Taking things as they came, good and bad, making the best of limited resources.

"I'm not ready to leave them with Heather again," she admitted. Then she smiled feebly, but the effort was valiant. "*She's* probably not ready yet, either."

"Josh has his cell phone," Logan reminded her. How could his voice sound so normal, with all he was feeling? It was as if a bucking bronc had been turned loose inside him, kicking down fence rails on all sides. "You have yours. If I turn out to be the baby-sitter from hell, he can call you."

She laughed at that, but there was a sob in there someplace, too. She'd been carrying a big load, alone, for a long time. It was hard for her to trust, hard to accept help, particularly from a relative stranger. "They can be a handful," she said, but she was wavering, and that pleased Logan in a way he hadn't expected. "Alec and Josh, I mean. They argue constantly—"

"I have brothers of my own," Logan said. "I can argue with the best of them." He paused, grinned, one hand on the doorknob, hesitant to go. "And I can whistle, too. Fit to split your eardrums."

"So I've heard," Briana replied, and now her smile was steady, though her eyes were still moist.

The need to stay and hold her through the night was almost visceral now. If ever a woman had needed holding—just that and nothing more, though God knew he *wanted* more—it was Briana Grant, but there were kids in the house. And he had two dogs at home, waiting for him, and horses to feed in the morning.

The rancher's life. He'd wanted it; now he had it.

"See you tomorrow," he said, and went out by sheer force of will.

The night was warm and dark, with just a sliver of a moon etched into the sprawling sky. He stood on the porch for a few moments, talking himself out of going back in.

Time enough, he thought, looking up at the clear country stars, following their ancient courses. There would be time enough.

"YOU'RE OKAY WITH THIS?" Briana asked her boys the next morning, as she flipped pancakes at the stove. "You don't mind going over to Logan's for the day?"

"Mind?" Josh said, slipping Wanda a morsel of bacon under the table. "It'll be fun."

Alec was downright chipper, for somebody who'd been hit by a van the night before. "I want him to sign my cast," he said. "Think he'd let us ride one of his horses?"

Briana stopped in midflip. "You are *not* to get on any horse, Alec Grant, unless I'm on it behind you."

Alec rolled his eyes. "I *know* how to ride, Mom. Dad taught me."

It was true. Although Vance hadn't owned a horse of his own for years, he'd had access to plenty of them through the rodeo, and the times he'd settled down for a month or two to take a job as a ranch hand on some spread. Briana had always wanted to stay; Vance had invariably gotten restless and insisted that it was time to move on.

Both Alec and Josh had been on horseback with their dad as soon as they could hold their heads up without help.

"Still," she said, setting the pancake platter in the center of the table with a thump. "No riding unless I'm there. Got it?"

Thinking of all the places they might have made a life, she and Vance, and all the times they'd packed up and pulled out, leaving some shabby but perfectly good little house behind, she ran square into the old reality. Vance was Vance, and he *would* be leaving Stillwater Springs one day soon, job or no job, wife or no wife—sons or no sons.

How could she prepare them for that?

She couldn't, of course. She'd have to pick up the pieces afterward, try to explain something she didn't understand herself, even after years of happy traveling with her dad—the mysterious pull of the rodeo circuit and the open road. The difference was she'd known Bill McIntyre loved her more than the gypsy life, more than the cheering, laughing spectators, more than the bulls and the broncs.

If she'd asked him to settle down, he would have done it.

The thing he *wouldn't* have done was leave her behind.

"Mom?" Josh prompted. "Aren't you going to eat?"

She smiled, shook off the what-makes-Vance-tick quandary. There was no figuring him out, and trying to was a habit she needed to break.

So she ate a pancake, and part of a fried egg, and drank her orange juice. She fed Wanda, let her out and then in again. Put together a peanut-butter-and-jelly sack lunch for the boys.

Then they all piled into the truck—Alec needed a little help—and headed along the county road, toward Logan's place.

He was straddling the gate beam when they arrived, setting the sign right. He'd ridden the buckskin down from the barn; it stood nearby, saddled and grazing on the high grass.

With a grin and a wave, Logan swung a leg over the beam, hung for a moment by his hands, then dropped to the ground—at least ten feet—to make a nimble landing on both feet.

Briana winced, rolled down the driver's-side window.

"The sign looks good," she said. *He* looked good—in jeans, boots and a sleeveless T-shirt that left his biceps gloriously bare.

"Check out the *horse!*" Alec spouted, from the backseat. "You're here, Mom. Does that mean I can ride it?"

"No," Briana said.

Logan, standing close enough that she could see the dare in his eyes, waited.

She peered through the windshield, studying the gelding.

"He's as gentle as they come," Logan said.

"*Please,* Mom," Alec wheedled. "I've been traumatized. I need positive reinforcement."

Logan chuckled at that, shoved a hand through his somewhat dusty hair.

"I'm not dressed to ride," Briana pointed out, referring to her customary casino getup, which amounted to a uniform. She couldn't show up with horse hair all over her slacks.

"Logan is," Alec said.

Logan raised both eyebrows.

"All right," Briana heard herself say, and was astounded.

Alec whooped with delight.

"Can I have a turn after Alec?" Josh wanted to know.

"If it's okay with your mom," Logan said. He rounded the truck, opened the left rear passenger door and whisked Alec out of the vehicle and onto the back of the gelding, all in a few strides. Before Briana could even catch her breath, he'd swung expertly into the saddle behind Alec and taken the reins.

The way Logan Creed looked on that horse, like he was part of it, cell for cell and breath for breath, was— Well, it should have been illegal.

Logan gestured toward the house with one hand. "After you," he said.

Alec beamed.

Josh scrambled out of his seat belt to kneel and watch through the back window of the truck as Briana continued up the driveway, Logan and Alec riding behind. "Cool," he said, sounding both impressed and resentful.

"You'll get your turn," Briana said, resigned.

She only glanced into the rearview mirror a couple of times, making sure Alec hadn't been bucked off. The second she'd parked in Logan's front yard, though, she was out of that truck and standing on the ground, shading her eyes from the morning sun and watching as Alec and Logan rode closer, the horse moving at an easy trot.

Sidekick and the Yorkie came to sniff at her pant legs—at least, she *thought* it was the Yorkie. Gone were the blue bow and the flowing dog-tresses.

"What happened to Snooks?" Briana asked, as Logan got down off the gelding's back and lifted Alec after him.

Logan's grin was as dazzling as that midsummer sun. "Found some shears in the attic and gave him a haircut this morning," he said, bending to pick up the dog. "He's still a scrawny little varmint, but at least he's got some dignity."

"Can I have my turn on the horse now?" Josh asked, trying to restrain his eagerness and not succeeding very well.

Briana sighed and took the brown-bag lunches she'd packed for the boys out of the truck. Handed them to Logan, who immediately set them aside on the hood of his Dodge to hold the buckskin's reins while Josh mounted up.

Why did she bother to set rules, when she always ended up changing them?

Still, she felt a flash of pride, seeing her boy on the back of a horse, and something very much like grief, too. Alec and Josh were growing up so fast. Before she knew it, they'd be men, following faraway dreams of their own. And she'd be on the perimeter of their lives, like a one-time planet demoted to moon status, always waiting for a phone call or an e-mail.

"I'll be back as soon as I can," she told Logan, who was watching Josh ride the buckskin around the yard at a walk. It was good of the man to look after the boys, but she couldn't expect him to do it every day.

"No hurry," Logan said easily.

Briana got into the truck, started it and headed for work.

Heather was waiting near the main entrance when she arrived, looking particularly forlorn. She wore the usual tight jeans, another skimpy top and a teensy denim jacket against the nonexistent chill.

Briana wondered, briefly and uncharitably, if the woman had developed a gambling habit—or already had one. It galled her that she was supposed to trust a virtual stranger with her children, but the reality was that Josh and Alec needed Vance, and Heather was part of the deal.

"Vance and I talked," Heather said hurriedly, walking fast to keep pace with Briana as she went toward the office to clock in, the brightly lit, noisy slot machines a colorful blur as she passed them. "And we agreed I shouldn't work until after school starts this fall. I'll make sure I'm off before they get out of class, so I can take care of them."

Briana stopped, speechless.

Heather had the good grace to avert her eyes.

"You did a great job of looking after them last night," Briana said evenly. Okay, so she wasn't at her most gracious, and the better angel was off somewhere, bugging somebody else, but Heather wasn't the only one who'd suffered a shock.

Briana was still jarred, could still hear Vance's voice, telling her Alec had been hurt.

Heather's clumpy mascara started turning to liquid.

Off to her left, at the edge of her vision, Briana saw Jim coming toward them, frowning a little.

"Is there a problem?" he asked when he drew up alongside Briana. He was general manager and, as such, chief of security, as well. Any sign of trouble, however subtle, was guaranteed to bring him on the double.

"I'm sorry," Heather told Briana, lower lip bobbing.

"No problem at all," Briana said, addressing Jim but looking at Heather.

"I didn't mean to hit Alec with the van!" Heather protested.

"She hit Alec with a van?" Jim gasped.

"He's going to be okay," Briana assured him. The better angel was back, damn it. "Look, Heather," she added reluctantly, "I'll stop by your place after work and we'll talk, okay?"

"Okay," Heather said moistly. Then the transformation came, startling and instantaneous; she turned a show-girl smile on Jim. "I dealt poker in Reno for a while. Maybe I could work here next fall—maybe seven to three?"

Briana's mouth fell open. Was the woman serious? She wanted to work with her husband's ex?

Jim looked from her to Heather and back again.

Briana glared at Jim.

He stifled a smile. Turned politely to Heather. "Fill out an application," he said, directing her to the customer service desk. "We have a fairly high turnover, and we're usually shorthanded in September, after all the grad students go back to school."

Heather nodded, smiled mistily at Briana and headed for the desk.

"Who *is* that?" Jim asked.

"My ex-husband's new wife," Briana said, "and if you hire her—"

Jim grinned, rocked back on his heels. Waited.

She huffed out a sigh. Like she had anything to say about hiring and firing. "I've got to clock in," she said.

But Jim took her by the arm and squired her into his private office, a virtual command post full of flickering monitors. Heather waggled her fingers at them as they passed, employment application in hand.

"If Alec was hit by a van," Jim said reasonably, once they were alone, "what are you doing here?"

"He's not in critical condition, Jim," Briana answered. "He broke an arm, and he and Josh are with Logan today."

A grin quirked Jim's mouth. "Logan's babysitting?"

"Don't let Josh and Alec hear you call it that."

Jim smiled, touched Briana's shoulder. "Go home," he said. "We can run this place without you."

"That's what I'm afraid of," Briana said.

"You can take sick leave, or vacation days."

"I'm not sick."

"You look sick to me," Jim said speculatively, tilting his head to one side as he studied her.

"Gee, thanks."

"Go," he said. "Your job will still be here when you get things under control."

"Things *are* under control."

"Are they?"

"Sort of," she said.

Five minutes later, Briana was back in the parking lot, watching Heather pull out in Vance's van. She'd follow her to the trailer, she decided, and get their talk out of the way before going back to Logan's to pick up the boys.

She nearly slammed into an old Corolla, she was so distracted.

Then Brett Turlow got out, smiling his smarmy smile, and came toward the truck. He'd tried to put the moves on her several times—it happened a lot, in her line of work—and so far she'd always been able to brush him off without making a big deal.

"Where you goin', Briana?" he asked. She'd automatically rolled down the window, because the truck didn't have air-conditioning, and now she regretted it.

"I'm taking the day off," she said, trying to smile, anxious to be gone already, if she was going.

"That's a pity," Brett answered, standing so close she was afraid he'd climb onto the running board. "You sure do brighten this place up."

Briana made a look-at-the-time motion, though she wasn't wearing a watch. She'd forgotten it that morning, when she'd taken it off to mix up the pancakes.

Brett's small eyes narrowed. He was only one of

a dozen pests, and Briana had never been afraid of him, but she felt uneasy now.

"Gotta be going," she said.

"There's a new movie startin' up at the drive-in Friday night," Brett ventured. "We could grab some supper in town and—"

"Sorry," Briana broke in cheerfully. "I have other plans."

Why did she always have to be so *nice?* Brett Turlow made her skin crawl, and she wouldn't be going anywhere with him Friday night or *any* night.

He looked petulant. Not to mention perpetually grungy. "You *always* have other plans, it seems to me."

Briana drew a deep breath, let it out, shifted the truck into gear and got ready to hit the gas pedal. "I don't date customers," she said moderately.

"You didn't mind dating Jim Huntinghorse," Brett taunted. "And he's nothin' but a damn Injun."

Something tripped inside Briana. "All right," she said. "Get lost. Is that clear enough?"

Brett stared at her, wheeled back from the side of the truck as if she'd reached through the window and slapped him.

Briana took that opportunity to boogie.

Glancing into her rearview mirror, she saw him watching her, and felt little invisible bugs creeping up and down her spine. With a shudder, she pressed down harder on the gas.

Suppose he followed her?

She spotted Heather up ahead, in Vance's van, stopped at a light. *Don't be paranoid,* she told herself, but she sped up just the same. Safety in numbers.

She'd planned to stay on Heather's bumper all the way to the trailer on the other side of Stillwater Springs, but Vance's bride surprised her by heading for the auto shop where he worked instead. And Briana knew the sick feeling in the pit of her stomach had nothing to do with the conversation she and Heather would have had. Would still have to have, at some point.

All the way home, she kept checking her rearview mirror.

THEY STOOD AT the fence for a while, Logan and Josh and Alec, after unsaddling the buckskin and turning him back into the corral. To Logan's amusement, Josh had gathered up Snooks and tucked him inside his T-shirt, "so he wouldn't get stepped on." Now, both the dog's and the boy's heads were sticking out of the neck-hole. Every so often, Snooks would lick Josh's cheek.

"Our lunches probably suck," Alec said.

After a moment, Logan realized the kid was talking about the two brown paper bags still sitting on the hood of his rig.

"Don't hint, butt-face," Josh told his brother.

"Who's hinting, jerk-wad?"

Logan grinned. "Do I have to whistle?" he asked.

Both boys shook their heads, though their eyes snapped with mischief.

"Are there really bears in the orchard?" Alec inquired, scuffing at the dirt with the toe of his sneaker as they started, by tacit agreement, toward the house.

"Sometimes," Logan said.

"What would you do if you met one?" Alec queried, his eyes huge. His cast was starting to look respectably grubby now—Logan had added his signature, as had all the guys working on the barn restoration.

"Return to the religion of my childhood, probably," Logan answered.

The two-headed creature—Josh and Snooks sharing a T-shirt—fell into step beside him. "Besides that, what?" Josh asked. "Would you shoot him?"

"I'd hate to do that," Logan said. He didn't hunt and, anyway, he'd had enough of guns in Iraq.

"But you would, wouldn't you?" Alec asked. "If he was going to eat you, or Sidekick, or Snooks or—"

"Or you?" Josh teased, raising both hands like claws and giving a growl.

Alec blushed. Logan's answer was important to him, that much was obvious.

He rubbed a hand over Alec's bristly haircut. Snooks's was almost as short, thanks to the buzz-job with the clippers. "If a buddy was in trouble, like you or Josh, here, I'd shoot the bear."

"You've got a gun?"

"Several," Logan said. "Old hunting rifles, mostly. Passed down through the family."

"Can we see them?" Josh asked, as they climbed the porch steps.

"Some other time," Logan replied. "Right now, we'd better rustle up some lunch. Then I thought we'd go out and see how that fence I'm building for old Cimarron is coming along."

Logan hadn't made too much progress on the inside of the house, but it was a comfortable place, without the charge of Jake's alcoholic temper to keep the air sizzling. He had a bed now, and the couch from his place in Vegas, and his computer was set up in the living room.

Josh immediately zeroed in on it. "Wow," he said. "State-of-the-art!"

Snooks started to squirm, and Josh took him out of his shirt and set him carefully on the floor, all the while gaping at the three oversize monitors and other gear.

"What do you *do* with this thing?" the boy enthused. "Run a government missile program or something?"

Logan chuckled. "Sometimes it seems that way," he admitted. "I sold my business recently, and I've had to help the new people iron out a few snags."

"*Our* computer is a dinosaur," Alec said.

"A dinosaur's *grampa,*" Josh agreed.

"How do chili dogs sound?" Logan asked, because the current drift of the conversation made him feel as though he'd sneaked a peek at Briana's checkbook balance or something. It had taken a lot for her to leave Alec and Josh with him, so she wouldn't miss work and suffer a corresponding hit to her paycheck.

After lunch, Logan piled the dishes in the sink and they headed for the pasture in the Dodge. The fence was three-quarters of the way finished, but the crew was nervous.

A glance told Logan why—Cimarron no longer stayed near the distant copse of birch trees; he was in the middle of the field, snorting and tossing his head every now and then.

"Stay here," Logan told the boys, climbing out of the truck.

They obeyed, peering over the backseat, along with Snooks and Sidekick.

"There's nothing in my contract," the crew boss told him, "that covers getting gored by a bull."

"The sooner you finish, the lower the risk," Logan answered, watching the bull thoughtfully. Damn, but that son of a bitch was *big*. Why did Dylan keep him around, anyhow? He was a freaking menace—or would be, if he ever got loose.

"I should have asked for hazard pay," the other man joked. His name was Dan Phillips, and he and Logan had gone to high school together, though Phillips had graduated three years before he did.

"Too late," Logan said, grinning. "I've got twenty head of cattle coming in a little under two weeks. The fence has to be done by then."

"Get 'em here early, why don't you?" Dan retorted. "Maybe they'd keep that sucker occupied. He's getting a little closer—and a little testier—every day. Damn near charged yesterday, when one of the guys hit a wasps' nest driving a post-hole. Ralph started jumpin' around, yellin' and wavin' his arms, and old Cimarron, he put his head down and headed straight for him. It was probably the wasps that turned him back."

"Probably," Logan agreed mildly.

He and Dan talked awhile longer, and then he went back to the truck.

"Gross!" Alec yelled, waving one hand in front of his face.

"You're the one who sneaked Sidekick some of your chili," Josh retorted.

Logan pretended to reel from the smell, which *was* pretty ripe.

Sidekick wagged his tail and looked innocent.

Alec and Josh scrambled out of the truck, Josh bringing Snooks along, out of mercy, Logan supposed.

"You should carry that spray stuff in the car," Alec said, as they all stood waiting for the miasma to dissipate. "Mom does."

Logan chuckled.

"Bet she'd love knowing you said *that,*" Josh hooted.

Alec flushed so red his freckles seemed to stand out on his face. "Because of *Wanda,*" he said. He looked up at Logan. "*Wanda* farts all the time!"

When it was safe to get back in the truck, they did.

"Ever seen a real teepee?" Logan asked.

The idea was a hit, so they motored for Cassie's place. She was outside when they arrived, clad in polyester shorts and a tank top and watering tomato plants with a bent green hose.

She smiled as boys and dogs tumbled out of the rig.

Logan made introductions, but Alec and Josh barely stood still for them. They were magnetized to the teepee, and Sidekick and Snooks were right on their heels.

"Is that a dog?" Cassie asked, squinting at Snooks.

Now that he'd been shaved within an inch of his hide, the miniature mutt looked even more like a rat than before.

"That's a dog, all right," Logan confirmed.

"I wouldn't take him to the pool hall or anything," Cassie observed. "Might get you beat up."

"Snooks and I can take care of ourselves," Logan said, handing over a dollar for the teepee admission fee.

Cassie waved it away. "A whole busload of tourists

stopped here this morning," she said. "This one's on the house." She smiled. "Or the teepee."

Logan looked around. "Nobody getting their cards read?" he asked.

"I could read yours."

"No, thanks."

Cassie watched as the boys and dogs dashed in and out of the teepee. "I don't need any cards," she said, "to know where *you're* headed, Logan Creed."

"Oh, yeah?" he challenged, though good-naturedly. "Where's that?"

"Right down the aisle," Cassie answered. But she seemed troubled all of the sudden, watching Alec and Josh. Maybe they reminded her of him and Dylan and Tyler, when they were young, playing the same kind of games. Innocent kids one day, trying to knock out each other's teeth after their father's funeral the next.

"What's the matter, Cassie?" Logan asked quietly, after a long time.

She met his gaze again. "I had a dream last night. Somebody wants to hurt you, Logan. Maybe hurt Briana and those babies of hers, too, if they happen to get in the way."

Logan would have discounted the warning, coming from anybody but Cassie. "Who?" he asked. He thought of Vance Grant, and then of Brett Turlow, and shook his head. Vance was a jerk, but mostly bluff. And Turlow was *all* bluff.

"I think it's got something to do with Jim Huntinghorse running for sheriff," Cassie murmured, and though she was standing right in front of Logan, she might as well have been beyond the farthest hills.

"As far as I know," Logan said, "Jim's the only one who wants the job."

"Then you don't *know* very much," Cassie responded. "You mark my words. Half a dozen people will be tacking signs on the power poles before Jim has the first bumper sticker printed. You've been away from Stillwater Springs for a while—" She held up a hand when he would have interrupted. "You don't know the things that go on around here. I know you like Jim, but you'd be better off to keep a low profile around this election. If he's meant to win it, he will."

"What 'things that go on around here,' Cassie?" Logan asked. If Stillwater Springs had become a hotbed of crime since he left, the *Courier* hadn't mentioned it. Nor had Jim, or Sheriff Book—although Floyd *had,* he remembered, asked him to stop by the office sometime soon.

He'd assumed that was part welcome, part warning—*good to have you back, boy, but don't think you're going to raise hell in my town.*

He moved the drop-in at the sheriff's office up a notch on his agenda.

"Why didn't you say anything about this before?" Logan asked, frowning.

"I just had the dream last night," Cassie told him, looking dead serious.

"I'll be careful," he said.

Cassie nodded. "Round up those yahoos," she said, gesturing toward Alec and Josh, "and we'll go inside and have a cold drink."

She was her old self again—and not.

He called the kids.

Josh's cell phone rang while they were all swilling cola on ice in Cassie's small, immaculate kitchen.

"We're with Logan, Mom," Josh explained patiently, after listening for a few moments. "We saw a real teepee—" His face changed, and his shoulders tensed. "Okay." He sighed. Then he ended the call and looked straight into Logan's face. "We've gotta go home," he said. "Wanda got out somehow, and Mom can't find her anyplace."

CHAPTER ELEVEN

"WANDA?" BRIANA CALLED, pocketing her cell phone as she reached the edge of the old cemetery. She shouldn't have worried the boys, but the truth was, she'd panicked when she got home and found the back door standing wide open and the dog gone. "Wanda!"

A low yip sounded from the direction of the orchard, and Briana hurried in that direction. "Wanda!"

Reaching the first row of gnarled old apple trees, she stopped cold. Wanda sat almost square in the middle, shadowed by overhanging branches heavy with bird-pecked fruit, looking up and shivering visibly. Her hackles stood straight up.

Instinct froze Briana's heart, midbeat. Made the tiny hairs rise on her forearms and her nape. The branches only a few feet over Wanda's head shook violently.

Briana barely dared to lift her eyes. When she did, she saw a massive brown bear clinging to the trunk of that apple tree and looking down at Wanda, almost curiously.

Were there cubs around? Briana had little—make that zero—experience with bears, but she knew if this was a sow, with a baby or two to protect, she and Wanda were in even bigger trouble than she'd thought.

Willing Wanda not to move, Briana slowly got

out her cell phone again. Thank God Josh had programmed the thing to speed-dial; she thumbed the
one-digit number and waited, her heart pounding so
loudly that she was sure the bear could hear it.

"Mom?" Josh said. "We're almost there—did you
find Wanda?"

"I'm in the orchard," Briana whispered, marveling
at the calm flow of her voice. "Wanda's here, too, and
there's a bear. *Tell Logan there's a bear.*"

Josh relayed the message, and Logan came on the
line before Briana could let out her breath.

"Do not move," he told her.

The tree branches began to shudder again, and
Wanda gave a soft whimper.

"Hurry," Briana pleaded. The phone was so slippery against her palm that she nearly dropped it.

"We're turning in at the ranch road right now,"
Logan said. "Stay on the phone with Josh—I need
both hands to drive."

Briana didn't stay on the line, she hung up. If that
bear mauled Wanda—or her—she didn't want her
son to hear it.

The phone didn't ring again, as she'd half expected, half feared. Logan would have better sense
than that—the shrill, unfamiliar sound might set the
bear off. And it was on the brink of rage *now*; the very
air seemed charged with a tremulous zing.

Wanda gathered the muscles in her haunches, as
if to stand on all fours and try to make it to Briana.
Her eyes were huge and full of trust. She believed
she'd be all right, if she could just get to her mistress.

Briana knew it wasn't that simple, and it grieved
her to think the dog's trust might be misplaced.

Hours seemed to pass, though it was surely only a matter of seconds. She thought she heard the roar of Logan's truck engine, but he was probably too far away to get to them in time.

Never show fear around a dangerous animal. The voice inside her head was her father's. He'd told her that a dozen times if he'd told her once, and he'd been an expert on the subject, called upon to face angry bulls and excited broncs every time he stepped into an arena in his silly clown getup.

The truck came closer, and Briana felt both exhilaration and alarm. The bear heard it, too, and started down the trunk of that ancient apple tree, the branches shaking so ferociously that it seemed the whole tree might be uprooted.

Wanda broke and ran just as the bear reached the ground.

It stood on hind legs, forepaws raised. A strange, almost mystical calm came over Briana, as some stronger, braver version of herself took charge.

"You will not hurt my dog." Had she spoken the words, or just thought them? In either case, the bear, still upright, regarded her with its huge head tipped slightly to one side.

Wanda ducked behind Briana; she felt the dog pressing close against the backs of her legs.

The bear gave a tentative growl. Lowered itself to all fours. Power rippled beneath the mangy fur on its haunches; it was gathering itself to spring.

Briana, desperate again, tried to grin.

At the same moment, Logan's truck came jostling overland at top speed, horn honking, veering right into the orchard.

The bear pondered its options, with an idle grace, and then bounded away, passing within a few feet of Briana and Wanda, in the general direction of the cemetery.

Logan slammed on the brakes and jumped out of the truck, running toward her. He pulled her hard against him, held her tight to his chest.

Briana's knees buckled; she would have crumpled to the ground if Logan hadn't been supporting her. Past his shoulder, she saw Josh and Alec in the truck, their faces pale circles against the windows.

"You're okay," Logan told her breathlessly. "You're okay."

She began to shake, hard. So did Wanda.

A cold sweat broke out all over Briana's body.

"I can walk," Briana managed to say. "I'm not so sure about the dog."

Logan held her a few moments longer, until he could be sure she wouldn't crumple to the ground. Then he reached down and hoisted Wanda into his arms.

Briana stumbled after him, looking back only once, to make sure the bear was still gone.

BRETT TURLOW HUNKERED in the shadowed back booth at Skivvie's Tavern, his guts roiling like a pot of rancid soup left too long on the stove. His credit was no good at Skivvie's, but earlier he'd stopped by the real estate office where his sister worked. Freida had been out showing a house to some sucker, so he'd borrowed a few dollars from the cigar box she kept in her desk drawer. Petty cash, she called it.

Everything about Freida was petty, as far as Brett was concerned.

Her constant harping that he ought to get his ass off her couch and into a job, for example. Freida still thought it meant something in Stillwater Springs to be a Turlow. Although three years ago now that snooty librarian, Kristy Madison, had bought the big family house on Maple Street for pennies on the dollar, Freida was saving up to get it back.

It didn't seem to bother Freida that Kristy had no intention of selling. She worked on the place from dawn 'til dusk, and sometimes longer, every time she had a day off from the library. Brett knew that because he sat out there on Maple in the dark sometimes, in Freida's ratty Corolla, remembering how things used to be, and the lights burned in that old wreck of a house 'til all hours.

Lived like a spinster, that Kristy. Good-looking woman, too. Prime piece of tail, librarian or not. Word on the street was, she'd gotten her heart good and broken by none other than Dylan Creed, and she was waiting for him to come back.

Made her sound like that pathetic woman in the song—"Delta Dawn," wasn't it?—meeting the train every day, hoping her long-lost lover would come rolling in on it.

Brett snorted under his breath and turned his second foaming brewski round and round between his hands, there on the scarred tabletop. Like *Dylan* would ever trouble himself to visit Stillwater Springs again, with everything going his way out there in the big world.

As for Kristy—well, if she was waiting for somebody, it was for her own reasons, and not because she was hung up on Dylan or anybody else. Brett had known her all his life, and she didn't care about anything besides books and horses and that old house.

He had to slow down on the beer, he told himself. This one had to last, because he was plum out of money—again.

He'd had all of that he needed once, back in the glory days when Turlow Timber was one of the biggest operations in the state. Briana Grant wouldn't have shut down *that* Brett Turlow, that was for sure. All right, so he'd had the Creed brothers' leavings when it came to women, but that hadn't been half-bad. He'd had a convertible and credit cards and all the best clothes, which was more than Logan or Dylan or Tyler could have claimed.

He'd done all right with the women *then*.

Brett rubbed his beard-stubbled chin. He was fairly slavering to guzzle down that second beer, feel it hit his jangly nerve endings and dull all the ugly regrets, but besides his empty wallet, there was another reason to hold off.

Every time he got even halfway drunk, he saw Jake Creed's ghost.

In fact, though he was still semisober, the specter loomed up on the other side of the table, right there in the back booth. Jake's whole chest was smashed to a bloody pulp under his tattered plaid work shirt, but he grinned.

Oh, the son of a bitch always grinned.

"I didn't kill you, you bastard," Brett mumbled, jumping a little when he realized he'd spoken aloud.

There had been an investigation after the accident, and he'd been cleared of any wrongdoing.

The ghost vanished, still grinning, but its disappearance wasn't the relief it should have been. Brett had been safe from Jake Creed's shade during the daylight, as long as he was sober, but he'd just seen him, and it wasn't much past noon—was it?

He leaned sideways in the booth seat, 'til he could see the beer-sign clock on the far wall. It had a light-up bear holding a can of brew in one paw on it, and the wire hands said five minutes to three.

Briana Grant appeared in Jake's seat in the next moment, looking all sexy and soft and female. She looked down her nose at Brett, like he stank or something, and then *blip,* she was gone.

Brett's benumbed brain groped for a memory that slithered away from him like wet soap in the bottom of a bathtub. Logan Creed. He'd seen Creed with Briana's boys, in the Mexican restaurant at the casino.

Holy shit.

No wonder Briana had turned him down when he'd asked her to the drive-in on Friday night. She was boinking the local hotshot.

Brett took a big gulp from his beer mug, hoping to steady himself.

He'd gone straight to Briana's place, after she'd cut him dead in the parking lot at the casino that morning—or had he? Sometimes, he got things he did mixed up with things he'd only *thought* about doing.

He took another taste of the beer, just a cautious sip this time. Had to make it last, he reminded himself. Freida refused to buy the stuff, stingy bitch; she had wine sometimes, but he always found it, and he'd finished off the last of her supply after he got back from Briana's.

If he'd *gone* to Briana's.

He shoved both hands into his hair.

Think.

Yes. He'd been there. The back door had been un-locked, and he'd gone inside, planning to move things around a bit, that was all. Give her a little jolt when she got home.

But an old black dog had come at him, first thing—hadn't even barked a warning, like a dog ought to do. He'd turned and hotfooted it for the Corolla, with that hound snarling and nipping at his ass.

"Hello, Brett," a familiar voice said, interrupting Brett's struggle to sort the real from the imaginary.

Brett blinked, looked up, saw Sheriff Floyd Book sitting across from him. At first, he thought he was imagining it, like before, when old Jake was there, and after him, Briana.

A few beats passed before Brett understood that the sheriff was flesh and blood.

"I ain't done nothin'," he said immediately.

Book smiled. Took off his hat and set it on the seat beside him, nodded his gratitude when Sally Jo, the barmaid, brought him the usual, a cola with extra ice. Sally Jo looked at Brett like she was scared of him, and scuttled back behind the bar as soon as she'd de-livered Book's beverage.

"Thought I'd give you a ride over to Freida's," Book said easily. "You're in no shape to drive, it ap-pears to me."

Rage swelled inside Brett, fit to burst him wide

open. "Sally Jo call you and tell you I was drunk?" he rasped.

"Don't you go blaming Sally Jo for my coming here," Book said, after taking a sip of his cola. Must have gone down good, since he closed his eyes for a moment, like he was savoring the taste or something. "Under state law, she's partly responsible if you get into an accident on the way home."

"I ain't gonna get in no accident," Brett said.

Book sighed. He was tired of his job, everybody knew that. Tired of Stillwater Springs, and probably tired of his crippled wife, too.

And Brett was tired of *him*.

Things would just go from bad to worse, though, if Jim Huntinghorse won the special election.

"You talk like a hillbilly. You need a shower and a shave. And those clothes…well. Those clothes." The sheriff interlaced his fingers, studied Brett thoughtfully. "Once, your name meant something in this town. What happened?"

Brett merely snorted. Book knew damn well *what happened.* The old man had died, leaving the company books in a tangle—turned out he'd had a whole nuther family squirreled away in Missoula—and then Jake Creed had gotten himself killed up in the woods on a fine summer day, just like this one. And after that, "Brett Turlow" meant fuck-all in Stillwater Springs and everywhere else.

"I'll finish my drink," Book said affably, as though they were two friends having a nice chat, "and give you a lift over to Freida's. You can hike back for the Corolla later on."

"I am not drunk," Brett said. "And I didn't cut that

logging chain and turn all that timber loose on Jake Creed, neither."

"Nobody said you did," the sheriff replied easily. He seemed loose, like his joint sockets were lubricated with motor oil, and Brett knew there was a younger, sharper man behind Book's eyes than most people ever guessed.

"Everybody *thinks* I did," Brett lamented. "Same as."

The sheriff glanced at Brett's beer, like he might take it away, hand it off to Sally Jo to be dumped down the drain back of the bar. So Brett grabbed it and chugged it right down.

Book just waited and watched.

He'd been doing it for years.

Waiting. Watching. Eyeballs peeled for a wrong move.

"Something has been eating at you all this time," the sheriff remarked. "That's for sure."

"You headed up the investigation yourself," Brett reminded him. "There was no proof that I killed Jake Creed."

Book leaned forward slightly on the booth seat, his hands still interlaced. "He was rolling in the hay with your girlfriend, as I remember."

"He 'rolled in the hay' with *everybody's* girlfriend," Brett said. Now, after downing what was left of his beer, his words were slurred, and there was a great, hollow ache expanding inside him—the knowledge that there wouldn't be more anytime soon. "And Jake didn't just screw girlfriends," he added. "He stuck it to plenty of other men's wives, too."

Let the sheriff chew on that one. Cocky old son

of a bitch. Did he think Brett didn't know about him and Freida? They'd almost run away together, once. Kicked off the traces, the both of them, and left town for good.

Would have done it, too, if Book's wife hadn't crashed her car into a bridge piling one snowy night and put herself in a wheelchair.

"You cut that chain," Book said quietly.

"I didn't," Brett said.

Another sigh, deep and heavy with the suffering of the ages. "You've finished your beer." Book reached for his hat, put it on and stood, leaving his cola unfinished. "Let's go," he said. "I've got things to do."

Brett went because he had no other choice, but he did so grudgingly.

The squad car was parked outside, where everybody could see it. Worse, there was a computer monitor on the front seat, so Brett had to sit in the back, like he was under arrest or something.

He seethed, sitting back there. Folks walking by on the sidewalk looked his way, and got those smartass smirks on their faces.

Brett sat as low as he could.

"Buckle up," the sheriff said. "Wouldn't want you getting hurt or anything."

Brett buckled up.

And Jake Creed appeared beside him, his normal bloody, grinning self.

Brett closed his eyes to shut him out, and suddenly he was back on the mountain again, up there in the lonesome woods. He *hadn't* cut that logging chain, but he hadn't fastened it right, either. Had intended to come back to it, after taking a quick piss in the brush.

He'd nearly wet himself, when he heard the thunder of those rolling logs. Actually felt the ground shake as he ran back toward the loaded truck, fumbling to zip up his pants as he stumbled along.

Any other man but Jake Creed would have been screaming, from fear if not from pain, but when Brett got there, he saw the bastard looking up at him between the gaps, grinning.

Brett had sworn a blue streak, danced around, this way and that, unable to stand still.

"Get somebody," Creed had said calmly.

Brett hadn't had a cell phone—practically nobody carried them in those days, especially up in the woods, where the service was patchy. He'd finally scrambled into the cab of the logging truck and pulled the cord on the air-horn until the rest of the crew came running.

Jake Creed had been haunting him ever since.

And now Logan would, too.

That was the real reason he'd come back, Brett decided. It figured.

THE DOG COULDN'T WALK. When Logan set Wanda on the ground, in front of his house, she made a puddle in the dirt and gazed up at him in helpless apology.

He looked into the truck, saw Briana was still sitting woodenly in the passenger seat, staring straight through the windshield.

"Stay here with your mother," he told Josh quietly. "I'll come back for her in a couple of minutes."

Standing beside him, Josh didn't move. Logan knew his instructions probably hadn't penetrated.

"Did the bear hurt Wanda?" the boy asked, his voice so small that Logan barely heard him.

Logan laid a hand on Josh's shoulder. "I don't think so," he said. "She's just scared."

Josh bit his lower lip, the way Logan had seen Briana do. Nodded his head. It wasn't hard to follow his line of thinking—first Alec had been hurt, and now his mother and his dog had come face-to-face with a bear. It was an uncertain world.

Anything could happen—to his mother, to his dog. Loving a person or an animal, needing them, didn't guarantee their safety.

Logan squeezed Josh's shoulder. He knew the feeling.

Jake's face bloomed in his mind, lying there in his hospital bed.

Shake it off, he heard the old man say, way in the back of his brain.

So he stooped and gathered Wanda up as gently as he could. Started for the house. Snooks and Sidekick jumped out of the truck and followed, and when he set the still-shuddering Lab in the middle of the kitchen floor, they sniffed at her, but otherwise kept their distance.

He went back for Briana—met her walking toward the house, Alec on one side of her, Josh on the other. They held her elbows solicitously, like little men.

She blinked when she saw Logan, stopped as though surprised to find herself standing in his yard. It was a good sign—she was coming out of it now.

Getting her bearings.

In the truck, she'd been practically catatonic, merely shaking her head while both boys pelted her with questions. Had she tried grinning at the bear? Did it have babies? Did she think it would have eaten her and Wanda both if they hadn't come across the field at top speed, with the horn honking?

Now, she seemed to be settling into herself, as if she'd been traveling outside her body.

Her skin felt clammy when Logan took her hand. He was tempted to carry her into the house, the way he had when she was wearing those teetery shoes, but she wouldn't want the fuss. She'd bristle, he knew, and tell him to keep his hands to himself, that she could walk just fine on her own, thank you very much.

So he stood back.

Led the way through the front door, on into the kitchen.

Once inside, Alec and Josh scuffled over the shared cell phone; Alec got it and ran, slamming out the back door into the yard. Josh didn't give chase, but sat down hard on the floor and wrapped a consoling arm around Wanda. She nuzzled him and licked his face. Sidekick and Snooks, completing the picture, were curled up on the old rug in front of the stove.

Logan ignored the boys and the dogs, and eased Briana into a chair at the table. What did you give a person who'd just had a close call with a bear? He'd have wanted a stiff shot of whiskey—did want one, in fact—but the female mind worked differently.

Tea, he thought.

Trouble was, he didn't have any on hand.

So he started a pot of coffee.

"Thank you," Briana said, like someone just hauled up out of a very deep, very dark well.

"Alec took the cell phone," Josh complained. "Bet he calls Dad."

Briana looked at the boy, nodded. "Bet he does," she agreed. She still didn't sound like herself, but her color was coming back. "Take Wanda outside," she told Josh. "If you don't, she'll be afraid to leave the house from now on."

Josh nodded, and half dragged poor Wanda to the door, out onto the porch.

Logan was still fiddling with the coffeepot.

Snooks and Sidekick followed Wanda's trail to the door, and he let them out.

"Vance will come," Briana said, in the same musing tone she might have used to remark on some small, subtle change in an otherwise familiar landscape. "For the boys, I mean."

Logan paused in the act of getting out the two coffee cups he owned. "Is that all right with you?"

Briana didn't shrug, but it was as if she had. "He's their father," she said. "He has rights."

Logan imagined Briana, the two boys and the dog stranded outside Wal-Mart in a strange town, with no money and nowhere to go. Saw all of them, watching Vance's taillights disappear into the night. He wished he'd been there, instead of Dylan.

Which was just plain useless thinking, and probably wouldn't have made a difference, anyhow. Two years ago, when Briana had been dumped, he'd still been trying to make it work with Laurie.

"Yeah," he said, with gravel in his voice. "He has rights."

"Can I stay?" Briana asked.

It was a moment before Logan registered what she'd said. "Stay?" he echoed.

"Here. With you. Just for tonight."

He crossed to her, crouched in front of her chair, took her hands. "You're pretty shook up right now," he told her. "Not thinking straight."

She laughed, even as tears filled her eyes.

"I was so scared," she said. And she leaned forward, and let her head rest on his shoulder, and Logan knew, sure as his dear old dad would have voted for a yellow dog before casting his ballot for a Republican, that Briana Grant was different from any other woman he'd ever known.

He patted her back. His knees were cramping up, but he was damned if he'd move. "I know," he said. "And that just shows you have good sense."

"I actually *grinned* at that bear," she confessed, the words cracking a little, muffled by his shirt and his shoulder.

Logan chuckled at the image, but it was a raw, shaky sound. He'd been scared, too. More scared than he would admit. "It's over," he reminded her—and himself. "It's over and you're okay."

She lifted her head off his shoulder, looked down into his face. Shook her head. "I'm not okay," she said. "I was strong before, and I'll be strong again, but right now, I need—"

Logan stood. "You don't know what you need, Briana," he said, because he had to put some distance between them, both verbally and physically. If the boys hadn't been right outside, he might have taken her straight to his bed. "You're in shock."

"Maybe so," she agreed, watching him as he retreated to the coffeepot. After that, she lapsed into a silence.

The boys came back in, bringing the dogs with them, and Logan made sandwiches, poured kibble into bowls. Set a mug of hot coffee in front of Briana.

Vance and Heather arrived, summoned via cell phone by Alec, as Josh had predicted. They only stayed a few minutes, then shooed the boys to the van and drove off, as hurriedly as if they expected that bear to track those kids right to Logan's kitchen and chew the flesh off their bones.

"May I stay?" Briana asked again, as soon as they were gone.

"Yes," Logan said. He did take her to his bed then, but it was different than he'd imagined. He straightened the covers, laid her down, pulled her shoes off and covered her with the bedspread.

She looked up at him, confused.

Wanda padded in, and he hoisted the dog onto the bed.

Woman. Dog.

No room for him.

"Rest awhile," he told her.

She closed her eyes.

He left the room, nearly tripping over Snooks and Sidekick in the doorway. Shut the door.

In the hallway, he shoved a hand through his hair.

He wanted Briana Grant. She was vulnerable right now, and that was exactly why he was taking his horny self back to the kitchen until she'd rested up a little, gotten over the whole bear incident.

Of course, it was more than the bear. Logan knew that. She was still reeling from Alec's accident the night before. There was only so much one woman could take without buckling under the strain.

So, he went back to the kitchen. Got out the *Our Family* album and looked at all the pictures again.

He looked at Jake.

He looked at his mother.

He looked at himself as a baby.

He ate another sandwich, and made one for Briana, in case she woke up hungry.

Twilight came, and hc went outside to feed the horses, taking the dogs with him.

When he got back, Briana was sitting at the kitchen table, wearing one of his T-shirts and eating the sandwich he'd built for her earlier. She'd showered and unwound her hair from its braid, and it burned like golden fire around her face and shoulders, tumbled down her back, nearly to her waist.

Logan's heart stopped, started again.

He stood clogging up the doorway, him and the dogs, unable to move.

Briana nodded to the album, still open on the table. Idly gave Wanda a corner of her sandwich as she spoke. "Is that you in those pictures?" she asked, as though it were a normal thing for her to be sitting in his kitchen, practically naked, with her hair loose and shiny and damp.

What would it smell like, all that hair? What would it feel like, flowing between his fingers?

"Some of them," he said, and he didn't sound like himself. But he did move out of the doorway, mainly because the dogs were pushing at him from behind, wanting in.

"If you don't want to make love to me," Briana said, "I'll understand."

"Oh, I want to make love to you," Logan answered, "but since I'm pretty sure you're not in your right mind, I probably won't."

She just looked at him, one eyebrow slightly raised.

He thought of the high-heeled shoes she'd worn the day before, and the short, gossamer sundress.

Maybe there *was* another side to Briana Grant.

"You think I'm still in shock," she said.

"Aren't you?"

"No," she answered.

"Until I'm absolutely sure of that," he said, after drumming up all the resolution he could, "I'm not touching you."

"Fair enough," she replied. She yawned, picked up her sandwich plate, carried it to the sink. Then she sashayed out of the kitchen, on into the living room.

When he worked up the nerve to follow, he found her in his bed, curled up on her side, sound asleep.

He took a shower, changed clothes.

Checked on Briana again.

Then he went back to the living room, checked his e-mail, surfed the Net for a while. He ate another sandwich, and after that, he couldn't think of anything else to keep himself busy.

So he found a blanket and stretched out on the couch.

Jake came to him as soon as he closed his eyes.

Are you crazy, boy? There's a warm and willing woman in your bed, and you're on the damned couch?

I'm not you, Dad, Logan answered silently. Jake

seemed so real, so present, that Logan thought he'd see him if he opened his eyes.

So he didn't.

You're damn right you're not me. I knew enough to take my pleasure where I found it—especially when it was right under my nose.

Logan shifted onto his side, with his back to the room. To his dead father. *Yeah, you did. And I'm trying to live that down, not follow in your footsteps. Go away.*

Something stirred the air.

Logan turned over, opened his eyes.

It wasn't Jake standing there; it was Briana.

Without a word, she crawled under the blanket with him, snuggled close.

"Hold me," she said.

Logan put his arms around her. Kissed the top of her head. "I'm here," he told her. "I'm here."

She nodded against his chest, bunching her fingers in the front of his shirt, and went back to sleep.

Eventually, he slept, too.

And when he woke up the next morning, she was still cuddled up close.

CHAPTER TWELVE

BEFORE SHE DARED to open her eyes, Briana let her mind race through the events that had brought her to that moment, pressed against Logan Creed on a narrow couch. The frustrating discussion with Heather, the then-disturbing encounter with Brett Turlow in the casino parking lot. Finding the door open at home, and Wanda gone. Wandering into the orchard. The bear. The oddly calm terror she'd felt. Logan's truck bumping and bucking over rough ground, wending between trees, horn blaring. And then…blessed safety, sanctuary in the ranch house that had stood empty for so long.

Her fingers were still knotted in the front of his shirt.

And he had a serious erection.

Was he awake?

She forced herself to look.

He was, dark eyes solemn. And smoldering.

She should get up off that couch, she told herself silently. Find her clothes, put them on and hightail it out of there, on foot if necessary.

On foot? She'd risk running into the bear again if she walked home, and, anyway, she couldn't expect Wanda to make that hike, bear or no bear.

Dylan's truck was still where she'd parked it the day before—next to the clothesline at the other place.

Briana gave a languid stretch, heard Logan groan under his breath. His erection, already hard and hot against her, searing through the only thing she was wearing—a T-shirt—grew harder still, and hotter.

The night before, he'd refused to make love to her. Said she wasn't in her "right mind," whatever that meant. Well, this morning she was, and she wanted him, if only this once, hurriedly, the two of them fumbling on his couch, like a pair of teenage lovers left unsupervised.

Her body was already expanding, warm and achy, to receive him.

She wasn't using birth control—there'd been no reason to—and even if Logan happened to have condoms on hand, she knew by his breathing, by the hard tension and the heat, that he might not take the time to find one and put it on.

But she was tired of the constant self-denial, and the need ran deep, a canyon in the center of her being, yawning and dangerous.

So she found his mouth with hers, and kissed him.

He held back at first, but then gave in.

Their tongues tangled, Logan shifted, and she was beneath him, squirming, arching her back. It wasn't yet dawn; they were blanketed in shadows, alone. Somewhere nearby, a clock ticked, marking off seconds like heartbeats.

Logan pulled back breathlessly. She saw his face clearly—there must have been a lamp burning, or maybe it was moonlight—and saw the reluctance and a need to match her own.

He didn't ask the question; she glimpsed it in his eyes.

Are you sure?

She nodded. Even then, with no foreplay save that horizon-bending kiss, she was on the brink of shattering. She wanted him inside her, filling her.

He moaned her name.

She wriggled beneath him.

He shifted, tugged the T-shirt up and off, over her head. Tossed it away.

She slid her hands up under *his* T-shirt, splayed her fingers across his solid, warm chest. Smooth. It was smooth, his chest. His nipples pressed like hard buttons against the palms of her hands.

He braced himself on either side of her, thrust his head far back with a ragged gasp. "Briana, I don't have—"

"Shh," she murmured.

She found the snap on his jeans, set him free, stroked him with a kind of shameless abandon she'd never felt before.

Logan made a raw, scratchy sound, deep in his throat, and allowed her to plunder him for several long, stretched-to-the-snapping-point moments. Then he fell to her, tongued her bare breasts, suckled on them, one and then the other.

Briana gave a low cry of sheer exultation, arching her back, grinding her hips where their bodies met. She parted her legs slightly, felt him settle between them.

And then, like the thrust of some fiery sword, he was inside her, deep, deep inside her.

"Yes!" she cried. *"Yes—"*

Her climax was immediate, as she had known it would be, and all-consuming, sucking the breath from her lungs, electrifying even the tiniest nerves, rippling like a current through every muscle. Even as she surrendered to the storm, as powerless as a bird caught up in a whirlwind, tears welled in her eyes.

It would be over so soon.

But it wasn't. She'd barely stopped shuddering, Logan holding himself still inside and above her, when the friction began to build again, more slowly this time.

"Easy," he groaned.

"Oh…my… *God*—" she pleaded, grasping at his shoulders, tossing beneath him. *"Logan—"*

He began to move again, but with excruciating slowness, consummate control. The second climax came several minutes later, more devastating than the first, wringing a long, crooning whine from Briana, but this time, there was no slow descent afterward. The orgasm spiked, and then began to climb.

As Logan increased his pace, Briana was utterly lost. Dazed, blinded, groping and begging senselessly, she practically disintegrated. Logan's own cry of satisfaction was a distant thing, an echo heard under deep water, more vibration than sound.

They strained against each other for what seemed a very long time, slowly coming back to themselves, and then collapsed in a tangle of arms and legs, speechless with exhaustion.

Even when they'd recovered, they didn't talk right away.

What was there to say?

Logan sprawled across Briana, though he'd been careful not to crush her under his full weight.

"Next time," he said, after a long time, "let's use the bed."

She laughed, savoring their closeness, her satiation and his. It would be gone soon enough, that magical, golden feeling of freedom, when reality reasserted itself. "Who says there's going to be a next time?"

He lifted his head, grinned at her. "After that? You've got to be kidding." He kissed her lightly. "Of *course* there's going to be a next time, and a time after that."

Briana felt the truth of her life prodding at the perimeters of her pleasure, looking for a way in. She would hold it at bay as long as she could, stay inside the bubble of contentment until it popped.

Before her befuddled brain came up with an answer for Logan's remark, though, his face contorted and he leaped over her, like a man on fire, hopping on one foot and howling.

Wanda, Sidekick and Snooks all came running, their barking fit to raise the roof.

"Charley horse!" Logan yelled.

And Briana laughed, full out, from the place far inside her, where her true self lived, the woman, the goddess, the unflappable One Who Knew. She laughed until she doubled over, until Logan stopped jumping around and Wanda came to the side of the couch and licked the tears off her face.

LOGAN LIMPED INTO the kitchen, the dogs following, to start the coffee brewing and give Briana a chance to collect herself. Once the java apparatus was in full chortle, he went outside, fed the horses, checked to make sure the water trough in the corral was full.

By the time he got back to the house, the sun was up, and Briana was dressed in her own clothes, frying bacon and eggs at the stove.

Logan had slept with a lot of women in his life, and he'd never been at a loss for words the morning after. This day, he was.

She'd tamed that wild, blazing blond hair of hers into the usual French braid—that part was a pity—but she seemed surrounded by a haze of soft light, as though she didn't quite belong in the ordinary, rough-and-tumble world, but had gone astray from some finer one.

"How's your leg?" she asked.

Logan was momentarily stymied. "My—?" Then he remembered the charley horse. The result of sleeping on the couch, probably, twisted like a snarl of rusty barbed wire, trying to avoid touching Briana and at the same time keep her from falling off onto the floor. "It's fine," he said.

"Are you just going to stand there all day, Logan Creed?" she asked, sounding for all the world like one of the long, long line of women who'd stood in that kitchen, turning the breakfast bacon in a skillet, urging some Creed husband to get moving. "Wash up and set the table. The food is almost ready."

The sweetness of that moment tightened the back of Logan's throat. It would have been so easy to imagine that this was a regular morning, that they were man and wife and her boys would be tromping in at any minute, fresh from their little-kid beds. Even that there might be a baby nearby, in a playpen or one of those cradlelike things that folded up for easy transport.

So easy, and so dangerous.

Logan put kibble out for all three dogs and re-filled their common water dish before washing his hands with soap and water at the sink, drying them on a wad of paper towels and setting plates and silverware on the table.

What now? He wanted to ask her that, and *Where do we go from here?*

But he didn't dare. Things seemed too delicately balanced for that, too fragile. Whatever was insulating the both of them from the real world was as flimsy, and as transparently beautiful, as a butterfly's wing.

Since there were no serving dishes to speak of, Briana shoveled the food onto their plates, straight from the big skillet and the smaller one she'd fried the eggs in.

Sitting down, she stole a glance at the Regulator clock on the wall separating the kitchen from the living room. Six-thirty.

Logan read her mind by reading her face. Her mouth puckered a little, as did her forehead, and then that slight shake of her head.

Too early to call Josh and Alec and find out if they'd survived the overnighter at Vance and Heather's.

"Sooner or later," Logan said, his voice sounding like five miles of dry gravel, "we're going to have to talk about what we just did."

She set her fork down. Frowned. But the pinkish tinge to her cheeks betrayed her. "We had sex."

"We made love."

Even though she didn't actually move, he saw her pull back inside herself, become the regular Briana—the hardworking single mother, barely making it from paycheck to paycheck. "What's the difference?" she asked.

Heat surged up Logan's neck. Was she *trying* to piss him off?

Sure she was.

She needed to throw up a barrier between them.

"What's the difference?" he echoed, determined not to let her pretend nothing had happened between them. Maybe *she* had resurrection sex all the time, but he'd *never* been hurled outside himself like that before. He still felt the jolt.

Briana bit her lower lip, wouldn't look at him.

"And where the hell did you get a name like Briana, anyway?" he sputtered, because, *damn it,* he had to say *something.*

Her green eyes twinkled a little. "Wild Man was quite a reader," she said, and it took Logan a second to make the connection that Wild Man was her dad's rodeo nickname. "He read a story with a character named Briana, and the name took his fancy."

The tension was ebbing, but it was a good-news/bad-news kind of thing. Now, the pretending would start.

Sure, they'd had sex, but they were two consenting adults, weren't they?

No big deal.

A pulsing sorrow welled up in Logan—he might have been onboard the *Titanic,* watching the last of the lifeboats skim away into the frigid Atlantic darkness. "Did your mother agree?"

"I don't know," Briana said. "She died when I was eight."

Logan glanced at the *Our Family* album, still lying on the other side of the table, where he'd left it the night before. Looked back at Briana. "I don't know much about my mother, either," he said. "I had stepmothers, though. They both tried to take up the slack."

Briana studied him. "Stepmothers, plural?"

He nodded, smiled wistfully at the memory of Dylan's mother, Maggie, puttering in this same kitchen, and then Tyler's mother, Angela. "Two of them," he confirmed. "Jake—my dad—seemed to think he could outrun his demons by marrying some good woman and getting her pregnant five minutes after the ceremony." He sighed. "It never worked."

Remember that.

Briana pushed her food around with the prongs of her fork. "Is that why you got married more than once, Logan? To outrun some demon?"

The question stung, striking bare nerves. He wondered briefly who'd told her about his marriages, decided it could have been anybody in Stillwater Springs. For all he knew, he'd told her himself.

"Maybe," he admitted. "Looking back, though, I'd have to say it just seemed like a good idea—*twice*."

She chuckled ruefully at that. "So many things *seem* like good ideas, at the time. When I met Vance, I didn't bother to find out who he was. I created an identity for him—the cowboy prince I'd read about in so many library books—and when that turned out to be false, I tried to change him into what I wanted."

"Good luck with that," Logan said.

"Didn't you want to change your wives? Ever?"

"No. But about six months in, I wouldn't have minded volunteering them both for long-term space flights. Say to Jupiter, or the asteroid belt on the other side of Pluto."

Briana laughed, swatted at his arm. Her touch made his nerves jangle under his flesh.

And then the phone rang.

Somebody had really lousy timing.

Logan sighed, got up and crossed the room. Barked a "Hello" into the receiver.

"Is my mom there?" Alec asked meekly.

Logan bit back the automatic *"Yeah"* that rolled to the tip of his tongue. It wasn't even seven in the morning, and young as Alec was, he might put two and two together, which would not, Logan knew by the look on Briana's face, be a good thing.

"She just stopped by for coffee," he said.

Briana was at his side in an instant; he surrendered the phone.

"Josh? Alec?"

Logan watched her face as she listened. Saw the anxiety drain from her eyes.

"You're fine?" she asked. "Really?" A long pause. "Yes. Yes, I'm going to work." More listening. Briana's gaze touched Logan, ricocheted off immediately. "Yes, I'll remember to charge my cell phone.... Sure, I'll see you tonight—bye."

She moved to hang up the phone, keeping her back to Logan.

"Can we act like this morning didn't happen?" she asked.

"No," he answered, without hesitation.

She turned, her eyes wide and troubled. "It was

wrong," she said. "You've already had to lie once because of it—"

He crossed to her, took her shoulders in a gentle grip. "It *wasn't* wrong, Briana," he said.

"Not for you, maybe," she retorted miserably. "You're a man. It's another notch in your bedpost. A score. For me—"

"What was it for you?" he demanded, loosening his hold on her shoulders but not willing, or able, to let her go. "And don't tell me it was 'just sex,' Briana, because I was *there*."

Color suffused her face. "Okay, so I enjoyed it," she said. "So did you."

For a long moment, they simply stared at each other, neither one knowing what else to say. Then they broke apart.

Briana started to clear the table.

Logan stopped her.

She found her purse and called her dog, he got his keys, and, by tacit agreement, he took her and Wanda home.

THE DOOR WAS open again.

Briana stared. She'd closed it when she went looking for Wanda the day before—she remembered that clearly.

Logan swore under his breath, shut off the truck and got out before she'd unbuckled her seat belt. After lifting Wanda off the backseat, he strode toward the back porch.

A shiver went down Briana's spine. Maybe, she thought, Vance and Heather had stopped by last night, so the boys could get their pajamas or something. In the rush, they'd forgotten to shut the door....

Only Josh wouldn't have done that. He was too security conscious. And Vance and Heather, while not exactly paragons of responsibility, would surely have noticed.

Wanda curled back her lips and growled, crouching a little in the grass.

"Stay here," Logan told Briana, as she got out of the truck.

He disappeared inside.

Briana fumbled for her new cell phone, remembered it needed charging. Tossed it back into her purse and inched toward the door, expecting shouts to erupt at any moment, or sounds of a scuffle—maybe even a gunshot.

"Logan?" she called uncertainly.

Wanda was still growling, still crouched, but apparently not inclined to spring at whomever, or whatever, was inside the house.

Briana was about to wade in, unable to bear the suspense any longer, when Logan reappeared on the porch, shoved a hand through his hair.

"Somebody was here," he said grimly. "But they're gone now."

Briana made her way up the steps, Wanda reluctantly following, almost at a crawl.

Nothing different in the kitchen, the living room, the boys' room, the bath.

But her bedroom...

Standing in the doorway, Briana gasped. And not because Logan, just behind her, laid a hand on her shoulder.

Her flimsiest nightgown—a little pink number Vance had given her one Valentine's Day—was the only thing out of place. It lay neatly in the middle of the bed, almost as if she were inside it.

She put a hand to her mouth.

"Vance?" Logan asked.

Briana shook her head. Vance wasn't capable of this kind of subtlety. No, someone else had rummaged through her bureau drawers, come across that long-forgotten nightgown, then arranged it with creepy, almost reverent care.

Someone who wanted to scare her.

But who—and why?

She flashed on Brett Turlow—she'd been pretty blunt with him, the day before—but it didn't feel right.

One of the men working on the pasture fence? A random passerby?

Briana turned, rested her forehead against Logan's chest, struggling to catch her breath.

He stroked her back with circular motions of one hand, opened his cell phone with the other.

"This is Logan Creed," he said. "I need to talk to Sheriff Book. Now."

"HELL OF A WAY for us to finally get to sit down and talk," Floyd Book told Logan, an hour later, at Briana's kitchen table. She'd talked to Jim on the telephone for a few minutes, then gone to town to get the boys, face still flaming with embarrassment over the nightgown incident as she got into Dylan's truck.

"Hell of a way," Logan agreed, distracted. It gave him the creeps, the way it did Briana, to think of somebody sneaking around in this house, handling her things. Setting up an intimate little tableau for her to find when she came home.

"You still suspect the ex-husband," the sheriff said. He consulted his notes. "Vance Grant."

"Briana ruled him out right away," Logan reminded the other man.

"I didn't ask who *she* suspects."

"The truth is, I don't have any idea."

"Wasn't Brett Turlow," Book said. "I took him home from Skivvie's Tavern myself, and that old Corolla he drives was still in the lot next to the bar every time I checked."

Briana had told both the sheriff and Logan how Turlow had asked her out the day before and she'd turned him down, politely at first, though when he'd made some remark about Jim, she'd cut him off at the knees.

And the sheriff had already recounted giving Turlow a ride from Skivvie's, and cruising past to make sure the Corolla hadn't gone anywhere.

They were running in circles.

"Chances are," Book said, "it was kids. Briana is a fine-looking woman, and she'd sure fuel a teenager's fantasies. Probably, some goof-off dared another one, and things just got out of hand."

"That's a nice theory, Sheriff," Logan said. "But suppose it's more serious than that?"

Book let out a long sigh. "You mean like a stalker? You've been living in the big city too long, Logan. This is Stillwater Springs, not Vegas."

"How did you know I was in Vegas?"

"Pull in your horns, boy. *Everybody* knows you

got hooked on the bright lights in your rodeo days, and went back there after you got out of the service."

Book grinned at the look of surprise on Logan's face. "My question is, how come you're driving that old truck out there, living and dressing like a ranch hand, when you founded a company that just sold for close to twenty million dollars?"

Logan didn't answer.

"Thought I didn't know that part?" Book asked. "I've been in law enforcement for a long time."

"What are you getting at, Floyd?"

"I'm just wondering," the older man said slowly, his eyes keen, "if maybe you came back here because you still think Brett Turlow dropped all those logs on your daddy on purpose. Man might keep a low financial profile, so as not to draw attention to himself, if he was looking to right an old wrong. The trouble with that idea is, soon as you crossed the county line, everybody knew."

"You think I came back to Stillwater Springs to get back at Turlow?"

"Did you?"

"Hell, no."

"Then why, Logan? Do you see Dylan hanging around? Tyler? No. Because they've got better things to do, in better places. And so do you." He paused. "Unless—"

"Unless what?"

"You were just passing through, and Briana Grant happened to catch your eye."

Logan narrowed his eyes. "Are you working your way around to accusing *me* of prowling around in this house, fingering Briana's lingerie?"

"If you're fingering her lingerie," the sheriff said, "it's your own business. And unless you've lost that famous Creed touch, you don't have to 'prowl around' to do it." Floyd took a noisy sip of his coffee. "I will be leaving office soon," he went on, when he was damned good and ready, "and I've got a perfect record, at least on paper. You know as well as I do that I always thought Brett Turlow cut that logging chain deliberately, but I could never prove it. I hate to let that go, but I can do it. Take my pension check, turn in my badge and call it good. What I cannot—and *will not*—ignore, is you taking the law into your own hands."

"Here's what *I* think, Sheriff," Logan said. "Brett Turlow didn't have the guts to cut that chain, even after he found out his girlfriend had been getting it on with Jake. He might have wanted to dance on the old man's grave after the fact, but to actually kill somebody? No way."

"Maybe it *was* an accident," the sheriff mused. "It would be a relief to know that."

Logan relented a little; he knew it was the sheriff's job to question his reasons for coming back to Stillwater Springs. And while he probably wouldn't have spit on Brett Turlow if he was on fire—well, maybe then—he had no intention of "taking the law into his own hands," as Floyd had put it. Even though he didn't practice, he was still a member of the bar, sworn to uphold the law, not break it.

"You ever consider running for my job?" Book asked cagily, a few moments later.

"I don't need a job, remember?" Logan replied. "And even if I did, I sure as hell wouldn't want yours."

Floyd laughed. "And you're Jim Huntinghorse's

best friend, at that. It would be awkward, running against him."

Logan thought fleetingly of Cassie's warning, that he was in danger and, through him, Briana and the boys might be, too. She'd asked him specifically not to get involved in the election, one way or the other.

"Jim's a good man."

"He is," Floyd agreed. "Always liked him. But there's already talk about how he'd look after the tribe first and the white folks in this county second, if not third."

"That's bullshit," Logan said.

"The bigots, like the poor, are always with us," Floyd reminded him. "And bigots vote—more often than other folks, probably." With that, Floyd picked up his hat, rose wearily out of his chair. Bent to pat Wanda on the head before going to the door. "If you say you didn't come back here to even the score with Brett Turlow," he said in parting, "then I believe you. Just don't prove me wrong, Logan. That's all I'm saying."

Logan nodded, not in agreement but to show he'd gotten the message. He *hadn't* come back to Stillwater Springs to avenge Jake's death—had he?

He rose, followed the sheriff outside, watched as his old friend and the nemesis of his younger years got into the squad car, ground the ignition and drove off.

It seemed strange, being at Briana's without her or the boys there, but he wasn't inclined to leave, either. He wished whoever had been creeping around the house later would come back so he could confront them, but since his truck was parked outside, in plain sight, he didn't think it was very likely.

"Just you and me," he said to the dog.

The wall phone rang, and he answered it automatically. "Logan Creed," he said.

No answer, except for some raspy breathing and then a quick hang-up.

Frowning, Logan punched star-sixty-nine, then realized it wouldn't work. Briana's phone system was as antiquated as the one at his place.

"Hello?" he barked, even though he knew there wouldn't be a response, beyond the frustrating dial tone droning in his ear. As the caller had, he hung up hard.

Wanda gave a concerned little whimper, head upturned, searching his face with those luminous brown eyes of hers. There was a problem, that much was obvious, and she needed reassurance.

"I know, girl," he told her. "I know."

The dog lumbered over to her bed and dropped onto it with a sigh.

"We need a plan."

Wanda sighed again.

Logan turned one of the kitchen chairs around backward, and sat astraddle of it. Rested his chin on his folded arms and narrowed his eyes.

Yep, they needed a plan.

And one was already taking shape in his head.

CHAPTER THIRTEEN

"THAT'S CRAZY!" BRIANA SAID, after she'd herded Alec and Josh into the kitchen and Logan had explained what he wanted to do. "Switch houses?"

She saw a muscle bunch in Logan's jaw. He needed a shave, but the effect was sexy as hell, and visceral recollections of their lovemaking rocketed unchecked through her entire body.

"Think about it," he said, keeping his voice low even though the boys were already in the living room, tumbling around with an elated Wanda. Alec's cast didn't seem to slow him down much, and all the excitement over the bear had pitched his energy into the frenetic zone. "You and the boys go stay at my place. We trade cars. Whoever laid your...lingerie...out on the bed sneaks in, and comes face-to-face with me instead of you." He threw up both hands. "Surprise!"

Briana started, reminded of the bear in the orchard, set her purse down on the counter with a distracted swing of one arm. "That's all fine—in theory," she replied, though the idea tingled along her spinal column. "Except that this...*person,* whoever they are, obviously chose a time when I wasn't around to come in here. What makes you think they'd try it again with my car parked outside?"

Logan laid his hands on her shoulders, and she

loved the weight and strength of them. Tried hard not to think the ways he'd used those hands to drive her crazy on his couch. "Things like this tend to escalate," he said. "This is a campaign, and it was only the opening shot."

Briana let out a long sigh, pushed her bangs back from her forehead, stepped away from Logan in the vain hope that the charge would stop arching back and forth between them like St. Elmo's fire. "You're probably right," she admitted. "But shouldn't we let Sheriff Book handle it?"

Logan's mouth contorted into a brief semblance of a grin, entirely void of amusement. "Sheriff Book thinks we're dealing with kids—that it was a one-time prank. And he's just marking time until his retirement, anyway."

"I can picture teenage boys doing something like this," Briana mused, but she wasn't convinced, and she knew Logan wasn't, either.

"So can I," Logan agreed. "And I wish my gut agreed with that scenario, but it doesn't. This is no prank, Briana. This is someone with an agenda. We have to do something besides wait for the next incident."

Briana dragged back a chair at the table, sank into it, suddenly weary.

"Has anything like this ever happened before?" Logan asked, turning another chair backward and sitting astride it. Was he *deliberately* pushing her buttons? If her sons hadn't been in the next room, Briana would have jumped his bones, right there in the kitchen. "Here in Stillwater Springs or elsewhere?"

Briana shook her head, trying to clear it. *Has any-*

thing like this ever happened before? He meant had anyone ever come into her house and gone through her most private belongings before, she knew that, but a big part of her wanted to answer, *"No. I've never wanted a man the way I want you."*

"Briana?" Logan prompted, his voice a low and inherently masculine rumble. If he touched her in any way, even to take her hand, she was done for, destined to melt into a quivering puddle of protoplasmic femininity.

He took her hand.

Briana drew in a sharp breath. "No," she managed to respond, feeling slow color climb her face.

Logan noticed, of course, and the slightest smile tilted a corner of his mouth. "And you're convinced it wasn't Vance?" He drawled the words, leaned in a little, as if he might nibble at her earlobe or trace the length of her neck with the lightest pass of his lips.

Briana gulped, fluttered one hand in front of her face. "Do you think it's warm in here?" she fretted.

Logan's grin flickered again. "Hotter than a two-bit pistol, as my dad used to say," he replied. "Stick with the subject at hand, will you? Who might want to rattle your cage a little, besides Brett Turlow or Vance? Some guy who hit on you at the casino, maybe?"

"Stop touching me," Briana said. "I can't concentrate."

He withdrew his hand from hers, but not before running the tips of his fingers along the underside of her wrist.

Another tremor snaked its way through her.

"Lots of guys hit on me at the casino," she said. "But so far, they've all taken no for an answer."

"Until Brett Turlow?"

"He seemed upset when I turned him down," she answered slowly, "but there's no reason to think he did anything about it. Especially since Sheriff Book gave him an alibi."

"Okay." Logan sighed the word. "As soon as it's dark, we switch houses and rigs and hope this yahoo makes a move."

Briana didn't think the idea would work, for a variety of reasons, but she *was* nervous about staying alone in that house, with the boys. Suppose the stalker, or whatever, did come back, and Alec and Josh were frightened out of their wits or even hurt? And, anyway, she didn't have a better plan to offer.

"I don't like it," she said, just the same.

Logan raised an eyebrow. "I don't like it, either," he replied, with exaggerated patience. "I'd much rather share your bed—or mine—but that isn't going to happen with the kids around."

"No," Briana said. It was amazing. She'd gotten along without sex all this time—hadn't really even had an opportunity to miss it—but now that she and Logan had done the deed, she was jonesing for more. Physically, she'd gone from a standstill to warp speed, and it was scary.

Logan stood, somewhat reluctantly, Briana thought. Shoved a hand through his hair. "I'd better go now," he said. "I'll be back after dark."

Briana merely nodded.

Logan bent, kissed the top of her head, patted her shoulder. She felt hesitation in that hand, knew he wanted to cup her breast but wouldn't. "There's one more thing," he added, in a whisper. "After you and the boys leave for my place, I'm going to hang that nightgown on your clothesline."

Briana twisted in her chair, looked up at him in consternation. "What? *Why?*"

"Trust me," Logan said. "I want to get this guy's attention. Make him think *you* want to get to know him better."

A violent shudder, revulsion mixed with fear, shook Briana to the core. "But I *don't*—"

"It might smoke him out." He sounded rueful, but determined.

Briana swallowed again, nodded again.

"Lock up behind me."

And, having given that order, Logan left.

Briana went and turned the dead bolt, then dropped back into her chair, her knees twitchy and weak.

Two seconds later, Alec appeared in the living room doorway. "Logan's gone?" he asked, his freckled face projecting his disappointment. "He didn't even say goodbye."

"He'll be back," Briana said.

Alec punched the air with his good arm and cheered. "Excellent!"

"You like Logan?" she asked cautiously. She hadn't told the boys about the nightgown incident and didn't intend to, nor had she mentioned it to Heather when she picked her sons up at the trailer. Some kind of explanation would be required when they traded spaces with Logan that night, but she was darned if she knew what it would be.

"He's great," Alec decreed. "Dad says he's on the prowl, though. What does that mean?"

Good old Vance. Always ready to confuse an issue.

"It's just a figure of speech," Briana said, in what she hoped was a light tone. "Nothing you need to worry about."

"Logan said we could name all his horses," Josh put in, pushing his way past Alec and making a bee-line for the refrigerator. "What's for supper?"

"Leftovers," Briana answered. Was it suppertime already? She'd lived a lifetime since morning.

"You get to name two, and I get to name two," Alec reminded his brother archly. "I'm calling the buck-skin Trigger and the gray Traveler."

"That's dumb," Josh argued. "Both those names start with a *T*."

"So what?" Alec shot back. Most kids wouldn't have associated Trigger with Roy Rogers, or a gray with Robert E. Lee's horse. Both people and horses had been well before their time, but hers were home-schooled, and the curriculum had been eclectic, to say the least.

"Stop bickering," Briana said. "You're giving me a headache."

"The guilt ploy," Josh said triumphantly. "Dirty pool, Mom."

In spite of the headache, her jangling nerves and an almost overwhelming need to go to bed with Logan Creed again, and the sooner the better, Briana chuck-led. Public school might turn out to be a good idea after all, she reflected. Keep the boys focused on read-ing, writing and arithmetic, and cool it with the pop psychology.

The guilt ploy? It was like living with two minia-ture Dr. Phils.

LOGAN TOOK CARE not to arrive at Briana's until well after the sun went down. He parked the Dodge behind the house and quietly unloaded Snooks and Sidekick, along with his shaving gear and a change of clothes stuffed into a grocery bag. He wondered if the freak was hiding in the trees, watching him, but his insides said no.

And he'd learned, in Iraq if not before, to trust his elemental instincts.

He rapped lightly at Briana's back door, wishing the whole scenario were different—that they would have supper together, maybe share a bottle of wine, then make love again, this time in a real bed. The boys were conveniently absent from the fantasy.

She opened the door to him, looking worried and a little pale. "I told Alec and Josh that a plumber was coming to fix something in the bathroom tomorrow," she whispered, like a spy imparting critical information to a colleague in the middle of some spooky bridge. "And that you're going to keep an eye on things. Did I mention that I *hate* lying to my children?"

"No," Logan replied, easing past her into the kitchen. "But I could have guessed it."

Wanda greeted Sidekick and Snooks with a few friendly sniffs.

Hearing Logan's voice, Alec and Josh immediately zoomed in from the living room, each lugging a backpack.

"This is cool," Josh said.

"Can we feed the horses?" Alec asked.

"Already fed them," Logan said.

Alec looked crestfallen. "Oh."

"But you can help me out as often as your mom allows," Logan was quick to add.

"Good save," Briana murmured.

"It's what I do best," Logan told her. "Or one of the things I do best, anyway."

She blushed. He'd couched a message in those words, and he saw that she'd gotten it.

"Here," she said, shoving a crumpled paper bag at him. He looked, saw the skimpy nightgown inside. The thing would cover about the same amount of territory as four squares of toilet paper, strategically aligned.

The leaving process was a jumble of confusion, which was probably for the best. Logan helped Wanda into his truck, and Briana gave Alec a boost, though he didn't appear to need one.

Logan stood on the running board, after Briana was behind the wheel, and leaned through the open window to plant a light kiss on her mouth.

Alec and Josh, having witnessed the exchange from the backseat, groaned in loud, prepubescent disgust, then made smooching sounds.

Briana ignored them, her eyes wide and serious and green as a tree-shaded pond as she looked into Logan's face. "Be careful," she said.

"Always," he said. He wanted to kiss her again, and mean business this time, but he didn't intend to set the kids off on another round of groaning and smacking.

She nodded, swallowed visibly.

He stepped down and back, watched as she ground the truck into gear and nearly wiped out one of the clothesline poles turning the rig around.

When she rounded the first bend, and the taillights

winked out of sight, Logan pulled the nightgown out of the paper bag and held it up between two fingers.

Briana must have worn it for Vance—or for some guy in between then and now. He was careful not to let *that* train of thought pull out of the station.

He draped the garment over the clothesline and secured it with a wooden pin. Then he turned, Snooks and Sidekick watching him from the back porch, and surveyed the surrounding trees.

Okay, punk, he thought. *Bring it on.*

LOGAN HAD LEFT sleeping bags out for the boys, on a wide air mattress in front of the living room fireplace, and the bed where he'd taken Briana after her meltdown over the bear sported crisp white sheets. Logan had turned the covers back enticingly, and there were flowers in a Mason jar on the nightstand.

All the comforts of home, Briana thought.

Except that Logan was missing, it looked perfect, in a homey, ranch-house sort of way.

She turned from the scene and almost stumbled over Wanda, who had padded up behind her without making a sound.

In the living room, the boys were arguing over what to name Logan's horses.

Briana wandered in that direction, nervous and at loose ends. Sleeping in Logan's bed was over-the-top, but the only alternative seemed to be the couch, and she wasn't going there.

"Quiet," she told her sons, more out of habit than any hope that they'd actually stop bickering for a few minutes.

Josh had gravitated to Logan's computer, fascinated by its multiple monitors, three printers and various electronic gizmos.

"It's on," he said, wriggling the wireless mouse a little. "Booted up and everything."

Briana knew where this was going, and put on the brakes immediately. "No," she said. "You may not use Logan's computer. It's private—and it's expensive."

"I don't think he'd mind," Josh persisted.

"And I don't think I was born yesterday," Briana countered. "Hands off, Josh. I mean it."

The boy's shoulders sagged a little. "Do you think we'll ever have a computer like this one?"

His tone was so forlorn that Briana went to him, laid a hand on top of his head. "I think you'll have all the things you really want," she said gently. "You don't have to be poor just because I am. You can go to college, get a great job—"

Josh's eyes were sad as he looked up at her. "I'll take care of you, Mom," he said, so earnestly that Briana's heart cracked and split right down the middle. "When I'm big, and I've been to college, I'll take care of you."

Briana hugged him, closed her eyes tightly, felt the tears seep through anyway. "I'll be fine," she insisted, after clearing her throat. "You won't have to take care of me, sweetie."

"But I want to," Josh said.

"I want to more than Josh does," Alec interjected. "I'll buy you a nice house and a horse of your own and pay off all your bills. You won't even have to go to that stupid casino anymore."

Briana blinked rapidly, sniffled and swiped the back of one hand across her eyes. "How about we table this discussion until you're both out of college and pulling down the big bucks?"

Josh agreed soberly.

Alec beamed, but dejection soon replaced the happy smile. "Logan," he said, his tone solemn, "doesn't have a *TV.*"

"Terrible!" Briana mocked, grinning moistly at her younger son. "Now we'll have to do something dreadfully old-fashioned, like *talk to each other!*"

"What are we going to talk about?" Josh asked.

"College?" Briana suggested.

"Too far in the future," Josh said, with a decisive shake of his head.

She forced herself to sit down on the couch, however gingerly. Then she patted the cushions on either side, and the boys joined her.

"Do you like visiting your dad and Heather?" she asked.

"It's okay," Josh said, typically taciturn.

"Heather lets us stay up later than you do," Alec volunteered, shifting his bulky cast. His eyes widened. "She didn't mean to hit me with the van, Mom."

"I know," Briana said, hugging him close for a moment, which was about all he would tolerate. The footed-pajama, teddy-bear, *Goodnight Moon* days, when it was okay to cuddle, were behind them now, a fact that never failed to sadden her, when she let herself think about it.

"Did you quit your job at the casino?" Josh asked. "You didn't go to work today."

Briana sighed. "No. After Alec broke his arm, I just decided to take some time off, that's all."

"Can we afford it?" This from Josh, the man of

the family. Little Atlas, balancing the world on his young shoulders.

"Not really," Briana answered, because she'd already lied to them about the reason they were staying at Logan's place that night, and she didn't want to compound that. When she *did* fib to Alec and Josh, she did so by omission, rather than putting a whopper into words. "But we'll be all right, like we always are, so I don't want you to worry."

"I like talking," Alec said.

"It's nice," Briana agreed.

"If Dad got married again," Alec continued, "why can't you?"

As many times as her smart boys pulled the rug out from under her, Briana was always surprised. "I guess I could," she said, after a few moments of thought. "But I don't know any potential husbands."

"You know Logan," Alec reasoned.

"He's too poor to buy a TV," Josh pointed out.

Briana laughed. Squeezed them both to her sides.

"No, he's not," Alec retorted, leaning around Briana to stare down his brother. "Look at that *computer,* doofus."

"No names," Briana said.

"If you married Logan, you could have babies," Alec said. "Heather wants to have a baby, but Dad said he's got his hands full with the ones he's already got."

Inwardly, Briana seethed. Vance had his hands full? Until a few days ago, he'd been perennially behind on his child support, and his communications with the boys had amounted to an occasional phone call—collect, as often as not—or a scrawled postcard.

Outwardly, though, she smiled. She had a bone to

pick with Vance and pick it she would, when she could get him alone, but Alec and Josh didn't.

"Babies are a lot of responsibility," she said moderately. The subject—and the couch she was sitting on—reminded her that she needed to get on birth-control pills, asap. She wasn't foolish enough to think what had happened that morning wouldn't happen again—or that she could get by with it for any length of time.

"Can we light a fire in the fireplace?" Josh inquired.

There was kindling in the grate, and crumpled newspapers, and a pile of logs rested next to the hearth. "It's kind of a warm night," Briana observed, wondering if Logan had laid the fire, the way he'd made the bed and turned back the covers.

"We could pretend we were camping," Alec said hopefully.

"Okay," Briana said, because she'd had to refuse them so many things in their short lives, and this was something she could say yes to.

They moved the air mattress and sleeping bags back, away from the fireplace, and Briana crouched to strike a match to the kindling. Soon, a happy blaze danced along the kindling, and she added a small log before putting the screen in place again and standing back to admire her handiwork.

When she turned around, Alec and Josh were in their sleeping bags, with Wanda ensconced between them on the air mattress. Chins cupped in their hands, they watched the flames.

"I like it here," Alec said, yawning.

"Me, too," Josh added.

Within fifteen minutes, they were sound asleep.

Briana got a library book out of her overnight bag, read for half an hour and then started to yawn herself. After checking to make sure the front and back doors were locked, she banked the fire and headed for Logan's bedroom.

In the adjoining bathroom, with its huge claw-foot tub and pedestal sink, she brushed her teeth, washed her face and successfully resisted an unbecoming urge to snoop in the medicine cabinet.

You could tell a lot about a person by what they kept in a medicine cabinet.

A variety of over-the-counter cold remedies and painkillers? Hypochondriac.

Prescription drugs from more than one doctor? Pill addict.

Colored or—God forbid—*flavored* condoms? Player.

Stalwartly, Briana turned her back on the cabinet and walked away.

Sleeping in Logan Creed's bed would be challenge enough, without scouting out his medicine cabinet.

SNOOKS AND SIDEKICK had long since passed out on the dog bed in the corner of the kitchen, leaving Logan to sit alone in the dark, trying to profile whomever had trespassed in Briana's house.

A little after midnight, he faced facts. His plan was a bust.

He wasn't exactly comfortable with the idea of sleeping on Briana's bed, but on the off chance the pervert showed up after all, that was where he'd head.

So Logan went in there, sat down on the edge of the mattress and kicked off his boots. Then he lay down.

The pillowcases smelled like Briana—flowery, with a touch of spice.

Logan turned onto one side, punched the pillows a couple of times, then turned onto the *other* side. That morning, he'd awakened with Briana, the two of them pressed together on the narrow couch in his living room. *Tomorrow* morning, he'd probably wake up with Snooks standing on his chest, licking his nose.

Lying there in moon-washed darkness, he thought about the gossamer nightgown, and the prowler, and Sheriff Book's admonition about taking the law into his own hands.

Logan hadn't come back to Stillwater Springs looking for trouble, but he didn't mean to shrink from it, either. That wasn't the Creed way. If Brett Turlow, or anybody else, came creeping around Briana, Logan would do whatever needed doing, including ass-kicking.

He closed his eyes, convinced he wouldn't sleep.

When the noise awakened him, he thought he'd dreamed it at first.

A glance at Briana's bedside clock told him it was after three.

Something thumped, out in the kitchen.

Sidekick—or possibly Snooks—gave a low, barely audible growl.

Logan frowned and sat up, making as little noise as he could.

Looking down, he saw two canine noses sticking out from under the bed.

A second thump sounded, and somebody muttered a raspy curse.

Logan stood, glad he wasn't wearing his boots, and soft-footed it out of the bedroom and into the hallway.

The corridor was pitch-dark, but he saw a shadow moving in the kitchen, and a weird, hot-damn kind of thrill raced through him. Adrenaline pumped.

Damned if the pervert hadn't taken the bait.

Logan inched closer, squinting, but all he saw was a man-shape, groping around in the kitchen, neatly skirting the shaft of moonlight coming in through the windows over the sink.

It never occurred to Logan that the intruder might be armed—he simply went after him, bare-knuckled, pounced on him and knocked him to the floor.

"What the fuck?" the prowler rasped.

A head of golden hair glinted in the light of the moon.

"Shit," Logan said, slowly removing his hands from the other man's throat.

Dylan sat up. *"Logan?"*

Logan stood, fumbled for a light switch and watched as Dylan got to his feet.

"What the hell are you doing here?" Dylan demanded, his blue eyes snapping with fury.

"I might ask the same question," Logan countered, folding his arms.

"I couldn't get a room in town," Dylan said, recovering his hat from the floor and slapping it once against his right leg. "I called Briana, but nobody answered, so I came out here hoping to sleep on the couch."

"And you're here—at Stillwater Springs, I mean—because…?"

"Because I damn well felt like it, that's why," Dylan growled. "I wasn't expecting a hundred and ninety pounds of cowboy to land on me out of nowhere, that's for sure."

Logan grinned, but he knew there wasn't much warmth in the expression. "And Briana probably wasn't expecting to find you snoring on her couch in the morning, either."

"I left a message," Dylan reminded him, hanging his hat on the peg next to the door like he—well—owned the place. He cocked his head toward the wall phone.

"Obviously, she didn't get that message," Logan said evenly. "Damn it, Dylan, you can't just go letting yourself into people's houses in the middle of the night. Some of them would shoot first and ask questions later."

Dylan spared him a slightly sour grin. "Or maybe just slam the poor bastard to the floor and try to choke him." His blue eyes, always full of the devil, narrowed a little. "Where is Briana, anyhow? And why are you here?"

Logan went to the cupboard, found a can of coffee and busied himself brewing a pot. "It's a long story," he said.

"I'm listening," Dylan replied, helping himself to a chair at the table. "Is there anything to eat?"

"No," Logan said.

"Okay. Just asking."

Snooks and Sidekick came slinking out of the hallway and approached Dylan, who greeted them with easy affection. Animals liked Dylan, and so did women and kids.

Logan started to feel downright territorial. Grudgingly, he opened Briana's fridge, found a carton of pansy-assed yogurt in a container the size of a shot glass and flung it at Dylan.

"Gee," Dylan said, catching the toss. "Thanks."

"You're hungry? Eat."

"You are really defensive, considering that this is my damned house and not yours."

"It's Briana's house," Logan said.

"Is this why you wanted me to come back to the ranch? So you could bite my head off?" Dylan asked affably. He got up, rooted through drawers until he found a spoon and tucked into the yogurt.

"Who said I wanted you to come back?"

Dylan stood leaning against a counter. Between bites of yogurt, he answered, "I don't hear a word from you for five years, and then all of a sudden you're calling me to tell me my bull is a menace and you're putting up fences. Why else would you do that if you weren't trying to provoke me into coming home?"

"Aren't you supposed to be falling off saloon roofs in a movie?" Logan countered, getting two mugs out of a cupboard and thunking them down on the table-top. He *had* wanted Dylan to come home, so why was he so pissed off?

The answer was uncomfortable. Vance was married, and presented no competition for Briana's attention. Dylan was another matter entirely.

Dylan's eyes sparkled; he'd always been good at reading Logan. "Finished the stunt job early," he said.

"I had some time on my hands, so I came to see what exactly you plan to do with this ranch."

The coffee wasn't finished, but Logan brought the carafe to the table and filled their cups anyway.

"What's going on, Logan?" Dylan asked quietly. "If Briana were here, the ruckus would have brought her out of hiding a while ago."

"She's at my place," Logan said. "With her kids and the dog."

"Why?"

Logan shoved a hand through his hair, sat down.

Dylan joined him at the table.

And Logan told his brother about the intruder.

Dylan listened intently. "You thought I was him," he said.

Logan smiled. "Yeah. And, frankly, I'm kind of disappointed that you aren't. Because I really wanted to get this yahoo by the ears and bounce his head off the floor a couple of dozen times."

Dylan took a thoughtful sip of his coffee, made a face at the taste. Logan had forgotten that his younger brother fancied himself a natural-born barista, and a natural-born everything else, too. "Cheap stuff," he muttered.

Logan leaned back in his chair. "Your tenant," he said, "isn't exactly rich. You expected the finest Colombian beans, personally delivered by Juan Valdez?"

"Man," Dylan said, "you are *really* on the peck. Are you sleeping with Briana?"

"What the hell kind of question is that?"

"A reasonable one. You're pretty touchy about her, it seems to me, and what's with the X-rated nightie hanging out there on the clothesline?"

Logan's jaw tightened of its own accord. "I told you what happened. I figured it might attract the pervert."

"It certainly worked on me," Dylan drawled.

"I rest my case," Logan said.

"Very funny."

"Oh, I'm a hoot."

"No, you're not," Dylan said. "You're still the same old tight-assed, judgmental son of a bitch you always were."

"Are we actually going there?" Logan leaned forward in his chair, arms folded, biceps quivering for action. "Because I've still got pissed-off to spare."

"I can see that."

"Why didn't you come to my place?"

"What are you talking about?"

Logan spread his hands. "When you found out you couldn't get a room in Stillwater Springs, why didn't you come to my place?"

"I wasn't sure what kind of reception I'd get," Dylan answered, weary humor flickering in his eyes, along with the usual fuck-you. He rubbed the back of his head, winced with pain. "Joke's on me. I had no idea how right I really was."

"Look, I'm sorry I jumped you. I thought you were a pervert."

Dylan chuckled, drank more coffee. "Like *that's* something new," he said.

"I never said you were a pervert."

"Yes, you did. When you were seventeen and you had all those naked Polaroids of your girlfriend— what was her name? Cindy? Suzanne? I posted them on the Internet, and you chased me halfway to the next county, yelling that I was a sick SOB. Translation—pervert."

"I still can't believe you did that."

"Believe it," Dylan said. "You stole that girl from *me*. Manly pride demanded reprisal."

"Her father would have killed you if Jake hadn't stepped in." Too late, Logan realized that mentioning their dad had been a mistake. After all, Jake was the sore point between the three brothers, and his death had sent them storming off in separate directions.

Dylan's face took on an expression of sorrow, and for a few moments, he looked much older than his thirty-two years. But his words surprised Logan. "What do you think made him so damn crazy?"

Logan didn't answer right away. This was ground he meant to tread lightly and besides, he wasn't sure he knew the truth. "You think he was crazy?" he finally countered. He'd learned that technique in marriage counseling, when he and Laurie still thought they could keep the ship from going down. It had some stupid psychobabble name he couldn't recall at the moment.

"Don't pull that lawyer shit on me, Logan," Dylan said. "What was wrong with Dad?"

Logan raised his shoulders, lowered them again. It wasn't a shrug, but a gesture of resignation. "He was an alcoholic, Dylan," he said carefully.

"But what made him that way? Was he abused as a kid or something?"

Logan sighed. Looked everywhere but directly into his brother's eyes. "Some people are just wired wrong, that's all. Maybe Jake was manic-depressive. Maybe he was just nuts. I really don't know and I'm tired as hell of trying to figure it out."

"So am I," Dylan said, after a long time. He stood. Stretched. "If you don't mind, I think I'll crash on the sofa."

"Wait a second," Logan said.

"What?"

"You might own this house, but right now, it's Briana's place. And she's got trouble enough without her landlord hanging around, eating up all the yogurt."

Dylan chuckled. "Okay," he said cheerfully. "I'll move into my old room at the main ranch house tomorrow."

So Dylan was staying, at least for a while.

Logan's feelings about that were decidedly mixed.

CHAPTER FOURTEEN

"WE FED THE HORSES!" Alec announced proudly, when Logan arrived at the main ranch house the next morning, driving Briana's old beater. Dylan followed in his gleaming, bright red pickup.

"Excellent," Logan said, grinning as Sidekick and Snooks jumped out after him and ran to greet Wanda and the boys.

Briana, looking like a rancher's dream, standing there by the corral fence, with the half-finished barn towering in the background, glanced uneasily at the other truck, then smiled in a way that made the pit of Logan's stomach clench when she saw Dylan spring to the ground.

Instant age-regression. Suddenly, Logan was fourteen and gangly, still catching up with the latest growth spurt, not quite filling out his hide.

Shit, he thought. *She likes him.*

Briana went to Dylan and hugged him—actually *hugged* him—and, being nobody's fool, Dylan hugged her right back. The old devilment shone in his eyes as he looked at Logan over the top of her head.

"Dylan!" both boys yelled in chorus, and raced toward him as Briana stepped back, smoothed her blouse and glanced, sidelong, at Logan.

Logan unclamped his back molars and managed a smile as she started toward him.

"Any luck?" she asked.

All of it bad, Logan thought, watching as Dylan chatted with Alec and Josh. They'd probably only met once or twice, Dylan and the boys, but you'd have thought they were old friends.

Dylan had that effect on people.

Briana touched his arm. "Logan?"

"Oh, you meant the pervert," he said, feeling like an idiot. He shook his head. "He was a no-show, but I half killed Dylan when he came in last night."

Briana bit her lower lip. "I suppose he wants his house back," she said, looking worried now. Logan might have been comforted by that remark if he hadn't known how hard it would be for her to make ends meet if she had to pay rent.

"For now," Logan said, "he plans to stay right here, with me."

"Oh," Briana said, looking as though she thought she ought to say something more, but didn't know what it would be.

"Look," Logan went on, in a low voice, "I still don't like the idea of you living over there alone. Maybe *you* should stay here, and let Dylan bunk in at your place."

She smiled wistfully. Shook her head. "Impossible."

He frowned.

"The boys," she reminded him.

Dylan was zeroing in; Logan had to hurry if he was going to make his case. "You could have your own room."

"How long do you think that would last?" Briana asked, running the tip of an index finger down his right bicep, a sure formula for spontaneous combustion.

He sighed, shoved a hand through his hair. "You're right," he said.

"I'm going to work today," she told him. "I'll take Alec and Josh with me."

"They hate hanging out in the coffee shop at the casino," Logan argued. "Why not leave them here?"

"Yeah!" Alec yelled.

"Yeah!" Josh added.

"Yeah," Dylan agreed, with a grin. The bastard. "After I say howdy to old Cimarron, we could hit the swimming hole."

Logan watched with some satisfaction as a frown furrowed Briana's brow. "What swimming hole?" she asked.

Dylan glanced at Logan, well aware he was getting under his skin, big-time. "You didn't tell them about the secret swimming hole?"

"No," Logan said tautly. "I've been a little busy."

Briana didn't roll over, God bless her. Maybe she was immune to Dylan's charms, though few women were. "Alec has a cast on his arm and—"

"Please, Mom!" Alec pleaded.

"A garbage bag and some duct tape," Dylan said, "and we're good to go."

"We're good swimmers, Mom," Josh reminded his mother.

Logan was still looking for a place to jump in when Briana suddenly cut loose with another dazzling smile. For Dylan.

Damn it.

"Okay," she said. "Go inside and fetch my purse, will you, Alec?"

Alec and Josh raced to do her bidding. Dylan hesitated a few moments, then followed them into the house.

"You're sure about this? Keeping the boys for the day, I mean?"

Logan was still watching Dylan.

"Logan?" Briana said, giving him a nudge to the midsection.

"I'm sure," he said.

Tiny vertical lines formed between her eyebrows. "Are you all right?"

"I'm fine. Are you?"

She sighed, looked away, met his gaze directly. "I'm not really going to work," she confessed.

Logan frowned. "Where then?"

"Over to Choteau, to the clinic. I need to get on birth-control pills, and if I fill a prescription here, it will be all over town in five minutes."

Logan blinked, felt a smile widen his mouth. Then it faded again. "You're planning on sleeping with somebody?"

She grinned, but her cheeks turned pink. "Yeah," she said. *"You."*

The smile came back. "Oh."

Briana leaned in, lowered her voice. "What were you thinking, Logan Creed?" She glanced back toward the house, and her expression changed again. To a glower. "Dylan?"

"He's death to women," Logan said ruefully.

"Not to *this* woman, he isn't," Briana replied, poking his solar plexus with her finger again, this time harder.

Alec came out of the house, lugging Briana's purse. He hurried across the yard and handed it over.

"You behave now," Briana told him. "Don't get that cast wet."

Alec rolled his eyes. "Mom, I'm not stupid."

She kissed his forehead, but nearly missed, because he immediately turned to Logan.

"Dylan says he's hungry enough to eat the north end of a southbound skunk. He wants to know if you've got any bacon."

Logan chuckled, shook his head.

Yes, indeed. Dylan was back.

Be careful what you wish for, Logan thought, *because you damn well might get it.*

WHEN BRIANA SHOWED up at the casino around lunchtime, she had a packet of birth-control pills in her purse and a load of worries on her mind.

She might already be pregnant.

Dylan Creed might want his house back.

Alec or Josh might drown in the "swimming hole" on the ranch.

Aliens might arrive in a giant spaceship and take over the governments of Earth. Well, there was one cheerful thought in the bunch, anyway.

The slot machines were doing their usual brisk business, with no less than three senior citizens' buses parked in the side lot, when Jim, who must have had eyes like the proverbial eagle, appeared out of nowhere.

"Hey," he said.

"Do I still have a job?" Briana asked.

Jim gave a slanted grin. "You can have mine if you want it," he quipped. He looked especially spiffy that day, in a new suit, obviously tailored to his impressive frame.

"Hot date?" Briana teased, heading for the office to clock in.

Jim straightened his tasteful tie. "I'm formally announcing my candidacy today," he said, keeping pace with her. "Somebody from the *Courier* is coming by later."

"Congratulations," she said, with a smile. "You've got my vote, for what that's worth."

"There is something I wanted to ask you," Jim said, sotto voce.

Briana stopped at the office door, one hand poised to push it open. "What?"

"I was wondering…well, if I get elected—"

"Jim," Briana said. "Spit it out."

"I'll need an office manager. It's a county job—lots of security, and benefits and—"

"You're offering me a job as your office manager?"

Jim nodded. "Of course, I have to win the election, but…yeah. Angie Wilson has held down that job through three administrations, but she wants to retire when Floyd does."

Briana put her hand out. "Sheriff Huntinghorse," she said, "you have a deal. Why, I'll even campaign for you."

He flushed slightly. Straightened his tie again. "There's something else," he said.

Here it comes, Briana thought. Working at the casino was going to represent some kind of conflict of interest. By the end of the day, she'd be unemployed *and* homeless, the way things were going.

Where the *heck* was that alien spaceship? Maybe she and the boys could hitch a ride to some planet where single mothers didn't have to juggle jobs and bills all the time.

"You worry way too much," Jim told her, evidently reading her face, taking her elbow and ushering her into the office. It rarely happened, but the place was empty except for them. "I was hoping you'd get my ex-wife to pose for some pictures with me—her and our son, Sam. You know, publicity shots for the news-paper and a few posters."

Briana blinked. "Jim, I don't *know* your ex-wife. Why would I have more sway with her than you do?"

"*Everybody* has more sway with Caroline than I do," Jim said. "This is important, Briana. Freida Tur-low is going to file her candidacy today, and Mike Danvers, from Danvers Chevrolet—"

Briana held up a hand. "Wait. What do Ms. Tur-low and the owner of the biggest car dealership in the county have to do with my talking to your ex-wife?"

"Freida's the last of a dynasty—the name Turlow still carries some weight around here, despite her bum of a brother. And Mike has a *family*—smiling blond wife, two-point-two winsome children and even a three-legged dog rescued from the pound, for Pete's sake."

"Her brother?" Briana echoed, feeling a little left behind.

"Brett," Jim said.

"Oh," Briana said. "*He's* bound to be a political liability."

"Freida's different—not like Brett at all. Everybody likes her. And Mike—"

"Jim," Briana broke in. "*Think.* Shots with your son are one thing, but dragging your *ex*-wife into the campaign might come off as...strange. Even deceitful."

"I've got to do *something.*"

"You'd be a great sheriff. That will be enough."

He craned his neck, so they were practically nose to nose. "I'm *Native American,*" he whispered.

Briana grinned. "Yeah," she said. "I noticed."

Jim straightened, took a slip of paper from the pocket of his immaculate suit jacket and shoved it into Briana's hand. "First duty as my future office manager. Call Caroline at that number and get her on board for the campaign."

"Jim—"

"Please?"

"Okay," Briana huffed out. "I'll call her. But she's probably going to tell me to take a flying leap."

"Call her now," Jim said. "I'll cover for you out on the floor. You can use the phone in my office."

"You've got to be kidding."

"Are you going to argue with me like this when I'm sheriff?"

"Clock me in," Briana said, resigned. "If I have to do this, I'm getting paid for it."

Jim grinned, watching as she ducked into his office.

Caroline Huntinghorse answered on the second ring. "Jim?"

Briana cleared her throat. "Er...no. My name is Briana Grant, and I work for your...er...ex-husband—"

"Oh," Caroline said. She had a nice voice, but she didn't sound too thrilled to get a call from a stranger. "I see."

Briana closed her eyes for a moment. Every button on Jim's phone was blinking. She sank into his desk chair, then immediately jumped out of it again.

"As you probably know," Briana began, wondering if she'd have to do things like this a lot in the if-I-win job Jim had offered her, "Jim's running for sheriff. I'm helping him with the campaign, and—"

"I'll just bet you are," Caroline interrupted.

"It isn't like that," Briana said.

"Are you telling me you never went out with my— With Jim?"

"We had dinner, went to the movies. It was nothing—"

Caroline let out a sigh. "Sorry," she said. "I still get possessive sometimes." There was something heart-breaking in the little laugh that came next. "So, Ms. Grant—what is it that Jim is so afraid to ask me that he put you up to it?"

I like this woman, Briana thought. "He wondered if you'd pose with him, for some campaign photos, with your son."

"Being divorced is a political advantage these days?"

Briana smiled. "My question, exactly," she said. "But Jim seems to think it's a good idea."

Caroline was quiet for so long that Briana thought she'd hung up, or they'd been disconnected somehow.

"Tell him," she finally said, "that he has to ask me himself."

Briana punched the air with one fist, the way she'd

seen her boys do when they were pleased. "You go, girl," she said.

Caroline laughed. "Tell him to call."

RIGGED UP IN his garbage bag/duct-tape/cast-protector, Alec splashed happily in the swimming hole, trying to drench Josh, while all three dogs barked like crazy on the bank.

"Reminds me of the old days," Dylan observed, taking a swig from a bottle of water as he sat beside Logan on the familiar log. "When you and Ty and I used to come here."

Pain knifed through Logan. For all Jake's disastrous drinking and brawling, and the progression of tender-hearted mothers, he and his brothers had enjoyed a lot of hot summer days in and around this hidden pond.

What happened?

He wanted to ask the question, but he couldn't force it past his damned Creed pride.

"Those were good times," he muttered, after a long silence.

Dylan nodded, not looking at him. "It's nice to see kids on the place," he said quietly. He turned then, met Logan's gaze. "You and Briana—?"

"What about us?"

"Come on, Logan. A blind man could see you're either sleeping with her, or you want to, real bad. Just how serious is this?"

"Serious enough," Logan said, "that I'll kick your ass if you mess with her."

Dylan laughed, shoved a hand through his damned golden hair, which was shaggy, as usual, the way women liked it. "Well, what do you know? I finally got a straight answer out of you." He fixed his attention on the boys and the dogs again, apparently enjoying *their* enjoyment. "Whatever else might be going on between you and me, Logan, I won't move in on your action, so stop worrying about that."

Logan bristled, realized he was acting like a rooster and made a concerted attempt to mellow out.

"You ever see Kristy around town?" Dylan asked, a few beats later.

"Kristy?"

"Kristy Madison," Dylan said. "You know, the librarian. When I left Stillwater Springs, she was engaged to Mike Danvers and all set to live the high life."

A slow smile overtook Logan, but he kept it on the inside, where Dylan wouldn't see it. Evidently, his brother didn't subscribe to the *Stillwater Springs Courier*. Dylan was smart as hell, but he'd been dyslexic as a kid, and he didn't read for pleasure.

"Mike Danvers married Becky Hammond," Logan said.

Dylan turned his head so quickly that Logan barely had a chance to change his expression. "No shit?"

"No shit," Logan confirmed.

"And Kristy—?"

"Far as I know, she's still working at the library." Kristy had been the subject of several human-interest stories in the *Courier* over the past couple of years, and everything Danvers did made the locals page. "Lives in the old Turlow house."

"I'll be damned."

"Probably," Logan joked, "but you could still re-pent and give your soul to Jesus."

"Coming from you, brother, that's ironic advice."

Logan took a swig from his own water bottle. All of a sudden, his throat felt as dry as August dust on a country road. "I'm sorry, Dylan," he said, and the words hurt like hell, scraping raw across his gullet the way they did. "For the things I said about Jake after the funeral, I mean—"

Dylan slapped his back.

Logan's eyes burned. He blinked a couple of times.

"He *was* a mean old son of a bitch," Dylan said. "But I wasn't in the mood to hear it the day we buried him."

"I know," Logan said grimly. "Neither was Ty. I should have kept my opinions to myself."

After that, neither of them talked for a good long while. Logan figured Dylan needed some recovery time, like he did. So they watched the boys and the dogs, still seated side by side on a fallen log, remembering other dogs, long gone now, and the boys they'd been themselves, once upon a time.

"What's up with that damn bull?" Logan asked, when he thought he could trust his voice.

Dylan gave a languid stretch, got to his feet. "Cimarron? He's the last bull I rode before I quit the rodeo. He had a perfect record—he'd never been ridden—and I'd never been thrown. He won that round, and they were going to retire him, so I bought him and had him trucked to the ranch. Figured to breed him one day."

Logan stood, too. Whistled for the boys and the dogs.

Reluctantly, Alec and Josh waded out of the swimming hole, and Sidekick, Snooks and Wanda trotted over to him, eager for the next great adventure.

"Chow time," Logan told the boys. When had he started to care so much about them?

Did Vance Grant even know what a lucky bastard he was?

"Can we go to town for lunch?" Alec asked, shivering in his wet jeans and an old, threadbare bath towel Logan had found in a bathroom cupboard before they left the house.

"Why not?" Logan grinned.

An hour later, they all rolled into the casino parking lot in Dylan's uptown, movie-cowboy ride. They'd stopped by Briana's, so the boys could put on dry clothes. Since there were no signs of breaking and entering, they'd left Wanda behind to sleep off the morning's excitement at the swimming hole.

Briana spotted them right away—mom-radar, Logan supposed. While Alec and Josh jostled for places in the nearest booth, he and Dylan stood, watching her approach.

"Hey, Mom," Alec crowed, "we went swimming and I didn't get my cast wet and Wanda swam out to get a stick and shook herself off all over everybody—"

Briana looked at the kid with an expression of such love that a whole new place opened up inside Logan. It felt like a seismic shift, and he actually put a hand to his chest, thinking he might be having a heart attack.

He was, he decided in the next moment, but it had nothing to do with clogged arteries.

"Oh, boy," Dylan breathed, watching him.

"That's great," Briana told Alec, but she was looking at Logan. "That thing I told you about this morning," she said. "I took care of it."

"Good," Logan said, and the word came out rough as gravel. He felt heat climb his neck. She'd gone to the clinic in Choteau, like she said she would, for birth-control pills. Which meant—

Don't go there.

"Join us?" Dylan asked. When it came to women, he always said the right thing, and he said it first.

Though maybe it hadn't been that way with Kristy Madison.

Briana shook her head. "Gotta work," she said. Then, with a twinkle, she added, "I'm angling for a promotion."

Logan wasn't thrilled. He was feeling pretty much like a caveman right then. He wanted to throw Briana Grant over one shoulder, haul her out of there, get her name changed to Creed and make a baby with her. Support her in style for the rest of her life.

Whoa back, he thought.

"See you tonight?" he said aloud.

"Depends," she answered. "I'm working late, to make up for some of the time I missed, and Vance called a little while ago." She turned that glowing goddess face of hers to Alec and Josh. "He and Heather are going to the drive-in tonight to see a movie, and you're both invited. Your dad has the weekend off, so you can stay over if you want."

Dylan looked from Briana to Logan, smiled to himself and sat down to open a menu.

"That would be great," Alec said, always the good-time guy.

"If you remember not to stand behind the van," Josh pointed out, with an eloquent roll of his eyes.

"I don't think Dad will let Heather drive if we're there," Alec remarked, serious as the heart attack Logan had thought he was having a couple of minutes before.

"Guess it's settled, then," Briana said.

"Guess it's settled," Logan agreed stupidly.

This time, it was Dylan who rolled his eyes.

WALTER, A PORTLY casino security guard old enough to be Briana's grandfather, walked her to her car when she got off work at nine that night. Vance had picked the boys up at five-thirty, when he was finished for the day, and except for feeding Wanda and letting her out, she was a free woman.

A free woman with birth-control pills in her purse.

"You just can't be too careful these days," Walter said kindly, waiting while Briana unlocked the truck.

True enough, she thought, thinking of the pills.

She hadn't seen Brett Turlow that day, but if Sheriff Book was right, Brett wasn't a problem, anyway. That only left about a hundred regulars who might be seething behind the understanding smiles they'd given when Briana told them she was too busy working and raising her boys to date.

"Lock up, now," Walter said, through the open window, when Briana was settled behind the wheel, with her seat belt buckled. It was a nice night, warm and soft. "With these old rigs, you have to push the buttons down manually."

Briana smiled, leaned across to lock the passenger-side door. If they'd been attacked, she would have had to save Walter, not vice versa, but his heart was in the right place and she liked him.

"All good," she said. Then she locked the driver's door, too, and rolled up the window. Tooted merrily at Walter as she drove away.

Conscious of Wanda waiting patiently at home for kibble and some lawn-time, Briana still made a quick pass by Heather and Vance's place. The van was missing from the driveway, and lights glowed at the trailer windows.

All quiet on the western front.

She headed for home, and was half-surprised, and half-not, to see Logan's truck parked near the house. The birth-control pills suddenly seemed to pulse inside her purse, like something nuclear about to blow.

After drawing a deep breath and letting it out again, Briana shut off the engine, unlocked the door and got out, pulling her loaded purse after her. She'd taken the first pill before she left the pharmacy in Choteau, washing it down with a glass of diet cola from the old-fashioned soda fountain, but she hadn't had the nerve to ask the busy doctor at the clinic how long it would be before the things kicked in.

Approaching the house, she decided not to worry. Dylan was probably in there with Logan, which meant there wouldn't be any sex.

No sex, no pregnancy.

Unless, of course, she and Logan had *already* conceived a child on his couch.

Her cheeks burned, but she smiled a little, too. She'd loved being pregnant with Alec and Josh, even though she and Vance had had their ups and downs.

Always moving from place to place, never enough money, never enough anything.

She'd loved the weight and scent and warmth of a baby nestled in her arms, though. It would be wonderful to have another child—a little girl.

Times change, she told herself, *and nobody has everything.*

The back door swung open just then, and Logan stood on the threshold, lit from behind. He was a rancher, a cowboy, the kind of man she knew and understood.

Or did she? There was a lot more to Logan Creed than he'd been willing to reveal to her so far, and that made her nervous.

She stopped, right there in the yard.

Wanda pushed past Logan and bounded toward her, wriggling with joy and wagging her tail.

She greeted the dog, steeled herself and started walking again.

"Dylan's at the other house," Logan said, though she hadn't asked.

Briana looked up at him, feeling shy.

He held out a hand, and she realized she'd stopped again.

Went to him.

He drew her up the porch steps and close against his chest, kissed her lightly but thoroughly before pulling her inside. Wanda trotted in behind her, lively as a pup.

"What did you give this dog?" Briana asked. "Speed?"

"It was a good day," Logan said. "She's happy."

Gripping her shoulders from behind, he steered Briana to a chair at the table, sat her down.

"What—"

"I made supper," Logan told her. "Well, actually, I *bought* supper." With a flourish, he opened the oven door, and the scent of take-out fried chicken wafted out.

Briana opened her mouth, closed it again.

He served up the feast—besides the chicken, he'd picked up biscuits, two kinds of pasta salad and a cheesecake.

"Are we celebrating something?" she asked, surveying all the food.

He grinned, executed a waiterlike bow. "Maybe," he said.

He brought plates and silverware to the table, then went back to the counter and tore off a couple of paper towels for napkins.

Since Briana was ravenous, despite the butterflies beating soft wings inside her stomach, she ate.

"Is this a seduction?" she asked, after the chicken and fixings and before the cheesecake.

"That's up to you," Logan replied. "If you're not too tired from work, I thought we could go out for a ride after supper. There are some places I'd like to show you."

Briana couldn't figure out if she was disappointed or relieved—both, probably. "Such as?"

"The swimming hole where Dylan and I took the kids today," he answered easily. "And a place up on the mountain where the stars seem so close you could almost reach up and grab one."

Great. On top of being sexy, Logan Creed was

romantic. He probably remembered birthdays and anniversaries and bought valentines before Groundhog Day.

The last valentine Vance had given her had been the skimpy nightgown, a gift for himself, not her. God only knew why she'd kept it, and knowing a stranger had handled it…next stop, the burn barrel out back.

"I'm not sure how soon the birth control will start working," she said, and then immediately wished she could evaporate on the spot.

"You're not the only one who stopped at a pharmacy today, Briana," Logan replied. "Relax, will you? Did anybody say we were going straight to bed?"

"You bought supper. You're talking about reaching out and grabbing stars—"

"And that means I'm going to jump you in the next two minutes?"

"Aren't you?"

His eyes smoldered with humor and heat as he leaned back in his chair and gave her a slow once-over. "Never let it be said," he told her, "that any Creed was ever less than a gentleman."

"Don't look now," Briana replied, getting up to clear the table, "but I think that's *already* been said."

Logan laid a hand, fingers splayed, to his chest, as though wounded, but his grin sizzled. "Our reputation precedes us," he lamented.

"Big-time," Briana replied, but she couldn't help smiling.

Logan got to his feet. "I'll clean up," he said. "You go change into something suitable for catching stars with both hands. We can consider the whole sex angle later."

"How much later?"

"Whenever you're ready, Briana. Tonight, tomorrow, next week, next year. It's gonna happen, we both know that, but there's no pressure, all right?"

"All right," she said.

She took a quick shower, put on jeans and a long-sleeved T-shirt. The nights could be cool around Stillwater Springs, even in the summer.

They locked up the house, loaded Wanda into the backseat of Logan's truck and went jostling through the countryside.

Logan was a country boy, Briana thought. Who needed a road?

They went to the swimming hole first, parked on a high bank with the headlights beaming out over the water. The place seemed almost magical, especially in the moonlight. There was an old, weathered wood raft out in the middle, and a rope hung from a tree branch, for swinging on.

Beyond that, Briana couldn't see much.

"My brothers and I used to come here a lot when we were kids," Logan said, gazing out through the windshield as if he could see into that other time.

"You and Dylan and—?"

"Tyler," Logan disclosed. His voice sounded hoarse. And very sad.

On impulse, Briana reached out, found his hand, squeezed it. "Feel like talking, cowboy?"

He turned his head, looked at her. "Dylan's leaving in a couple of days," he said. "He just came back to check on the bull and make sure I wasn't putting up any fences where he didn't want them."

"Is that good or bad?"

Logan thrust a hand through his hair, stared straight ahead for a moment, before starting the truck's engine again and shifting into Reverse. "Both, I guess. I was hoping—"

"What, Logan? What were you hoping?"

"I guess that things could be different. Between Dylan and Tyler and me."

"And what happened?"

"Dylan and I came to an understanding—at least, the start of one," Logan said, as they bounced off through the trees, presumably headed for the place where the stars were close enough to catch. He shook his head. "Tyler, though—that's going to be harder."

"What exactly happened between you and your brother?" It was too personal a question, Briana knew, but she'd already asked it, so she simply waited.

Logan let out a ragged sigh. The truck rattled and banged up a steep hill, and he brought the rig to a stop.

Overhead, in the big Montana sky, millions of stars shimmered, huge and silvery.

"There were some hard words spoken," Logan finally said, "the day of our dad's funeral. I was grieving, and still a little drunk from the wake the night before. Tyler sang a eulogy at the funeral, all about what a great guy Jake was." Logan didn't seem to notice the stars, for all the buildup he'd given them earlier; his profile was rock-hard. "Dylan showed up at the services with the floozy-du-jour—some showgirl in a low-cut red dress—and the three of us passed a flask after everybody else left the graveside."

Briana waited, wanting to take Logan's hand again but not quite daring.

"After that, we repaired to Skivvies to get drunk

in earnest," Logan went on. "Even the floozy cut out eventually—took off with some truck driver passing through. And Tyler got out his guitar and started singing that damned song again—"

"Go on," Briana said gently.

"I couldn't take it anymore," Logan finished. "I jerked Tyler's guitar out of his hands and smashed it against the bar, yelling that it was all bullshit, that Jake was nothing but a drunk and we were no better." He paused, dragged in a shaky breath. "It was a piece of junk, that guitar. It was also the only thing Tyler's mother left behind that Jake didn't break, give away or burn in the backyard. That's when the fight broke out. Sheriff Book and two deputies he recruited on the spot dragged us off to jail. End of story."

Briana took Logan's hand again, held it. After a while, she said, "What do you say we get out of this truck and have a firsthand look at those stars?"

CHAPTER FIFTEEN

THEY LAY ON their backs in the deep grass, holding hands and gazing up at the stars, while Briana's old dog slept peacefully in the truck. The moment was as nearly perfect as any Logan had ever lived, and he wished it could last forever.

It was like some kind of holy benediction, that sprawling sky, black and velvety and sprinkled with a billion other worlds.

Briana sighed, warm against his side. They hadn't made love, but it seemed as if they had—as if they'd joined souls in some inexplicable way, just by lying together under all that eternity. "You're right," she whispered. "It's beautiful."

He drew her nearer, so she rested her head on his shoulder. Ran his hand the length of her braid. Dylan would have had some line ready, Logan supposed, but *his* throat was too thick for speech, too constricted with the sheer wonder of just being alive, and with this particular woman beside him.

"Are you okay?" she asked, spreading her fingers wide on his chest, probably feeling the steady thud of his heartbeat through her palm.

Women. If you weren't talking, they thought there was something wrong.

Logan smiled. "More than okay," he said.

She fell silent again.

He kissed her forehead, propped his chin on her crown.

A long time passed.

Briana broke the silence. "Who are you, Logan Creed?" she asked, very softly.

"Good question," he answered. "Member of the Nevada State Bar Association. Wannabe rancher. Son of Jake Creed. Beyond that, I really couldn't tell you."

"You lived a different life, before you came back to Stillwater Springs, didn't you?"

He gently displaced her to roll onto his side and, propping himself up on one elbow, looked down into her face. "Yeah," he said. "I have a place in Vegas. I was married a couple of times." He traced the curve of her cheek. "Wondering if I've got any dark secrets?"

Even in the delicate light of the stars and the moon, he saw her blush. She shook her head. "I'm just trying to understand."

"What is there to understand?"

"You. You have another life, in another place. Why did you come back here?"

"If I tell you," he said, "I might scare you off."

She smiled. "Give it a shot."

"I came back because I can lie in the grass here, and watch the stars. Because this is where I was born, and where I belong."

"Not very scary so far," Briana said.

He chuckled, kissed her. "Here's the scary part. I want to rebuild the ranch—return it to its former glory, so to speak. I want a wife and a passel of rowdy kids, and I want to prove—to myself if no one else—that I'm not the kind of man my father was."

She absorbed all that. Didn't jump right up and run for the main road, which was encouraging. "What kind of man *was* your father?"

"He was a d—"

Briana stopped him, put a finger to his lips. "Besides the drinking," she said, her eyes luminous and flecked with stray shards of starlight.

Logan thought. "Tough. Jake was tough. He had a temper. He worked as a logger his whole life, and even though we barely held on to the ranch, especially when he got laid off for the winter, we never missed a meal. We had shoes and went to the dentist every six months."

"Was he abusive?" She'd worked up her nerve to ask that question; Logan knew that by the sudden tension in her body.

"Not so much physically," he said. "He hauled us off to the woodshed a time or two, but it was that way for most kids, back then. When he got drunk, though, and that was often, he went berserk. He couldn't hold in the rage then, the way he could when he was sober. We always went into hiding at the first sign of a bottle, Dylan and Ty and me, and lay low 'til it blew over."

Briana's hand made a slow circle on his chest. "I haven't noticed you getting drunk and going berserk," she said quietly. "Do you?"

"Not since the funeral," Logan said, closing his eyes against the memory. "Swore off hard liquor the next day—God, what a hangover *that* was—and now I can barely finish a beer."

"Did your dad want to build up the ranch and have more kids?"

His throat went tight again. He shook his head.

"He didn't want the three of us, let alone more, and he hated the ranch—a carryover from *his* father, I guess. The ranch thrived for generations, but when the Depression hit, nobody bought beef. Gradually, they shot and ate the few skinny cattle they had left, and I don't think my grandparents ever got over it. Jake didn't, either. Said the land was an albatross around his neck. After Tyler's mother killed herself, things got a whole lot worse. He drank more, if that was possible."

"Logan, can't you see how different you are? From your father, I mean?"

"Can we talk about your dad for a while?" Logan countered. Just talking about Jake depressed him, made him feel hopeless, even with more money than he could ever spend. He'd expected wealth to make him happy.

It hadn't.

She smiled, no doubt seeing images of Bill "Wild Man" McIntyre, king of the rodeo clowns, in her mind. "He liked to read," she said. "We had a whole shoebox full of library cards, all from different towns, in half a dozen states. Once, he forgot to return a book before we left for the next rodeo, and we backtracked almost a hundred miles to turn it in and pay the fine. Fifty cents."

"It never bothered you, growing up on the road that way?"

"I wouldn't want to do it again," she said, after a long time. "Not at this point in my life. But it was a wonderful way to live, watching the highway unroll in front of us, singing along with the radio while it blared Johnny Cash, or Patsy Cline, or George Jones. Our favorite was Tom T. Hall's 'Old Dogs, Children and Watermelon Wine,' though." She paused, sighed again. "Every Christmas," she went on, "we headed back to Boise to visit my Aunt Barbara and her family. There was always a big tree, and special food, and lots of presents, but I could barely enjoy it, because I was so afraid my aunt would finally convince Dad to leave me behind so I could go to 'real' school. He never did, though. Not even when I hit my teens. He traded the camper in for a two-bedroom trailer—second- or thirdhand, of course—when I turned twelve. Before that, I slept on a fold-down bunk, and he took the couch."

"You never wished he'd settle down someplace? Not even once?"

"A few times, I did. Like when I'd see a bunch of girls my age, giggling in a mall, having lunch with their moms or their friends in the food court. And it would have been nice to have a mother—especially when I got my period, and I started thinking about boys."

Logan felt a pang for the girl Briana had been, gave her a slight squeeze.

"Right before Dad decided to stop following the rodeo and stay in Boise, I met Vance."

"Love at first sight?"

"More like lust," Briana said.

Logan chuckled. "I can identify," he said. "I married both my wives because I was young and stupid and I wanted to have sex with them. It never occurred to me—or to them, either, I guess—that we'd have been better off skipping the weddings and hitting the sack instead."

As soon as he'd uttered those words, Logan wondered if he'd regret them.

"I guess things happen for a reason," Briana said. "It didn't work out with Vance, but I have Josh and Alec, so it was worth it."

"They're terrific kids," Logan said. "And—"

"And?"

"And it's getting cold out here. Let's go back to your place."

Logan sat up, got to his feet, pulled Briana after him.

"This," she said, grinning impishly, "would have been a fantastic place to have sex."

He laughed, kissed her. "A bed would be better."

A WEIRD LITTLE THRILL jiggled in the pit of Briana's stomach as they turned off the county road, headed for her house. In the backseat, Wanda gave a low growl.

Even before they pulled in and saw the back door standing open, Briana knew something was wrong.

Her first thought, as always, was of the boys. It was irrational to worry, she knew—they were at the drive-in movie, with Heather and Vance, probably gorging themselves on popcorn. Still, she groped for her cell phone as Logan slammed on the brakes, shut off the engine and hurtled out of the truck to sprint toward the house.

No one answered Josh and Alec's shared cell phone.

Most likely, they'd shut it off to watch the movie.

Briana got out of the truck and hurried after Logan,

forgetting Wanda, turning to go back for her, then thinking better of it.

"Logan?" she called.

He was just coming out of the hallway leading to her bedroom and the bath, and if she hadn't known he was on her side, the expression on his face would have scared her half to death.

Someone had been there—and this time, they'd ransacked the kitchen. Emptied all the drawers. Broken every dish and cup.

She whirled to look at the lock on the back door, but it wasn't broken. Had the intruder had a key?

Briana thought of the photo album, with all the pictures of her dad, her younger self, her babies, and ran into the living room.

The contents of the album were scattered all over the floor, some of them torn. Briana dropped to her knees with a cry of dismay, and started gathering them up with frantic scooping motions of her hands.

Behind her, she heard Logan on his cell phone, talking to Sheriff Book.

Her wedding picture, a memento she'd planned to duplicate and pass on to the boys when they were older, had been ripped down the middle. Alec's first baby photo was in tatters, pieces no bigger than bits of confetti, Josh's crumpled into a tight little ball.

Tears slipped down Briana's cheeks, and she couldn't stop making those awful sounds, those soft, keening wails of protest and despair and helpless fury.

Logan pulled her to her feet, wrapped his arms around her. She shuddered violently, trying to get her breath.

"Why would someone *do* this?" she cried, against his chest.

"I don't know," he said. "Sheriff Book will be here in a few minutes."

Briana shoved back from Logan. *"Sheriff Book!"* she ranted. "What *good* is that going to do?" In the distance, Wanda's bark, though muffled, grew more urgent.

"I'll get her," Logan said.

Briana nodded, made herself look around the living room, past the pool of ruined pictures in the middle of the floor.

The couch cushions had been ripped open, the curtains torn down. The TV screen was smashed to glinting shards.

Briana put a hand to her mouth, turning in a slow circle, her stomach roiling. She was on her way through the kitchen, determined to see what had been destroyed in the boys' room and her own, when Logan came in with Wanda.

"Don't," he said. "Don't go in there."

She broke and ran, trying to beat him to the hall, but he was faster. He caught her by the arm.

"No, Briana. Not yet."

"It's that bad?"

"It's worse than bad."

She began to shake.

Logan led her to the table, sat her down in the nearest chair. Handed her her purse.

She found her cell phone, dialed again.

Still no answer.

Her children. What if this person had somehow gotten to Alec and Josh?

"What's Vance's number?" Logan asked calmly.

Wanda had slumped heavily onto Briana's feet. She was scared. That made two of them—three, counting Logan, who had turned a dangerous shade of gray at the jawline.

Briana struggled to remember the number, gave it to Logan when she did. In the distance, a siren shrieked.

"Vance?" Logan said, into his phone. "Logan Creed. Are Josh and Alec with you?"

A frown creased his forehead.

Briana got hold of the phone in a single grab. "Vance?" she croaked. *Where are my children?"*

"Relax," Vance said. "I got a chance to put in some overtime, so Heather went ahead and took them to the movies."

Logan stood still as death, even as the siren grew louder and Wanda began to bark.

"They're not answering their cell phone," Briana said, raising her voice to be heard over the dog and the sheriff's arrival.

"They must have gone to that multiscreen place out on the highway," Vance said. "They'd have had to turn it off. And stop yelling."

Sheriff Book loomed in the doorway, then came over the threshold. His gaze sweeping the demolished kitchen, he gave a low whistle.

"I need to talk to Alec and Josh," Briana insisted. "If you can get hold of Heather, do it!"

A bulb must have gone on in Vance's head around then. "Is something wrong?"

Duh, Briana thought. "Someone's been in the house," she said, finally catching her breath. "They trashed the place. *I have to know Alec and Josh are all right,* Vance."

"I'll go get them, bring them there—"

"No!" Briana cried. She forced herself to take a deep, calming breath. It didn't help much. "Not until I can get this place cleaned up. I don't want them to see it the way it is."

"Are you alone out there?" Vance asked.

"No," Briana said. "Logan's here, and Sheriff Book. Track Heather down, Vance. Ask her to have the boys call me right away. Okay? Can you do that?"

"I can do that," Vance said wearily.

They hung up without goodbyes.

By that time, Sheriff Book and Logan had disappeared from sight. They were in her bedroom, by the sound of it, their words muffled and sharp around the edges. She caught the occasional muttered expletive.

Briana clasped her cell phone tightly in her right hand and willed it to ring. She stood, whispered to Wanda that everything would be all right, and made for the bedroom.

What she saw when she reached the threshold stopped her cold.

The word *bitch* was scrawled on closet doors, in what looked like lipstick.

The bed, the window and the walls were covered in shining red, and Briana thought it was blood, for one terrible moment, before she caught the fumes in the air.

Spray paint.

"Oh my God," she whispered, bending to pick up a small tube lying at her feet, halfway under the dresser.

The lipstick was hers—she'd bought it at the drugstore in Choteau, when she picked up the birth-control pills.

Birth-control pills.

Had she really been lying on the ground with Logan, in a mountain clearing, not even an hour before, marveling at a sky so full of stars it could barely hold them all?

Logan slipped an arm around her shoulders.

"That's it," Sheriff Book said, snapping his radio off his belt. "I'm having Brett Turlow brought in for questioning. Try not to touch anything until I've had the state police bring in their crime-scene people."

Briana bit her lower lip, nodded numbly.

The cell phone rang, vibrating against her palm.

She answered immediately. "Alec? Josh?"

"Mom?" Josh said urgently. "Are you okay? Dad said somebody broke into our house—"

"I'm okay," Briana said, dizzy with relief. "So is Wanda. H-how was the movie?"

"We didn't go," Josh said. His voice sounded small, and a little shaky.

Briana's heartbeat quickened again, like a racehorse hitting its stride on the stretch. "Where are you?"

"Dad said not to tell you."

"I don't care what your dad said," Briana retorted. "I want to know where you are—right now."

Sheriff Book had left the bedroom, though his radio could be heard crackling in the kitchen, along with the orders he was barking into it. Logan remained at Briana's side, his arm still around her.

"He's on his way to get us, Mom," Josh said, wheedling now. "Can't we just leave it at that? I don't want to break my word."

Briana closed her eyes, counted to ten, opened them again. "Joshua William Grant," she said, "start talking."

"We're at the casino."

"What?"

"In the coffee shop." Josh began to cry. "Alec's here, and we're okay. Honest."

"Where's Heather?"

Logan frowned, listening intently to Briana's end of the conversation.

"She said she had to play some blackjack, and then we'd go to the movie, and we shouldn't tell you or Dad because you'd just get all bent out of shape."

Briana swallowed hard, looking up into Logan's troubled eyes. "Listen, honey, you're not in any trouble, and neither is Alec. Why did you shut off your cell phone, though? I was worried when I couldn't reach you."

"Heather borrowed it," Josh answered. "She forgot to charge hers. She must have called Dad or something, because she came back and slammed it down on the table and said she hoped we were satisfied because now all three of us were going to catch hell. I called Dad because we were supposed to be staying with him, and he told me not to say—"

"Is Heather there now?"

"No," Josh said. "Alec wants to talk to you."

"Put him on in a second," Briana said. "Listen to me, Josh. I want you to ask the nearest casino employee to get Jim if he's around, or a security guard. You will not leave that place with your dad, do you understand? And you will *definitely* not leave with Heather."

"O-okay," Josh said. "But how are we going to get home?"

"Logan and I will come and get you."

Logan nodded as she spoke.

"Do you understand?" she repeated, when Josh didn't respond.

"Dad's here," he said. The next voice she heard was Alec's.

"Mom? I'm scared. Dad looks really mad. Heather's back, and he's yelling at her—"

She and Logan were already moving, Wanda following while the sheriff waited for the crime-scene people. "Hold on, sweetie," she said. "I'm on my way."

Logan hoisted Wanda into the back of the truck and got behind the wheel, thumbing in a number on his own cell phone. "Dylan?" he said, as Briana buckled her seat belt, half listening, still trying to reassure Alec.

"I have to go now," Alec said.

"Wait!" Briana cried.

But the call was disconnected.

"For once," she heard Logan telling his brother, "I'm glad you're a poker shark. Alec and Josh are in the coffee shop, and something is going down—I'm not sure what. Will you make sure nobody—and I mean *nobody*—takes them away before Briana and I get there?"

Briana's heart was pounding, and she'd broken out in a cold sweat. Fumbling with her phone, she dropped it and had to grapple around for it on the floor.

"Thanks," Logan said, and ended his call, shifting gears so fast that Briana was almost flung against the dashboard.

"Are you thinking what I'm thinking?" he asked, prying the cell phone out of her hand.

"Heather," she said.

"Yeah."

Logan's phone rang as they careened onto the county road. Poor Wanda was probably holding on for dear life in the backseat.

"Okay," he said, after listening for a few moments. "Be right there."

"Is Dylan with them?" Briana demanded.

"Yes," Logan said. "Jim's there, too. The kids are all right, Briana. Just a little shaken up and confused."

"Vance...?"

"He and Heather got into a shouting match," Logan said reluctantly. "They're being held by the security people until everything gets sorted out." He concentrated on the road, a long ribbon of moon-washed pavement that seemed never-ending to Briana. "Take a breath, Briana. You're okay, and so are the boys. Right now, nothing else matters."

"I don't care what Vance says," Briana ranted, "I'm *not* letting that woman near my children again!"

"Let's wait 'til we hear everybody's side of the story," Logan reasoned. "It could all be a misunderstanding of some kind."

"Thanks, Counselor," Briana snapped, "but weren't you the one who just implied that Heather might have been the one who trashed my house? She could have done it while the boys were sitting in the coffee shop waiting for her to finish playing blackjack. *Blackjack!*"

"I was thinking out loud. We don't really know what happened yet, and it isn't going to help if you blow a blood vessel before we can find out."

Briana folded her arms. "Give me that cell phone," she said, the contradiction between her words and her body language barely registering.

"No," Logan said. "Alec and Josh are upset enough as it is."

"That's why I need to talk to them!"

"You can talk to them face-to-face in five minutes."

"Can't you drive any faster?"

"Not without breaking the sound barrier, no," Logan said.

He'd barely stopped in front of the casino when she leaped out of the truck and ran inside, pushing past the valet who'd tried to open the door for her.

She found Alec and Josh in the coffee shop, sitting in a booth with Dylan, drinking milk shakes. They were both pale, and a little scruffy, but neither of them was bleeding.

Briana reached the table, opened her mouth to speak and nearly fainted. When the blackness and the circling stars receded, Dylan was holding her up and Alec and Josh were watching her with wide, frightened eyes.

"Sit down," Dylan told her, easing her into the booth seat and handing her a glass of water from the next table over.

"Where's Jim?" she managed to ask when the room stopped spinning.

"In the security room, with the happy couple," Dylan said, as Logan burst into the equation.

Somewhat to Briana's chagrin, both boys rushed to Logan, bypassing her completely. She saw him squeeze his eyes shut briefly as he held them against his sides.

"Can we go home now?" Alec asked, tilting his head back to look up at Logan, and still clinging to him as best he could with a cast on one arm.

"As soon as your mother can stand up," Logan said.

Briana guzzled the last of the water Dylan had given her. "I want a word with Vance first," she said.

"That can wait," Logan said.

A stare-down ensued.

Logan won it. Briana was at the end of her rope, physically and emotionally, and she needed to get the boys out of there.

There had been enough crazy drama as it was.

"Thanks," she said to Dylan.

He and Logan exchanged looks.

"I'll explain later," Logan said.

Dylan nodded. "Guess I'll get back to my poker game," he said. "Last hand, I had an inside straight."

With that, he grinned at the boys, turned and walked away to return to the poker room at the back of the casino.

ALEC AND JOSH were too worn-out to tell the story. Logan made scrambled eggs and toast when they reached the main ranch house, while Briana got their sleeping bags ready in the living room.

They ate—though Wanda, Snooks and Sidekick got most of what was on their plates—and Briana put them to bed.

Logan waited in the kitchen, sipping coffee and

giving her time with the kids. When she finally re-appeared, she looked worn to a frazzle.

"I guess I overreacted," she said.

"You're a mother," Logan replied, pouring coffee for her, because he still didn't have any tea. "That's what mothers do, isn't it?"

She sat down at the table. "Thanks," she said, as he handed her the coffee. "For calling Dylan. For driving me to town and—"

"Briana," Logan interrupted. *"Stop."*

Tears welled in her eyes. "If anything had happened to them—"

"They're in the living room, Briana. They're safe. Unless you want them to be nervous wrecks for the rest of their lives, you'd better reframe this as an adventure, not a kidnapping with potentially dire consequences."

Her face was wet, but she was trying to smile. "You're such a...such a—"

He grinned. "What?"

"Lawyer," she finished.

He chuckled. "That could come in handy," he said. "If it turns out you're right about Heather, there will be some legal issues."

She looked back over one shoulder, as if expecting to catch the boys eavesdropping. "Custody?"

"Suppose we talk about that tomorrow," he suggested. "You're a wreck right now. You won't be able to think straight anyway."

She considered that, nodded.

Logan cupped her cheeks in his hands, stroked away her tears with the sides of his thumbs. "Just for tonight," he said, "let me make the decisions."

She nodded again.

He stood, pulled her to her feet, steered her out of the kitchen, past the already sleeping boys, and along the hall, into his room.

"Extenuating circumstances," he said, when she balked at lying down on the bed. "You won't fit on the air mattress, and Dylan's got dibs on the couch."

He undressed her, shoes first, then jeans, then the shirt.

"The boys—"

Damn, but she looked good in those lacy panties and that fussy pink bra. He'd figured her for the white cotton briefs and sports bra type, but he'd sure been wrong.

"They're dead to the world," Logan reminded her. "And I'm making all the decisions tonight, remember?"

"I remember," she said, shimmying to get under the covers.

Logan sat down on the edge of the mattress, took off his boots. Hauled his shirt off over his head, stood to unbutton his jeans and let them fall to the floor.

Briana drew in a sharp breath.

"Sorry." Logan grinned. "I forgot to pack underwear when I left Vegas."

He switched off the bedside lamp and got into bed beside her.

She felt cold, so he pulled her into his arms.

"All the decisions?" she asked.

He kissed the top of her head. "All of them," he confirmed.

They lay still for a long time, listening to the

sounds of the old house settling as the temperature dropped.

When Briana was warm again, Logan kissed her, working the front catch on her bra as he plundered her mouth. She stiffened briefly, then wrapped her arms around his neck and kissed him back.

He moved down, to her breasts, tongued her nipples, one and then the other, until she moaned, entangling her fingers in his hair.

Then he progressed to her navel.

She arched her back and gasped his name.

"The walls are thick," he murmured, against her soft, warm flesh. "Let go, Briana. It's all right to *let go.*"

"Oh my God," she whimpered, when he reached the juncture of her thighs. "Logan... I—"

"Shh," he whispered, into the sweet, moist nest of curls he was about to part with his tongue.

She gave a strangled cry when he took her full into his mouth and suckled, his hands resting under her firm buttocks. He drank of her, like a thirsty man kneeling beside a stream.

She writhed, and pressed herself against him, her hips undulating.

He brought her to a climax, stayed with her until she'd stopped buckling with the violent force of her release. When he looked up, he saw that she was gripping the rails in the headboard with both hands. Her breasts and belly and thighs were damp with perspiration.

"That was—" she gasped "—that was..."

"What?"

"Wonderful," she said.

"Good," he answered, still holding her high, nibbling at the insides of her thighs. "Because I'm about to do it again."

"Logan—"

"Hmm?"

"I don't know if I can be quiet this time—"

He tasted her, made her groan again. "Like I said, the walls are thick."

"But I—"

He took her again.

And the sturdy Montana logs surrounding that room absorbed her cries of pleasure, as they'd done so many times before over so many years, with so many other lovers.

CHAPTER SIXTEEN

DYLAN WAS UP, pouring himself a cup of freshly brewed coffee, when Logan wandered into the kitchen the next morning, well before dawn. He'd either put in a hard night on the couch or not slept at all.

Seeing Logan, he raised his mug in a toast. His eyes were watchful, and quietly amused, as he took in Logan's misbuttoned shirt and the jeans he'd hauled on after picking them up off the floor next to his bed.

Snooks, Sidekick and Wanda had already been outside, apparently. They were all noshing on kibble in the far corner of the room.

"Gotta feed the horses," Logan said, addressing Dylan but not looking at him. He carried his boots in one hand, sat down at the table to tug them on.

"Already done," Dylan replied. "Coffee?"

Logan pushed out a sigh. Last night, after all that had happened, sharing his bed with Briana had seemed like a good idea. Now, he knew she'd probably be ashamed to face Dylan, not to mention her sons.

"Thanks," he growled.

Dylan chuckled, brought him a mug. Nodded toward the *Our Family* album still sitting on the table. "I'd like to have copies of those pictures," he said. "Ty would, too, I imagine."

Logan nodded, swallowed a scalding gulp of java.

"There are more. I haven't gotten around to going through them yet."

Dylan hauled back a chair, turned it backward and sat. "What happened last night, Logan?" he asked quietly. Seeing Logan's hackles rise, he held up a hand and added quickly, "Not between you and Briana. What was up with the kids? I tried to get the story out of them while we were waiting for you in the coffee shop at the casino, but they weren't talking, even after I bribed them with milk shakes."

"Good news first, or bad?" Logan asked, with a halfhearted grin.

"Bad news."

"Your house is going to need major work. Somebody trashed it last night. Painted the whole bedroom red." He thought of Briana, trying to gather up her cherished pictures from the living room floor, and winced. "Briana panicked, for obvious reasons, and couldn't reach the kids on the cell phone she gave them. They were supposed to be at a movie with their stepmother, but she took them to the casino instead and left them in the coffee shop to go play some blackjack. Right now, that's all I know."

Dylan absorbed it. Ruminated for a few moments, scratching the back of his neck, shaking his head. "Same yo-yo who pilfered her lingerie drawer?"

Logan nodded grimly. "Probably."

"Any locks or windows broken?"

"No," Logan said. "Whoever did this had a key."

Dylan sighed. "I didn't have the locks changed when Briana moved in," he said. "It was kind of a hurry-up deal, since she needed someplace to stay. Hell, nobody I rented to before bothered to lock up anyway, as far as I know. There could be keys to those doors all over Stillwater Springs."

"That's comforting," Logan told him.

"I've got another movie to shoot, down in Cheyenne," Dylan said. "Have the locks changed and get the bedroom repainted—any color but red—and I'll settle up with you when I come back through." Again, he sighed. "Fact is, I'd have the place bulldozed to the ground and build another house, if Briana didn't need to live there."

"She's not going back until it's safe."

Dylan rubbed his gold-stubbled chin. "Where else can she go?"

"She can stay here."

"If she agrees to that," Dylan said doubtfully. "And from what I've seen of Briana Grant, she's not only proud, she's devoted to those kids. My guess? She won't shack up with you, no matter how much she wants to, because of Alec and Josh."

"Thanks for the input," Logan said, annoyed because he knew Dylan was right. Briana would rather take her chances at Dylan's place, even risk encountering a stalker face-to-face, than set what she surely regarded as a poor moral example for her children.

On the other hand, if she was in danger at the other house, so were Alec and Josh. And that might well tip the balance.

"I guess you could get the furniture out of storage and set her up in Tyler's old room," Dylan speculated, his eyes twinkling. "Get some beds for the boys and put them in mine. That would ease her mind where Alec and Josh were concerned, but there would still be talk about it. You know how word gets around in a place like Stillwater Springs."

"I don't give a rat's ass what people say," Logan growled.

"No," Dylan said agreeably, "but I'll bet Briana does."

The door to the living room swung open, and Briana came in, fully dressed and pink to her hairline.

"Briana does what?" she asked irritably, marching to the cupboard for a cup and helping herself to coffee.

"I'm staying out of this," Dylan said, standing and holding his hands out wide, like a calf-roper trying to beat a clock at the rodeo. "Mind if I saddle that buckskin and ride over for a confab with Cimarron?"

"Suit yourself," Logan replied, relieved when Dylan immediately left the house, headed for the corral.

Briana joined him at the table. "He knows we slept together," she said miserably.

"He knows you spent the night," Logan said reasonably. "There's a difference. Besides, we're not kids, Briana."

She put both elbows on the table and rubbed her face with her hands. "What am I going to do?" she asked, probably talking to herself more than to Logan. *"What am I going to do?"*

"Move in with me?"

"Call me old-fashioned," she said, in a sharp whisper, lowering her hands to glare at him, "but I don't live with men I'm not—" She lost some steam. "Married to," she finished.

"Actually, Dylan offered a half-decent suggestion, for once in his life. We could set up beds in his old

room, and Tyler's. You can't seriously be thinking of
going back—"

"Everyone in town would know, within a day. And
they wouldn't believe for a minute that we were sleeping in separate bedrooms."

"I didn't say it was a *perfect* suggestion, Briana.
Does gossip really matter that much to you? More
than being safe and—" he went ahead and played the
trump card, though it pained his conscience a little
"—knowing Alec and Josh are safe, too?"

"You know *perfectly well* that we'd have sex—"

"I prefer to think of it as 'making love,'" Logan
said loftily.

"Whatever," Briana answered, in that same hissing
whisper. "I know lots of good people live together,
Logan. I know I'm way behind the times. But I'm not
living under the same roof with you unless—" She
broke off, blushing even harder than before.

"Unless we're married?"

"Like *that's* going to happen. We've known each
other for a *week,* Logan." Her hands flew out at her
sides. "Sure, the sex is good—it's *better* than good—
but…"

He took her hand. "But…?" he prompted.

"I don't know," she said. "Why are we even talking about this, anyway? It's crazy!"

"Is it?" Logan countered. He probably looked and
sounded calm on the outside, but inside his heart was
thrumming and his brain was echoing Briana's senti-
ment—it *was* crazy. He was a two-time loser, when
it came to marriage. They were virtually strangers to
each other. And yet—

Briana gaped at him, speechless.

"We could be married in three days," he heard himself say. "Approach it like a business deal. You get what you want—security and a good name—and I get what I want. A wife and kids."

"You're *serious!*"

By God, he *was* serious. He grinned at the realization of it. "I'll set up trust funds for both Alec and Josh," he said, on a roll now. "And instead of a prenup, I could set aside a couple of million in your name—"

"A *couple of million?*" She looked around the kitchen, with its peeling wallpaper, outdated cupboards and battered wood floors.

"Did I forget to mention that I'm rich?" Logan asked.

"Yeah," Briana said. "You neglected that little detail."

"What do you have to lose, Briana?" Logan reasoned.

She opened her mouth, closed it again. Glanced toward the inside door, most likely making sure the boys weren't listening in.

"On the other hand, look what you have to gain. Several million dollars. Hefty college funds for your sons. You'd never lack for anything, even if the whole marriage thing went bust, and neither would they."

She blinked. "What's in this for you?"

"I told you. A wife. Kids."

"Alec and Josh are *Vance's* sons," Briana reminded him. "And while I don't mind admitting I wish they weren't, reality is reality."

"Kids of our own," Logan proposed. "At least two. The first one within the year."

Her green eyes fairly popped. *My God, those eyes.*

A man could tumble right into them, end over end, and never be sane again.

"You're nuts if you think I'd have babies with you and leave them behind if things went sour," she warned. "I'd want the children, *not* the money."

"That's one of the reasons I think I could love you," Logan said. "We wouldn't be the first people who ever got married for practical reasons, you know, and fell in love after the fact."

"That is the craziest thing I've ever—"

Logan folded his arms, arched one eyebrow. "Think about it," he said. Then he stood up and headed for the back door. Maybe Dylan hadn't ridden out yet; if he had, Logan meant to catch up with him. It had been too long since they'd raced each other across a field, in the light of a new dawn, yelping like a couple of Sioux braves on the warpath.

Way too long.

"Where'd Logan go?" Alec asked, peeking through the doorway to the living room and still blinking a night's sleep out of his eyes. Josh pushed through behind him.

Briana stood at the stove, frying up some bacon and eggs. It seemed an oddly normal thing to be doing, making breakfast in that shabby but spacious old ranch house, with all its history.

"I think he's gone riding with Dylan," she said carefully. The truth was, she'd looked out the window and seen the two men riding out together just as the sun came up, Dylan on the buckskin, Logan riding bareback on the gray.

"Are you mad at Heather?" Alec asked, creeping into the room, dragging back a chair at the table.

"I'm not sure *mad* is the right word," Briana said moderately. "What happened last night, guys?"

Josh plunked down in the midst of all three dogs, and began ruffling ears. A tentative grin eased the strain in his face as he relaxed. "Somebody called Heather at the trailer, after Dad went back to work his overtime shift," he said. "She started crying."

"We didn't know what to do," Alec said solemnly.

Briana pushed the skillets off the burners. Breakfast could wait. "Of course you didn't," she said gently, going to Alec, touching his face, looking over at Josh in the next moment. "Do you know why she was crying?"

"She said her mom was real sick," Josh said.

"I'm sorry to hear that," Briana replied, very softly.

"We were going to have supper at the casino before we went to the movie," Josh added. "Heather said she needed to play some blackjack, and then we'd go. But then she brought the phone back, and she was real mad and crying again, and she said Dad called and we were all in trouble. I called Dad, and he said he was coming to get us and we shouldn't tell you what happened—"

"But you *told,*" Alec said accusingly.

"Hold it," Briana said. "Josh did the right thing."

"Heather just wanted to win some money so she could help her mom," Alec maintained. "That's what she said."

Explaining Heather's convoluted logic wasn't Briana's job, even if she'd known how to go about it in the first place. She'd discuss that part with Vance, and with Heather, too, but not in front of her children.

"She isn't a bad person, Mom," Alec insisted. "She was just scared, that's all."

"Are you going to make us stop seeing Dad?" Josh asked.

"No," Briana said, struck by her elder son's apparent change of heart where Vance was concerned. "But we grown-ups are going to have to work some things out."

"Do we have to go back to our house?" Alec wanted to know.

"I think we'll stay here for a few days," Briana said, concentrating on making breakfast again because she needed something to do to keep from coming unraveled.

"What happened over there, Mom?"

Had she told them about the break-in, the destruction of their belongings? She couldn't remember. "Who said anything happened?"

"Something did," Alec said, staring at her.

Briana sighed. "Somebody messed the place up," she said, conscious of both boys watching her now, and unable to look at either one of them directly.

"Who?"

"I don't know," Briana said. She'd suspected Heather, but now that she'd heard part of what had gone on—Heather getting a call that would upset anybody—she wasn't so certain. Maybe it *had* been Brett Turlow, indulging in some kind of nutzoid reprisal because he'd been questioned about the first incident with the nightgown. If so, he'd probably feel obligated to strike again, if Sheriff Book had brought him in like he'd said he was going to do.

"Did they want to hurt us?" Alec asked.

She couldn't bring herself to let them think that, even though it might be true.

"No," she lied, hating herself for it. "I think it was just a prank."

Alec shivered visibly. "When Logan is around," he said, "nothing can get us. Not even a *bear*."

That wasn't entirely true, either, but Josh and Alec were too young to understand. Let them have their illusions, Briana thought, for as long as they could.

"I've got some things I have to do today," she said, dishing up a plate for each of her children. "Logan might be too busy to look after you—if he is, you'll have to spend a few hours at the day-care center in town."

This announcement elicited a chorus of loud groans.

"Mom!" Alec wailed. "The day-care center is full of *little kids in diapers!*"

"Yeah," Josh agreed. "Soggy ones that droop."

Briana rolled her eyes. "Life is hard," she said. She hoped they'd never find out *how* hard. Had Logan *meant* what he'd told her about the trust funds for Alec and Josh?

You'd never lack for anything, even if the whole marriage thing went bust, and neither would they.

She left a note for Logan, after washing up the breakfast dishes and hurrying the boys into getting dressed to go out.

The people at Happy Dale Day-care Center agreed to look after them, and Briana drove straight to the trailer, noting immediately that the van was gone, parked Dylan's truck and walked up to knock smartly on the tinny door.

Heather opened it slowly, bundled into a lavender chenille bathrobe that, like the trailer, had seen better days. She hadn't washed off her makeup from the night before, so there were black patches under her eyes, and old lipstick clung to the cracks in her lips.

"Vance isn't here," she said, sounding groggy.

"I didn't stop by to see Vance," Briana answered. "May I come in?"

Heather gave a great, noisy sigh. "Why not?" she asked, stepping back.

The inside of the trailer was remarkably clean. There were cheap knickknacks, hopefully arranged, on every surface. A grubby crocheted afghan covered the back of the couch.

"I haven't made coffee yet," Heather said.

"I don't need any," Briana replied.

Heather gestured toward a black recliner patched here and there with duct tape—probably Vance's TV chair.

Briana sat down, keeping to the front edge and folding her hands to keep them still. "The kids told me you got some bad news about your mother last night," she began.

Heather flopped onto the couch. Her slippers had high plastic heels, and grungy purple feathers fluttered atop her insteps. In Heather-world, this probably represented glamour. "Yeah," she said. "I got pretty upset. I'm not used to having kids around."

I'm not used to having kids around.

Briana kept her temper. "I take my children's safety

and well-being *very* seriously, Heather," she said. "Why did you decide to go to the casino?"

Heather's face crumpled. "I thought you might be there," she replied.

That made more sense than Briana cared to admit, and it had a ring of truth to it. "To take them off your hands?"

"It wasn't like that," Heather insisted, sniffling once and raising her chin a notch. The other woman had had to fight a lot of battles in her life, Briana realized, and many of them had been tough. "I like Alec and Josh, I really do. And Vance wants so much to have a chance to make things up to them." Tears welled in her puffy eyes, making the mascara situation that much worse. "After that fuss at the casino last night, he'll probably get fired. Then he'll want to move on, and I can forget convincing him that we ought to have a kid of our own—"

"Do you really think you're ready for that?" Briana asked gently. "A baby, I mean?" The thought of a helpless infant at the mercy of this mercurial woman-child gave her chills.

Heather didn't seem to hear her. She was hugging herself and staring through the trailer wall at something far, far away. "I'll be lucky if he even takes me with him when he goes," she muttered.

Briana tilted her head, trying to catch Heather's eye. "All of that is your business," she said. "Alec and Josh are mine. Vance isn't going to be happy about this, but I can't help that. Until things settle down a little, Heather, I can't leave my children with you again."

"You can't keep Vance from seeing his own kids!"

"No, I probably can't. But I *can* get a lawyer and restrict visitation."

"You don't understand," Heather almost wailed. "Vance is already furious with me. When he hears this—"

Briana stood. "I guess you should have thought of that," she said evenly, "before you left Alec and Josh at the casino to fend for themselves while you played blackjack."

"I told you, I thought you'd be there!" Heather was on her feet, following Briana to the door.

"You could have called," Briana pointed out, "and you didn't."

"But—"

Briana opened the door, went out. "What time does Vance get off work?" she asked.

"He's not *at* work," Heather burst out. "He's down at the sheriff's office, trying to get both of us out of dutch with the casino."

"Thanks," Briana said.

"Wait!" Heather called, from the slapdash porch.

Briana simply got back in the truck, turned the ignition key and drove away.

Sure enough, Vance's van was parked in the side lot at Sheriff Book's office. She ran straight into him at the front door as he was leaving.

Seeing her, he came to a stop, swept off his hat, ran a hand through his hair.

"Did they drop the charges?" Briana asked.

He nodded, looked away, looked back again. "We need to talk," he said finally.

"You're telling me," Briana said.

They went, in separate cars, to the Birdhouse Café,

on Main Street. Even though Briana hadn't eaten any of the breakfast she'd made for the boys, the thought of food, or even coffee, was more than she could take. So she sipped water while Vance ordered the ham-and-eggs special.

"Is Heather mentally ill, Vance?" she asked quietly, when the waitress had gone and a private space had opened around their table. "Is she a compulsive gambler? A drunk?"

"No. She's just not all that smart," Vance said, using too much salt on his eggs. When he felt defensive, he had to be doing something.

"She hit Alec with a car," Briana reminded him. "And then she left our children on their own at the casino."

"You do it all the time," Vance challenged, glaring at her. "Did you think they wouldn't tell me that, Briana?"

"I kept an eye on them," Briana said. Now who was defensive? "So did the other employees. It isn't the same thing and you know it."

"Isn't it?" Vance clenched his fists on either side of his plate and leaned forward, his gaze boring into her face. "Are you saying somebody couldn't have taken them right out of there when you and 'the other employees' weren't looking?"

Briana bit her lower lip. "I couldn't afford day care," she said. "Small matter of child support."

Vance reddened. "I was doing the best I could."

"So was I."

"Where are they right now?"

"In day care." She smiled. "And do they ever hate

it. They wanted to stay at Logan's place, but we've imposed on him enough as it is."

A muscle bunched in Vance's jaw. He picked up his fork and jabbed at a piece of ham as though it had suddenly come to life and he meant to kill it. "What you do with Logan Creed, or anybody else, is your own business," he said.

"You've got that right," Briana answered. "Logan has nothing to do with this. Heather has *everything* to do with it. She's clearly unstable, Vance, and until she settles down, I don't want Alec and Josh left alone with her."

"You think I'd let her take them anyplace, without me, after what happened last night?"

"I don't know, Vance. Would you?"

"No."

"And I should believe that, and put our children at risk, because—?"

All the starch went out of Vance in a whoosh of breath. His broad shoulders sagged, and he hung his head for a long moment. "Because," he rasped, after several seconds, "I'm *trying,* damn it." He met her eyes, and she saw sincerity there, even a certain force of character she'd never guessed was in him. "I don't know much about being a father. Heather and I probably got married too soon after we met. But when I won that money, Briana… When I won that money, when something went right for me for the first time since I can remember, it felt—it felt like a sign from God or something. It was a chance to start over."

Briana reached across the table, touched his hand. "The boys love you," she said gently. "Don't be too quick to give up."

"My boss is going to hear about that fuss at the casino," Vance reflected, his voice sad and gruff, his eyes averted again. "He goes to church three times a week. He might just decide I'm a poor moral influence and show me the road."

"If he goes to church three times a week," Briana speculated lightly, "maybe he's the forgiving type."

"Have you been to a church lately?" Vance snapped.

Briana let the question pass unanswered. When she was young, on the road with Wild Man, they'd dropped in for a lot of different church services, in different places. The people had invariably welcomed them, encouraged them to stay. In some cases, they'd even offered housing, a job, food.

And Briana had always been relieved when her dad shook his head and said they'd be moving on as planned.

"Not to overstep or anything," she said, about to overstep, "but there's one more thing. I know Heather wants to have a baby. That's neither here nor there. According to the boys, though, you said you had enough trouble taking care of the children you already have."

Vance looked completely deflated now, and Briana did not feel good about it, even though she'd had plenty of fantasies, over the last two years, of bursting his bubble.

"I didn't think they heard that."

"It wasn't exactly reassuring to them, Vance."

A cord of muscle stood out in his neck. "Are you through?"

Briana got to her feet. Stood beside the table, looking down at a man she'd married for a lot worse reasons than what Logan was proposing. "Almost," she said. "I don't want this to turn nasty, Vance, but if you don't personally look after Alec and Josh when they're with you, I'll get a lawyer."

"Word down at the shop," Vance said crisply, "is that you're already sleeping with one."

Briana shook her head. Small towns. Keeping a secret was impossible.

Refusing to dignify the comment with an answer, especially since it was true, she simply walked away. She'd said what she needed to say, and it remained to be seen whether or not she'd gotten her point across.

AFTER THAT RIDE, Logan had a lot to think about, and a lot of time to do it in.

Dylan loaded up his gear, got in his truck and drove off, headed for Cheyenne, where he'd be riding bulls for a rodeo movie. The pay was good, he'd said, but he'd been thinking of settling down, working something out with Sharlene, his former girlfriend, so he could spend more time with his little girl.

He carried a picture of Bonnie in his wallet. She had curly hair and Dylan's eyes, complete with that look of devilment that was better proof of paternity than a DNA test.

They hadn't settled everything, he and Dylan, not by a long shot, but it had been good, riding the range together, like old times. Talking a little.

There was a lot Dylan hadn't told him, of course.

And a lot he hadn't told Dylan.

But they'd made a start.

If only that could happen with Tyler.

After rereading Briana's note for about the fourth time—she'd taken the boys to day care and gone to have a chat with Vance and Heather—he thought suddenly of the pictures scattered on her floor at the other house.

Standing in the kitchen, he called Sheriff Book on the wall phone, asked if he'd be compromising evidence if he went over there.

Floyd replied that the state police had taken all the pictures that they needed, and he'd held Brett all night, but had to let him go that morning, since he couldn't charge him without some kind of proof.

Logan said he understood.

Then he got in the truck, drove over to Briana's and gathered up the pictures and the ruined album. Took them back to his place and piled them, as neatly as he could, next to his computer.

After that, he made a sandwich, ate it, took the dogs out, brought them in again.

Sat down at his desk and booted up the photo-doctoring program.

He'd used it a lot, while he was building his company, to make brochures and design a Web site, and navigating it was second nature. He began mending pictures as best he could, scanning them in, smoothing out tears and wrinkles.

Perhaps because Briana was an only child, Wild Man had taken a lot of pictures of his daughter. Working with those images was like watching her grow up—she'd been cute as a very little girl, then an awkward tomboy, always on a horse. As a teenager, she'd been drop-dead gorgeous, and garnered herself a couple of rodeo queen titles.

There were scores of snapshots of Alec and Josh, as babies, as toddlers, as small boys. Their clothes were shabby in those pictures, and the backgrounds showed a succession of trailers and old houses, but they'd looked happy. Secure.

Kids were resilient. Alec and Josh were proof of that—and so were he and Dylan and Tyler.

Logan began to hope that, by scanning in the Creed pictures he'd found in the attic, and giving disks to Tyler and Dylan, he might open the way back to being brothers. Real brothers.

He worked until his eyes felt as though they'd cross, then took a break to check on the progress with the barn. It was going well.

Briana drove in, when he was just thinking it might be time to rustle up supper, with the boys in the back-seat.

He was ridiculously glad to see her, and it had nothing to do with the cosmic sex they'd had the night before, or the prospect of more.

"Hey," he said.

Alec and Josh clamored out of the truck. "We had to go to *day care*," Josh complained.

"Like *babies*," Alec added.

Then they hurried off to greet the dogs. So much for the Day-Care Trauma.

Logan ran his hands down the thighs of his jeans, suddenly awkward now that he and Briana were alone.

"Did you mean what you said this morning?" she asked, very quietly. Her expression was solemn, and she seemed to be holding her breath. "About getting married?"

"Yes," he said. "I think I did."

"When can we get the license?"

CHAPTER SEVENTEEN

LOGAN SADDLED THE pinto gelding, still unnamed, for Briana. Put a bridle on Traveler, the gray. Alec and Josh, happy because they'd had corn dogs for supper, watched from their perches on the corral fence.

"Out of practice?" Logan asked, as Briana hesitated beside the pinto.

She raised her chin a notch. "I haven't forgotten how to ride a horse," she said. Then, to prove it, she stuck a foot in the stirrup and hauled herself up into the saddle. The late-in-the-day sunshine rimmed her like the aura of some stray saint. "I don't like leaving the boys here alone, that's all."

"We'll stay close by," Logan assured her. He knew she was worried about running into that bear again—it was enough of a possibility that he'd cleaned and loaded one of Jake's old hunting rifles and attached the tooled leather scabbard to her saddle, since he didn't have one.

"We're okay, Mom," Alec called.

Logan mounted the gray, Indian-style, gripping the mane in one hand and making a swinging leap.

"Pretty fancy horsemanship," Briana said. She'd been skittery as water droplets on a hot griddle, since agreeing to his proposal when she got home from town, and the pinto picked up on that, fidgeting a little beneath her.

"Jim Huntinghorse taught me that move," he answered, riding in close to grip the pinto's bridle strap for a moment, so it would settle down. "When we were seven."

She smiled, but looked pointedly at his hand, where he was holding on to the bridle. "I'm not a greenhorn, Logan. Let go."

He let go. Smiled. "Ready?"

She nodded.

He leaned to open the corral gate, waited as she rode through ahead of him. Josh came around the fence to close it behind them.

"Stay close to the house," Briana called over one shoulder.

Logan gave her a look. "They're *okay,*" he told her.

She smiled. "Race you," she said. "Across the field, through the orchard to the graveyard and back again."

"You're on," Logan said, and bent low over the gray's neck, urging the animal into a run with light taps of his boot heels. He shot ahead of Briana, but she was soon streaking along beside him, poetry on horseback, as fiercely beautiful as he could bear for her to be.

Logan was so busy watching Briana, in fact, that he was almost thrown over Traveler's head when the horse came to a fallen log and paused for a split second before making a clean jump.

Through the orchard they raced—the horses would have caught the scent of a bear if there had been one around—but neither animal hesitated. They seemed to revel in speed and freedom, the pinto and the gray.

As they cleared the orchard, though, and the graveyard was in sight, a shot sounded, somewhere up ahead.

Logan immediately reined in his own horse and grabbed for Briana's reins, too. Deftly, he bent sideways to wrench the rifle free of its scabbard.

"Probably just a poacher," he said. "Go back to the house, Briana."

"Let's *both* go back to the house," Briana replied.

Another shot boomed through the still afternoon, a muffled, reverberating *ka-boom,* soon followed by a second blast, then a third.

Logan rode forward, the rifle resting crosswise in front of him.

That was when he saw Brett Turlow, through the trees edging the cemetery, standing astride Jake's grave and pointing a shotgun at the ground.

The damn fool was trying to shoot a corpse.

Logan imagined the top of the coffin splintering, Jake's dust-and-bones body buckling under a spray of buckshot. He knew the lead wouldn't penetrate six feet of hard Montana dirt, but that didn't stop the gruesome pictures from forming in his mind.

"Call the sheriff," he said evenly, handing his cell phone to Briana because he knew she'd left her own at home, charging on the kitchen counter. "And get the hell out of here before he sees you."

It was too late for that, though.

Brett looked up, hesitated and then stormed toward them, still holding the shotgun.

"Go," Logan rasped. "I'll be okay. Just *go,* and get hold of Sheriff Book as soon as you're out of range."

Her eyes gleamed with tears. "Logan—"

Brett was closer now. He cocked the shotgun.

"Put it down, Brett," Logan said, feeling relieved when Briana finally turned the pinto and rode back through the orchard. "Put it down."

Brett ignored him. As he drew nearer, Logan could see that his face was ravaged—by drink, by rage and despair, and God knew what else. "I never killed your old man!" he wailed. "But I wish to Christ I *had,* because at least I wouldn't have spent all these years payin' for somethin' *I didn't do!*"

"You're drunk, Brett," Logan said easily, though his finger was hooked around the trigger of his rifle and he'd taken the safety off. "Lay down the shotgun, and we'll talk."

Brett stopped, took wavering aim. He was pretty unsteady, so any shot he fired would probably clear both Logan and the gray, but *probably* wasn't good enough. And Logan couldn't take even a moment to look back to see if Briana had ridden beyond the range of that shotgun. He sensed her, back there in the orchard, felt her presence, a strange, harried energy, in the skin of his back and the pit of his stomach.

His hand tensed on the rifle. He didn't want to shoot Brett Turlow, or anybody else. But he'd do it if he had to—and he suspected Turlow was trying to provoke him into killing him. Guilt-free suicide—he'd seen the phenomenon in Iraq, on the American side as well as the enemy's.

It was a game he didn't intend to play.

Brett pulled the trigger, and Logan swung his rifle wide just in time to keep from putting the poor bastard out of his misery by sheer reflex. Turlow's gun had jammed, or he'd forgotten to reload after firing the last round into Jake's grave.

Logan was off the horse in an instant, tossing his rifle aside in the process, and grappled with Turlow to get the shotgun away from him.

The struggle was brief, but Turlow was stronger than he looked, and he put up a fight.

Finally, Logan managed to rip the shotgun out of Turlow's grasp and fling it away, into the grass. He sat astraddle of the other man's belly, knees pressing hard into the underside of his upper arms.

Turlow gave a keening shriek, a trapped-animal sound that chilled Logan, deep down.

"Easy," he said gruffly. "I'm not going to hurt you, Brett."

Briana rode up then—Logan had been right in guessing she hadn't gone back to the ranch house, and he was both annoyed and proud. "The sheriff's on his way with a couple of deputies," she said calmly, swinging down from the saddle and then collecting the fallen rifle and shotgun, carrying them out of reach and leaning them against the trunk of a tree.

"Did you break into my house, Brett?" she asked quietly, when she came back.

Turlow struggled, spat at her feet, and Logan pressed his knees in a little harder.

"Answer the lady," he growled.

"I didn't mean nothin' by it," Turlow protested. "I just wanted to hold that little nightgown in my hands. I put it on the bed so I could imagine you lying there, wearing it, and wanting me."

Bile scalded the back of Logan's throat, left a bitter taste on his tongue. "Sheriff Book said your car never left Skivvie's parking lot that night."

Turlow gave a soblike laugh. "I used our next-door neighbor's Blazer," he said. "Always leaves her keys in the ignition. She never even missed it."

Logan willed himself not to lose control. "The spray paint was a nice touch," he said.

"I don't know nothin' about no spray paint!" Turlow gasped out. "Let up on my arms a little, will you? You're gonna break 'em."

Logan and Briana exchanged glances.

Logan let up, but only slightly.

"You didn't come to my place a second time?" she asked Turlow.

He shook his head. Tears glistened in the craggy lines at the sides of his eyes. "Floyd picked me up and harassed me about it, 'cause that's what he does best, but I was helping Freida put up campaign posters that night, and my sister will vouch that it's true!"

"What the hell were you doing, plunking away at Jake's grave with a shotgun?" Logan demanded, still breathing hard from the struggle. He was out of shape—too much soft living in Vegas. Chopping wood and digging post holes would fix that. "You ever heard the word *ricochet?* You're damn lucky none of that buckshot struck a rock and doubled back on you."

"The bastard's been haunting me since the day he died!" Brett cried, and the hoarse conviction in his voice was painful to hear. "I can't stand it anymore!" He flung his head back and screamed, *"Do you hear me, Jake? I can't stand it anymore!"*

Logan shifted, got to his feet, looking pityingly down at Brett Turlow.

Briana moved to stand beside him, touch his arm. "I'm going back to the house to watch for the sheriff and make sure the boys are all right—they must have heard the shots, and they're probably scared to death."

Logan nodded. "Go," he said, his gaze still fixed on Turlow. The poor, crazy son of a bitch needed medical attention, not a stretch in the county jail.

After Briana had gone, Turlow struggled up onto one elbow. His billed cap lay beside him on the ground. "You believe in ghosts, Creed?" he asked, in an eerie, disjointed tone.

"Not the kind you're seeing," Logan answered. "And don't make any sudden moves. I'm still more inclined to choke the life out of you than leave you be."

Far off in the distance, a siren droned, an almost weary sound in the humid summer air, thickening into twilight.

Logan crouched a few feet from where Turlow sat, interlaced his fingers. He'd seen Jim Huntinghorse sit like that for hours. Logan's thighs cramped, and he had to stand up again.

A crafty expression crossed Turlow's face. "I know things," he said.

"Hard to believe," Logan replied, wishing the sheriff would hurry up. If Brett Turlow hadn't spray-painted Briana's bedroom bloodred, and Logan's deepest instincts said he hadn't, that meant the real vandal was still out there someplace. He didn't like having Briana and the boys out of his sight, knowing that.

And it would be dark soon.

"I know, for instance," Turlow went on, "that the

high-and-mighty Sheriff Book sweated up some sheets with my sister."

"Not exactly news," Logan said. The *Courier* certainly hadn't run the scandal; it wasn't that kind of newspaper. He'd heard the gossip around the time of Jake's funeral—hadn't given a rat's ass then, didn't give one now.

With every passing moment, the anxious tension inside him mounted.

Briana.

She'd taken his cell phone, so he couldn't call the house, make sure she and Alec and Josh were safe.

The siren sliced the stillness; Turlow covered both ears with his hands and rocked back and forth.

A few moments later, Sheriff Book came through the orchard on foot, at a lumbering trot, one hand on his holster to keep it from bouncing against his leg.

"I'll be goddammed, Brett," he sputtered, slowing to a walk and jerking his cuffs off his utility belt, "you're a regular one-man James gang, aren't you?" He turned to Logan. "You better get on back to the house. Briana's got Deputy Jenkins by the shirtfront—says somebody snatched her kids—"

Logan swore and raced for his horse, grazing a dozen yards away, and sprang onto its back.

While Floyd arrested Turlow, he and the gray cut through the brush as though they'd been catapulted.

Reaching the corral, Logan jumped off the gelding and landed running. He vaulted over the fence and hurried toward Briana, who was struggling with Deputy Jenkins—Stillwater Springs' version of Barney Fife—next to the squad car.

Logan pulled the deputy away, flung him back so

hard that he thumped against the second squad car. Red and blue lights still flashed dizzyingly along the bar bolted to the cruiser's roof.

Freed, Briana immediately headed for Dylan's truck.

Logan caught up to her in a few strides, grabbed hold of her arm.

She kicked and fought; holding her was like trying to stuff a feral cat into a gunnysack.

"Stop," Logan ordered. He hadn't shouted the word, he'd whispered it, but his throat felt as raw as if he'd yelled at the top of his lungs.

Miraculously, Briana went still. She dragged in great gulps of air, and she was trembling. "The kids—" she finally managed "—gone…"

"I was just trying to keep her from hurting herself," Deputy Jenkins interjected, from somewhere nearby, sounding put-upon. "Nobody ought to drive when they're that upset, and soon as Sheriff Book gets back—"

"We'll find the kids," Logan told Briana, gripping both her shoulders and looking directly into her face. *"We'll find them."*

Desperate hope flickered in her green eyes, and she swallowed again, nodded.

"Now don't you go off half-cocked, Logan," Jenkins reasoned hastily. "Soon as Sheriff Book gets back here—"

"We can't wait," Logan told him. The keys to his truck were in his front pocket; he got them out with a jingle. "Do me a favor, Deputy, and put this pinto back in the corral."

Jenkins flushed, from the base of his scrawny neck

to the roots of his hair. "We've got to follow procedure!" he protested, even as he got the pinto by the reins and led it toward the corral. "You can't go taking the law into your own hands—"

Briana scrambled into the truck on the passenger side.

Logan got behind the wheel. The dogs were nowhere in sight—for the time being, anyway, they were on their own.

"Talk to me, Briana," Logan said, making the rear tires scream and fling up dirt on all sides as he backed into a hard turn.

Her hair was coming loose from that tight braid; she pushed her bangs back with a swift motion of one hand. "I went inside the house," she said, like someone hypnotized, or talking in their sleep. "Wh-when I didn't see Alec and Josh in the yard. The—the dogs were there, but—"

"Did you get your cell phone off the counter?" Logan marveled at how calm he sounded; everything inside him was in a churning panic. If Alec and Josh had been his own sons, blood of his blood and flesh of his flesh, he couldn't have been more frightened than he was.

She nodded, felt around, visibly realized she had her handbag. Fumbled through it, clasped the phone. Almost simultaneously, she raised her backside off the seat, straining against the seat belt, and pried Logan's phone out of her hip pocket.

He took it as they careened down the long driveway.

NAUSEA ROILED IN Briana's stomach. Her palms were clammy with sweat, and somewhere inside her, someone was screaming in helpless hysteria.

Logan.

Thank God for Logan.

At the gate, he wheeled the truck in the direction of town.

And the cell phone rang in Briana's hand.

She nearly dropped the thing, trying to open it. "Hello?" she blurted. "Josh? Alec?"

"Mom," Josh said, barely whispering. "I'm scared."

The back of her throat scalded. She looked frantically at Logan, nodded once. Somehow had the presence of mind to put the phone on Speaker. "Where—where are you?" she croaked.

"In—in the van," Josh answered, starting to cry. "It's dark in here, Mom, and Heather—Heather hit Alec when we stopped at the gas station 'cause he yelled for help and now I can't wake him up—"

Be calm, urged the better angel.

Logan was already thumbing a number into his cell phone. Quietly describing the van to someone, probably the dispatcher at the sheriff's office.

"Is your dad there?" Briana asked, fighting another rush of panic.

"No," Josh whispered. "She's coming back, Mom—I have to hang up—"

"Josh," Briana said hastily, "put the phone on Vibrate—"

"I already did that— Bye—"

He was gone. Riding in the back of Vance and Heather's van.

It's dark in here, Mom... Heather hit Alec... I can't wake him up...

"My babies," Briana rasped. "My babies!"

"She couldn't have gotten far," Logan pointed out.

"The dispatcher is contacting Sheriff Book by radio. She said he'll have the state patrol block both highways out of town."

"You heard what Josh said—Alec is hurt…"

Logan reached across, lightly squeezed the back of her neck. "Call Vance," he said. "He might have some idea where she'd go, and if I were him, I'd sure as hell want to know what was going on."

Briana opened her phone, begrudging every moment it was tied up because Josh wouldn't be able to get through if he tried to call again. She didn't recall her ex-husband's number, but Josh, the technological wiz, had programmed it in.

Vance answered on the second ring. "What now?" he snapped.

Briana drew a deep breath, let it out slowly, because she'd have screamed until her throat bled if she hadn't. "Heather has the kids, Vance. She hit Alec. Josh says he can't wake him up."

"What the—"

"Do you know anything about this, Vance? Because if you do, you'd damned well better tell me!"

"That broad is certifiable," Vance growled. "We had a fight, and this is her way of getting back at me—"

"Vance. She has the kids."

"I'll borrow a rig from one of the guys here at work and find her. Just chill out, will you?"

"No! I will not 'chill out'! *Where would she go, Vance?*"

"My guess?" Vance barked. "The casino. She'll think she can parlay what's left of the grocery money into a stake—"

"The casino!" Briana yelled at Logan, so loudly that he winced.

Briana shut her phone with a snap, immediately dialed Jim.

"Jim Huntinghorse, your best bet for sheriff!"

"Jim, this is Briana and—"

"A vote for me is a vote for law and order—"

Dear God. It was his voice mail.

Shaking with exasperation and that incipient panic, Briana rang off and called the casino's main number, asked to be connected to the security desk.

By then, they were speeding along the highway, with both Sheriff Book and Deputy Jenkins hot on their trail in their separate squad cars, sirens shrieking.

Briana explained the situation to casino security as coherently as she could and then hung up, praying Josh would call again, say that Heather had come to her senses, let them go, that he and Alec were all right....

But Josh didn't call.

The battered van was parked at a reckless slant outside the casino's west door, in a handicapped-only zone.

Briana bounded from Logan's truck as the two squad cars screeched in alongside. She was aware of Floyd and the deputy only peripherally—her entire being was focused on getting to that van, pulling open the back doors.

Somehow, Logan and Vance got there first.

Alec and Josh lay inside on the floorboards, blinking in the darkness.

Vance hauled Josh out, since he was closer, and

the boy clung to him with both arms, big as he was, hiccuping and saying "Dad," over and over. Logan stepped aside, and Alec scrabbled, crablike, to Briana, whimpering, his cast thumping against the floor of the van as he moved.

"She—she was going to s-steal us," Alec murmured, into the curve of Briana's neck. "She said we'd n-never see you and Dad and Logan again—"

Vance eased Josh to his feet, kept an arm around his son's shoulders, his gaze bleak as he watched Briana comforting Alec. "I'm sorry, Briana—I never thought she'd—"

Briana silenced him with a look, over the top of Alec's head. Noted distractedly that Brett Turlow was sitting in the backseat of Sheriff Book's car. If Floyd and Deputy Jenkins were around, they were somewhere beyond the frayed edges of her vision.

A scuffle at the casino door got everybody's attention.

Briana, Logan, Vance and the boys all turned, just in time to see Heather being led outside, the sheriff holding one arm, the deputy holding the other. They were flanked by casino security, and Heather fought and screamed shrill invective, trying in vain to break free.

Alec held on tighter to Briana. "Don't let her get us, Mom," he pleaded. "Don't let her get us—"

It was then that Vance broke away from Josh, barreling toward Heather like a charging bull.

"Uh-oh," Logan said, and went after him at a run, tackled him just before he would have flung himself on Heather in a fury.

"Is Logan going to hurt Dad?" Josh asked anxiously, pressed against Briana's side.

"No, honey," Briana said. The adrenaline rush was
subsiding now; she felt almost light-headed. She had
to set Alec on the floorboard of the van again and grip
one of the doors to keep herself upright.

Vance struggled, but Logan was stronger, and re-
strained him from behind, by the arms.

"You took my *kids!*" Vance raged at Heather, who
walked with her chin high now, between the sheriff
and the deputy. She'd stopped fighting them and assumed an almost regal dignity; she seemed to *like* all
the attention she was getting. *"You took my kids!"*

Logan said something; Vance stiffened, then shook
his head.

Logan let him go.

Deputy Jenkins settled Heather in the back of his
squad car, and she sat there like some rock-queen
about to be whisked away after a sold-out concert.

Sheriff Book approached Briana and the boys, and
Logan and Vance took their places nearby, Logan
at Briana's right elbow, Vance a few feet to the left.

"You boys all right?" the sheriff asked, favoring
Alec and Josh with an engaging, no-big-deal, hap-
pens-every-day kind of grin.

Alec nodded.

So did Josh.

Neither of them seemed certain.

"Best take these kids by the clinic for a checkup,
just to make sure," the sheriff said. "Then I'd like
you all to come by the office, so we can get to the
bottom of this."

"I've got to get that rig back to my buddy," Vance

said, as both squad cars pulled out, lights and sirens blessedly stilled, and the three plainclothes security guards disappeared inside the casino.

Logan, somewhat to Briana's surprise, laid a hand on Vance's shoulder. "I'll drop Briana and the boys off at the clinic, then pick you up at the shop," he said.

Vance nodded his appreciation, gave Briana a sheepish glance, then went to Alec and Josh and hugged them awkwardly. A few moments later, he climbed into a subcompact and drove away.

Josh, Briana and Alec rode in the backseat of Logan's truck, Briana keeping an arm around each of her boys as they headed for the clinic.

She didn't talk, and neither did the kids. There would be plenty of time for that later. Thank God, there would be plenty of time.

BETWEEN THE EXAMS both boys received at the clinic—physically, they were both fine—and the stint in Sheriff Book's office, hours had passed by the time they got back to the ranch house.

Logan carried a sleeping Alec inside, Josh and Briana following, all of them greeted by three barking dogs.

At Briana's direction, Logan laid Alec on the air mattress in the living room.

"The horses—" he began.

She smiled wearily. "Feed them," she said, already helping Josh to get undressed for bed. "I can manage this part."

Logan left the house, taking the dogs with him. The pinto stood, still saddled, in the corral, the gray nearby, reins dangling from his bridle.

He put out hay first, then unsaddled the pinto, removed his bridle and then the gray's, and set the tack inside his half-finished barn.

While the horses ate and the dogs did what dogs do after being inside for too long, Logan stood at the corral fence, looking up at the star-splattered sky.

Montana, he thought. It was home.

He glanced toward the house, saw the lights glowing golden in the windows. Yes, Montana and this ranch were home—to his body, anyhow. But to the intangible part of him—soul, spirit, whatever—*Briana* was the center of all universes.

When had he fallen in love with her?

At first sight, that day in the cemetery?

Over supper, at her place?

When they made love on his couch, and rockets went off?

He didn't know, didn't care.

He wanted to tell her how he felt, but she'd been through enough that day.

She'd already agreed to marry him, and until right now, that had been enough for Logan. Now, it wasn't.

Both boys were sleeping when he and the dogs went back into the house, and Briana was in the shower.

Too rattled to sleep, Logan lowered the attic stairs, climbed them and lugged down three more plastic containers full of photographs, letters and other Creed memorabilia.

He was at the table, bent over the last box of pictures, when Briana came in, wearing one of his T-shirts. Her hair was freshly washed, and blazing like fire around her face.

"Hungry?" she asked, sounding for all the world like a wife, at the end of a long day.

"I could eat," Logan admitted, but the words came out sounding gravelly and rough.

She paused beside his chair, laid a hand on his shoulder, bent to kiss the top of his head.

I love you, he told her silently.

"Scrambled eggs?" she asked.

He smiled, nodded. "That would be good," he said.

While she cooked, he turned back to the photographs. Dylan. Tyler. Himself. All at different ages—wearing Halloween costumes. Starting school in some long-gone, leaf-fiery September. Even a few shots of them opening presents on Christmas morning, in those glorious years when Jake hadn't taken a chain saw to the tree.

"What do you suppose will happen to Heather?" Briana asked, almost idly, cracking eggs into a skillet Logan's great-grandmother had probably used.

"I don't know," Logan said, picking up the last picture packet. Two sets of negatives, with an envelope tucked in between. "She needs help, that's obvious."

"Vance is pressing charges against Heather," Briana remarked. "For kidnapping."

Logan was only vaguely aware of her now—he'd taken the envelope out of the photo packet, seen the names scrawled on the front of it in Jake's familiar hand.

To my sons.

"That's nice," he said.

She came to him, sat down. Smiled. "Logan Creed," she accused good-naturedly, "you are not listening to me."

He blinked.

She noticed the envelope. Fell silent.

Hands shaking slightly, Logan opened the letter.

If you've looked this far, Jake had written, *you're ready to read this pitiful missive from your soon-to-be dearly departed father...*

A chill rippled down Logan's spine, then back up again.

Briana dragged her chair closer to his and wrapped an arm around his shoulders.

I tried, the letter went on, *but I could never get the hang of living. It was just too damn hard. So today, I mean to go up on the mountain, just like always, and rig a logging chain...*

The kitchen whirled around Logan.

Fragmented images blipped across his brain— Tyler, so young, lapsing into a year-long silence when they told him his mother was dead by her own hand. Dylan, baffled by grief. Himself, sobbing in the privacy of his room for poor, benighted Angela, who had always set out cookies and milk as soon as she heard the school bus squeaking to a loud halt at the end of the long driveway.

"Weak," Jake had said, the day of Angela's funeral. "She was weak."

"Logan?" Briana's hand rested on the nape of his neck; he realized he'd lowered his head to rest on his folded arms, amidst all those badly focused snapshots. "Logan—?"

"He killed himself," he said. "Made it look like an accident, so we could collect the insurance money."

"What?" she asked.

Logan raised his head, feeling drunk. Pole-axed.

"That chickenshit, selfish son of a bitch *killed himself*." He slammed a hand down on the brief letter lying on the table. "Read it for yourself. He thought he was being *noble*—"

She scooted her chair nearer, pressed her face into his hair. "Who, Logan? Who killed himself?"

"My father," Logan answered, after a long time. He straightened. "My father."

Her eyes were green pools of confusion, concern. "Your *father*—?"

He shoved the letter at her. He could handle this, once he'd had a little time to absorb the shock. Dylan would handle it, too, though he'd be as pissed as Logan was, for a while. But Tyler? Ty, who had lost his mother to suicide—how was *he* supposed to take news like that?

While Briana read the letter, tears welling in her eyes as she took in the full meaning of what Jake had written, Logan pulled his cell phone from his shirt pocket.

Dialed Dylan's number.

"Yo, Logan," Dylan said cheerfully, after the second ring. "What's up? Did Cimarron get out? I really thought that fence would hold—"

"It isn't that," Logan broke in.

"What, then? Look, we just finished shooting a rodeo scene a few minutes ago and I've got a party in half an hour and—"

"Dylan," Logan said. "This is about Dad's…accident."

He heard Dylan draw in a breath. And he couldn't go on.

Briana cupped his face in her hands, looked deeply into his eyes.

"Logan?" Dylan called from inside the phone, sounding as if he were on another planet, not just in another state.

Logan nodded to Briana.

She took the phone. "Dylan? This is Briana. You need to come home—as soon as you can."

CHAPTER EIGHTEEN

SHERIFF BOOK ACCEPTED the cup of coffee Briana offered him, there in Logan's kitchen the next morning, with a grateful nod of his head. Logan, who had been at the computer since he'd come in from feeding the horses, joined them.

He immediately produced Jake's letter, handed it to the sheriff. Book sat down to read it.

"I've already contacted the insurance company," Logan said, leaning against the counter and folding his arms. "I'll be reimbursing them, with interest, as soon as they give me the numbers."

The sheriff gave a low whistle. His whole countenance seemed to brighten, as though he'd shed some crushing weight. He set the letter carefully aside. "I came out here to tell you folks how things stand with Brett Turlow and that Heather woman," he said. "I sure didn't expect *this*."

Briana cast a sidelong glance at Logan, pulled up a chair at the table. Waited. She needed to know whether or not Heather had been released, if she still presented a continuing danger to Alec and Josh, but for the moment, Jake Creed's suicide took precedence over everything else.

Sheriff Book sighed heavily. "I'm sorry, Logan," he said. "It's a hell of a thing, finding out something like this. Poor Jake—it just seemed like he could never get in step with the rest of the world." He paused, regarding Logan thoughtfully. "You tell Dylan and Tyler yet?"

Logan shook his head. "Dylan's on his way—he'll be here in a few days. Tyler still isn't returning my calls."

"Ty's gonna take this hard," Book said. He'd been the one to find Angela lying dead in a seedy motel room, according to Logan, and he had to be remembering that now. Briana felt almost as sorry for the lawman as she did for Logan and his brothers. "*Real* hard."

A muscle bunched in Logan's jaw—his eyes glinted with weariness and shock. In the night, Briana had comforted him in the only way she knew how—with her body. He'd alternately lost himself in her and lay staring up at the ceiling, his hands cupped behind his head.

"At least Brett Turlow's off the hook," Logan said. "For killing Jake, anyway."

"Freida says she'll slap him in long-term treatment if Briana doesn't press charges for the break-in," Floyd said. "She's pretty embarrassed. Already pulled her name out of the hat. Too bad—she'd have made a good sheriff. Just Jim Huntinghorse and Mike Danvers running for my job now. Welcome to it, either one of them."

"Can we keep the charges pending until we're sure Turlow follows through on the treatment program?" Briana asked.

"Long as I'm sheriff, we can. After that, it'll be up to Mike or Jim."

"What about Heather?" Logan wanted to know.

Book sighed again. "Well," he said regretfully, causing Briana to tense, "that's a whole other kettle of fish. Ran her information last night. Seems she has a record, that one—various cons, some petty thefts and the like. At least three aliases that we know about. Skipped out on her bail the last time, after a drug bust—Nevada wants her badly enough to send a couple of suits up here to take her off our hands." Floyd paused, cleared his throat. "Seems she never bothered to divorce her last husband before she took up with your ex."

Briana closed her eyes for a moment, relieved, but stricken, too. Poor Vance. He really *had* been trying to start over, put down roots, build a relationship with the boys.

What would he do now? He'd be humiliated, as soon as word of Heather's rap sheet and extra spouse hit the streets, if it hadn't already. Past history indicated that he'd simply leave town, find himself another rodeo, and another after that.

Same old, same old.

Alec and Josh would be crushed.

After that, they talked about ordinary things—the weather, cattle prices, the new barn and the pasture fence.

Presently, Sheriff Book finished his coffee, asked Logan for a copy of Jake's letter and left with the evidence that Brett Turlow, whatever else he might be guilty of, hadn't murdered Jake Creed.

"You'd better go talk to Vance," Logan said, surprising Briana. "I'll take care of Alec and Josh."

Briana swallowed, nodded. Got her purse and the keys to Dylan's rig.

She found Vance at the trailer, after stopping briefly at his job and learning that he wasn't working that day. The front door stood open, and through the gap, Briana saw her ex-husband hurling things into a beat-up suitcase.

She knocked, remaining on the porch.

He turned, scowled at her. Flushed to the roots of his hair. "I guess you're happy now," he said. "You got the last laugh, didn't you?"

Briana stepped over the threshold. "Vance."

He stopped, looked at her again.

"Nobody's laughing," she said.

He flung a pair of jeans into the suitcase and sagged into the patched leather chair where Briana had sat during her recent visit with Heather. Bracing his elbows on his thighs, Vance shoved both hands into his hair and stared at the floor.

Briana remained standing. "So this is it? You're just going to leave?"

Vance didn't look up. "Isn't that what you want?"

"This isn't about what I want, Vance. It's about the boys. You're their father, and they need you."

"Best if I just move on," Vance said. "You're going to marry Logan Creed, aren't you? He'll make a decent stepfather—"

"Will you, just for once, stop thinking about yourself? Logan *will* make a good stepfather—probably a great one. You bail out now, and he'll take up the slack, because that's the sort of man he is. But is that really what you want, Vance? What matters more? Your stupid masculine pride, or Alec and Josh?"

When Vance raised his eyes to Briana's face, she saw tears there. "After what happened last night—" He paused, shook his head. "After all the mistakes and the missed birthdays and the crazy stuff—" Another pause. "How am I supposed to face them, Briana?"

"Like a man," Briana said, but gently, choking up a little herself. "Like a *father*."

"You'd still let me see them?"

"Yes," Briana said, though that part wasn't easy for her. "Provided you don't do anything stupid, like reconcile with Heather."

Vance gave a raw, bitter laugh. "That's the only good thing about this mess," he said. "Finding out I'm not married to that maniac after all. She's going to be in jail for a while, and when she gets out—*if* she gets out, 'cuz if the kidnapping charges stick, it's federal, according to Floyd Book—she'll take up with some other sucker and make *his* life hell."

"Then how about standing your ground, Vance? How about being a real father—present and accounted for—to your sons?"

Vance raised one eyebrow, watching her speculatively. "Wouldn't it be easier for you if I just signed off, and your new husband adopted Alec and Josh?"

"Much easier," Briana said, in all honesty. "For me. But we're not talking about what's good for me, *or* for you. We're talking about what's best for our children." She shrugged one shoulder. "Maybe Alec and Josh would be better off without you. And maybe there would be a Vance-shaped hole in their lives from 'so long, Charlie' on."

Vance got slowly to his feet. So many emotions

moved in his face that Briana couldn't read any of them.

"If you're going to leave, I can't stop you," Briana went on, when he didn't say anything. "But at least say goodbye this time. They deserve that much, Vance." She swallowed a sob. "They deserve that much, damn it!"

"I guess they're at Creed's place right now?" Vance asked hoarsely, after a very long time.

Briana bit her lower lip, nodded.

"Then I'll go out and talk with them," Vance said, clearly making the decision as he spoke. "See if they even want me to stick around."

"They want you to stick around," Briana said, swiping at her cheeks with the back of one hand. "Just ask them, and you'll know."

Vance approached her, checking his hip pocket for his wallet, snatching up his keys from the top of the TV. The gestures were familiar ones, the residue of a marriage that had died a long time before the divorce papers were filed. "You love this Logan Creed yahoo, Briana?" he asked gruffly. "You really love him?"

She did, she realized, with dizzying clarity, but Vance certainly wasn't going to hear it first. Logan was—when the time was right.

"See you at the ranch," she said, turning to go.

DYLAN SOUNDED DOWNRIGHT beside himself. "Is this important, Logan?" he demanded, over his cell phone. "Something came up and I—"

"It's about Jake," Logan said. He was in the living room, watching as Josh and Alec battled cyber-monsters on all three monitors of his computer.

He eased away, out of the boys' earshot.

"Did somebody finally prove that shit-heel Brett Turd-low dumped two tons of logs on Dad up in the woods that day?"

The play on Brett's last name was by no means original. Thinking of what the other man had endured over the years, Logan squeezed his eyes shut for a moment. *Old man,* he thought, *you fucked up so many people's lives.* "No," Logan said quietly. "He's been cleared."

"Then *what,* damn it?" Dylan shot back.

"It's not something I can tell you over the phone," Logan replied.

"Is this another gambit to get me back to the home-place?" Dylan asked, sounding distracted. "Because, brother, I am in no mood for games right now."

"I did kind of hope you'd show up for the wedding," Logan said, surprised to feel one corner of his mouth tug upward in a grin.

"The wedding? You and Briana?"

"Yeah."

"Isn't it a little soon—?"

"Can't be soon enough to suit me," Logan answered.

"Do I have to remind you that you've already got two strikes against you?"

"This is different."

"That's what they all say," Dylan argued. "'This is different.' Hell, I've said it myself."

"As soon as we get the license and explain things to the kids," Logan said, "Briana and I are getting married. That would be three or four days from now, give or take ten minutes. Be there, or be square."

"'Be there, or be *square'*?" Dylan groaned comically. "Have you been watching vintage TV or something? I think they said that in *Dad's* generation."

Logan chuckled, but his eyes burned at the mention of his dad, at the reminder. Life had been too painful for Jake, so he'd just checked out. It would take some doing to get over that.

"Is Jim going to be your best man, or is the job open?" Dylan asked.

Logan sensed that everything teetered in the balance, as far as his relationship with Dylan—or lack of one—was concerned. "Job's open," Logan said. "If you get here in time, that is."

"I'll try," Dylan grumbled. That was probably as close as he'd get to a promise. He still sounded strange—not just distracted, but beleaguered.

"Is everything all right?" Logan asked.

"Oh, it's just *peachy,*" Dylan snapped.

"Talk about vintage lingo."

"Look, Logan, I— *Stop that, damn it*—"

Another grin warmed Logan's face. "Are you with a woman?"

"I wish," Dylan said. "I've got to hang up now—I said *stop it*—but I'll get there when I can. If I don't show up in time, go ahead without me."

Logan chuckled, rubbed his eyes with his thumb and forefinger. "Trust me, I will. Vegas is always an option—we wouldn't have to wait for a license there."

Dylan sighed in a very un-Dylanlike way. "Vegas," he muttered. "Bright lights. Good-looking women. Twenty-four-hour poker games. Silver buckles at the National Finals Rodeo. Those, my brother, were the days."

"Do me one favor," Logan said quickly, sensing that Dylan was about to hang up.

"What?"

"Get word to Tyler, if you can. Tell him I need to talk to him, in person."

"He's not speaking to *me,* Logan—I told you that. Wait— Oh, *shit*—"

"Just do it, Dylan."

Dylan rang off without a goodbye—or a promise.

What the hell was going on with him, anyway? Woman trouble, most likely, though he hadn't been willing to admit it.

Logan had no time to ponder the question further, because all three dogs started barking, and the boys rushed to the front windows, and in the next moment, they were yelling, "Dad's here!"

Time to make yourself scarce, Logan told himself.

He left by the back way, made for the barn, stealing a glance at the new arrivals as he went.

Briana got out of Dylan's truck, and Vance got out of the van.

Vance put a hand on each of his sons' shoulders and then the three of them crouched in the yard, like a posse picking up a trail in the dirt, and powwowed.

Briana reached the barn a few moments after Logan did, her face puffy, her eyes red-rimmed, smiling from ear-to-ear. Sticking both hands into the pockets of the lightweight pink hoodie she'd put on that morning, along with jeans and sneakers, she tilted her head back to look up at the new beams overhead.

"Looks pretty sturdy," she said, with a sniffle.

"Built to last," Logan agreed, watching her. "You all right?"

She met his gaze again. Sniffled again. "There's something I need to tell you," she said.

Logan braced himself. He'd lost a lot in his life—his mother, Jake, two wives and a lot of dreams. If Briana backed out, said she wasn't going to marry him after all, it would be worse than all the other things combined.

They stood about a dozen feet apart, in the shadowy coolness of the barn, with its new stalls and roof. It had stood more than a hundred years, that barn, and now it could stand a hundred more.

None of which would matter, without Briana, without Alec and Josh. Even without *Wanda,* for Pete's sake.

"I—" She stopped, moistened her lips. She wasn't wearing a lick of makeup, and yet she looked Botticelli-beautiful. "I think you should know—"

"Briana, you're driving me crazy here."

"I love you," she blurted.

The whole universe ground to a stop. "What—?"

Color flared in her cheeks. "I know it's crazy, but—"

He closed the distance between them, picked her up by the waist and spun her around, with a shout of joy. And then he kissed her.

Really kissed her.

She was gasping when he finally let her come up for air. "Are you— Do you—?"

"I love *you,* Briana Grant," he said. And then he flung back his head and yelled it, because he couldn't keep it inside. *"I love this woman!"*

She beamed up at him. "Guess we won't have to

worry about breaking the news to the kids," she said. "Or any of the neighbors, either."

He laughed. "Guess not," he said.

One small figure appeared in the doorway of the barn, then another.

"Are you and Logan getting *married?*" Alec asked.

"If that's all right with you," Logan said, praying to God it was. If the boys had objections, they'd really be getting off on the wrong foot.

"You'd be our dad?" Josh inquired cautiously.

"You've got a dad," Logan replied. "I'd be your stepfather."

Silence.

Logan waited. Briana waited.

"Yee-haw!" Alec yelled suddenly, punching the air with one fist.

"Ya-hoo!" Josh bellowed.

"They seem to approve," Briana said dryly.

"Can we spend the night at Dad's place?" Josh wanted to know. "Heather's gone, so the coast is clear."

"It's a little soon for that," Briana answered. "Let's wait 'til things settle down a bit."

"Like *that's* ever going to happen," Alec remarked.

"He's got a point," Logan told Briana.

"Not tonight," Briana said firmly.

The boys were only momentarily disappointed, zooming back out into the sunlight.

"Mom said 'not tonight,'" Alec reported.

"She's going to marry Logan!" Josh announced.

Logan slipped an arm around Briana's waist, and they followed the kids.

Vance was standing by the corral fence, watching the horses.

After exchanging glances with Briana, Logan approached Vance while she steered the boys toward the house.

"That's some fine horseflesh there," Vance said, without looking at Logan.

"Thanks," Logan answered, bracing both arms on the top fence rail. "In a day or two, I'll have cattle, too. Not a herd, but the start of one."

Vance nodded, his gaze still fixed on the horses. "Briana's a good woman," he said. "You give her any grief, and you'll have me to deal with, cowboy."

"I was about to tell you the same thing," Logan said. "You planning to head out?"

"I was," Vance answered. "But I don't think I can leave those boys of mine. I've got a job and the trailer and my old van—not much, but something—so I reckon I'll stay put."

"That's good," Logan said, and he knew he'd caught Vance off guard. Out of the corner of his eye, he saw the other man staring at him.

"Good?" Vance echoed.

"Josh and Alec are great kids," Logan replied. "If they were mine, I wouldn't leave them, either. No way, no how."

"Briana told you—about Wal-Mart?"

Logan nodded. "She told me."

"It was a damn fool thing to do, leaving them like that."

"No argument there," Logan said mildly. "But that's in the past. What matters is what you do now."

"Yeah," Vance said, looking toward the house

again. "You tell my boys I'll be back another day, will you?"

"I'll tell them," Logan answered.

Vance turned and walked away, toward his van.

And Logan headed for the house, where Briana waited, and the boys were probably playing games at the computer again.

She was sitting at the kitchen table, sipping coffee, looking at the collection of Creed pictures, smiling every once in a while.

Once again, she'd stopped Logan in his tracks. Taken his breath away.

"You," she said, looking up at him with a twinkle in her green eyes, "were one *seriously* cute little kid."

"I was angelic, too," he said, grinning.

"Don't push it," Briana replied wryly.

"I have something for you," he told her. He went into the living room, interrupted an intergalactic battle long enough to pull a folder from his desk drawer, returned to the kitchen.

He set the folder on the table, in front of Briana.

She looked up at him curiously. "What—? Tell me these aren't legal papers...."

"Take a look," he urged, with a grin, drawing up a second chair and sitting down. Breathing in the scent of her hair and her skin.

Slowly, Briana opened the folder. Then she gasped.

"The pictures," she marveled, staring down at a sheet of snapshots showing Josh and Alec as toddlers, splashing in a plastic swimming pool. She turned to the next sheet, and then the next, and a tear slipped down her right cheek.

Logan didn't wipe it away, as much as he wanted to.

"Oh, Logan," she whispered, looking at him mistily. His wild-west Madonna. She probably had no clue how lovely she was—and that was part of her charm. "You fixed them—"

"The originals are still in pretty bad shape," he said. "But I did what I could."

She closed the folder, scooted off her chair and onto his lap. Wrapped her arms around his neck and pressed her forehead into his cheek. They sat like that until Alec bombed in.

"Josh!" he whooped, delighted. "Mom is sitting on Logan's *lap!*"

"Yuckaroo!" Josh yelled from the living room.

Briana laughed, and the vibrations wreaked havoc on Logan's senses.

"And they're *snuggling!*" Alec reported triumphantly.

"Film at eleven," Logan joked.

"Like I'd let you film what's going to be happening by then," Briana murmured, this time into his neck.

At eleven that night, as it happened, both boys had been asleep for several hours.

And the venerable walls of the master bedroom absorbed the sounds of unrestrained pleasure, the cries of a man and a woman who loved each other, and knew it.

EPILOGUE

Three days later...

FRANKLY, BRIANA WAS a little intimidated.

Logan's house in Las Vegas could have housed the main concourse of a major shopping mall, with room to spare. The floor-to-ceiling windows in the living room overlooked the gleaming spectacle of the city by night, punctuated by the forms of colossal cacti and rock formations that could only have carried God's byline.

The boys were at home, with Vance—Kristy had promised to look in on them and call in case of an emergency, and Josh, as always, had his cell phone.

Logan handed Briana a champagne flute bubbling with ginger ale. He'd worn a tux to their wedding, at a chapel on the Strip, and swapped it out for slacks and a sports shirt after the ceremony. Briana was still sporting the sleek emerald-green evening gown she'd chosen for the occasion, the day before, in one of the Forum shops at Caesar's.

Briana tapped her flute against Logan's, studying his face closely for any signs of regret. He bent his head, kissed her with light, lingering leisure.

"I'm sorry Dylan didn't make it," she said, once

she'd caught her breath. This world—*Logan's* world—was so different from anything she'd ever known.

Thank God they'd be going home to Stillwater Springs Ranch first thing in the morning.

Logan chuckled against her mouth. "Classic Dylan," he murmured. "He'll turn up when he's damn good and ready, and so will Tyler."

"Are we crazy?" Briana asked.

"If this is crazy," Logan said, "bring on the strait-jackets and all the rest."

Briana giggled, tipsy from the excitement of their delightfully tacky Vegas wedding. Because they were already trying to have a baby, she preferred to skip the champagne. "I love you," she said. "Did I mention that?"

"Once or twice," Logan confirmed. Then he took the champagne glass out of her hand. "Did I reply that I love you, too?"

She slipped her arms around his neck, snuggled close, nodded. "It's been at least two hours since you made love to me, Mr. Creed," she responded.

He reached behind her, unzipped the back of the gossamer dress, pushed it downward until it pooled at her feet. She kicked off her high-heeled shoes, pulled his shirt off over his head.

"Two hours?" he marveled. "Reprehensible neglect on my part."

They'd had a penthouse suite at a glitzy downtown hotel, changed into their marital finery there. Only the process had been delayed, because Logan had remarked that a bride ought to glow at her wedding, and he'd brought her to four screaming orgasms over the back of the couch to make sure she did.

Intending to honeymoon in the suite, they'd decided to spend the night at Logan's house instead. *End of the old life, beginning of the new,* he'd told her.

Now, he bent his head, found her right nipple and suckled.

Briana drew in a sharp breath. No matter how many times Logan pleasured her, it was always new, always a surprise. And he invariably took her to new heights.

Idly, Logan enjoyed her breasts, one and then the other.

All of Vegas, all the world, it seemed, glittered and glowed beneath them, a colorful panorama.

And Logan knelt.

Briana whimpered, knowing what was coming. Craving it, and yet wondering if, this time, she would lose herself completely, and for good.

He drew down her lacy panties, tossed them aside.

"Logan—"

"Shh." He parted her, flicked her lightly with his tongue, slid her lacy garter down her thigh.

She gave a guttural cry. "Can anyone—will anyone—?"

"No one can see us," Logan said.

He'd used his mouth on her before, but this was different, more intense. Perhaps because they were married, for better or worse. She groaned and leaned back, his strong hands cupping her bare buttocks, holding her upright.

Oh, this was definitely the "better" part.

He drew on her until she writhed and twisted against his tongue, until her knees threatened to give out. And then he brought her to a shattering climax;

she flexed helplessly, her fingers buried in his thick hair as she cried out his name, over and over again, in utter, delicious abandon.

When her knees did give way, Logan eased her gently to the floor, with its sumptuous carpet. He took off his own clothes, and she felt his naked warmth against her flesh and gloried in it.

He was deep inside her in a single, breath-stopping thrust, and all the lights of the city spread out below and around them melded into one dazzling, iridescent flare of color.

The earth and the sky changed places, and in the midst of the maelstrom, a million tiny fragments came together, and Briana Creed was whole in a way she'd never been before. And even as Logan lost control, she knew he'd been transformed, as well, by the same sweet alchemy.

THE CATTLE BAWLED and stirred up dust as they streamed out of the back of the livestock truck and into the newly fenced pasture. Briana watched, mounted on the pinto, while Logan rode the big gray. Alec and Josh, riding tall in the new saddles Logan had brought back from Vegas, especially for them, did a fair job of cowboying.

In the week since he and Briana had gotten back from their honeymoon, there had been no word from Dylan at all, and certainly none from Tyler.

The house was being renovated, and the boys had real beds now, set up in Dylan's old room, but daily life still felt like a campout. That was fine with Alec and Josh, and Logan had never been happier. Never even dreamed it was possible to feel the things Briana brought out in him, and not just when they were making love.

With her, cooking supper or folding laundry or any of a thousand other ordinary tasks seemed sacred.

Every day he thought it couldn't possibly get better. And every day, it did.

Vance had decided to stay on in Stillwater Springs, and the boys were cautiously pleased about that. Like all kids, they lived from moment to moment, fully engaged in the right-now.

Jim Huntinghorse and Mike Danvers were squaring off for a lively campaign, with the special election coming up in a few weeks, and Sheriff Book couldn't wait to turn in his badge. He and the wife, he said, were signed up for one of those Alaskan cruises, two full weeks, with all the extras. As soon as the new sheriff was sworn in, the Books were out of there.

Logan smiled at the thought. He didn't mind the dust, or the bawling, or any of it. Because the woman riding that little pinto was his.

His.

"What do you think of that, old man?" he asked Jake, under his breath. The cattle were all in the pasture now, and Briana and the boys had fallen back, turned their horses for the gate. Cimarron was already checking out the heifers.

Logan caught up with his wife and stepsons. "Something I have to do," he told Briana, shifting in the saddle. She'd given up her job at the casino, to his great relief, and planned on having babies for a few years, maybe taking a college course or two online when time permitted. In the meantime, she'd promised to help Jim with his campaign, though she'd already broken the news that she wouldn't be signing on as his office manager if Jim was elected.

She nodded, leaned from her saddle to kiss his cheek. "See you at home," she said. "I've got some reading to do. Kristy's book group meets at the library tonight."

Logan veered off toward the cemetery, found Jake's buckshot-pocked grave and swung down out of the saddle. His face was wet; he ran one forearm across it to clear away the sweat.

"I'm going to make the Creed name mean something again, old man," he said, crouching to pluck a few stray weeds away from the base of the headstone. "Live down everything you did, if it takes me the rest of my life."

There was no answer, of course. Just a soft breeze, playing in his hair and cooling the back of his neck.

"I forgive you, you old son of a bitch." Logan sniffled, wiped his face again. More than sweat, this time, but it didn't matter. "I forgive you for everything you did, and everything you should have done and didn't. I can't speak for Dylan and Tyler—I don't know how the hell I'm going to explain the way you died to Ty— but for my own sake, and for Briana's and those two boys, I'm not going to hate you anymore. I'm not going to try to figure you out. Any kids I have, I'll tell them the truth about you."

He stopped, tilted his head back, studied the sprawling Montana sky, bluer than blue, wider than wide.

"And the truth is, Dad," he went on, when he could, "in spite of all of it, I loved you. Which is not to say, if you were here right now, I wouldn't try to knock your teeth down your throat on general principle."

The breeze danced in the grass, and somewhere nearby, a bird sang a lonesome, poignantly beautiful song.

"There's a new Mrs. Creed now," Logan told Jake, after some time had passed. "And years and years from now, when they lay me to rest in this place, too, she'll be here, in widow-black, with my ring still on her finger. And my children, men and women by then, maybe with kids of their own—they'll have no cause to wonder if I loved them, the way Dylan and Tyler and I wondered about you."

He stood.

"That was quite a speech," drawled a voice behind him.

Startled, Logan whirled.

And there was Tyler. His kid brother.

He was tall now, over six feet. His hair was dark, like Logan's own, his eyes ferociously blue—and snapping with that Creed temper.

Tyler was mad as hell, as likely to take a swing at Logan as not, from the look of him.

Logan grinned. Shoved a hand through his filthy hair.

Tyler was back.

For now, that was all that mattered.

* * * * *

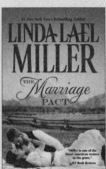 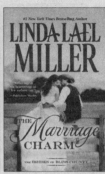 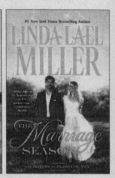

  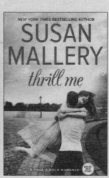

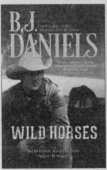
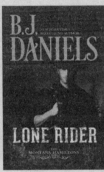
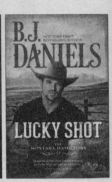

GET 2 FREE BOOKS, PLUS 2 FREE GIFTS

just for trying the Reader Service!

ESSENTIAL ROMANCE:
Indulge in sweeping romance stories and contemporary relationship novels by today's bestselling authors and new voices.

ESSENTIAL SUSPENSE:
Enjoy edge of your seat thrillers and heart-stopping romantic suspense stories, from today's bestselling authors and new voices.

You'll be delighted to know that in addition to getting 2 FREE books, you'll get 2 free mystery gifts (approx. retail value of $10) and also get to choose the type of reading you prefer most.

Your 2 free books and free gifts have a combined retail value of over $25 and they're yours to keep without any obligation to buy anything, ever!

See for yourself why thousands of women enjoy these captivating novels. Get your 2 free books and 2 free gifts today!

Conditions apply. See website for details.

Visit: www.TryReaderService.com/2Free

ROM15W

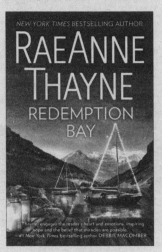

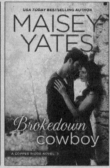

LINDA LAEL MILLER

HQN™